Trudi Pacter is a former Fleet Street journalist, now a full-time writer. She is married to Baronet Sir Nigel Seely, and divides her time between London and Leicestershire.

GN00356855

By The Same Author

Kiss and Tell
Screen Kisses
The Sleeping Partner
Living Doll
Yellow Bird

WILD CHILD

Trudi Pacter

POCKET BOOKS

New York London Toronto Sydney Tokyo Singapore

First published in Great Britain by Simon & Schuster Ltd, 1995
First published in paperback by Pocket Books, 1996
An imprint of Simon & Schuster Ltd
A Viacom Company

Copyright © Trudi Pacter, 1995

This book is copyright under the Berne Convention
No reproduction without permission
All rights reserved

The right of Trudi Pacter to be identified as author of this work
has been asserted in accordance with sections 77 and 78 of the
Copyright, Designs and Patents Act 1988

Simon & Schuster Ltd
West Garden Place
Kendal Street
London W2 2AQ

Simon & Schuster of Australia Pty Ltd
Sydney

A CIP catalogue record for this book is available from the British
Library.

ISBN 0 671 85444 5

Printed and bound in Great Britain by
Caledonian International Book Manufacturing, Glasgow

For my husband, Nigel

1

The long black limousine purred its way round Trafalgar Square, past the National Gallery, pausing briefly at St Martin-in-the-Fields until the lights changed. Then it made its slow, majestic progress into the Strand.

Curled up in the back seat, Holly held her breath and waited. From where she was, she could almost see the lights of the Adelphi. Then unexpectedly the traffic speeded up and they pulled up right in front of it.

She made out the pictures first, fuzzy black and white stills of the production that showed her mother in a lacy white crinoline playing the part of Queen Victoria.

If she hadn't been in the car, Holly might have lingered to look at them. But the traffic was thinning, and would soon move on, so she raised her eyes to the title of the play. Then she looked above it, and her mother's name blazed out at her. 'Eve Adams', the bright red letters proclaimed, 'Starring Eve Adams'.

She had been gazing at that name for years now, ever since she was a little girl. Sometimes it was in black lettering, sometimes there were other names surrounding it, and sometimes, like tonight, it was in glowing neon, dominating the title of the play itself.

For a few moments Holly couldn't take her eyes off it. It seemed to draw her in, almost to hypnotize her, and she wondered why it was having this effect.

She was going to see her mother tonight. She was going

to sit down and have dinner with both her parents. And what was even more important, she was going to be the centre of attention, for today was her birthday.

She was fourteen, grown up enough to celebrate in style, grown up enough to be taken to the Savoy. She dragged her eyes away from the flashy neon sign. She was grown up enough to stop behaving like a star-struck groupie.

The car was gathering speed now, rolling down the Strand, leaving the theatre behind them. Soon she would be at the hotel, sitting in the grand dining room with her parents. She could almost see her mother, dressed up to the nines and slightly out of breath because she'd had to dash over from the theatre. Her father would be tanned from his trip to California. They would be sitting at the best table in the restaurant.

They'd hurry over to her the minute she came through the door. There'd be kisses and congratulations. Then musicians would strike up 'Happy Birthday to You'.

Holly sighed. it wouldn't happen that way, of course. It never did. Mummy and Daddy were far too busy with their own lives to make a fuss of her.

This morning, when she came down for breakfast, she had been quite convinced they hadn't even remembered it was her birthday.

Her mother was still in bed, as usual, and her father crouched over the phone, talking to some business contact. She heard him yelling about Californian law as she passed the drawing room.

In the kitchen, Lola, the Spanish housekeeper, had set a place for her. Holly could smell the bacon frying – only she had no appetite. It was her birthday and nobody seemed to care.

She poured herself some coffee and was searching around for a piece of toast when she saw it. It was poking out from underneath her plate – a plain, square, velvet box. She pushed the plate aside and regarded it in wonder.

'What on earth . . .' she said.

Lola looked up from what she was doing. 'Open it,' she instructed. 'It's for you.'

Holly did as she was told and found a single strand of pearls. They were obviously real, for they had that special translucent sheen. Even she knew that. Very gingerly, she took them out. At the same time, she saw the note. It was folded underneath the pearls and she opened it to find a message from her mother.

'Your first grown-up present,' it said in Eve's scrawly handwriting. 'For your first grown-up birthday. Wear them tonight, my darling, when we take you out to celebrate over dinner at the Savoy.'

Suddenly the day which had been so dismal seemed bright and brilliant. Her mother did care after all.

Holly was seized with the impulse to run up the stairs, burst into Eve's bedroom and cover her with kisses. Then she thought again. She wasn't dealing with a normal mother. She was dealing with a star, tired from last night's performance.

Reluctantly, Holly ditched the idea and went into the drawing room in search of her father. She caught him as he came off the phone.

'Did you find them?' Jason asked anxiously.

Holly pretended she hadn't understood him. 'Did I find what?'

'The pearls, you noodle. Your birthday present. I came down early and put them on the kitchen table.'

She flung her arms round his neck. 'Daddy, they're lovely. They're more than lovely, they're the best present I ever had.'

'So you'll wear them tonight?'

'I can't wait.'

After that her questions came out in an excited gabble. She'd never been to the Savoy so she wanted to know what to wear, how she was going to get there . . .

Her father laughed. 'I would take you myself,' he told her, 'but I've got a late meeting. Would you mind very much if I sent a car and a driver?'

3

Holly swallowed her disappointment with as much grace as she could. Her father was an important theatrical agent and her mother was a famous actress. When you had parents like that, you had to make allowances.

2

Holly arrived at the Savoy on the dot of nine thirty. As the car pulled into the forecourt of the hotel, Holly's sense of anticipation started to build.

A uniformed porter stood to attention and opened the car door for her, and she was ushered through revolving glass doors into the grandest lobby she'd ever seen.

There were two reception desks taking up an entire wall, a vast expanse of carpet, and in the background she could hear the sound of a string quartet.

Feeling rather overwhelmed, Holly approached the imposing walnut counter and caught the eye of the uniformed man nearest to her.

'Could you tell me where the Grill Room is, please?' she asked.

The receptionist looked at her from what seemed like a great height.

'Who are you meeting?'

'My father,' she said, 'Jason Fielding.'

The words came out louder than she intended, making her feel a fool. Then she waited awkwardly while the man consulted a list.

It seemed to satisfy him, for he called a minion and told him to escort her to the Grill.

The room was bigger than Holly had imagined, and busier. She had had visions of a cosy, clubby little place where the three of them could be private.

I should have known better, she thought, surveying the

acres of linen-covered tables. When the fabulous Fieldings go out to dine, they want the world to know about it.

She stifled her resentment. It wasn't their fault that her parents were public property. It wasn't anybody's fault that their lives had been woven into a legend.

She thought back over the acres of newspaper clippings that had littered her childhood. They all told the same story. Beautiful drama student catches the eye of successful young agent, who knows immediately she has what it takes to be a star. And he sets about turning her into one. Somewhere along the way, the two of them fall in love. And like all good fairy stories, they end up getting married and living happily ever after.

Then I came along, Holly thought, and became part of all that. Just for a moment, despite everything, she felt privileged.

The sound of her name being called jolted her back to the present. Her father was sitting in the corner of the restaurant, doing his best to attract her attention.

Her mother wasn't there yet, she saw. A bottle of champagne in an ice bucket stood ready and waiting and as Holly wove her way between the tables, she wondered whether she'd be allowed a glass.

She didn't have to wonder too long. The minute she sat down, her father handed her a tall flute.

'Happy birthday, darling,' Jason said. Holly lifted the champagne to her lips.

'Shouldn't we wait for Mummy?' she asked.

Jason didn't say anything for a moment, but pushed his hand through his curly black hair, a sure sign he was nervous.

'Mummy's going to be delayed,' he told her softly.

'How delayed?' Holly demanded.

'About half an hour, I should think. She's with some American producer who's interested in her show.'

All the excitement Holly felt earlier started to ebb away.

'Half an hour means an hour,' she said hollowly.

'Not necessarily,' Jason insisted. 'She knows it's your birthday.'

'Whenever did that mean anything to her?' Holly retorted bitterly. 'When Mummy's talking about her career, it could be the most important day of my life and she wouldn't even notice.'

She hadn't meant to get angry with her mother, but when something like this happened she simply couldn't help it.

Holly cast her mind back to the first time her mother had let her down. She had been six, just old enough to know that Mummy wasn't always there when she needed her — just bright enough to understand that Mummy had important work that took her away. Except she didn't think Mummy would actually leave home on her birthday.

She had been looking forward to it for ages. She was going to have a cake with icing and six candles. Lola, the house-keeper, was going to make it for her specially.

And of course there would be her present. She'd dropped hints about what she wanted for ages now. It had to be a dolls' house like the one her best friend at school had, with a real live kitchen and proper stairs and rooms with curtains at the windows.

Holly's mind had been so full of her present that she didn't really hear her mother when she said she was going away. She even got up from where she was sitting and started to make her way across the room, when Eve restrained her.

'Darling,' she said, 'I'm not going to be here for your birthday.'

Holly hadn't believed it. She *refused* to believe it. And when her mother tried to tell her where she was going, she put her hands over her ears and cried her heart out.

It didn't change Eve's mind. She went off the next day, accompanied by two huge trunks. And Holly was shattered.

She was so miserable that she even forgot her own birth-day. In the end her father reminded her what day it was, hugging and kissing her and calling her his grown-up girl.

'Does Mummy know about today?' she had asked, wide-eyed.

'Of course she knows,' Jason responded. 'She's planned a special surprise for you.'

Suddenly everything was all right again. Mummy hadn't forgotten. She was coming home after all. How silly of Holly to think Mummy would do anything else.

Holly hung onto her father's hand. 'When is Mummy's surprise?' she asked.

'When do you want it to be?'

'Now, of course.'

Without another word, her father marched her into the big room at the front of the house. Then he let go of her and went over to the table by the window. On it was a package wrapped up in shiny silver paper.

'It's for you,' he told her. 'Mummy sent it all the way from Scotland.'

The truth of what had happened suddenly hit her. Mummy wasn't coming home at all. Her idea of a surprise was to send this silver monster.

She turned away. 'I don't want it,' she said.

Her father made an attempt to be cheerful. 'Why don't you open it first, and then decide?'

Holly went on standing there, her hands clenched by her sides. So in the end Jason went over, took the silver parcel and put it down in front of her.

When she still didn't respond, he stripped the paper off so she could see for herself what was inside.

Holly gave a little gasp. It was everything she'd dreamed about. The biggest, most perfect doll's house in the world. Her mother must have searched for miles to find it. She'd even put furniture in all the rooms.

She saw her father looking at her anxiously. 'It's what you wanted, isn't it?' he said.

She felt the tears gather in the corners of her eyes.

'Yes, but I wanted Mummy more,' she told him.

Holly brought herself back to the Savoy, forcing herself to look around the expensive, wood panelled room. It did nothing for her, just as the dolls' house had done nothing for her. Without her mother, she could have been in Buckingham Palace and still not given a damn.

Jason must have sensed what was going through her mind,

for he leaned across the table and took the champagne out of her hand.

'The booze is making you maudlin,' he said.

The anger Holly had directed towards her mother suddenly transferred itself to him.

'What do you know about disappointment?' she asked. 'Mummy's nice as pie when it comes to you.'

'Not always.'

'What do you mean, not always? She's dotty about you. She does everything you say.'

She saw her father smile. 'You've been reading too many newspapers. Your mother and I are like any other old married couple. We love each other, but we also understand each other. I know Eve puts the theatre above everything else she does – she often puts it above me – but I don't fight it the way you do.'

Holly looked at her father in surprise. 'Why not?'

'Because there's no point. Your mother has an incredible talent which controls her. It's uncomfortable to live with sometimes, but it's part of her, like an arm or a leg.'

Holly was just pondering the significance of this, when she was distracted. Everyone at the tables around her was applauding.

She craned her neck to see what all the fuss was about and she was greeted by the sight of her mother.

Eve had pulled out all the stops that night. Most of her long dark hair had been twisted into a chignon and she was sporting the diamond earrings Jason had bought to celebrate her latest award.

On anyone else the whole thing might have looked over the top, but Eve knew how to carry herself. It was a trick she'd acquired in the theatre. She could put on the most elaborate costume and make it appear as if it was as ordinary as a pair of jeans. Tonight she was wearing her Bruce Old-field, slashed to the thigh and plunging in the front.

Eve arrived at the table now, bending to kiss Holly, enveloping her with the heady scent of Joy, which she always wore.

More than anything, Holly wanted to forgive her for being late, but something stopped her. Her mother wasn't alone. There was a man with her, a tall, craggy man with a drinker's face. Before Holly could wonder who he was, Eve made the introductions.

'This is Al Goldman, the American producer.' She said it the way other people might say, 'This is Alfred Hitchcock,' or 'This is Cecil B. De Mille.' So Holly guessed he must be important.

When her mother gestured for him to sit down, she knew her hunch was right, but she resented his presence all the same.

'Why is Al here?' she whispered to her father. 'I thought it was my evening.'

'It *is* your evening, darling. Just be patient for a few minutes and it'll come right.'

Holly did her best, but it was hard going. Al Goldman turned out to be the most boring man on the face of the earth. All he could talk about was her mother's play, which she'd seen five times and knew off by heart.

'New York would eat it up,' he drawled. 'It's got everything us Yankees love.'

Now Holly thought she'd heard everything. The play was about Queen Victoria. Half the Americans he was talking about wouldn't even be interested in her. She turned to her mother, expecting her to put the ignorant fool on the right track, but Eve did nothing of the sort. She just signalled to the waiter for another bottle of champagne.

The girl's heart sank. If they didn't get started soon, the whole evening would be wasted.

She moved closer to her father. 'Can't you get rid of him?' she whispered from behind her hand.

Jason looked at his daughter, all done up for her big night out. The dark dress, the discreet touches of make-up, had all conspired to turn her into a woman. The least he could do was treat her like one.

He took her hand and squeezed it. 'I'll do my best, darling,' he said kindly.

The next time there was a gap in the conversation, Jason turned to his wife.

'Darling,' he said. 'It's getting late. Don't you think we should do something about dinner?'

Eve smiled. 'Of course we should. You don't mind if Al joins us, do you?'

Jason was shaken, though he made a good job of hiding it.

'I don't mind,' he told her, 'but you'd better ask Holly how she feels. It is her big night.'

Eve turned to her daughter and saw she was going to have trouble. Holly was looking daggers at Al Goldman and she knew unless she could defuse the situation there would be a first-rate scene. She rose from her chair and took hold of Holly's hand.

'Come on,' she said. 'You and I are going to the ladies' room for a second.'

Then, before the girl could object, Eve had her on her feet and was pulling her towards the back of the restaurant.

The cloakroom was deserted, to Eve's eternal relief. She sat her daughter down in front of the mirror and pulled up a second chair for herself.

'I know you hate this, don't you?' she said.

Holly looked tearful. 'What do you think?'

'I think you've every reason to feel the way you do. If it was my birthday I'd scream blue murder.'

'So why are you doing this to me?'

Eve sighed. 'Because I don't have any choice. Al Goldman flew in from New York specially to see me and I can't just tell him to get lost.'

Holly rubbed her eyes, smearing mascara all the way down her face.

'You could if you cared about me.'

Eve looked at her daughter in despair. 'You know I care about you, you silly goose. But this is business. What's happening tonight could affect my whole future.'

Holly suddenly looked suspicious.

'This Al Goldman character,' she said. 'He doesn't want to take the play to New York, does he?'

11

Absent-mindedly Eve started to wipe the mascara off her daughter's cheeks.

'He might do,' she ventured. 'That's what he wants to talk to your father about tonight.'

Now everything clicked into place. Her mother had wanted Broadway for ages now, but Jason had talked her out of it, because of her. She was too young to be left for months on end. Holly could see her father's influence didn't count for much any more.

'When did you first know about this?' she asked her mother.

'About a week ago,' Eve told her, 'Al rang me to say he was interested in the play.'

'Did he ring Daddy too?'

Holly could see she'd hit a nerve. For an instant, a look of absolute fury passed across the flawless mask of her mother's face.

'He didn't have to ring him,' Eve said crossly. 'He knew he'd be seeing him tonight.'

Holly felt slightly sick. Mummy was planning to go away to America and she'd picked her birthday to finalize things.

She should have walked out then and there. Mummy was abandoning her. She deserved to have her nose rubbed in it. But then she realized there was little point. She could shout and scream all she liked and it wouldn't make the slightest bit of difference. Eve would do exactly as she wanted to do.

Holly checked herself in the cloakroom mirror and saw that Eve had done a good job of patching her up.

'I think it's time we went back to the restaurant,' she told her mother. 'Mr Goldman and Daddy will be talking business by now. You won't want to miss any of it, will you?'

3

Holly had always lived her life on a seesaw. At one end of it was bad news. At the other, counterbalancing it, was good.

So when she heard the bad news – that her mother was taking off for Broadway – she wasn't entirely devastated. In her bones she knew the game wasn't over yet. Something else was bound to happen, something that would take the sting out of her mother's defection.

It happened three days after her birthday. Her father broke the news to her. The management of the Adelphi had decided to hold Eve to her contract. She couldn't leave for the States until the end of the run.

Holly did her best to hide her jubilation. 'I suppose that means Al Goldman will have to find someone else for Mummy's part.'

Jason felt weary. 'It looked like that two days ago. Then Al rang this morning to say he's going to postpone everything until your mother can get there.'

'So she's going?'

Her father nodded. 'It doesn't look like anything's going to stop her now.'

Holly turned on her heel and headed for the door. That's what you think, she thought.

Holly had no idea what made her start to eat. She didn't develop strange cravings for toffee pudding and condensed milk. All that happened was that she got hungry.

13

Almost from the day she knew she was going to lose her mother she felt ravenous. She found herself nibbling almost non-stop — sandwiches, biscuits, leftovers from dinner. It was as if she had a bottomless pit where her stomach used to be, and she had to fill it or she felt unhappy.

Nobody at home noticed there was anything wrong at first. Holly was a teenager. She was at the age when overeating was perfectly normal. So Lola, the housekeeper, brought in extra supplies when she did the weekly shop. Eve pretended she didn't notice when her daughter raided the fridge almost every night.

Then Holly started to get fat and everything changed.

The weight seemed to go on overnight. One day she was her normal self, running around in blue jeans and skinny T-shirts, the next, she couldn't get into anything.

At this point Eve decided she had to take action.

'You're eating all the wrong things,' she said, not mincing her words. 'It's time I put you on a diet.'

Eve devised a whole regime which she wrote out in careful longhand and pinned on the fridge door. Breakfast consisted of prunes and fat-free yogurt. Two boiled eggs and a crispbread passed for lunch. And supper was always a piece of grilled fish with a salad.

In the normal way, the diet wouldn't have bothered Holly. She had never been all that interested in food and if her mother wanted her to eat crispbreads and prunes she would have been happy to oblige.

Now it was different. She looked to what she ate for comfort and solace, and she didn't find it in prunes. The things she was looking for existed in fried potatoes and chocolate milk, so she incorporated them into her mother's diet.

Holly didn't tell Eve about all the extras. There was no point in upsetting her mother after all the trouble she had gone to, so she became secretive.

Her pocket money, which she used to spend on clothes, went on a secret hoard of food. She would buy packets of biscuits and tins of salted peanuts and hide them away in the top of her wardrobe.

For a while her ruse went undetected. When she didn't get any thinner, Eve simply thought the diet was taking time to work. After three weeks, she realized something was seriously amiss.

She had been on enough slimming cures to know that her daughter was cheating. Nobody who stuck to the regime she had devised could fail to maintain eight stone. She went out and bought some scales for Holly's bathroom. Then, so her daughter couldn't get out of it, she insisted on being there every morning when she recorded her weight.

To help Holly concentrate on her body, she started taking her to the gym. Eve made herself work out at least three times a week. Now she put her daughter through the same routine.

They would sit beside each other pedalling away on exercise bikes. Holly, instead of resenting it, found she was having a good time. Her mother had never been so concerned for her before. She would continually summon up the gym manager to monitor her daughter's progress. When she was satisfied Holly was making a real effort to be slim, she treated her to a Swedish massage once a week.

When Holly looked back on these last days with her mother, she knew they were the happiest she had known. Eve wasn't focusing on the theatre any more. She was focusing on *her*. Holly wanted it to go on for ever, so she formulated a plan.

She would keep her mother so busy, so concerned, so upset about her, that when the time came to leave for New York, she would have to postpone her trip, even cancel it altogether.

She invented problems associated with her fatness. Shyness was one. She refused to go out because she said she felt awkward and ungainly with other people. When her mother tried to talk her out of it, she threw tantrums.

From being a docile, eager-to-please adolescent, Holly changed overnight into a monster. She didn't like herself for doing what she was doing, and she vowed that once she had persuaded Eve to stay at home, she would go back to being herself. Right now, the end justified the means.

15

As the time approached for Eve's departure, Holly became aware of her parents quarrelling. She would listen to their raised voices through the door. Her father was unhappy about Eve going away.

'Holly needs you more than ever. If you desert her now, she could be in real trouble.'

Holly found it difficult to make out what her mother said in reply, because she spoke very quickly and her voice was shrill and almost unintelligible. Whatever it was, Holly knew her behaviour was having an effect. It's only a matter of time now, she thought, before I'm home and dry.

She began to have her doubts when her mother started shopping. She laid in stocks of her favourite soap and a handcream that you could only buy from Fortnum's. When she came back from her weekly trip to the hairdresser, Holly saw she had bought two huge bottles of the tint she used on her hair.

'Are you going to start doing your hair at home?' she asked.

Eve looked at her and told her not to be naïve.

'I'm off in ten days,' she told her daughter, 'and I can't trust the hairdressers in New York to get the colour exactly right.'

Holly felt as if she had been hit from behind. So she's going after all, she thought bitterly. She wanted to cry, but choked her feelings back.

'I never thought you'd really do it,' she said.

Her mother looked genuinely surprised.

'Why ever not?' she asked. 'I'm all set to open at the Plymouth in three weeks.'

The girl gave her mother her full attention then, concentrating on the way she looked as if it could give her some clue about what was going on inside. She was perfectly put together in a cream Chanel suit with all the pearls and gold chains that went with it. If Holly hadn't known she had just come back from the hairdresser, she might have assumed Eve had been at some charity lunch.

She has to dress up to the nines wherever she goes, the girl

16

thought bitterly. It's as if the whole world is her audience. It was then she realized she had never really stood a chance. Whatever she did, her mother would always be an actress first.

'You weren't even tempted to put it off,' Holly said sharply. 'Even though you knew I'd be heartbroken without you.'

She expected her mother to look guilty, but Eve didn't even flinch. 'You won't fall apart,' she said matter-of-factly. Then, without even looking at her, Eve took hold of a bottle of crimson nail polish and started painting her nails.

There was something about the way she did it that made Holly want to strangle her. Her stupid nails were more important than her daughter's feelings.

'You're so sure of yourself,' she said. 'You're so convinced you can swan off into the sunset and nothing will happen.'

Eve looked up from what she was doing. 'What do you have in mind?' she asked. 'Are you going to put another seven pounds on your hips? Or will it be a full-scale nervous breakdown?'

Holly couldn't hold the tears back any longer, and they coursed down her cheeks like a river in full flood.

'You don't care,' she wept. 'You don't give a damn about me.'

Eve sighed. 'You know that's not true.'

'Then prove it. Cancel New York.'

When Eve spoke next there was ice in her voice. 'If I cancel New York,' she said, 'the only thing it will prove is I'm frightened of you.' She softened slightly. 'Look, darling, I know it's hard when I go away, but you've managed without me before. Going to New York isn't any different than going on a provincial tour. It might take a bit longer but that's as bad as it will get.'

Holly listened while her mother tried to make light of the trip. But there was no denying it. Eve was going to the other side of the world. There was no way she could pop down and see Holly for the odd weekend. Even if she phoned her, she would have to calculate the time difference.

17

'I suppose you'll be saying next I can come and see you in the school holidays.'

Eve shrugged. 'You can if you like, though I'll be working most of the time.'

Holly knew when she was beaten. 'Don't worry,' she said. 'I wouldn't dream of barging in on your precious Broadway debut. I'm only your daughter. I wouldn't want to spoil things for you.'

4

The words would haunt Eve for as long as she lived, making her feel guilty and miserable as hell.

'I'm only your daughter. I wouldn't want to spoil things for you.'

Holly had looked so broken when she said it that all Eve had wanted to do was fold her in her arms and promise to stay for ever.

But she had not been able to. She wondered how she had summoned up the strength to be so hard. Only a monster would say the things she had said to her daughter, a nerveless, unfeeling, selfish monster. Or an actress.

Eve replayed the scene in her head for the hundredth time, and she felt sad, for it had been one of her better performances. By now Holly would be utterly convinced that Eve didn't care whether she lived or died. The gulf between them, the gulf that had been growing with every year of her daughter's life, would be that much wider.

Eve stared out of the window of her New York apartment, absent-mindedly noting the Chrysler Building, its Art Deco frontage glowing in the last rays of the sun.

Soon it would be night and all the lights in the glass and chrome skyscrapers would come on, twinkling merrily in the dark, turning the city into a fairyland.

Normally it would have excited the hell out of her. Tonight Eve didn't have the heart for it, for superimposed on the image of the city was her daughter's face. It was a mind's eye picture, all pouting mouth and tear-stained eyes, and try as she might, she couldn't get rid of it. It haunted her and she knew at that moment she could never be what Holly needed.

She wants a full-time mother, Eve thought. And what she's landed up with is a Broadway actress first, a mother second. And there's not a damn thing I can do about it.

She thought back to how it all started with her own childhood, wondering if she could have changed things then. And she realized she was being a fool.

I couldn't have stopped my father leaving home, she thought, just as I couldn't have prevented all those solid, suburban little girls I went to school with teasing me about it.

It was the teasing that got to her. Her classmates called her Orphan Annie and rag doll. And when one of them found out her mother cleaned people's houses to earn money to live on, the taunts became unbearable. As far as Croydon High School was concerned, Eve was an outcast, friendless, unloved and unwelcome.

She might have dropped out of school if it hadn't been for the new English teacher. He was forever experimenting with ways to encourage his pupils to express themselves and one of his favourite exercises was charades. He would get the girls in his class to imitate a TV personality or a movie star.

Nobody much liked these games, because they felt silly and self-conscious. But Eve had the peculiar knack of being able to reproduce almost anyone.

She could be Benny Hill or Marilyn Monroe right down to the last mannerism. She was so good at it that she was asked to do it again and again. After class, the girls would beg her to sing 'I Wanna Be Loved by You' in Monroe's wispy, sad little voice.

Eve found herself obliging, at first unwillingly, then with increasing confidence, as she discovered it was the key to popularity. When she was herself, she was despised and ignored, but when she became another person, everyone wanted to know her.

She decided to become an actress then and there. It was

20

such an easy way to make people like her, a sure-fire way of getting people's attention.

She brought herself back to the present. Nothing has really changed, she reflected. No matter how grown up I get, I still need people to love me.

Eve looked out of her apartment window, seeing the glittering city spread out before her like a piece of expensive jewellery. Dusk had faded into night and below her on the street the traffic was building up, taking people to restaurants and bars and theatres.

Some of those people, she thought, will want to come and see me. If I'm good they'll applaud and throw bouquets and persuade their friends to come to the play.

She knew then she couldn't go home, for no matter how much her daughter needed her, she had to stay for the applause.

5

Eve got up at lunchtime the next day, spent the afternoon going over changes to the text for the New York production, and then went to the theatre.

Broadway was sleazier than she'd imagined. In London the playhouses were near the vice centre, but somehow they'd managed to rise above it. Out here the girlie shows and the porno movie houses had infiltrated and the theatres had to take their chances as best they could.

She saw a peep-show next door to a grand old Victorian building with a billboard advertising a Shakespeare play. Further along the street she saw two theatres with their original façades, the carved angels and cupids jostling for attention with all the cheap neon. The whole thing made Eve feel uneasy. There was no respect for the theatre here. It was just another form of entertainment.

She thought for a moment about the play she was opening in – *Portrait of a Queen*, the life story of Queen Victoria.

What the hell am I doing? she wondered. What the hell is Al Goldman doing bringing it over here? Nobody in New York could care less about English history.

Her doubts took on a new shape when she reached the theatre. The minute she walked through the door of the Green Room, she was confronted by a member of the cast sounding off about the play. He was surrounded by the rest of the production, who were hanging on his every word.

'It's not American enough,' he told the assembled players. 'Nobody will make any sense of it.'

Eve recognized who he was now. His name was Brett Weston and if her memory was right, he had been cast as her leading man.

This is all I need, she thought, a leading man who doesn't believe in the play. If he goes on like this, we'll fall flat on our faces.

She turned to Brett. 'You're talking rubbish,' she said. 'Not everything here plays to the suburbs. What about Pinter's *The Homecoming*? What about *Rosencrantz and Guildenstern*?'

'There are always exceptions—' the man said sulkily.

Al Goldman interrupted him. 'Those plays weren't exceptions. Over the years there have been lots like them. They're known as snob hits in the business.'

Brett looked disbelieving. 'Don't tell me *Portrait of a Queen* is going to be a snob hit.'

Eve held her breath. It was the sixty-four-thousand-dollar question.

Al didn't even look concerned. 'Why did you think I brought it over?' he demanded. 'It's got nothing to do with the lives of the people here. If you judged it against *Fiddler on the Roof* you'd have to vote it a no-no. But you don't do that. Instead you think about the people who queued to see *Fiddler* and ask if they want something apart from being entertained.'

Eve looked at him curiously. 'Do they?'

'You bet they do. They want to be admired. They want to be thought of as intelligent and classy, and buying a ticket for *Portrait of a Queen* gives them that kind of kudos. Of course, half of our audience could well be bored to tears, but they're never going to admit it. They'll tell their neighbours in New Jersey how uplifted they were, how intellectually challenged. Then the neighbours will want tickets, and before you know it, you've sold out.'

Brett stood up and made to leave. 'I hope you're right,' he said, 'for all our sakes.'

'Of course he's right,' Eve said. 'Wait till I tell you about some of the audiences we had in London.'

The actor looked her up and down and she saw for the

first time how striking he was. There was an earthy quality about him that reminded her of Robert De Niro. When he next spoke she was conscious that everyone's eyes were on them.

'Why should I wait to hear about your London audiences?' he said. 'If you come across the street with me, you can tell me about them over a glass of beer.'

6

Brett took Eve to an Irish bar where most of the cast gathered after rehearsals. It was a crowded, smoky hole full of other theatre people. Eve slid into a booth, feeling very at ease.

She'd hung around places like this all her working life. When she was touring the provinces all she did every night was prop up the bar and gossip about the play. Now she was doing the same in New York.

She saw her new leading man was making himself at home, waving to acquaintances grouped around the long wooden bar, and she decided it was time she found out a bit more about him.

It wasn't exactly difficult. Brett loved talking about himself. Even though he was a method actor by training, he had none of the complications that came with it. By the time he and Eve were on to their second beer, he was well into his life story.

He had grown up in California surrounded on all sides by the film business: his sister was a wardrobe mistress at one of the big studios; his father worked for a big agent as an accountant . . . It was somehow inevitable that Brett would go to drama school as soon as he graduated from college.

As he rambled on about his early life, Eve felt her attention wandering.

She had heard the story a hundred times before. She knew it so well that if Brett lost his memory for a second, she could have easily ad-libbed for him.

Then he said something that had her hooked. 'Two years

ago,' he confessed, 'when I was down on my luck, a magazine offered me a thousand dollars to take my clothes off.'

'Did you do it?' Eve asked him, fascinated.

Brett smiled, teasing her with his silence. 'Sure I did it,' he said finally. 'It was the turning point of my career.'

Soon after the spread appeared, an influential model agent spotted him and put him up for a cigarette commercial. It featured a cowboy riding into the sunset. The agency thought he was just the man they were looking for. He had the right outdoor look without coming on like a bonehead, and they featured him in a national campaign.

Overnight, Brett's face appeared not just on television, but on posters and in women's magazines as well. There was something about him that took the public's imagination.

He became a minor celebrity, opening supermarkets and appearing in the gossip columns, and he took advantage of his new status by moving to a hotshot agent who could get him acting jobs.

It was a shrewd move. Notoriety got him the breaks that hard work had failed to do. There were a couple of meaty roles in low-budget television followed by a small part on Broadway.

The stage role showed he could act. There followed other, not-so-small parts, and now this: his first lead.

As Eve listened to Brett talking about his career, she realized she had been wrong about him. He didn't need any coaxing to pull his weight in this production. This was his big chance. He needed the play to be a success and she had an idea he would do almost anything to make it so.

It was getting late and before she could object, Brett signalled the waiter and ordered a couple of hamburgers.

'You do eat meat?' he said, looking at Eve's face. 'You wouldn't prefer a salad or something?'

'No, I wouldn't prefer a salad,' she said crossly. 'But I think you might have asked if I was free for dinner first.'

He spread his hands. 'I decided to take a chance,' he told her. 'I know you're new in this town, so I didn't think you'd have a hot date.'

'You do know I'm married?' Eve asked him.

'Sure I know you're married, but most people don't care about that when they're on the road.'

'Well, I care,' she told him, suddenly feeling insulted. 'I don't go on dates and I don't cheat on my husband. I'd like you to remember that.'

Brett looked at her then, appraisingly. There was no mistaking the message in his eyes.

'What if I choose not to remember it?'

'You'll be on a hiding to nothing.' Eve snapped back.

He leaned against the padded leather cubicle and she was reminded of a cat, a big self-satisfied tom, crouched and ready to move in for the kill.

'I don't believe you,' he said. 'New York can be a lonely town, particularly when you're stuck here on your own.'

'But I'm not on my own. There's Al Goldman, and I guess I'll make friends in the company.'

'It may work in the beginning, but people have their own lives. Al has a wife in Connecticut and a girlfriend in the city. The kids in the cast have already started pairing off. If you're not careful you'll end up with the television set for company.'

'Maybe that's the best solution.'

Brett looked scornful. 'No way it's the best solution. You're a woman, aren't you? You're young and you're warm and you need to keep the fires burning. Everyone does.'

'And I suppose any minute now, you're going to tell me you're just the man to do it.'

There was a silence.

'I don't have to tell you that,' he said eventually. 'You already know it.'

Eve walked around in a rage for the next week. Brett's presumption took her breath away. She was a new face in a new town and suddenly she was a target for every stud on the make.

If she was being strictly honest with herself, Brett was the only stud who had tried it on, but it didn't stop her from losing her balance. She found it hard to rehearse with him, particularly when they had to play a love scene, and she started to wonder what was happening to her.

Eve had always had admirers and it had never bothered her before. If the truth were known, they had boosted her ego. They flirted, but they knew how to take no for an answer. And when she got home she would tell Jason all about them and they would both laugh about it.

Brett was different. For a start, he was American, so he didn't really know about her reputation. He didn't give a damn about it either. She was just an English actress in for a limited run and that's the way he treated her.

He made her increasingly nervous, so much so that the cracks started to show on stage. Where Eve had been confident in London, she was stiff and uptight in New York. What made it even worse were the changes to the script. They shouldn't have rattled her, but inexplicably she couldn't seem to remember the new lines at all.

Al Goldman was seriously worried. He had a lot riding on this English play. If it failed it wouldn't just deplete his bank balance; his credibility would take a tumble as well, and he couldn't afford that. The business on Broadway was full of sharks. Once he seemed vulnerable, he'd find it harder to raise money for other projects, and nobody would back him in another English venture. This didn't please him at all, for he had already had his eye on an Andrew Lloyd Webber show.

A week before they previewed, he decided to take Eve on one side. He had his own office at the back of the theatre and after a particularly disastrous dress rehearsal, he invited Eve there for a glass of champagne.

As soon as she walked in, she was on the defensive. Al only saw bankers and people he was about to fire in his office. She had no doubt which category she fell into, so she positioned herself on his overstuffed plush sofa and waited for the axe to fall.

Al was taking his time. He made a great production of filling her glass and when she sneaked a look at the label, she saw he had gone to the trouble of getting in vintage Bollinger, which he knew was her favourite.

What's he up to? she wondered. It didn't take her long to find out.

'I've noticed you have a problem,' he said, getting to the point. 'Do you think we might talk about it?'

Eve took a sip of her champagne. 'If you like,' she told him, 'but it won't do any good. I just can't seem to function over here.'

'I don't buy that. You were superb in London and nothing has changed since then apart from a couple of little adjustments, and you should have taken those in your stride.'

Eve sat perfectly still. 'Something else has changed,' she said. 'The cast is different.'

For a moment Al was thrown. This was a professional experienced actress telling him she was bothered about a New York cast. Then he realized he was missing the point.

It wasn't the cast that was bothering this prima donna, it was a *member* of the cast. Eve had taken against somebody and it was hurting her performance. He racked his brains to think who it could be. None of the women appeared to be stealing her thunder. He hadn't heard any of the usual backstage squabbles.

So it has to be Brett, he thought. Either he's fucking her and they've had a fight, or he isn't fucking her and she wants him to.

It was a delicate subject and the producer approached it the only way he knew.

'Do you want me to get rid of Brett?' he asked. Eve did a double take. 'How did you know about Brett?' she demanded. 'I haven't told anyone about it.'

'Well, what if you did tell me?' Al replied. 'I'm only the poor schmuck who's putting up the money for the show.'

Eve knew when she was cornered. Al might be pouring her favourite champagne and coming on like a father, but he was quite capable of terminating her contract if she didn't play straight with him. So she told him about the evening she spent with her leading man.

29

'It wasn't the proposition that upset me,' she said. 'I've had enough of those in my time. It was his attitude. He was so sure of himself, so convinced that if he bided his time, I'd fall into his bed.'

The producer looked at her. 'And will you?'

Eve was shocked. 'How can you even think that?'

'I'm not the one who's doing the thinking,' Al smiled. 'You are. If you weren't interested, you wouldn't be reacting like this.'

Eve rounded on him then. 'You've got a dirty mind, Al Goldman. You shouldn't judge everybody by your own standards.'

He sighed. 'I'm not going to argue with you any more. We all know what the problem is and it's not going to go away until you and Brett make it.' He paused. 'How you do it is none of my business. But I can promise you one thing: if you can't work this one out I'm pulling the plug on the show. I can do without making a fool of myself in this city.'

7

Eve hardly slept that night. She tossed and turned, going over what the producer had said to her. If she and Brett didn't come to terms, it would all be over.

It was a tough ultimatum because Al knew how much this show meant to her. She had dreamed of making it on Broadway ever since she started. Now her chance had come, she was going to blow it.

The nightmare was, she could do nothing about it. At every rehearsal she could feel the part slipping further and further away from her. Every time she froze, she would see Brett looking at her, watching and waiting until she reached out for him to rescue her.

Well, she wasn't going to do it. She was too old and too experienced to need props like Brett. She'd grown out of that sort of thing years ago.

She closed her eyes, praying for sleep, and her prayers were answered. She fell into a light doze, but even then her troubles wouldn't leave her alone. They wove themselves into her dreams.

Now Eve was just twenty-one, a promising drama student at her first real-life audition. She knew the part off by heart. She could have recited it in her sleep. All she had to do was go out on stage and knock 'em dead. She'd been doing it all her life, hadn't she? What was so different about today?

Without meaning to, she thought about her mother and she knew exactly what was different. If Pearl had been with her now, she'd be reading her cues and checking she was word-perfect. She would have told her what she was up against and that she had nothing to worry about because she was far and away the best thing in the theatre.

But Mummy wasn't here now, because her smart new agent couldn't live with her. She was all on her own and the realisation made her fearful. Then she pulled herself together. I'm not a little girl any more, she told herself.

She saw the stage manager was standing beside her.

'You're on next,' he told her. 'Go out in two minutes.'

She took a deep breath and put down the script. Then she thought herself into the part she was playing. She was a young girl breaking up with her lover. He had been the only man she had slept with and the wrench was tearing her apart.

She waited for change to come over her. For the moment when she actually became the girl she was playing. Only it didn't happen.

As Eve stood in the wings of the theatre, she felt like nobody but herself. This is ridiculous she thought. I know this part off backwards. I know the character; I've *been* the character. So why can't I be her now?

She saw the stage manager looking at her. 'You're meant to be on now,' he whispered.

She pulled herself together and did as she was told, but she was out of character, and the stage which she had always been so at ease with suddenly terrified her.

Why didn't I notice it was so big before? she wondered. There's acres of it. And the lights, they're dazzling. Blinding, almost.

A voice somewhere below her asked if she was ready and Eve nodded. Then she started the speech she had memorized.

The words came back to her with no difficulty. She was fluent and smooth but there was no heart in what she was saying. Each time she tried to find the girl she was playing, the character eluded her. So she relied on tricks: she made clever little gestures and used her face to convey the emotions she seemed incapable of feeling. Half-way through her performance, she was told to stop and leave her name and number with the man on the door. Then she was dismissed.

Eve walked off the stage in a state of shock. This had never happened to her before. At drama school all the other competitive students hung on her performances. Everyone who had heard her wanted her to go on and on reading everything.

Only this man was bored by what she had done. He wanted her off the stage and out of his sight as quickly as possible.

Eve struggled to hold back the tears. If Mummy had been there she would never have gone on stage in the state she was in.

Eve woke up from the nightmare in a cold sweat, and for a split second she wasn't sure what was real and what was her dream.

Groggily she reached for the light switch, sitting up in bed. I was on stage, she thought, and I froze. I couldn't deliver a performance. That was yesterday, wasn't it?

The bedside lamp came on, flooding the room with soft golden light. She rubbed her eyes. It wasn't yesterday, she realized. She had been dreaming about what happened years ago.

She suddenly felt helpless, for she knew history was repeating itself.

The phone was ringing when Jason walked into his office. He sighed. Why wasn't his girl there to take the call? It was ten in the morning; there was no excuse.

He had reached his desk now, but the phone was still going, demanding his attention, insisting on being answered. He sat down and picked up the receiver.

'Jason Fielding,' he said. 'Can I help you?'

He thought he heard a sob on the end of the line. Then Eve's voice came on.

'Darling, thank God I got you.'

All his senses were on alert. Something had gone wrong.

'What is it?' he asked, doing his best to remain calm. 'What's the problem?'

Eve started to cry in earnest. 'New York's the problem. I can't stand it here on my own.'

Jason waited for a few moments while she collected herself. Then, when the sobbing subsided, he tried to get to the bottom of things. 'When did you start feeling like this? The last time we spoke, you seemed to be having a fine time.'

'It was never fine. I pretended it was because I didn't want to worry you, but from the moment I set foot over here everything's gone wrong.'

'Like what?'

He sensed her hesitation. 'I can't sleep,' she said finally. 'I lie awake at night worrying about what's going on at home. I think about Holly and that eating problem of hers. I think about you. I think about the house. The whole thing drives me crazy and when I get up in the morning, I feel like I've been run over by a truck.'

Jason thought for a moment. 'You always feel like that when you first go away. Things will settle down.'

'They won't settle down.' She sounded hysterical now, and for the first time he was seriously worried.

'You're not thinking of quitting, are you?'

'That's exactly what I'm thinking of. I want you to see if you can get me out of my contract. I've had it with New York.'

None of what she was saying made sense. She'd been waiting for this break all her life. She'd worked herself silly for it. And now there was a serious chance of her dreams coming true, she was throwing in the towel.

There's more to this than meets the eye, Jason thought. She's not missing me and Holly any more than she did before. There's something she's not telling me.

Out of the corner of his eye, he saw his secretary appear in his doorway. She was signalling frantically, the way she did when there was a crisis in the office.

He sighed. Whatever else was happening, his wife came first.

'Darling,' he said, 'I can't make you any promises until I take a look at your agreement with Al Goldman. If you give me an hour, I'll get back to you.'

It seemed to mollify her. 'I know you'll sort something out for me,' she told him. 'You always do.'

Jason put the phone down. There was something he'd missed, but if he went back over things, he knew the answer would come.

8

LONDON, 1968

The girl on the bare rehearsal stage was playing a tart. It was a sluttish, let-it-all-hang-out performance, and the man watching her assumed it was based on her own experience. After all, where else could she have learned it? She hadn't been treading the boards long enough to fake all that sensuality.

No, thought Jason as he settled into his uncomfortable tip-back seat, that one's been around the tracks. Yet she intrigued him: years of watching actresses had given him a sixth sense for talent. The girl might be playing herself, but she had presence. When she was walking across the stage, you didn't look at anyone else, because you couldn't look at anyone else. To pull that off you needed more than sex appeal.

Then he reminded himself where he was. He was watching a drama school, for Christ's sake. All the actors in this show were students strutting their stuff at the end of the course. They were short on technique and needed knocking into shape. He decided to reserve his judgement until he saw what else the girl on stage could do.

At LAMDA that year, all the kids had two bites at the cherry. If they blew it on the first reading, then at least they had a second chance. Jason wondered what the girl was going to go for next. It was bound to be something sexy. He was so convinced she would go for the obvious that when she came on next he almost didn't recognize her. She was done up like a Victorian matron in trailing skirts and she had padded herself to look heavier than she was.

He thought she'd probably make a complete fool of herself. Students never knew when to leave well alone.

Jason looked up to see the girl had come right into the centre of the stage. And she held it. For some reason she'd managed to grab the attention of everyone in the audience, and he supposed it was the usual lust for blood. His profession, the profession, loved to see a newcomer take a fall. It made them feel better about themselves.

He listened intently as she started her first speech and he noticed the voice had changed. When she was playing a tart she used a throaty, street-smart accent. Now the vowels were pure cut glass. He wondered how the hell she did it. She was playing the Lady Bracknell part from *The Importance of Being Earnest* and the performance she was turning in had everyone on the edge of their seats. Nobody was expecting her to mess up any more.

Jason looked around him. There was the usual mishmash of old actors and proud parents that made up the passing out parades from the big schools, but they weren't what interested Jason. What he was looking for were other professionals – producers, casting directors, agents like him.

Unerringly, he found them. Two of his competitors were sitting in the front row, furiously taking notes. He didn't bother to look any further. Experience told him there would be at least half a dozen people after this clever little student by the end of the afternoon. He mentally added his name to the list. If she was as good as she looked he could earn a lot of money out of a girl like that.

In the six years he had been in business, Jason Fielding had made quite a killing out of drama school students. He had started small in two tiny offices at the top of St Martin's Lane, and his hunger, his greed and his talent had done the rest for him.

Now, at the age of twenty-eight, he occupied one floor of the converted house he'd started out in. He had a staff which included receptionists, secretaries, and junior executives who did his running around for him. Most important of all, he had stars.

Of the two dozen actors he'd started out with, two had made it across the Atlantic to Hollywood and five were currently starring in the West End. His competitors called him a toffee-nosed Hooray Henry who had made it on chutzpah and luck. His admirers simply referred to Jason as 'the starmaker'.

When he thought about it, Jason realized none of it was true. He didn't make stars, he merely found them. He was too reserved to have chutzpah, and he was no luckier than anyone else. The Hooray Henry accusation was another illusion. Jason came from a middle-class army family, who had the good sense to send him to Eton. This provided him with a commanding air and perfect manners, all of which he proceeded to throw away when he pursued a career in the theatre.

His father, a brigadier, told him he was a bloody fool but it didn't put him off. Jason had no intention of ending up with a safe job in the City, so he kept writing off for stage management jobs and hoped for the best.

His break came when a Birmingham company lost their assistant stage manager at the beginning of the season. The man had just walked out, leaving them with a pile of scenery to hump and a production to organize.

If Jason had any luck in his life, it boiled down to one gift: he had rugger player's shoulders, so when he walked into the Birmingham Alhambra, he was exactly what the management were looking for. He was hired on the spot. For the next four years he humped scenery and read prompts.

It all ended when he discovered he didn't have what it took to become an actor. It had been his dream ever since Eton, and his reason for turning down the City and falling out with his father. But when his chance came he simply couldn't handle it.

He had been understudying one of the supporting actors. It was a small, showy part and one on which the entire play revolved. So when the actor went off sick with flu, the cast were understandably nervous.

38

Jason did his best to reassure everyone. 'I know the part backwards,' he had said. 'Depend on me.'

So they did. And he let them down. The worst part about his performance was his nervousness. From the moment he walked on stage, to the moment he walked off, Jason was wooden with terror. He was perfectly adequate in rehearsals but the presence of an audience destroyed him.

The play was a disaster. After his debut, the theatre manager begged him never to act again. Jason said he wouldn't. Then he handed in his notice.

He loved the theatre, but he knew he had no place in it. All he could do – all he was capable of doing – was to love it from a distance. So he considered his options and, at last, he wondered about becoming an agent. He'd spent four years watching actors, and though he couldn't do the job himself, he knew how it should be done. It was a flimsy qualification for a life's work – he hadn't even put it into practice – but it was all he had. So he took a chance.

It paid off. Almost from the start he realized he could pick a winner. The actor didn't have to be experienced or street-wise. In fact, the greener the talent was, the more Jason liked it because it put him ahead of the competition.

Time after time, Jason would pick someone out of a provincial touring company or a drama school and within months they would be getting TV work.

Nobody he favoured ever flunked a casting. As his strike rate was so high, he was on the top of every student's list.

Now, as he sat behind his desk and glanced at his diary, his mind returned to the girl he had seen a week ago.

He had little doubt he was on the top of her list and that was why he had delayed contacting her. By now she would have seen all the other agents, listened to their lies and their promises, and she would have an idea of her value.

It would be a totally false idea, of course, and he would have to put her right about herself, but that gave him an advantage. If she listened to what he had to say, he could do something with her. If she told him to go to hell, then neither of them had lost anything.

Jason picked up the phone and pressed the button that connected him with his secretary.

'Has the LAMDA student arrived yet?' he asked.

As always the girl was sharp with him. 'The LAMDA student has a name, you know. She's a human being, not a number on a call sheet.'

He suppressed his irritation. 'Then tell me this human being's name, will you?'

'She's called Eve Adams,' the secretary told him victoriously. 'And she hasn't come on her own.'

Jason groaned. This was all he needed. 'Don't tell me, let me guess. She's with her boyfriend. Either that or her mother.'

He heard a giggle on the other end of the line and knew his instincts had been right.

'Send them both in,' he barked into the phone, not bothering to find out which of the two evils accompanied this talent. 'The sooner we get this over with, the better.'

If Jason hated anything, he hated hangers-on. He looked up as the door opened, admitting Eve Adams and a small blonde woman. So she's with her mother, he thought. This could be worse than I imagined. He stood up and did his best to look welcoming.

'Why don't you both sit down and make yourselves comfortable.'

There was a sofa at the end of the office that Jason used for interviews. The two women made a great business of settling down on it. Both took their coats off and searched around for a spot to dump their big leather handbags, and while they were fussing, Jason did a fast assessment.

They came from the suburbs. Women who lived in the city didn't try as hard as these two did. He made a mental note to do something about the girl's image. He couldn't have her walking into a casting looking as if she'd come up to town for the day to do her shopping.

He studied the girl for a moment longer, taking in the tousled dark hair and the perfect oval of her face. There was a look of Vivien Leigh about her and that reassured him.

Those kind of looks were in fashion right now. He'd have no trouble selling her.

It was the older woman who opened the conversation. She wanted Jason to know her daughter had been in demand, and she went through the whole list of agents they had been in to see.

He decided to shoot her down while he still could.

'If you've had so many offers,' he observed, 'what are you doing here?'

It didn't put her off.

'We heard you were the best,' the woman replied, 'and that's what I want for Evie. The very best the theatre can offer.'

He looked at her, sliding his reading glasses down to the end of his nose in an attempt to look older.

'And what does Evie want?'

The girl looked at her mother for some signal, but there was none forthcoming so she improvised.

'I want the West End,' she said.

He smiled. 'I suppose you want to be a leading lady too?'

She nodded, shaking the great mane of hair around her shoulders. 'I have the talent for it,' she told him. 'Why shouldn't I want it?'

There was something very sure about the way she stated her ambitions. A lot of other actresses had sat in his office and shot for the moon, but none of them had been as convincing as this girl. He decided to probe a little further.

'What's your game plan?' he asked.

She looked confused. 'Mummy knows all about the business side of things,' she said, a little unsurely. 'I just do what I'm told.'

He turned to the blonde. 'What's your game plan then?'

It was a trap, baited and primed and she fell right into it.

'I thought it would be a good idea to start her off in television,' the woman said. 'There are a lot of commercials that need good-looking girls, and Evie would be just right for them.'

There was a brief silence, but Jason eased her over it.

'And when Evie was the queen of the commercial break, then what would you do with her?'

The woman was leaning forward now, flattered by all the attention she was getting.

'I'd see if the film companies were interested in her,' she said. 'Her face would be well-known, she could easily be picked as a Bond girl.'

'That's what you want for Eve, TV exposure and glamour parts. I suppose you'd think it was a good idea if she opened supermarkets as well.'

The blonde nodded vigorously. 'It's all money, isn't it?'

Jason made his expression neutral. 'Of course it's all money. Prostitution's all money too. Have you ever considered that for your daughter?'

The woman realized she'd been played for a fool.

'What's prostitution got to do with it?' she snapped at Jason. 'My daughter's an actress.'

'She may be an actress now,' he replied, still neutral, still amiable, 'but with you directing her career she won't be one for much longer.'

The woman made to get to her feet, but before she could do so, Jason moved out of his chair and went back to his desk.

It was important for him to be in charge now. They both had to see him as an authority figure, otherwise all this would have been for nothing.

It was the girl who spoke next: 'Are you saying Mummy doesn't know what she's doing?'

He smiled. 'She knows what she's doing if you want to be a starlet, but you told me you wanted more than that. You wanted to be a West End actress.'

'And you don't think getting my face on television is the way to do it?'

'I don't *think* it's not the way to do it. I *know* it's not the way to do it.'

Her mother came back into the conversation then. 'If you're such a big shot,' she said, 'you tell me how you'd make my daughter a famous actress.'

Jason turned to her, mustering up every ounce of charm he had. 'I'd start by sending her out of town. Eve's still raw. She needs the edges knocked off her and a few years in provincial rep will do that.'

The older woman narrowed her eyes. 'How many years does Evie have to do this for?'

'It depends how fast she learns. Two, maybe five years.'

'Then she'd play the West End.'

'In little parts, yes. She won't walk into a leading lady's part overnight.'

The blonde looked doubtful. 'That's not what I heard. If a girl has the right introduction, if she mixes in the right circles, she can be discovered just like that.'

She fixed Jason with hard brown eyes, reminding him of a large predatory bird. 'You know what I think your problem is?' she said. 'You're too young. You haven't been around long enough to make the proper connections. Look, I know you've put people on the map, but a lot of agents make stars. You just got lucky a few times.' She paused. 'I need more than some fly-by-night with a flashy reputation for my Evie. I need proof that something can be done for her.'

For one wild moment, Jason was tempted to call in one of his assistants with a list of the current casting calls. There were two requests from major Hollywood studios, a West End director needed a second lead and he had the exclusive rights to cast a BBC *Play of the Week*.

He ditched the idea the moment it came into his mind. He didn't have to prove anything to this grasping stage mother. If she had known the smallest thing about the business she would have respected his reputation instead of rubbishing it.

He concentrated his attention on the girl. 'Do you agree with what your mother has to say?' he asked.

Eve was caught between a rock and a hard place and she didn't have the slightest idea of how to talk herself out of it.

'It's not fair of you to ask me that,' she said tearfully. 'My mother's done everything for me.'

The older woman looked fierce. 'Damn right I have. You'd be nowhere on your own.'

43

It was an old cry. He'd been hearing it from stage mothers for years and it sounded as false now as it always had.

Jason hunched behind his desk and got his thoughts together. He wanted the girl. He'd lied when he'd said she'd have to trail round the provinces for years. With what she had, she could make it much faster than that. But this was no time to start promising things.

Eve Adams knew what he had to offer. She also knew if she took him up on it, her mother would never speak to him again, and that was exactly what he wanted. If he was going to do anything with this girl, he needed her free and unencumbered. If she didn't have the balls to break away, then that was her problem.

He stood up, indicating the interview was over.

'You've both got a lot of sorting out to do,' he said, 'so I'll leave you to it. Why don't you get in touch when you've made up your minds?'

He watched as the two women stood up. Nobody had shown the mother how to get out of a sofa and she made a mess of it, struggling and nearly losing a shoe before she made it to her feet. The girl, on the other hand, was a pro. She did the whole action in one seamless movement and Jason felt genuine regret that he probably wouldn't see her again. With a mother like that there was no way she'd get any further.

Eve turned up at his office three weeks later. It was the end of the day and Jason was on his way out to a cocktail party when his secretary buzzed him through and told him Eve was waiting for him.

His first instinct was to put her off till the next day. Most actresses, if they were ambitious enough, didn't mind being messed around. Then he remembered Eve's mother, the tough lady. The girl had probably been through hell with her before she made it to St Martin's Lane. She'd be bruised and feeling sorry for herself. The last thing she needed was another rejection. He decided to cut the party.

44

'Tell Eve to come through,' he instructed his secretary, 'and hold all my calls.'

She was even prettier than he remembered. He realized it was because she wasn't trying. When he'd seen her last she was all done up in a little wool suit that made her look slightly matronly. Now she was in blue jeans, without a vestige of make-up, and it suited her better.

'So you finally made it,' he said.

She nodded and said nothing. So in the end he filled in the silence.

'Are you happy about leaving your mother?' he asked. 'You have left her, haven't you?'

Once more she gave the same miserable little nod.

'She threw me out, actually. I told her I was going to put myself in your hands and she said if that was the case I could leave.'

His heart went out to her. 'Where are you staying?' he asked as gently as he could.

'I've got a girlfriend with a flat in Fulham. All I need is the rent and I've got a base for life.'

He suddenly felt worried for her. 'Have you got the rent?'

She threw herself on to his sofa, running her hands through her wild black hair until it started to look like a haystack.

'Of course I haven't got it,' she told him. 'I've got fifty pounds in savings certificates and that's my lot. After I've been through it, I'll have to start drawing social security.'

'The clever thing to do is start drawing the dole now. You're entitled to it.'

'Does that mean you won't be able to find me any work?'

'Of course it doesn't, but I can't give you any guarantees. You could land a TV series tomorrow, or you could be living on your savings for another few months.'

He paused for a moment. 'Is it totally hopeless with your mother? Or could you patch things up?'

She looked confused. 'Why are you asking me that?'

'Because it would help if you buried the hatchet. A little financial support from the parents is what every aspiring actress needs.'

'The parent,' she said. 'My father left when I was ten.'
She let this fact sink in before going on.

'Mummy brought me up on her own, which is why it was so difficult to go against her, but I did. I stood up for myself, so I can't really go crawling back begging for hand-outs.'

Jason reached into the top drawer of his desk and drew out his cheque book. He didn't like lending money to people he hardly knew, but this one was going to starve if he didn't.

'I'm going to give you an advance against your future earnings,' he told her. 'It's not a loan and it's not charity. In fact, the instant you sign a contract, I'll want you to start paying me back. Is that understood?'

She jumped up from the couch and ran over to where he was sitting.

'How can I thank you?' she asked.

Jason did his best to look stern. 'You can thank me by keeping out of trouble and turning up on time for auditions.'

His coolness didn't fool her for one minute. This agent liked her. He believed in her and he was prepared to put his money where his mouth was.

She snatched the cheque up and stuffed it into the pocket of her jeans. Then she flashed him a dazzling smile and got out the door before he could change his mind.

Only when she was sitting safely on the tube, en route to Fulham, did she dare to take the cheque out and see what he had given her. She couldn't believe it. Five hundred pounds.

So Jason Fielding really is going to make me famous, she thought. The notion buoyed her up all the way to the flat.

She hadn't meant to blow every audition. Eve thought the stage fright was something she'd get over, the way she was getting over her mother. For it was fun living on her own for the first time. She could eat what she wanted and sleep where she wanted. And best of all, she didn't have to account for everything else she chose to do.

She was her own boss now . . . except when she went on stage. Then her soul cried out into the darkness. She was looking for reassurance, she knew that. She needed to know there was someone rooting for her. Someone who cared whether she lived or died. And when she found no one at all, she went into a kind of panic.

Eve did her best to explain this to Jason when he asked to see her. The agent was worried she wasn't getting any work and had asked her to come in, so they could talk about what was going wrong.

'With your talent,' he told her the minute she came in the door, 'you should be tied up for the rest of the year. There has to be a reason why nobody seems to want you.'

She told him about it then. What really touched Jason was that she didn't bleat. Eve knew she had to stand on her own without her mother to hold her hand and he kicked himself for being such a fool.

Why didn't I spot this problem in the first place, he wondered. Maybe I could have done something about it then.

9

Jason sat in his office high above St Martins Lane and remembered the first time Eve had told him about her stage fright. She had been so ashamed of it then. As if she was the first actress in the world ever to go through this torture.

No wonder my heart went out to her, he thought. It would have been less than human not to feel her pain, or to want to help her through it. But I didn't have to ask her out to dinner, he chided himself. That was beyond the call of duty. And I didn't have to make love to her afterwards. That broke every rule in the book.

He looked back at Eve as she was then, and realised he couldn't rewrite the past. However hard he had tried to resist her, there was no way she would have let him.

For it wasn't lust that propelled her in to his bed. It was need.

The memories of that first night flooded in on him. He had taken her to the Ivy and spoiled her with champagne. Then to make her feel at ease in his world he had introduced her to every actor and producer who walked into the place. Eve was in her element and as he sat and watched her having the time of her life, something in him changed.

This wasn't just another actress he was trying to impress. This pale, scrawny little thing reminded him of an orphaned kitten — a kitten which could easily perish without him to watch over her. And it was then he knew he could never let her fend for herself.

He would get her on her feet again. And somehow he

would take away her terror of the stage. Though if anyone had asked him at that precise moment how he intended to do it, he wouldn't have known the answer.

The solution came two months later when Eve had moved into his flat in Covent Garden. He had been asked to find someone for a little part in a TV play. It was no more than a walk on, really. So he sent Eve along to the audition. She hadn't tried for anything since they got together and he half expected her to come back with her tail between her legs. Only she didn't. The director gave her the part on the spot.

'How did you do it,' he asked in wonderment, 'what turned you back into an actress?'

As long as he lived, he would never forget her answer.

'You turned me back into an actress,' she told him. 'You loved me out of my stage fright.'

The memory of how he had saved Eve jolted Jason back into the present. Of course, he thought, Eve's problem with Broadway is nothing new at all. It's the same old terror she's always had and its come back to haunt her because she's on her own.

He frowned and wondered what he was going to do about it. He couldn't drop his entire business to go and hold her hand.

But he couldn't let her fail in New York either. He'd nurtured and built her talent over too many years to let her give up before she'd started.

If she came home now, Eve would be saddled with mediocrity for the rest of her life. She'd go on appearing in the West End, but without an international name, the parts would get less and less important.

I need to get her functioning again, Jason decided. He picked up the phone.

As soon as Eve answered, she wanted to know about her contract. He knew she was close to hysteria, but he wasn't going to pander to it.

'I haven't even spoken to Al Goldman yet,' he told her, 'and I won't until you tell me the real reason you want to come home.'

'You know the real reason.'

'You mean that baloney about missing the family. I'm sorry, I'm not buying it. You never missed us when you were succeeding.'

'I'm not failing now,' she said sharply.

He didn't say anything for a moment. Then he hit her with the truth.

'So why are you so damned scared?'

That took the wind out of her sails. 'I didn't know you had any idea,' she whispered.

'Then you're a bigger fool than I took you for.'

'You're right,' she said, 'I am a fool, but this time you're not going to be able to wave your magic wand and make everything come good.'

'I wouldn't bet on it.'

Now Eve sounded bitter.

'What can you do for me in London?'

Jason thought for a moment.

'I can jog your memory,' he told her. 'How did you cope with stage fright when you left your mother?'

'I had you.'

'Not all the time you didn't. I couldn't come to every audition.'

She cut in on him.

'But I still had you in my head.'

'Has flying aross the Atlantic driven me out of your head?'

This time she stopped to think about it. 'I suppose in a way it has,' she said slowly. 'You're not there for me in London. Not in the same way.'

'You're wrong,' he said softly. 'I'm there for you wherever I am. I love you and I believe in you and I know you can do this part.'

He paused, 'You've got to hold on to that Eve.'

As he said it, he wondered if he was reaching her. Then she spoke again and he knew something was beginning to make sense.

'If I get through the first night,' she said, 'can I come home if it still feels bad?'

'Of course you can, but it won't come to that.'

She laughed hollowly. 'You haven't met my leading man.'

Jason thought about Brett Weston and tried to remember his track record. But it was no good, it was as much as he could do to keep up with English actors.

'You'd better tell me what his problem is.'

'Ego,' she said shortly. 'Every time we do a scene, he fights me.'

'And what do you do?'

'You know what I do. I crumple up.'

'That's no way to deal with an egomaniac. Either you fight back, or you make friends with the bastard.'

'You really think I should do that?'

Jason laughed. 'You haven't told me which you're going for yet.'

'I thought I'd try being friends,' she said slowly. 'It could help with the other problem too.'

He thought about that for a long time after they said good-bye. How could Brett Weston help with Eve's stage nerves? He could see they needed to call a truce, but that old trouble of hers needed more than just friendship. It needed care and intimacy. The kind of intimacy you only got from a lover.

He wondered whether he had been right to make her stay in New York.

Eve decided to cook Brett Sunday lunch. It was a casual, informal sort of meal — not like dinner, where there could be all sorts of undercurrents. They would wear jeans and drink Bloody Marys and set the world to rights. And after-wards, she promised herself, the show would go on.

Brett arrived at her flat just after one o'clock clutching a big bunch of flowers.

'Peace offering,' he said thrusting them at her.

Then before she could react, he strode past her into the big shabby drawing room.

Once again his attitude astounded her. The first time they met, he had ordered dinner without consulting her. Now he took charge of her drinks cabinet.

51

'I mix a mean martini,' he told her. 'All I need you to do is bring me some crushed ice.'

Eve went into the kitchen and fetched the ice and a tray of bits and pieces she'd picked up from the local deli on West Side.

They could nibble their way through lunch American style, she'd decided. It would save her the distractions of cooking and serving.

When they were onto their second martini, Eve brought up the subject of the play.

'I had a meeting with Al on Friday,' she said. 'He didn't seem all that happy with things.'

Brett looked up from his drink. 'I'm not surprised. I don't think anyone's happy. Are you happy?'

'You know damn well I'm not.'

He reached across her and selected a bagel covered in cream cheese and pickled herring.

'So what are you going to do about it?'

'I thought I'd talk to you and find out what was going wrong.'

The bagel was half-way to his mouth when he changed his mind and put it down.

'I can't help you, lady,' he said. 'I'm not the one who's blowing my lines.'

'So you think I'm doing the whole thing on my own,' Eve retorted angrily. 'My nerves, my stiffness on stage – that's nothing to do with you at all.'

Brett looked interested. 'You're telling me I'm the cause of all this? I'm flattered, I never had this much effect on anyone before.'

Eve felt like hitting him.

'This isn't funny. Al's seriously considering pulling the plug if we don't get this right.'

'I know about Al's plans. You weren't the only one he talked to on Friday.'

He pushed both hands through his mane of dirty-blond hair as if he was considering what to do next. Then he got to his feet and came over to where she sat.

'Get up,' he said.

'Why? I'm not going anywhere.'

'Just do it.'

She put her glass down and did as he asked. Then before she realized what was happening, he put both hands on her shoulders and drew her towards him.

A thousand protests rose up inside her. But Brett kissed her before she could express any of them. It was a warm, rough kiss and she felt her mouth come open. Then she felt his tongue, probing and insistent. And after that she knew she was lost.

Another lover might have prolonged the moment, but Brett wasn't that kind of man. Instead, still keeping hold of Eve's shoulders, he turned her round and propelled her down the hall towards the bedroom.

She knew if she wanted she could still change her mind. She felt ashamed of herself for not struggling a little but her will had somehow deserted her as she allowed him to sit her down on the bed.

Then he started to undress. He shrugged off his shirt and unbuttoned his jeans and she stared at him mesmerized. I've waited for this moment, she realized, almost from the first time I saw him. And suddenly she knew what she had to do.

She pulled her dress over her head and stood in front of him clothed only in lace panties, her stockings, and a little half-bra. She leaned forwards and ran her hands down the length of his body.

Brett came erect right at that moment. It was like lighting the blue touchpaper, a fire seemed to build inside him and he pushed her back onto the bed and started to tear at the fragile French lace.

Eve's bra came apart almost instantly. Then her panties came tumbling down to her knees. Then Brett left the rest of it alone. Whether he was in a hurry, or whether he just liked taking her with her stockings and suspenders in place, she never knew. Before she could wonder, she was on her back with her legs apart and Brett was pushing into her.

53

It was like nothing she had ever experienced before. The fire that burned through this man woke up her own passion, and she realized that all her life this feeling had lived inside her, waiting for someone to release it.

Just for a moment she felt genuine regret that her husband hadn't been the man to do it.

Then she stopped thinking about her husband. She stopped thinking about anything except the man who was astride her on the bed.

The following day Eve gave the performance of her life. She was relaxed, confident and word-perfect, but that wasn't all of it. What shone through everything she did was the fact she was in complete harmony with her leading man.

Al, who was watching from the stalls, heaved a sigh of relief. So Brett had listened to him after all. Not only had he listened, but he'd done as instructed. For a moment he wondered whether the pair of them had had a fun time or whether it was all in the cause of their art.

Then he laughed at himself. Brett wasn't the type to read poetry. If Al knew him as well as he thought he knew him, Brett would have fucked the English dame's brains out and asked questions afterwards.

10

Jason came to New York for the critics' night. It was the ultimate test of the play. If the reviews were behind them, Eve would have no problems. She could look ahead to a comfortable run on Broadway, followed by a triumphant return home.

He prayed for a good press. She had finally got her performance right. She had even thanked him for making her stay with it.

'All I needed was time,' she told him. 'Time and bloody hard work.'

Jason believed her, because it suited him to believe her. Now, he rushed across town to the theatre. Eve had got him a seat in the front row, as she always did, so he could study everything that was happening on stage.

The play had changed a lot since London. It was wordier now, and more pretentious. Eve was doing her best with it, but the sheer plodding heaviness of the script got Jason down.

They'll never buy it over here, he decided. I'd better start booking Eve's ticket back to London.

He sneaked a look across at the critics. They were seven rows behind him in the stalls. They all seemed curiously intense.

Frank Rich, the so-called Butcher of Broadway, was scribbling hard in his notebook and that pulled Jason up short. Rich normally didn't bother to take a note. Either he disliked a play or he hated it, and he didn't need references to tear a piece apart.

Jason looked into the audience to see if they were reacting the same way and he found they were. Everyone was concentrating on the turgid prose as if their lives depended on it.

Do they like it? he wondered. Or are they simply finding the whole thing impossible to follow?

In the end he gave up second-guessing. It would only be a matter of hours before they knew which way the wind was blowing. Until then all he could do was admire Eve's performance and praise God that she had finally got it right.

The curtain came down at nine thirty to polite applause. Jason struggled his way through the first-night crowd to Eve's dressing room. She wasn't alone. Al Goldman was there pouring champagne. The theatre manager was there looking anxious and pretending there was nothing to worry about. The leading man had just come through the door.

Brett was still in his stage make-up, but he'd managed to get out of his costume and was wearing the actor's uniform of T-shirt and jeans. He pushed his way past everyone until he got to Eve. Then he went down on one knee and took her hand in his.

'Darling, you were wonderful,' he intoned. 'I wanted to be the first one to tell you.'

It was a typical piece of actorish first-night nonsense and Jason was surprised to see his wife blush. She'd had enough young men throw themselves at her feet to be used to it by now. He decided it was time to rescue her.

'Eve,' he said, moving up to them, 'you were marvellous. We'll talk later, but now we've got to rush to the critics' night party.'

Eve was on her feet then, pushing the growing crowd out of her dressing room.

'I'll see you all in Lexington Avenue,' she kept saying. 'If you ever allow me to get changed.'

She was in better shape than Jason expected. Usually the strain of opening in a play showed on her face. Tonight she seemed radiant. There was a sparkle about her he hadn't seen before and he put it down to New York. Making it in this city had been one of her dreams and he realized how badly she had wanted this success.

All the way over to the party, she babbled on about the play and Jason praised everything to the skies. He knew it was expected of him, and he also knew she was only half listening to what he was saying.

From now until the first reviews came through, his wife was going to be in a state of mild hysteria.

The moment they got to the restaurant, Eve was surrounded. The backers, the cast, the friends of the production all wanted to tell her how marvellous she was. Jason retired to the bar and left her to it, and suddenly he felt sorry for all actresses. They were so fragile. So infinitely destructible. All it took was one bad review and they fell apart. He thought back to the tedious play and the way Frank Rich was scribbling in his notebook. Please God, he prayed, spare her a massacre.

Eve couldn't see Jason from where she was standing and it made her feel vulnerable. She knew he was probably at the bar. He always stayed there on first-night parties and normally she didn't mind, but tonight she wanted him by her side. There were too many people here, too many people asking too many questions, and she was in no mood to deal with them on her own.

Al had started it. He had come over minutes after she'd arrived and virtually asked her point-blank if she was having a thing with Brett.

'You were touched by magic tonight, darling,' he told her. 'There has to be something behind it.'

She smiled demurely. 'The muse was with me.'

The producer chuckled. 'If the muse's name is Brett Weston I'll believe you. You two seem a lot closer suddenly.'

She had ducked out of that conversation, turning to sign her autograph for someone. Then the cast started to group around her and she had a moment of feeling safe — until Brett's name came up again.

'You two were dynamite tonight. How do you do it? Or is that classified information?'

Eve pushed her way free from the solid wedge of people around her, and headed towards the bar and the safety of her husband but was stopped by Brett himself. She knew instinctively he had been waiting for her all evening. She screwed her face into a smile and mumbled that she was in a hurry to get to the reviews, but he wouldn't be put off.

'Is that your husband over there?' he said, pointing in the direction of the bar.

She nodded, doing her best to edge past him. He caught hold of her hand and hung on.

'Tell me,' he said, 'will you be sharing a bed with him tonight?'

Eve felt as if she was holding an unexploded bomb. One wrong word, one false move and the whole mess would blow up in her face.

'It's none of your business what I'll be doing tonight,' she said stiffly.

'It's all of my business,' Brett replied, 'or have you forgotten the last few days?'

'Of course I haven't forgotten,' Eve said softly, close to tears. She prayed Jason wasn't looking in her direction. Then she pulled her hand free, just in case he was, and faced Brett. 'I think this has gone far enough,' she told him. 'You know the score with me — mutual satisfaction; so try behaving like a grown-up for once.'

Then, before he could say anything else, she shoved him out of her way and hurried over to Jason.

The crowd in the room was already thinning out as people hurried over to the Sardi Building to catch the first TV reviews. Eve was relieved to see Jason had both their coats over his arm.

'You're cutting it fine,' he said. 'Brett Weston couldn't have been saying anything that important.'

'He was fussed about a couple of his cues,' Eve said quickly. 'You know actors.'

Jason grinned. 'I should do by now.'

They made their way out of the restaurant and when they got to the Sardi Building, took the elevator to the publicity agency handling their show.

For opening night, the agency had lent out their suite of offices to the production, filling it with champagne and Scotch and late night snacks.

Extra TV sets had been specially brought in and all the guests filled their glasses and huddled round them.

Channel Five was the first to give its verdict, a few minutes after eleven.

'Tonight at the theatre I was moved,' the critic pronounced. 'This new English import brings sensitivity back to the Broadway stage.'

Eve turned to Jason, not daring to smile. 'I think that's a yes,' she said.

No more theatre news came up for another fifteen minutes. Then all at once three reviews came on at the same time.

Everyone liked what they saw and a buzz started to go through the offices. They were winning now and they knew it. Jason bagged a bottle of champagne, but Eve stopped him from opening it.

'There's a way to go yet,' she warned.

NBC came on next, pronouncing the play a worthy look at English history. Then Channel Seven called it a jewel.

Jason went ahead and opened the champagne. There was still the *Times* to come, but even if Frank Rich rubbished them, they were still ahead of the game, he said.

Eve didn't agree. 'The *Times* could close us if they hated it. I've heard of it happening before.'

She refused to touch a drop of champagne until their contact called them from the *Times* building.

The tension seemed to affect everyone. All conversation had stopped. People were just standing waiting for the call to come through. Then the phone jangled.

Jason was the first to pick it up and as soon as he knew it was their man at the *Times*, he passed the receiver to Al Goldman.

Everyone knew they were home and dry just by looking at his face, but just to clinch it, the producer read over the review to the assembled company.

'I left the theatre,' wrote Rich, 'with a pleasant tingling sensation. What I saw tonight raised my opinion of British imports.'

He went on in the same vein, praising the production to the skies. Then he focused on the players. Eve got the biggest rave. In Rich's opinion, Eve had the looks of Vivien Leigh and the power of Dame Edith Evans.

'She and Brett Weston set the stage on fire, particularly in the love scenes.' He pronounced the leading man to be the perfect foil for 'this brilliant English actress', and predicted the play would be the hit of the season.

The moment the producer put the phone down the whole place seemed to go mad. Champagne was opened, conservative men in Ivy League suits let out great whoops of joy and fell on each other's necks. And Eve disappeared.

One moment she was standing next to Jason looking nervous. The next she was nowhere to be found. Jason knew better than to fight his way through the mêlée, so he climbed up on to a desk for a bird's-eye view of the whole party.

He spotted Eve immediately. She was flanked by her producer on one side and her leading man on the other. All three of them had their heads together and just for a moment Jason wished none of this had happened. Now things would never be normal again. This kind of hit could run for nearly a year. Then there would be more Broadway offers, perhaps even an approach from Hollywood. Eve would have to start deciding where her loyalties lay.

Jason couldn't be expected to give up his business and follow her around the world. He wasn't that kind of man. So it was Eve who would have to make the sacrifices.

His eyes searched through the crowd until he found her again. She was still in the same huddle with Al and Brett and she was laughing now, as if she could see her whole future spread out in front of her and she liked what she saw.

He wondered where he fitted in this brave new world of hers. Or *if* he fitted in.

11

LONDON, 1983

Ron Beattie looked at his daughter and thought he was going to have an apoplexy. He was on his way to the pub for his usual Sunday session when she told him she wanted a word.

'Can't it wait?' he told her. 'The lads will be down there by now. If I don't get a move on, I'll miss the first shout.'

Linda had stood fast. 'Dad,' she said, 'it's important.'

So he sat down again at the Formica table that passed for a centrepiece in their kitchen and listened to what she had to say.

It didn't take long. His daughter had it all planned out. She'd probably been organizing herself for months, and she'd chosen to tell him what was going on when it was all over.

'I want to leave Epping,' she told him. 'I want to live in London.'

At first it didn't sink in. Why would a girl of eighteen, a girl with a comfortable home on a council estate, want to live somewhere where she had to pay rent?

'You've got to be joking,' he told her. 'Who put that idea in your head?'

She picked up the old brown teapot in front of her and filled her mug. As she did it, he noticed she was wearing her hair in a different style. Normally it was backcombed to within an inch of its life and held in place with glittery ornaments. Now she'd abandoned all that, letting it hang straight and natural to her shoulders.

She must have been in a hurry this morning, he thought. He fixed her with his eye.

'You haven't answered my question,' he said. 'Why do you want to run off all of a sudden?'

'I won't be running off,' Linda said, looking uncomfortable. 'I'll still come home at weekends.'

'Sod weekends,' he said. 'I want to know why you're going in the first place.'

Linda regarded her father warily, wondering how much of the truth she could let him in on. If she told him she'd been offered a job with the BBC, a job in a television studio, would he be impressed?

'I've been offered a job in the West End,' she ventured, 'so I can't commute up and down to Essex every day.'

Ron didn't say anything for a bit. Instead he took out one of his foul-smelling mini-cigars and lit up.

'What kind of a job are you up for?' he asked, looking suspicious. 'It's not page three modelling, is it?'

Linda prayed for patience. 'I won't be taking my clothes off in London,' she said. 'I'll be working as a secretary, the same as always.'

'A secretary for who?'

Now he'd pinned her down, there was no way out of it.

'I'm going into television,' she explained. 'My new boss is the big cheese on a current affairs programme.'

Ron bit the end off his cigar and spat it out.

'A current affairs programme,' he mimicked. 'Get you. I'd be happier with the nude modelling, if you want to know.'

'Come off it, Dad. You hate the idea.'

'Not as much as I hate the notion of you mixing with all those ponces in television. They'll put funny ideas in your head. They'll have you believing you're something you're not.'

She started to get angry.

'You'll be saying next I'm not good enough for the BBC. It's what you mean, isn't it?'

Ron sighed and wished his other daughters were in the house to back him up, but they'd all pushed off the minute they got pregnant. None of them was going to pass up the chances of a council flat.

63

So now he had to tell his youngest the facts of life, on his own.

'I'm not saying you're not good enough,' he began. 'What I'm saying is, you won't belong. The sort of characters who work for television have an education. They read books and they watch films with subtitles. You'll be like a fish out of water the minute you walk in there.'

'I could learn. I'm not a complete dummy.'

'It's not about learning. It's what you're fit for. Look, I drive a minicab. It's not the best job in the world, but it suits me. If I was a brain surgeon, none of my mates would talk to me.'

Linda looked at her father in his jeans and trainers and battered old anorak, and decided they were poles apart.

Ron didn't want to get on in the world because he was frightened of what they'd say in the pub. It didn't occur to him that if he had a success – any success – he might not want to hang out with the old crowd.

'I don't care what you think,' Linda said stubbornly. 'I'm going to London and I'll take my chances.'

Ron got up, scraping his chair across the worn lino as he went.

'You'll be sorry,' he said.

12

Linda had been at the BBC for six months before she realized she was indispensable. It was Edmund Stern who finally convinced her.

A researcher, he never made a move without consulting her. If he had to talk a cabinet minister into appearing on the programme, he went to Linda first and she fixed him up with the names and telephone numbers of the middlemen he needed to contact.

If he needed to know the state of the stock market, Linda could find out. Today the stock market was the last thing on his mind. The editor-in-chief had put him to work on a story about cot deaths, and he hadn't a clue where to start.

When he took his problem to Linda, she was vaguely irritated. Far too many of Edmund's colleagues had been coming to her recently with tales of woe.

The requests came so often, she didn't have time to do her own work. Now Edmund was looking for bereaved mothers.

She looked up from her word processor to see him standing over her, looking helpless.

'For Christ's sake, Edmund,' she said, 'why don't you phone around some of the counselling groups, or the welfare services? They're bound to come up with something.'

'It will take ages,' he told her. 'Anyway, I've got a meeting.'

'I've got a news schedule to type, I've got letters to do, and there's a long memo to the Director General.'

The researcher made a face. 'There's no need to make a fuss,' he said. 'I'll go and ask one of the other girls.'

Linda reconsidered. In her heart she knew none of the other secretaries could possibly come up with the goods the way she did but she didn't want to put it to the test.

'Don't do that,' she said quickly. 'I'll find your cot death mothers. When do you want them by?'

He looked at his watch. 'Would four o'clock be pushing it?'

It would, but she'd committed herself now, so she told him it was no trouble and sent him on his way.

She watched Edmund swagger out of the newsroom and felt genuinely confused. How could somebody as clever as him, somebody with a degree from Oxford, not know the first thing about doing his job?

He was terrific in meetings. She'd seen him bring a whole room to a standstill when he talked about an idea he'd been developing. The fact was, though, Linda had done all the donkey-work, and he'd taken the credit for it.

Linda brushed back her long mane of ash-blonde hair and reflected on what her father had told her before she left Epping.

In order to succeed, you have to be born to it. She'd disagreed with him at the time. Now she'd seen a bit of the world, she was beginning to think she was wrong.

Edmund, with his posh accent and fancy education, was living proof of her father's words. He didn't have an ounce of initiative in his head, but he looked as if he had, he talked as if he had, so he was taken on trust.

Nobody paid her that compliment. From the day she moved to London, she had to prove herself every inch of the way.

The girls she shared a flat with in Fulham made her pay a month in advance. If she slipped behind even one week, there were searching questions.

Linda felt sad. I come from the minicab driving, beer swilling, working classes. What chance do I have? she asked herself.

At four on the dot, Edmund was back at her desk.

'Have you got them?' he asked. 'The cot death mothers?'

Wordlessly she reached into her top drawer and pulled out a sheet of typewritten paper.

Edmund scanned it quickly and let out a whoop of joy.

'You've actually talked to two of them. Have they agreed to come on?'

Linda nodded. 'They just need you to confirm a time.'

He leaned forward and patted her on the shoulder.

'You're a good girl, you know. I don't think I appreciate you enough.' He paused, considering what he could do to reward her. 'Would you let me buy you a drink tonight?'

For the first time that day, Linda smiled. Edmund had never wanted to know her socially before. Maybe she was getting somewhere after all.

'I'd love to have a drink with you,' she said.

'Fine, then it's all fixed. 'I'll see you in Raffles at six. Don't be late.'

She was there on the dot. Though when she walked in the door of the BBC's favourite wine bar, there was no sign of Edmund.

She walked up to the bar and got herself a gin and Italian which she sipped as slowly as she knew how. Half an hour later there was still no Edmund, so she ordered herself another drink.

When it arrived, she looked up to see a group of reporters she knew vaguely waving and looking friendly. She was tempted to join them, but thought if Edmund turned up, he'd think her an easy pick-up. So she shook her head and said she had a date.

At half-past seven, she knew she'd been mistaken. Edmund wasn't there. He hadn't even phoned to make an excuse.

I'm not good enough, she thought, picking up her bag and making to go. I should have realized it before I accepted his charity.

For days afterwards, Edmund felt like a bit of a bastard. He'd wanted to buy Linda a drink. The girl genuinely deserved it, but in the end, he couldn't bear anyone he worked with seeing them together.

It's all that make-up she uses, he thought, and those clingy dresses. If the news editor saw me sharing a bottle of wine with Linda I'd never live it down.

Hurting her feelings had a price, of course. After he stood her up, Linda had studiously ignored him, so he had to do his own dirty work.

It was so tedious. All that searching through directories and pleading with people's assistants wasn't his style at all. He didn't have the patience to stand in line and be fobbed off with excuses. Once he actually shouted when some minion told him her boss was in a meeting.

He botched up three stories before he realized he had to make his peace with Linda. She might look like a scrubber, but she was too useful to be cast aside. So he put on all his charm and asked if she'd have dinner with him.

She turned him down flat.

'After the last time when you didn't turn up, I don't trust you,' she said.

'But I can explain that,' Edmund told her. 'My mother was taken ill and I had to shoot down to the country. I know I should have called you but I was so distracted, it didn't occur to me.'

Linda looked doubtful. 'Why didn't you tell me this the next day?'

'I didn't dare come near you the next day. You looked so fierce, I thought you'd bite my head off.'

In the end he got round her by promising to take her to a trendy French restaurant in Battersea. He intended to fill her up with gourmet cooking and flatter her to death, so that his career at the BBC would be safe for ever.

He only hoped he didn't run into anyone he knew. That night his luck was in. The place was full of strangers, all of them enjoying French food at its best. All of them except for Linda, who pushed her food round her plate and looked embarrassed. Edmund realized he'd made a mistake bringing her here. She would have been more at home in a hamburger bar. He fought down his irritation with her.

It's not her fault she's unsophisticated, he thought. To

make her more at ease he ordered lots to drink. They'd already had two champagne cocktails to start, then a bottle of white wine came with the starter, and a bottle of red with the main course. When the coffee arrived he insisted she had a brandy balloon of Armagnac.

By the end of the meal Linda was beginning to look slightly flushed and Edmund wondered if he hadn't overdone things. If she staggered into work tomorrow bleary-eyed and dry-mouthed she wouldn't be any use at all. And he had a major favour he wanted to ask her.

He looked across at Linda, who was starting to giggle, and realized he had to do something fast. The girl was about to pass out.

He signalled for the bill, then got up and began to help her out of her seat.

It wasn't easy. Linda was all arms and legs, and when he finally got her to her feet she had to lean against him to stop herself from falling over.

He had never realized quite how big she was, or how heavy. Her blonde, little girl looks concealed the fact that she was buxom and without really knowing what he was doing, he started to wonder what Linda would look like undressed.

She'd be ripe, he thought, and soft with the sort of flesh you'd want to bury yourself in. It was at that precise moment, Edmund made up his mind he was going to have her. He thought about the next morning and the fact that she'd be even less use than he feared. Then he thought, it can't be helped; I'm not made of steel. No man in his right mind would pass up this opportunity.

He managed to get her into his car, which was mercifully parked outside, and when the night air hit her, she started to sober up a little.

'What time is it?' she asked. 'I mustn't miss the last tube.'

He looked at his watch and saw that she had fifteen minutes to get to the station.

'You've got oceans of time,' he said. 'I thought we'd have a coffee at my place before you finally hit the road.'

She seemed to hesitate, so he made up her mind for her, revving up his Jaguar sports car and heading for home. It was only when he pulled up outside his conversion in Pimlico that he saw Linda was fast asleep. Somewhere between Battersea and home, she had quietly drowned in all the alcohol he had given her.

Christ, he thought, if I can't get her to wake up, it won't be any fun at all.

He took her by both shoulders and shook her till her eyes came open. Then with no ceremony at all he hustled her out on to the pavement and into his front lobby.

She stayed awake all the way up in the lift. She even made it down the hall to his flat. But by the time she got into his living room, the effort had proved too much for her. She curled up on his sofa and went right back to sleep and there was nothing Edmund could do to rouse her. So he left her where she was and stomped off to bed.

She woke him in the early hours of the morning. It was obvious she was still drunk for she had wandered into his bedroom thinking she was back in her own house. He got himself into a sitting position and watched while she shrugged off her clothes.

The dress was the first thing to go and as she pulled it over her head, he realized he had been right about her. Her body was one of the most erotic things he had ever seen. She was wearing little lacy pants and a matching bra and it was all he could do to stop himself grabbing hold of her and tearing them off, but he willed himself to be patient.

Linda could be just sober enough to push him away and he didn't want to risk that. So he let her get completely undressed and climb into his bed. Then when there was no turning back, he made his move.

To Edmund's intense relief, Linda seemed to like what he was doing to her. She sighed and cuddled in closer. As she did he could smell the scent of her coming at him in great waves. It was a very earthy, animal smell and he could feel himself going out of control.

When he seduced a girl, Edmund liked to take his time.

Foreplay was important to him and he liked to stroke and nibble and make a thorough exploration of the territory about to be conquered.

With Linda he didn't get the chance. Lust overcame him. In a way he was glad she was still drunk for he wasn't as gentle as he should have been, and as he turned her on her back and parted her legs he felt a moment of remorse. Then he eased himself into her and all his finer feelings disappeared.

He took her quickly and selfishly, and when she cried out he pretended he hadn't heard her. He knew what he was doing was strictly against the rules, but he promised himself he would make it up to her. In the morning, he decided, I'll behave like a perfect gentleman.

Edmund made sure to set his alarm half an hour earlier than usual. Then, while Linda was still asleep, he crept out of bed and went to fix breakfast.

He took a certain amount of trouble with it, so the first thing the girl saw when she opened her eyes was Edmund staggering under the weight of a heavy tray. She had never seen such an array of food. There was a grapefruit perfectly sliced and sugared. A bowl of muesli, hot buttered toast and freshly made coffee in a cafetière.

He's behaving like a bridegroom, she thought. She cast her mind back to the night before, looking for clues to his behaviour, but she could remember nothing.

All she knew was she had had too much to drink in the restaurant and Edmund had taken her back to his flat for a sobering cup of coffee.

I must have passed out, she thought. Though if I did, what am I doing in Edmund's bed stark naked? She didn't know for sure, but she sensed she had been made love to. Her body rather than her mind told her that, and she felt ashamed.

'I suppose you think I'm easy,' she said harshly.

Edmund didn't say anything, but put the tray down on the bed and started pouring coffee.

'Here,' he said handing her a cup. 'Get this down. It will make you feel better.'

71

She took it, gulping most of the hot liquid down in one go. Then she listened to the thudding in her head and felt it decrease a decibel.

'Edmund,' she said, 'we have to talk.'

Edmund wasn't interested in conversation. His main concern seemed to be that she ploughed her way through the breakfast he had prepared, and because she felt so weak, she didn't put up a fight.

When she finished the last mouthful, he whisked the covers aside, and pulled her out of bed.

'I've run you a bath,' he told her. 'If you hurry, it might still be warm.'

Linda put herself together in a kind of daze. This man had taken her over completely. He had wined her, dined her, seduced her and now he was fussing around her like a mother hen.

She wasn't quite sure how she felt about it all, though as her headache receded, one of the emotions that surfaced was gratitude. Where she came from, the opposite sex wasn't quite as willing to please as Edmund. If she had woken up in the morning with one of the local lads, she would have been kicked out of bed and sent to make the toast, and he wouldn't have given a damn about her headache either.

She looked at her companion with a new curiosity. He was good-looking, if you liked the intellectual type, though his hair was receding a bit and he didn't have much chin.

She began to feel pleased he was going out of his way to be nice to her. It was obvious he wanted an affair and the prospect started to appeal to her.

I wonder if he knows how to make bacon and eggs, she thought. I can't stomach the thought of any more muesli.

Edmund never made as much fuss of Linda again, and she realized that the posh French restaurant and the slap-up breakfast had been his attempts at courtship.

Now he had got her, there was no need to make an impression. So they went to curry houses and hamburger joints and the local wine bar. And Linda made breakfast.

72

She didn't complain. Edmund was way out of her class and she knew it. The sort of girls he was usually seen around with had private incomes and a groomed, glossy style she could never come within a million miles of.

Over the next few weeks, she heard about the big house his parents had in the country, the house that would one day be his when he inherited his family title.

He told her about his schooldays at Eton, and the way he was taught to ride to hounds. At the end of it she was left speechless. There seemed no reason in the world why he would want to know her, let alone have her as his girlfriend.

She said as much to him one night when they were having dinner at his flat. He laughed her out of it and took her to bed.

It didn't stop her wondering about the relationship. Why me? she thought a dozen times a day. Why not some Sloane or one of the clever producers he works with? Surely they could do more for him than me.

As the weeks wore on, she realized they probably couldn't. A horsy girl from his own class couldn't talk to him about television, and a colleague wouldn't put herself out to help him the way she did.

Linda didn't stop working for Edmund. In the office the extra chores he gave her took up most of her time. And now there was more. Increasingly, Edmund wanted to come up with ideas of his own. For inspiration he turned to Linda.

She never failed him, and she knew that her usefulness was part of her attraction. When Edmund put up a project she'd suggested she was on tenterhooks until she knew it had been accepted. Then she relaxed till the next time, knowing nobody else could do what she did.

She was his right hand, the reason he managed to hold on to his job, as necessary to him as breathing.

She might have convinced herself this was true, if she hadn't agreed to let Edmund take her to dinner at Le Suquet.

It was an expensive outing by anyone's standards. The only reason they were going there was to celebrate Edmund's impending advancement. He had landed an interview for a high-flying posting at the BBC, and he was so convinced he would get it he had decided to splash out.

Linda had been uneasy about the evening right from the start. She suspected Edmund was jumping the gun and making a fool of himself. She knew without a doubt he was trying to make a fool of her. She couldn't cope with restaurants like Le Suquet. They were for the nobs and the upper classes, not Essex girls like her. She wouldn't fit in in a million years. She would walk into the overdecorated restaurant with its wall-to-wall carpeting and giant fish tank and everyone would think she was working there as the hat check girl.

She thought about pretending she was ill that night, but Edmund had gone to so much trouble with advance bookings and making sure there was champagne on the table, that she didn't have the heart. So in the end she did the best she could with a dress she had bought from Richard Shops the year before.

She had worn it for her sister's wedding and it was a copy of an Alaïa — or so the woman who served her had said. It was certainly tight enough to be and if she hadn't just been on a diet she wouldn't have dared put it on.

As it was, when she changed into it in the ladies' room after work, she felt pleased with her choice. In her little overnight case she had brought some costume jewellery to compliment the dress: a Chanel-style necklace with yards of chains, interspersed with little pearls; a bracelet to match, and a pair of earrings with the classic twinned Cs. If you didn't know, you couldn't tell it from the real thing, Linda thought.

She took one last look at herself in the mirror and knew she had the effect she wanted. Big hair, wild-looking jewellery and a dress that fitted where it touched. You'll do, she told herself. There's no restaurant in town where I'd go unnoticed.

She was right. When she arrived at the fish restaurant in Chelsea, the man who showed her in let his eyes travel the length of her. If it had been anywhere else but this stuffy place, he would have probably whistled. Instead he asked whom she was meeting.

74

She gave him Edmund's name and was directed through to the conservatory which looked out on to the street.

She thought, rather worried, that Edmund had pushed the boat out. It was the smartest room in the place.

Edmund was sitting at the table as Linda walked in. Just for a moment, she thought he looked startled when he saw her, but by the time she got to him, he had rearranged his expression.

As soon as she sat down, he thrust a glass of champagne in her hand. Then he proposed a toast.

'To my new job,' he said. 'The next rung up the ladder.'

Linda took a tiny sip of the wine and the bubbles fizzed all the way up her nose. For an awful moment she thought she was going to sneeze. She paused, then asked about the big break. Edmund had been remarkably tight-lipped about it and now she wanted a few details.

He wasn't forthcoming. 'It's all a bit hush-hush,' he said, looking shifty. 'I shouldn't be going for this job at all, but a friend wangled me on to the list. So I'm not meant to talk about it.'

Linda looked at him from under her eyelashes. Clever Dick, she thought. Always getting people to do things for you.

She was about to ask who was helping him when her attention was distracted by a large group coming into the restaurant.

They could have just come from Ascot, for all the women were dressed in bright silk dresses and elaborate hats. Linda smiled to herself. They looked as if they had been kitted out by Harrods twenty years ago.

She touched Edmund's elbow. 'Have you seen the crowd of "Hoorays" that's just arrived?'

Her companion turned to follow her gaze and as he did a change came over him. The easy self-confidence he wore like a second skin seemed to melt away.

He suddenly looked pale and terribly nervous. 'My parents are in that group,' he said faintly.

Linda looked at them with interest. 'Which ones are they?' she enquired politely.

Edmund indicated a large woman in a turquoise hat, accompanied by a tall thin man. They were obviously on their way over, but before they could get anywhere near, Edmund was on his feet.

'Wait here,' he whispered. 'I'll just go and say hello.'

For the next twenty minutes, Linda sat and sipped her champagne while her escort talked to his parents.

He clearly hadn't seen them for some time, for he seemed to have a lot to say to them. He's talking about his job interview, Linda thought. I'll give him a few more minutes.

After half an hour she decided enough was enough. If he was going to be all this time, he might have included me, she thought. I am his girlfriend, after all.

She decided to take matters into her own hands. If Edmund won't introduce me, she thought, I'll introduce myself. Then she knocked back the rest of the champagne, struggled to her feet, and holding her head high, she marched across the room.

The matron in the turquoise hat viewed Linda's approach with a certain curiosity. She had seen girls like this before serving behind the counter of the local pub. But she never in a million years imagined her son would keep company with such a creature. For a moment Edmund's mother wondered if she was a tart. Then she dismissed the idea. Edmund might be a rebel, but he wasn't a fool.

The girl was standing beside them now and was pressing herself up against her son.

'I'm Linda,' she said brightly, jangling a wristful of cheap jewellery.

'Oh yes?' said the woman, shortly. Then she turned to her son. 'Edmund,' she said, 'who on earth is this?' She gave him one of her penetrating looks. The sort of look that had reduced him to tears when he was a little boy. And she saw with satisfaction he had gone beet red and was shuffling his feet.

'Linda and I work together,' he muttered. But the answer didn't cut any ice.

'I don't believe a word of it,' she said. 'Girls like her don't work at the BBC.'

'Yes they bloody well do,' Linda said regretting the words as soon as they popped out of her mouth. 'I've been helping Edmund do his job for ages now.'

'Is that all you've been helping him with?' the woman retorted cattily.

Linda decided it was now nor never. 'No, actually,' she admitted. 'I'm Edmund's girlfriend too. Though that's more recent.'

It was the information the woman seemed to have been waiting for.

'So it's sex,' she said. 'I might have known.'

Linda thought about all the pundits she'd dragged on to the programme in Edmund's name. All the overtime she'd worked doing his typing. All the ideas she'd filled his head with and let him take the credit for.

She turned to Edmund. 'I think you should tell your mother exactly where I stand in your life,' she said.

He gave her the same shifty look she'd seen earlier when she'd asked about his interview and in that moment she knew he was going to let her down.

'I think you should stop getting your knickers in a twist,' he said shortly. 'We work in the same office and sometimes we sleep together. It's no big deal.'

Linda looked at Edmund and his parents and thought she had never seen such a load of shits in the whole of her life. They had bags of charm when they wanted something, but underneath the surface they were no different from the people she had grown up with in Essex. In a way they were worse. The people she grew up with had a rough kind of honesty. This crew didn't know the meaning of the word.

She started back towards the table and was surprised to see Edmund scuttling behind her.

'Sorry about all that,' he said as they sat down. 'Mummy can be very difficult sometimes.'

'Mummy's not the only one. What was all that garbage about us sometimes sleeping together? Are you seeing anyone else?'

'Of course I'm not seeing someone else. You know me better than that.'

But Linda didn't know him any more. She thought she knew him, but tonight had proved her wrong.

For the first time she saw their relationship for what it really was. Edmund was using her — that she'd suspected already. What she hadn't known was that he was using her without any heart. He took everything she offered, but it didn't mean anything to him. He didn't value her for it.

Linda was just a means to an end as far as Edmund was concerned. When he landed his new job, her role in his life would be over.

I can't help him on another programme, she thought. So he'll go and find some other girl to share his bed and give him a leg up the BBC ladder. Then it will be goodbye Linda. And good luck.

She felt the rage rise up inside her. I deserve better than that, she thought.

13

Linda stopped seeing Edmund after that. He thought she had gone mad, of course, and used every trick in the book to get her to change her mind. But there was no way he was going to sweet-talk his way back into her bed. He could bloody well do his job on his own, Linda thought. She wasn't his slave.

Her rage gave her the push she needed. If she was good enough to cover for Edmund, maybe she could be Edmund. She knew the ropes, after all. All she had to do was apply for the next research job that came up.

It wasn't that simple. The people that hired researchers were all looking for graduates. It didn't matter that she could do the job standing on her head. As far as the BBC was concerned, Linda was a secretary, employed to type schedules and answer the phone.

She got turned down so many times she almost began to believe she really was incapable of anything but typing. Then she got a letter from a regional programme she had written to on the off-chance. It had been an act of desperation really, for the advertisement wasn't for a researcher at all, but for a reporter.

She might have forgotten all about it if the regional people hadn't written to her, and the biggest surprise of all was that they didn't tell her to go away. The producer of *Manchester Today* was actually inviting her to be interviewed.

She looked at the letter and checked the date. They wanted to see her at the end of the week at the studios in White City.

I might as well go, she thought. They'll turn me down, of course. But I could learn something from the experience.

For all her other interviews she had gone in with all guns blazing. She had curled her hair up and piled on the mascara. And even though they killed her, she had put on her high white patent leather shoes, the ones she went dancing in.

On Friday she didn't make that kind of effort. She threw on a pair of flannel trousers she wore most days, and an old navy blazer.

I'll go through the motions, she thought, but that's all.

She had been summoned to see David Berger, the news editor of *Manchester Today*, who was holding his interviews somewhere in the basement of the building. Linda sighed when the receptionist told her where the office was. She had been here before for two of her other interviews, and she knew she had to hike down three flights of stairs and along miles of corridor to get there.

Because she had made the journey before, she was slightly blasé when she finally got to the office Berger was using, and sauntered through the door.

'Linda Beattie,' she said to the secretary, 'for *Manchester Today*.'

There was a sharp explosion from among the line-up of applicants sitting along the far wall.

'What in hell's name are you doing here?' said a familiar voice.

She turned to see Edmund Stern staring at her.

'I've come for a job interview,' she replied, shaken. 'Is there a law against it?'

He did not look pleased. 'They're looking for reporters,' he said crossly, 'not secretaries. You must have got the wrong day.'

She considered walking out there and then. There wasn't a chance of anyone hiring her and she could do without Edmund's mockery, but something made her dig her heels in.

I've had enough of this, she thought. I've had enough of people telling me I'm not good enough, or educated enough, or experienced enough. I'm better than anyone going up for this interview. And I'm bloody well going to prove it.

She pushed past Edmund and grabbed the last vacant seat. Then she turned to him.

'I haven't got the wrong day,' she said sweetly, 'and I'm not going up for a secretary's job either.'

If they had been alone in the room, she imagined Edmund would have said something rude. Only there were three other applicants waiting with them, so he kept quiet and just glared at her.

It didn't put her off. And when it was his turn to be interviewed, she blew him a little kiss and wished him luck. He could talk all he wanted about his posh school and his exam results, but if David Berger was worth anything, he'd see right through him.

To keep herself going she made a list of her achievements. Britt Ekland had been on the programme because Linda had talked her agent round. David Owen turned out for the same reason. As the names flashed past her, Linda realized she was looking at a kaleidoscope of her life. People did that when they where about to die, she thought. Normally the notion would have frightened her, but today she couldn't care less.

She heard her name being called and looked up to see a fat man wearing pebble glasses and a sports jacket standing in the doorway.

'David Berger,' he said extending a hand. 'Come through will you.'

Linda followed him into the bare office she had visited before. She had sat through two interviews here, and been turned down for both jobs. Now that didn't matter either. The only thing that really counted was what happened right here, at this precise moment.

For the first time ever, she started to give an honest account of herself. When the news editor asked her about her education, she didn't fudge the details the way she had done before.

She came right out with the fact she had been to the local school and from there to secretarial college.

'I can't supply any fancy qualifications,' she told Berger, 'because I don't have any.'

The fat man seemed amused. 'What can you supply?' he asked her. 'There must be some reason why you're applying for this job.'

She wondered if he was patronizing her.

'I'll tell you what I've got that the others haven't,' she said. 'I've got street sense. While they were sitting passing exams, I was out there getting on with things. So when the programme editor yells for an expert on brain tumours or a man who performs in circuses, I know just where to look for them. None of the graduates I've ever worked for had a clue what to do in a crisis. I was always the one who pulled them out of the shit.'

She noticed the look of surprise on the news editor's face and wondered if he was going to throw her out.

Instead, he wanted to know about everything she had done since she joined the corporation – details of the stories she had worked on, names of the researchers and reporters she claimed to have helped – and when he had drained her dry of her last few months with the BBC, he leaned back in his chair and regarded her.

'If what you say is true,' he said, 'I'm very tempted to offer you the job. You've got the guts for it and you'll look pretty on screen.'

Linda started to smile. 'And if I made it all up?'

'Then I'll recommend you move over to Light Entertainment. Anyone who can invent that lot should be writing scripts.'

A week later Linda received a formal letter offering her the post of reporter for *Manchester Today*. She would have to find her own digs and her salary wasn't all that much more than she was getting in her secretarial job. But she didn't think twice about accepting it. It was one in the eye for Edmund and all the other Edmunds who had used her over the years.

Besides, she thought, I might just enjoy the job.

14

1984

It was a very small item right at the bottom of a page. Normally Holly would have turned it over and got on with the rest of the paper, but the picture that went with the item stopped her.

It showed her mother and a tall blond man coming out of a restaurant. It wasn't the usual glamorous publicity shot she was used to seeing. Mummy wasn't all dolled up in an evening dress smiling at the cameras. She looked rather scruffy, Holly thought, in blue jeans and a rumpled leather jacket. Her hair was scruffed back in a ponytail and she was scowling. Now Holly was really intrigued. Mummy never scowled at photographers. Even when Holly was quite little, she remembered Eve posing when some intrusive lensman snapped them shopping in Harrods.

'It's all part of keeping up an image,' her mother would tell her. 'The public have a certain idea of me and I have to go along with it.'

Holly studied the smudged, slightly out-of-focus picture. Mummy wasn't keeping up her famous image here. If anything she was going a long way towards destroying it.

The caption underneath didn't tell her anything she didn't already know. Mummy was coming out of Joe Allen with Brett, her leading man, who was meant to be her good friend.

The rest of the story went on to say that she wasn't seeing much of Jason since her success on Broadway. Holly snorted in disgust. Talk about stating the obvious. Of course she wasn't seeing much of Daddy. He had a business to run in

London. He couldn't just put it on hold because his wife was cavorting on the stage in New York every night.

Holly tore the story out of the paper and put it in her pocket. She'd show it to Daddy over supper tonight. It would be interesting to know what he had to say about it.

She didn't bring it up immediately. When Jason got home he had seemed a bit preoccupied, so she left it until he'd relaxed and had a drink or two. Then she produced the newspaper cutting when Lola was clearing the dishes away.

'I saw this in the *Mail* this morning,' she said, carefully unfolding it and laying it out on the table. 'What do you think?'

Her father didn't say anything for a bit. Instead he made a big production of taking out a cigar and cutting the end off it. Finally, when he'd lit it and was puffing away, he pronounced judgement.

'I think it's a rotten shot of your mother,' he said. 'She should know better than to go out in public dressed like that.'

Holly wrinkled her brow. 'I wonder why she did.'

'Why does anyone do anything? Maybe she was tired after the show. It could be she was feeling a bit off colour as well and all she really wanted was to have a quiet hamburger and go home. Nobody's perfect, you know.'

But Holly wasn't satisfied with that. 'What did they mean about Brett being Mummy's good friend? I thought he was just an actor she was working with.'

Her father started to look impatient. 'Grow up, Holly,' he said. 'Every time Eve has a leading man who's the least bit good-looking the papers always try to make a story out of it. Remember when she was doing that TV series with Nigel Havers? You never stopped seeing pictures of them together.'

'But that was different,' she said.

Jason pushed his chair away from the dining table and got up to leave.

'It wasn't in the least bit different,' he told her firmly.

Eve hadn't been looking to have an affair. When she came to New York all she wanted to do was make a name for herself and impress a few casting directors. Climbing in bed with a stranger was the last thing on her mind. Which is why she didn't see Brett coming.

Eve sighed and stared at her reflection in the dressing-room mirror. She had creamed her make-up off and the face that looked back at her seemed anonymous, devoid of character.

In London when she looked at her reflection she knew who she was. She had a past and a reputation, and they gave her a better idea of herself. Here she was just another actress in a popular hit.

With an effort, she pulled herself together. I'm getting maudlin, she thought. I'm letting this whole sordid little drama get to me.

Jason had phoned her that morning and told her about the picture in the *Mail*. The fact that it had appeared at all came as a surprise to her, for none of the New York papers had bothered with it.

'Was it a good likeness?' she had enquired, playing for time. 'Did it flatter me?'

Her husband was not taken in for a second. He knew when Eve was trying to hide something, and he wasn't going to let her get away with it.

'It was terrible of you,' Jason told her. 'And it was even worse of your boyfriend. If you were going to have an affair, you might have picked someone better looking.'

His voice was light and bantering but Eve knew he wasn't joking.

'Brett isn't my boyfriend,' she said crossly. 'Whatever gave you that idea?'

She thought she heard Jason laugh, but it could have been static.

'You looked so guilty, my darling. When the cameraman pounced, the pair of you looked as if you had got straight out of bed.'

They had too, but it was the last thing she was going to tell her husband, so she worked herself into a state of righteous indignation.

'How dare you?' she said. 'You sound like one of the gossip hounds I'm always trying to avoid.'

'Maybe you should try a little harder the next time you go out slumming. It's not your style at all.'

'And it's not your style to question every paparazzo picture you see in the papers.' She paused. 'Actually there's a perfectly innocent explanation if you want to hear it.'

'Try me,' Jason said.

'For a start,' Eve said, wading right in, 'it wasn't just me and Brett coming out of the restaurant. Three of the cast were right behind us, though I don't suppose you can tell that from the pictures. As for looking embarrassed, so would you be if you'd just come off stage and didn't want to be seen. I had no idea there would be cameramen outside Joe Allen at that hour.'

There was nothing wrong with her story. So why, Jason wondered, did he think his wife was lying?

'I'm still not happy about you running around Manhattan at all hours,' he persisted. 'I told you just now it isn't your style and I meant it.'

'Styles change,' Eve said carelessly.

Not yours, he thought. Not unless there's an outside influence altering you — one who goes by the name of Brett Weston.

There was no way he was going to get to the bottom of things sitting in London. They could go on arguing over the phone till kingdom come and he'd still be no wiser.

No, Jason decided. One day soon he was going to have to visit his wife in New York and see what was really happening.

It was Al Goldman who told Eve about Jason's visit.

'He's coming to New York Friday,' he said. 'You'd better start laying out the red carpet.'

The news threw Eve into a panic. It wasn't like Jason to spring that sort of surprise on her. They talked almost every day, so why hadn't he told her about his plans?

Then she remembered the paparazzo picture. She'd lied her way out of it as best she could, but clearly she hadn't convinced Jason. So now he was going to descend on New York in the hope of catching her out.

He would, of course. The affair was an open secret among the cast. There was bound to be somebody who would say something compromising. They wouldn't intend to, but it would come out anyway. These things always did.

Eve wondered what she was going to do about the situation. This was her first time in New York, her first hit, her first run-of-play affair. These three milestones in her life had addled her brain. She could hardly cope with one of them, let alone all three.

Then she had an idea. When there was a problem with a production, the man you always called on to sort it out was the producer. Well, you could say an irate husband was a very real problem. Eve decided to invite Al Goldman to lunch.

He accepted almost too readily, and she realized he knew what was up. In a way it was almost a relief. She didn't want to waste time pussyfooting around the place. At least if the problem was out in the open, they might be able to find some way of dealing with it.

Eve started agonizing about where to take Goldman. The Russian Tea Room was the obvious choice. It was chic and theatrical and everybody there would know who she was.

But it had its downside. There would be a queue of table hoppers interrupting them every five minutes. In the end she called Brett and asked for help.

'Where would you go if you wanted to talk business and not be interrupted?'

The actor considered for a moment. 'It depends who you're talking business with. You're not thinking of taking another lover, are you?'

She laughed. 'Not right now. The man I'm lunching with is the producer.'

'Then that's easy. You take him to Lutece. It's the nearest thing this town has to a private club. Nobody would dare cut in on you if you went there.'

Eve thanked him and put the phone down. Then she called the restaurant and reserved a table. The nice thing about starring in a hit show was that you could always get a table in the best places, with no notice at all.

She arrived at the converted townhouse on East Fiftieth a good ten minutes ahead of time. She had never eaten here before and she wanted to get a measure of the place. If she was going to be in control today, she needed to look as if she had been coming to Lutece all her life.

When Eve discovered that the chef was the owner, she immediately sent for him and piled on the charm. She praised his food, which she hadn't tasted, and the pretty conservatory room where he served it. By the time Al arrived, Eve was really getting quite intimate with André Soltner. It had the desired effect.

The producer immediately deferred to Eve, and she allowed him to do it. She was beginning to enjoy being treated like a star.

By the time they ordered lunch, she was all ready to start talking about what was on her mind. But even then, Al was anxious to save her any embarrassment.

'You don't have to discuss the Brett thing if you don't want to,' he told her. 'I appreciate how private it is to you.'

Eve laughed. 'It might be private to me, but it's not to anyone else. Everyone on the production knows about it. You seemed to know about it on the night we opened.'

'And you're dead scared your husband is going to find out the minute he hits New York,' the producer finished for her.

Eve took a sip of her drink and did her best to keep calm.

'I've been worrying myself sick about it, ever since I knew Jason was coming,' she admitted. 'I don't see there's any way I can keep it from him.'

Al looked at her and realized Eve was as neurotic as every other actress he had dealt with. It would be the easiest thing in the world to keep the affair from Jason. All she had to do was brief the cast and tell Brett to toe the line, and everything would be sweetness and light.

Only she couldn't do that – not on her own, at any rate. And he wasn't sure whether it was in his interests to help her.

Eve had gone down better in New York than Goldman had bargained on. If he wanted to make some money out of her, the best thing he could do would be to put her straight into a new show when this one closed. He had two possibles already lined up, but she wouldn't go for either of them if she was still attached to her husband.

He reached out and put a hand on her arm. 'Eve honey,' he said, 'I think you're going to have to face this situation head on. Grab it by the balls.'

'How do you mean, grab it by the balls?'

Goldman gave her his most innocent smile. 'I mean you're going to have to level with your old man – take the initiative. That way you'll be in the driving seat.'

'That way I'll be in the divorce court.'

The producer leaned back in his chair. 'So tell me what alternative you have. You said yourself, somebody's bound to spill the beans sooner or later.'

'I was exaggerating, playing the drama queen. I didn't seriously think he'd find out that easily.'

Goldman decided that he was going to have to take this one very carefully. He'd pushed her too hard, too quickly. He'd have to soften her up a little.

'You're getting frazzled,' he said, looking concerned. 'There's nothing worse for you and I won't have it. So I'm going to take you through to our table right now, give you a glass of André's excellent Chablis, then do every damn thing I can to cure your nerves. I can't allow my leading lady to have a breakdown.'

Eve let him lead her through to the conservatory she'd admired earlier. Then she sat back and relaxed while Al told her what kind of effect she was having on New York. A number of society hostesses were sending her invitations and the producer urged her to accept one in every three.

'That way you look busy. And if you look busy and you're hard to get, they'll want you even more.'

As she listened to the producer, Eve started to feel safer. This man knew what he was doing. He wasn't going to let her make a fool of herself over a little indiscretion.

When they had finished the main course and the dishes had been taken away, she raised the subject of Brett again.

'Do I really have to come clean about him?' she asked.

Al hesitated. 'Not if it's going to make you unhappy. You could always let your husband pick up the rumours and deny the whole thing.'

Eve remembered the last rumour Jason had picked up, the one in the *Daily Mail*. If her husband hadn't believed her denial the first time round, there was no way he would take her seriously now.

Maybe Al was right. Maybe her only choice was to get her story in first.

'If I decided to take the other course,' she said warily, 'what the hell do I say? There's no excuse for what I did.'

'Then find an excuse. And make it a good one.'

Jason had broken all the rules for transatlantic flights. He had had wine with his dinner – quite a lot of wine – then he'd watched the film instead of putting on the complimentary sleeping mask and trying to get some rest.

Now, as the plane approached New York, he felt like yesterday's leftovers. The headache, which he'd been vaguely aware of all night, had somehow expanded and was threatening to split his skull, and the pale morning light filtering through the laminated windows hurt his eyes. He wondered if he'd be in any state to cope with his wife.

Eve had called him as soon as she'd heard he was coming over and she'd sounded nervous. The old Eve would have given him hell for telling Al about his visit before he got round to her, but now she was playing her cards close to her chest. She wanted to know exactly when he was arriving, how long he was staying, and what his plans were.

'I have no plans,' Jason had told her, 'except for you.'

That made her even more jumpy and she went on at length about how busy she was at the theatre.

'We'll have hardly any time to talk,' she protested.

'I didn't know we needed to,' he countered.

Eve didn't say very much after that, except to suggest he

took the flight out on Saturday night. It would get him in on Sunday morning in time to spend the day with her. The theatre was closed on Sunday so they could talk from early morning till late at night. He had never looked forward to anything less in his life.

Jason got into the city just before lunch, and instead of going straight to the apartment, he stopped off at an Irish bar on Seventh Avenue.

He needed a stiff Martini to steady his nerves and kill his hangover. Then he had to do some tough thinking before he faced Eve.

She was having an affair with Brett Weston. Jason was more or less convinced of that now and he was furious he hadn't picked up on it before.

I should have suspected her on opening night, he berated himself. All that whispering in corners with Brett was far beyond the call of duty. But what could I have done if I had known? Threatened her with divorce if she didn't come home? She would have laughed in my face.

Jason realized his wife's life was already racing far beyond his control. And he felt helpless and defeated.

I should cut my losses, he decided. I should get out now while I still have some dignity.

But he couldn't do it. Their lives had been too close, they had depended on each other too much to end everything with a lawyer's cold letter. No, they had to talk it out. He had to hear why she had done the unforgivable — and whether it was unforgivable.

If she's straight with me, he thought, we might stand a chance. Anyone can make a mistake, and there's Holly to think about. I can't leave her stranded without a mother because my pride has been wounded.

Afterwards, when Jason looked back on that day, one thing stuck in his mind: he didn't consider for one moment that his daughter would be going with her mother. He knew, even then, that if Eve wanted out of the marriage she'd walk away from everything.

*   *   *

Jason got to the apartment on West Side prepared for a row. He was late and Eve was entitled to complain, but she didn't say a word. Instead, she ushered him through to the main room. Then she set about preparing a pitcher of Martini.

He considered telling her he'd had enough of that particular drink, but she'd obviously gone to a lot of trouble with fresh limes and London gin, and despite himself he was flattered. If she was making this kind of effort, maybe she did care after all.

He took the glass out of her hand and noticed it was shaking. Maybe she's just feeling guilty, he thought.

Jason took a closer look at Eve and decided he didn't like what he saw. She had lost weight since she'd been away. She had never been plump, but now she was positively skeletal. The hair was different too. She'd braided it like an Indian squaw and it made her look modern and tough. He could see she hung out with the arty crowd – fringe actors and pseudo-intellectuals – and he blamed the whole thing on Brett.

Brett was taking Eve away from her roots, seducing her with the novelty of the unfamiliar, and Jason realized he had to get her back while he still knew who she was.

He let her make small talk for the next hour or so until her hand stopped shaking and her smile came back. Bit by bit the frost started to melt, so that by the time lunch was finished and Eve was making coffee, they were almost at ease with each other.

Jason tackled her about Brett over brandy in front of the fire. She put her glass down as if she had been stung.

'What are you trying to prove?' she demanded.

'I'm not trying to prove anything. I don't have to.'

There was a silence.

'So you know?' Eve asked.

Jason nodded, and she looked so stricken he wished there was a way he could make it easier for her.

'I don't want to fight about this,' he said finally. 'There's no point in yelling about something that's already done.'

Eve reached for her drink again. 'What do you want to do?'

'I want to find out how I failed you,' Jason told her. 'I must have done something wrong to drive you into another man's bed.'

That took the wind out of her sails. She had been geared up for a confrontation and all she had was an apology. All the elaborate lies she had been rehearsing flew out of her mind, and she found herself telling the plain unvarnished truth.

She'd had no one to confess to until now — there were no close women friends in the company — and Al Goldman was too cynical to grasp what she was really going through. So she dumped everything on her husband.

Eve talked about Brett making a pass at her over a drink, about her panic when she realized she was vulnerable to him, and most of all about her nerves.

'There was no way I could act with Brett,' she confided. 'Everyone saw it. Even Al saw it and threatened to postpone the opening.'

'And going to bed with your leading man solved all this?'

She fiddled with one of her plaits. 'It did actually.'

Jason looked at his wife, suddenly seeing her for what she was.

'Do you want to know why it helped?' he asked bitterly.

'Tell me.'

'It wasn't really Brett you were fucking. It was the theatre itself. Do you remember the first time you got stage fright? When you walked away from your mother? You were falling apart then, and the only way I could put you back together again was to make love to you. It wouldn't have worked if I'd been just anyone — your boyfriend or a stranger you picked up at a party. What you needed at that moment was someone who was someone in the theatre to show they approved of you. It cancelled out your mother. Now it's happened all over again, only this time you needed to cancel me out, because you were moving on again.'

Eve got up from where she was sitting and went to find the brandy bottle.

'That all sounds terribly final,' she said.

94

Jason took the Hennessy out of her hands and topped up their glasses.

'It's only final,' he told her, 'if you want it to be. You could give up being the toast of Broadway and come back home. I could find you a nice tour or a television play and we could forget this ever happened.'

'And if I don't come home?'

Jason looked at his wife. 'We get a divorce,' he said levelly. 'We don't have any other choice.'

15

Holly should have known something was wrong, because no matter how far Eve's work took her, when she said she was coming home, she always kept her word.

Holly said as much to Jason when he broke the news about New York.

'There's no need for Mummy to stay to the end of the run,' she protested. 'She told me herself six months was long enough to make her mark.'

'Well, she's changed her mind,' Jason told her. 'She'll explain why when she's back.'

But Eve's play closed and she went straight into another Broadway production.

'Something's keeping her out there,' Holly said when Jason broke the news. 'Something you haven't told me about.'

Jason wondered whether to level with his daughter. She was fifteen now, old enough to understand that love doesn't always last the course. Yet now it had actually come to it, he found it hard to admit that he and Eve no longer wanted to live together.

He cast his mind back to the last time he had seen her.

Eve was in the middle of rehearsals for a new play, so they didn't have very long together. In a way Jason was relieved, for he had run out of things to say to her.

They met in a bar in the theatre district and he noticed the change in her the minute she came through the door. She had cut her hair very short and was wearing it brushed back off her face. The last time he saw her she had been looking like an Indian squaw because Brett liked her that way.

She'll have finished that affair by now, Jason thought. This butch look is for somebody else.

He was tempted to ask her who, but he knew it would only lead to trouble, so he asked her about the play instead.

Eve shrugged and told him the same story he had heard a million times before. They were having teething problems.

'You'll get to grips with them on the out-of-town run,' he told her. 'You always do.'

'I suppose so,' she sighed.

The barman approached and Eve asked him for a glass of wine. She turned to Jason.

'Will you have the same, or do you want something stronger?'

He told her wine would be fine.

Then he asked her how long she expected the new play to run. She shrugged.

'We have advance bookings for three months. It can only build from there.'

'So we won't be expecting you home?' Jason had come all this way to ask Eve that one question, yet when it came out, it sounded more brutal than he intended. Not that it seemed to bother her.

'I think we both know where we stand on that one.'

He looked at her for a long time after that, searching in vain for some sign of warmth, and found none. It was as if a switch had been turned off inside her and he knew that no matter how hard he tried it was too late to change things.

'I suppose you want a divorce,' he said.

Eve nodded. 'It would make things tidier.'

Jason looked at the woman he had married and wondered when she had turned into a stranger. It started with Brett, he thought bitterly. If Brett hadn't happened, it would have been different.

But Jason knew he was blaming the wrong person. Brett hadn't taken her away. Eve had taken herself away.

He remembered the look on her face when he suggested she came home and he would find her a television play. He knew then she would rather go to the gallows than step down from where she was.

'What are we going to do about Holly?' he asked.

Eve looked him in the eye. 'What do you think we should do about her?'

'I wish I could tell you, but I haven't got a clue. It's been a difficult few months.'

For the first time since they met, Eve softened.

'What's she been up to?' she asked.

'What hasn't she been up to? She's still eating like it's going out of fashion. Then she moans that she's getting too fat — as if the whole thing were my fault.'

Neither of them said anything for a moment. Then Eve turned to him. 'It's not your fault,' she said softly. 'I'm the one to blame for this problem. When teenage girls feel they're being neglected they turn to the biscuit tin for comfort. I saw the signs before I went away, but I hoped she'd grow out of it.'

Jason took hold of his drink, downing half of it in one gulp.

'If it was just the eating thing, I could cope with it,' he said. 'But there's more. She's moody, the way she used to be when she was a little girl and she couldn't get what she wanted. I do everything I can to make life easy for her, but she acts as if I'm some kind of enemy.'

He made to drain the rest of his wine, but Eve reached out and took the drink out of his hand.

'We're not going to solve anything by you getting sozzled.'

He laughed hollowly. 'Tell me something I don't know.'

'You don't know how much your daughter needs you right now. All this acting up is a way of testing you. She wants to be sure that no matter what she does, you'll still be there for her.'

'What about you?' Jason asked. 'Will you be there for Holly as she grows up?'

Just for a moment he thought he saw a tear glinting in the corner of Eve's eye.

'How can I be?' she said. 'With my itinerary I won't have a moment to breathe.'

'So you'll leave her with me in London?'

Eve nodded. 'I wish it was different. I wish I could offer her more.'

The hardness that she wore like a mantle had dropped away completely now, and Jason got a glimpse of the real Eve, the one he had known before all the success had come between them. Part of him ached to take her in his arms and beg her to try again, but he knew it was too late for that now.

Instead he ordered them both another glass of wine and started to lay out a plan for their daughter's future.

'I'd like her to spend her school holidays with you, if you can find the time.'

'I'll make the time,' Eve said firmly. 'It's the least I can do for her.'

'Do it because you love her, not because you feel guilty.'

She looked at him. 'You're never going to believe this, but I love both of you. Silly, isn't it?'

Jason took hold of her hand then. 'Yes,' he told her, 'it is silly. Because there's not a damn thing we can do about it.'

Jason decided to have it out with Holly the day after his daughter had confronted him. The divorce would be final in a month or so and he didn't want her finding out about it from some gossip column.

Holly was in the kitchen when he got in, gossiping to Lola while she prepared the supper. What he had to say couldn't be discussed in front of the housekeeper, so he asked Holly to come up to his study at the top of the house.

She grabbed a Coke for herself and a bottle of claret for him, and followed him up the stairs. It was ages since she and Daddy had really talked, and she wondered what was on his mind. It's probably about Mummy, she thought. She sat herself down in one of his big antique leather chairs and looked across at him.

There was something excited and expectant about her and Jason suddenly found himself lost for words. In the end it was Holly who rescued him.

'This is something to do with Mummy's new play, isn't it?'

He nodded. 'It looks like she'll be staying on in New York for a bit.'

The child looked wary. 'How long is a bit?'

'It depends on the play she's in. If it's as big a hit as the last one, it could be some time.'

Holly slid out of the high-backed chair and went over to her father. 'Stop telling me lies,' she said. 'I know Mummy's in New York because of Brett Weston. I'm not a complete nerd.'

Jason raised an eyebrow. 'How do you know all this?'

'There was a story in the *News of the World*. One of the girls at school showed me.'

'And you swallowed it whole? You didn't even come to me and discuss it?'

Holly looked uncomfortable. 'How could I?' she demanded. 'It was a horrible story and I thought you'd be angry.'

Jason put an arm round her and held her close, searching his mind for what to say next.

He had read somewhere that modern parents talked out all their problems with the children. Apparently it gave them a better understanding of how the world worked. He looked at the soft, believing face of his daughter and decided the social workers could go to hell. He would tell her what he wanted her to know now. When she was grown up she could piece the rest of the story together for herself.

'The story in the *News of the World* wasn't just horrible,' he told Holly, 'it was wrong. Mummy isn't in New York because of Brett Weston. She's there because of her career. She's just starting to be known in America. If she comes home now, she'll never make her name.'

'But it could take years to make her name,' Holly said. 'What are we going to do in the meantime?'

Jason breathed deeply. 'We're going to be brave and soldier on without her.'

Holly started to feel frightened. Her father had never talked like this before. Something was terribly wrong.

'This isn't just about Mummy making her name?'

A feeling of despair swept over Jason. This was the moment he had been dreading.

'No it isn't,' he said, as reasonably as he could. 'I've decided, that is we've both decided, we don't want to be married any more. So there's no point in Mummy coming home.'

Holly looked at him with such anguish, such disappointment, that he felt like a murderer.

'You're getting divorced, aren't you?' she said.

He nodded, then he watched helplessly while his daughter fell apart in front of him.

16

Before any storm, there is an ominous silence. Holly's sudden retreat into herself should have alerted Jason to a potential problem, but he was busy. Two major Hollywood studios were making costume dramas, big historical epics that required English accents, and Jason was expected to come up with a list of suitable candidates — two lists actually, one for each film.

Every moment of every day was taken up with phone calls and interviews and last-minute dashes across town to see the talent on stage.

Most nights he didn't get in until past twelve, so he missed his daughter, only catching up with her at weekends when they usually went for a walk in Hyde Park or caught a movie.

Looking back on it, Jason supposed he should have been more observant, but his mind was so full of the actors he was putting up for Hollywood that he hardly noticed Holly at all.

In the end it was Lola who alerted him.

'Miss Holly isn't well,' she said. 'She has problems with her digestion.'

Jason was mystified. Since when was indigestion an illness? He decided to tackle Holly about it.

'Lola tells me you've got some kind of tummy upset,' he said.

The girl looked at him wide-eyed. 'She must be dreaming. There's nothing wrong at all.'

There was a false note in her voice and Jason started to worry. She's hiding something, he thought.

He looked at her then, seeing her properly for the first time in months. And what he saw didn't make him happy. She was very peaky, with dark shadows under her eyes. And the puppy fat that she complained about seemed to have disappeared entirely. He could see her cheekbones now. And he suspected that if she got undressed he would probably be able to see her ribs.

'Have you got on the scales recently?' he asked her.

Holly looked rebellious. 'I weigh myself every day. First thing in the morning.'

'Then you won't object if I ask you to do it again?'

She shrugged. 'Why don't I just tell you what I weigh? It will save you the trouble of going upstairs.'

He took her by the arm. 'It's no trouble,' he said.

He weighed her in his bathroom, on the scales Eve used to use. And what he saw stopped him in his tracks. His healthy teenage daughter was under seven stone.

'Why didn't you tell me you were ill?' he demanded. 'I would have done something about it ages ago.'

She looked at the carpet, fidgeting from one foot to another.

'I'm not ill,' she said finally. 'I'm just thin.'

Jason did a double take. 'Thin is an understatement, isn't it? I'd say you were skeletal. How the hell did you get like this?'

She looked up at him then, and he saw the triumph in her eyes.

'I went on a diet,' she said. 'It was time I did something about the puppy fat.'

A horrible suspicion started to grow in Jason's mind. He'd heard about girls starving themselves to death because they wanted to look like fashion plates. Was his daughter one of those? He chose his words carefully.

'Do you like the way you look?'

'It's okay. It's better than looking like a lump.'

He knew she needed help then. She was like a prisoner from Belsen, yet in her eyes that was okay.

103

I have to get her to a doctor, he decided, before she gets into real trouble.

Holly stared balefully at Geoffrey Bolan and wondered when he would put a sock in it. So far he had told her she was suffering from malnutrition, her metabolism was shot to pieces and if she didn't get a hold on herself she would do herself real damage.

'What makes you think you know everything?' she demanded. 'I've been in your surgery for half an hour and already you've got my whole life history off pat.'

'I've every reason to know what makes you tick,' he told her. 'I was there when you were born. I knew your mother before you knew her.'

'Fat lot of good that did,' she said. 'She didn't exactly stick around, did she?'

It was obvious to Dr Bolan what was wrong with the girl. She wanted to be loved, and when her mother wouldn't pay attention to her, she found another way of getting heard.

He remembered the conversation he'd had with Jason before he saw Holly. The girl had been using food as a weapon for months now. First she'd gorged herself silly, then when she lost her mother she did the other thing. She starved. It was a classic story. If he wrote it up for the *Journal*, it would probably be rated as a textbook case.

He looked through the copious notes he had made and felt worried. Holly might be a textbook case, but the textbook treatment wasn't going to go down well at all.

'How do you feel about a stay in hospital?' he asked.

Her reaction was just as he expected.

'I won't do it,' she said.

He looked at her over the top of his spectacles. 'Why not?'

'Because I know what they'll do to me. Some bossy nurse will start stuffing me full of food. And if I refuse to accept it, I'll be strapped down and forced to eat.'

Geoffrey Bolan smiled. 'You've missed out the intravenous feeding,' he said, 'when they push an needle into you and drip nourishment through your system.'

Holly looked as if she was going to be sick. 'You won't let them do that to me, will you?'

The doctor leaned forward and looked serious. 'It all depends,' he said. 'If you make an effort to mend your ways, I might not send you to hospital after all.'

There was a silence. Then: 'You want me to get fat again?'

'Not fat – normal. Tell me, Holly, do you remember how much you weighed before you starting stuffing yourself?'

The girl considered for a moment. 'I think it was about eight stone.'

'Fine. I need you to be eight stone again.'

'But that's gross.'

'Not half as gross as being force-fed in hospital for the rest of your life.'

The doctor supplied Holly with a vile-tasting liquid food that she had to drink four times a day after meals. He also put her on a course of pills designed to increase her appetite. And as a final insult he gave her a menu card.

She was to eat three big meals a day consisting of porridge and cream for breakfast. Some kind of pie and greens for lunch. And in the evening she was expected to lay into a great hunk of meat with all the trimmings.

The sight of Dr Bolan's menu card made her feel quite ill. I'll never get through this, she thought. If the liquid food doesn't kill me, the solids are bound to finish me off.

Holly went to find her father. If she sat him down and explained how impossible this scheme was, he was bound to let her off the hook. Jason wasn't in, however. It was nearly nine o'clock, which meant he wouldn't be home for dinner now. For a moment Holly felt utterly defeated.

Since her troubles, Jason had made an effort to be home in the evenings. But now she'd seen the doctor and been given a cure, he'd forgotten about her again.

He'll be out in some posh restaurant with his theatre friends, she decided. When he comes in he'll insist it was a business evening, only I know better. He likes talking showbiz. It's fun for him, a damn sight more fun than keeping an eye on an anorexic daughter.

Holly dragged herself down to the kitchen. So far she'd stuck to Dr Bolan's plan for two meals, feeling queasy every time she put something into her mouth. She wondered what Lola had in store for dinner. As she came through the door, she was assailed by a wonderful smell – not the meat she was expecting, but something altogether more appetizing.

'What's cooking?' she asked the Spanish woman, who was busy laying the table.

'You'll find out when it's ready,' Lola smiled.

It wasn't like her to be mysterious.

'I suppose you're following Dr Bolan's menu card,' Holly said, fishing for clues.

But Lola wouldn't be drawn. Instead she handed her a packet of breadsticks.

'You can nibble on those while you're waiting.'

Normally Holly wouldn't have looked at a breadstick, but she was being made to wait for dinner, so almost absentmindedly she worked her way through the packet. They were grissini, she noticed, Italian and light as air.

I'd better enjoy them while I can, she thought. Dinner is bound to sit on my stomach like a stone.

Only she was wrong. When Lola finally opened the oven door, Holly was greeted by the sight of an enormous cheese soufflé. It was steaming and fragrant, and despite herself, the girl felt hungry.

'Surely Dr Bolan didn't say I could have this,' she protested.

'No, he didn't,' Lola told her, 'but I'm sick already of preparing the doctor's meals.' She rolled her eyes. 'They're so boring.'

Holly didn't look a gift horse in the mouth. Instead she reached over and dug into the soufflé. It wasn't like eating real food – it was too insubstantial to take seriously – and when Lola pushed the dish towards her a second time, Holly helped herself to some more.

Lola followed the soufflé with a pile of finely sliced apples on a wafer of pastry. Holly devoured that as well.

106

'That was wonderful,' she said, when she had quite finished. 'Thank you for giving me the night off from Dr Bolan.'

Lola started to clear the plates away. 'If you like,' she said, 'we could take tomorrow off as well.'

Holly felt a stab of guilt. 'Won't we get into trouble?'

'Not if we don't tell anyone.'

For the next week Holly and Lola were conspirators. The vile-tasting liquid food was put in front of her as the doctor ordered after every meal, and Lola would pour it down the sink before she stacked the dishwasher.

The doctor's menu card suffered a similar fate. Not one item on it ever found its way on to the table. Instead, the Spanish housekeeper served the kind of light food you find in five-star restaurants.

By Friday, Holly started to panic. Jason was taking her to Dr Bolan to be weighed. And when they saw she hadn't gained an ounce, there was bound to be an almighty row.

She took a decision then. She was going to lie about Lola's part in the deception. Since her mother had left, Lola had been Holly's only consolation. Even when Holly was a little girl, Lola had always been there for her. But now she was taking a bigger part in her life.

She probably isn't doing me any good, Holly thought, but at least she's on my side. She cares when I'm miserable.

She was due at the doctor's surgery in Harley Street at eight o'clock on Friday morning. It was ridiculously early, but it fitted in with her father's plans. They could be in and out of there in half an hour and Jason could still be in the office for his first meeting.

Holly wondered whether her father would feel like taking a meeting when he realized she'd been cheating. Then she thought, the hell with it, I own my body. What I put into it is my business.

Nevertheless she felt quite nervous all the way from St John's Wood to the West End. By the time they arrived at Dr Bolan's she and her father were hardly saying a word to each other.

107

Holly stole a sideways glance at Jason. He's on to me, she thought. He suspects something's up.

They were the first appointment that day, so there wasn't long to wait. Holly was just starting to leaf through a property magazine when her name was called.

'You don't have to come in with me,' she said to Jason. 'I'm big enough to go through this on my own.'

It was a nice try but it didn't cut any ice. Jason simply stood up, took her by the hand and led the way into the doctor's surgery.

Holly's heart sank when she saw Geoffrey Bolan sitting behind his desk. He was so big, so unsmiling – what would he do to her when he found out she'd thrown away his diet sheet?

She sat in the slippery leather seat that faced him and did her best to look innocent.

'How's the eating?' he asked her.

'Fine,' she said quickly.

'You are eating, I take it?'

At least she didn't have to lie this time. 'Of course I am. Three times a day, the way you told me.'

To her relief he didn't make any comment about the liquid food. Instead he got up and indicated the scales in the corner of the room.

'Hop on,' he instructed. 'We'll see what effect my treatment is having.'

Numbly she did as she was told. It was one of those new-fangled scales with a digital face that printed out the pounds and ounces. Last week she had been ninety-six pounds on this machine. She prayed she hadn't lost anything.

With an effort she looked down at the digital face. The black figures in front of her said ninety-nine pounds, four ounces.

She did a double take. It had to be wrong. She'd hardly eaten a thing all week. There was no way she could have gained over three pounds. Then she felt her father's arm around her.

'That's my girl,' he said. 'I knew you could do it if you put your mind to it.'

Jason was looking at her with such love, such concern, that her heart turned over. She'd just put on three pounds of fat and he was behaving as if she'd just passed her university entrance. For a moment she felt panicky. She hated being overweight. Even to please her father, she wouldn't let herself get like a blimp.

She looked at the scales again. She was just over seven stone. She knew as long as she kept her head, there was hope for her.

In the next two days Holly achieved two things: she found a brand of laxative that acted faster than any other, and she discovered how to make herself sick.

If she combined the two techniques, she could go on eating Lola's meals and not damage her figure at all.

The whole scheme worked like a charm. The beauty of it was that nobody caught on to what she was up to. When her father checked with Lola, she could tell him quite truthfully Holly was eating three meals a day, so he didn't hassle his daughter. He didn't even insist on coming with her to Dr Bolan for her next weigh-in. This was a relief, for when Holly next stepped onto the scales, the read-out was ninety-nine pounds, the same as the week before.

'What have you been up to?' the doctor asked.

Holly widened her eyes. 'I haven't been up to anything,' she lied. 'I can't put on weight every week.'

Geoffrey Bolan narrowed his eyes. 'If you'd been eating properly you could.'

Holly was about to tell him she wasn't a machine, when she remembered his threat about taking her into hospital. She decided to compromise.

'If I put on a few pounds next week, will you promise you won't say anything to Daddy?'

'I'll keep quiet for a week,' the doctor said, 'but that's all.'

The following week Holly had gained one and a half pounds. It had been an effort, but she'd done it because she knew she had to. The week after that she put on just half a pound, but a week later she'd lost it again.

'I'm doing my best with the diet,' she told the doctor, 'but nothing happens.'

Geoffrey Bolan wasn't fooled for a moment. He had no doubt she was eating, but he'd seen too many girls like her not to know what else she was doing. It was time to have a quiet word with Jason. The two men met at Dr Bolan's club in St James's one evening after work.

After ordering drinks for both of them, the doctor came straight to the point.

'It's about Holly. I'm afraid I'm not having any success with her.'

Jason looked mystified. 'I thought she was doing fine.'

'She was for five minutes. Then she slipped back into her old ways. Teenage eating problems aren't easily solved. The patient has to want to get better, otherwise whatever anyone does, she'll sabotage it.'

Jason began to feel helpless. He was bringing up his daughter as well as he knew how, yet no matter how hard he tried, he couldn't be both parents.

He regarded his old friend. 'Do you think it would help if I sent her to see her mother?'

'It might. Anything's worth a try.'

Eve's schedule flashed into his mind. She was touring in a Pinter play right now. But in ten days, she was due to open in New York. Then she'll be back in the apartment she always rents on the West Side, he thought, and there'll be room for Holly.

17

Holly looked around her mother's New York sitting room and decided Eve couldn't care about it much. The sofa and the matching armchairs had seen better days, yet Eve had done nothing to disguise the tatty chintz. In the old days, Mummy wouldn't have given them house room, nor made her home in such a dreary place.

Holly had hated the apartment the moment she'd set foot in it three days before. 'It smells musty here,' she'd told Eve, as she struggled with her suitcase through the door.

'It smells musty all over New York,' her mother told her. 'Even in the Ritz Tower it smells musty.'

Holly suspected Eve was making it up. It was obvious she was embarrassed about bringing her daughter back there. As they struggled down the narrow hall she turned to her mother.

'Why are you living like this?' she asked. 'I thought you were doing well over here.'

Eve didn't say anything until they reached the sitting room.

'I am doing well,' she finally replied. 'Only the theatre doesn't pay that much and I have to manage on what I earn.'

'What about Daddy? Surely he gives you something?'

Now her mother really did look embarrassed. 'I didn't take a penny from your father.'

'Why not?'

Eve sighed. 'Because Jason gave me everything. Without him I wouldn't be on Broadway. I probably wouldn't be acting at all.'

'But you were married to him, Mummy. You had me. Surely that deserves something?'

Eve sat down on the big shabby sofa. She looked sad when she next spoke.

'I wasn't much of a wife, just as I'm not much of a mother. And now if you don't mind, I'd rather not talk about it any more.'

After that they'd stayed away from the subject of her parents' divorce, yet Holly couldn't get Eve's sacrifice out of her head.

Now, as she sat in the big untidy drawing room over-looking the West Side, she wondered what had possessed her mother. Maybe she still loves Jason, she thought. It's the only reason I can think of for not taking what's rightfully hers.

She pondered her parents' relationship. They didn't behave like any divorced couple she'd ever heard of. They still spoke on the phone once a week, and, what was even stranger, Daddy went on working as Mummy's agent.

Maybe, deep down, Holly thought, they know they've made a mistake and they're playing for time. They're probably working on being friends again before they take the final step and get back together.

It was a fantasy, she knew, but she couldn't let it go.

Later, when she left the apartment to meet her mother at the theatre, she was still imagining what it would be like if her parents lived together again. All the way on the subway to Times Square, she saw them in her mind's eye, the way they used to be – Jason, tall and protective; Eve clinging to his arm, looking up at him.

Holly was so taken up with her dream that she didn't really come to until she reached the theatre. Then the hustle of people in the foyer brought her down to earth with a bang. She literally had to fight her way through to the box office. Then she had to repeat her name twice before the man behind the glass cubicle recognized who she was.

'Aren't you Eve Adams' kid?' he said finally.

Holly nodded vigorously. 'You should be holding my

house seat.' She waited while the clerk rummaged around before producing what she'd come for.

Then, her ticket in her hand, she hurried through the double doors into the theatre. So far she'd seen the play every night since she'd been here, and repetition didn't improve it. Pinter was dull, dull, dull. She'd always hated him. But she knew better than to tell Eve.

As long as Holly pretended to enjoy the performance she got to meet her mother every night. That was well worth sitting still for two hours and being bored out of her skull.

After the theatre Eve liked going to a little Italian restaurant off Seventh Avenue. It was run by a family from Naples and all the waiters went out of their way to make a huge fuss of her.

Tonight was no exception. Alfredo, a big black-haired man who seemed to run the place, came over to them the minute they were through the door.

He had a table all ready. A bottle of Frascati was chilling on ice. Whatever either of them wanted he would break his balls to provide.

Holly looked at the Italian fawning over her mother and wished he'd cool it. These late-night dinners were precious to her. They were her only chance to get close to Eve. All she needed was some waiter butting in all the time.

Finally Alfredo got the message and went off to fetch the menu, and Holly started to relax. She'd made her mind up to talk about her illness. She needed her mother to know about it because, try as she might, she couldn't explain it to her father. Lola was a dead loss now too. All the Spanish woman did was try and make her eat.

Eve won't do that, Holly decided. She cares more about her figure than she does about food. As the evening went on, though, Holly started to wonder.

When Alfredo came back her mother began to ask him about the pasta. For ten minutes the two of them discussed some of the most fattening dishes in the world, before Eve finally made up her mind.

113

'I'll have the lasagne,' she pronounced. 'And bring me a bottle of Barolo to go with it.'

Holly couldn't believe her ears. If she made a habit of going to this restaurant Mummy would end up as big as a house.

She made a face when it was her turn to order, deliberately opting for plain grilled fish and a salad. She couldn't tell Eve not to touch the pasta, but she could make her feel ashamed she was having it.

Eve watched while her daughter gave strict instructions to the waiter. There was to be no butter on the fish, and no dressing on the salad. Holly had obviously been cutting down on her calories for some time now, for she was painfully thin and wasted-looking, exactly the way Jason had described her when he called and told Eve about the problem.

'I'm at my wits' end,' he had told her. 'The doctor's done all he can – even Lola's tried to help – but none of us can persuade her to put on a pound. I sometimes think Holly actually gets a kick out of all the worry she causes. She sees us running around in circles and she feels in control.'

Now, as the waiter arrived with the wine she'd ordered, Eve reflected on these last words. The more upset we get, she thought, the more we encourage her in this insanity. There has to be another way.

She glanced up to see her daughter looking at her.

'Mummy,' Holly said, 'there's something I want to talk to you about.'

Eve took a sip of her wine. 'Go ahead, I'm listening.'

Now her words came out in a rush. 'I have this problem with food. I really want to be thin, so I don't want it round me all the time, but Daddy and Lola think I'm making myself ill and they insist on stuffing me like a goose.'

'You don't look all that stuffed to me.'

Holly smiled. 'That's because I'm smart.'

Eve looked curious. 'Tell me what you do that's so smart.'

'I make myself sick,' Holly said brightly. 'Daddy can force me to eat, but he can't insist I keep it down.'

Eve made herself stay calm. She's winding me up, she

thought. She's looking for a reaction, and I'm damned if I'll give it to her.

'Do you enjoy doing that to yourself?' she asked levelly.

The girl made a face. 'Not really, but it has to be done.'

Eve shrugged. 'So what's your problem? You seem to have things all worked out from what I can see.'

She noticed the dismay on her daughter's face.

'But I'm making myself ill,' Holly said. 'Dr Bolan keeps threatening to take me into hospital.'

'I'll have to have a word with Geoffrey. You don't seem the least bit ill to me.'

'You mean you'll put a stop to the weigh-ins and the three meals a day?'

Eve nodded. 'It's all a complete waste of time. You're a grown-up girl now. How you live your life is your affair.'

Holly started to say something, but Eve cut her short. A group of people had just come into the restaurant and she wanted to attract their attention.

They saw her after a couple of minutes, and made a beeline for the table. Then everyone started kissing everyone else. The waiter had got them all chairs and Eve made the introductions.

'This is Ida,' she told Holly, indicating a matronly woman covered with flashy jewellery. 'She's my very best friend in New York.' She turned to a jowly man in a shiny suit. 'This is Ida's husband, Frank.'

The other introductions were drowned out by the welter of small talk. Everyone was busy catching up, dropping names, repeating choice bits of gossip, everyone, that is, except for Ida, the leader of the pack.

'Poor baby,' she said, looking at Holly. 'We didn't mean to home in on your party.'

'It's not a party,' Eve said quickly. 'We were just grabbing a quick bite after the theatre.'

'So we haven't interrupted anything.'

Eve grinned and signalled the waiter for another bottle of Barolo. 'We weren't talking about anything important,' she said.

Five minutes later, Holly made an excuse and headed for the washrooms. As she left the table she looked to see if her mother noticed what she was doing. But Eve seemed totally oblivious to her.

Nothing's changed, she thought bitterly. Mummy's so wound up with being a star, she couldn't care if I was on my way to cut my wrists.

She was in such a rage that she almost pushed down the door of the ladies' room. And she was relieved to see there was no one else in there. What she had to do needed privacy and space.

There were three cubicles and Holly chose the one furthest away. Then she shut herself in and kneeled down in front of the toilet bowl. She was about to do what she always did, when something made her stop.

There was a long strip of mirror opposite her and she could see her reflection. She was on her knees sticking her fingers down her throat. The sight should have horrified her, but it didn't. It made her feel stupid. There was something pointless about what she was doing. She was hurting herself, but for what? So her mother could lose sleep worrying about her? The thought almost made her laugh. The only thing Mummy lost sleep over was the size of her billing. Holly could fade away in front of her and Eve probably wouldn't even notice.

Slowly, still staring at her reflection, Holly got to her feet. As she did so, she saw herself as she really was. The shock made her catch her breath.

It can't be me, she thought. My hair never looked like string before, and there was colour in my cheeks.

She stepped closer to the glass, seeing for the first time the black circles under her eyes, the way her cheeks caved in like a dead person's.

If I go on like this, she realized, I'll end up in hospital whether I want to go there or not.

Holly remembered her mother's words then: 'You're a grown-up girl now. How you live your life is your affair.'

She hated Eve for that. She hated her mother for telling

her she was finally on her own. Yet instead of destroying her, the emotion gave her purpose.

So my mother doesn't love me, Holly thought. It's not worth lying down and dying for.

18

MANCHESTER, 1984

Julian, programme director of *Manchester Today*, watched the blonde as she went through her paces. She was a pretty little thing, a bit on the tarty side, but underneath all the lip gloss and chunky gold jewellery, he suspected she was probably quite bright.

His news editor wouldn't have picked her out from all the other hopefuls if she didn't have something.

The camera was on her now, so Julian paid attention to what she was saying. It was the standard dummy interview, the one they gave to all trainees, but the girl couldn't get the hang of it at all.

She kept making little speeches to an invisible audience, so her interview subject didn't get a look-in.

What the hell's she playing at? Julian wondered. I thought this one had worked on a programme.

When it was obvious Linda Beattie had no conception of what she was doing, Julian stepped in and stopped the proceedings.

'That will do for today,' he told her. 'Tomorrow I'll send you out on a real story.'

Then without telling her any more, he turned on his heel and went into his office.

Educating Linda wasn't going to be easy, the programme director decided. She was nervous, she was awkward and he suspected if he put her anywhere near a camera team, she'd get under everyone's feet. If he had any say in it at all, he would have sent her straight back to where she came from, but his hands were tied. The BBC were committed to taking in trainees, so, like it or not, *Manchester Today* was lumbered with this one.

He reached into a drawer and got out the schedule for the following day. There were two firm dates on it. The National Front were holding a demo in Leeds, and Eric Morecambe was getting some kind of gong from Lancaster University.

She'd better go on the Eric Morecambe assignment, he thought. It's a soft story, she won't get hurt, and if she does make a nuisance of herself, someone can always send her to sit in the camera van.

When he got into the studio the next morning, Julian discovered the Eric Morecambe story had grown in importance. The Duke of Kent was going to be at the ceremony, which lifted it to the top of the schedule, particularly as the National Front had backed off at the last moment.

Apart from a knobbly knees competition in Blackpool and a church rally in the city, Eric Morecambe was now all they had.

Julian cursed himself for involving the trainee. The team he was sending didn't need any distractions. Then he took a decision.

It was too late to pull the girl out – she'd already been fixed up with a press pass to the University – but it wasn't too late to go along himself as the director. All they needed was a reporter, a cameraman and a researcher.

Linda discovered going out on her first real story was a lonely experience. Julian, who seemed to be in charge, organized everyone on the team to sit up front in the van. Linda was parked in the back along with the cameras and the video equipment. That wouldn't have been so bad if somebody had talked to her, but she might as well have been made of wood for all the attention she got.

Everyone else there seemed to know each other and when they weren't gossiping about the other people on the programme, they were talking technicalities. There was a lot of jargon about camera angles and sound levels and after half an hour of it, Linda felt completely at sea.

119

I should ask a question, she thought, something that makes me look as if I'm involved with this story. Nothing came to mind, so she stayed silent and stared out of the window as the black industrial scenery went rolling past.

When they got within a couple of miles of the University, Julian decided they all had time to stop off for a drink. He knew a little country pub nearby, and when they got there, Linda started to feel a bit better.

They had long passed the factories and been over moorland. All around her Linda could see open fields. The pub had a garden, and Julian managed to organize a big table just for them.

Everyone seemed more friendly when they'd had a glass of wine. The cameraman asked her which programme she worked on in London, and seemed really interested when she told him it was the six o'clock news.

They gossiped a bit about the BBC and discovered they had a couple of friends in common. Then the reporter joined in, and by the time Julian came out with more drinks she began to feel part of the team.

I should look interested in this story, she thought. So she turned to the director and dredged up the only thing she could think of.

'How much film will you shoot today?' she asked. 'I know it's always more than you actually use.'

She realized she'd put her foot in it when she saw Julian's face.

'How the hell do I know what I'm going to shoot?' he demanded. 'Eric Morecambe might tell a feeble joke. Or he might assault the University Dean.' He paused. 'Next time you've got a dumb question, I suggest you put it in writing and give it to me at the end of the day. That way you won't waste any more of my time.'

He got up indicating it was time for them to get a move on. So everyone left their drinks and trailed back to the van. Linda brought up the rear feeling about two foot tall.

This was the second time she'd got on this man's nerves. When she'd done her run-through for the cameras, she could see she was bungling it just from the look on his face. And now she couldn't even ask a question without his biting her head off.

Linda was tempted to admit defeat and bow out gracefully. She was only a secretary, after all. She didn't have the background or the education for this sort of job.

Then something inside her rebelled. I haven't come all this way, she thought, I haven't suffered all the insults, all the petty injustices to go running back home the first time somebody shouts at me.

No, she thought, if my boss thinks I'm a deadhead, I'm going to have to change his mind for him.

They got to the University just before lunch. Word had gone out that the Duke of Kent would be there and a huge crowd had gathered in the forecourt of the building.

There were women in hats and children carrying Union Jacks. There were also several representatives of the national press hanging around looking extremely uncomfortable.

'What are they doing outside?' Julian asked no one in particular. 'They should be in the main hall taking photographs and talking to Eric Morecambe.'

The researcher said she'd check what was happening. Five minutes later she was back, looking worried.

'The University have decided to put a block on the media,' she told Julian. 'The Dean doesn't want the Duke embarrassed by all the reporters –'

Linda interrupted them. 'Is the Dean the tall man standing by the entrance?'

The researcher nodded impatiently. 'But there's no point in arguing with him. He won't treat us any different than the newspapers.'

Linda smiled pleasantly. Then before anyone could stop her, she was out of the van and heading towards the building.

If she could have heard what Julian had to say about what she was doing, she might have faltered. But the crowd swallowed her up and blotted out the van and all her companions.

121

She was on her own now. Whatever happened next was in the hands of the gods and her own ingenuity.

Julian looked out of the front window of the van and felt true despair. The tarty little trainee had obviously come unglued. Any minute now she was going to bring disgrace down on the programme, the BBC, and his head.

What on earth had possessed her to go over to the Dean of Lancaster University? he asked himself. She knows he's made his mind up about the press.

From his elevated position, he regarded Linda's bright blonde head next to the Dean's grey one in the main doorway. She was looking very earnest and talking fifteen to the dozen.

What on earth is she saying? he wondered. What dumb inanity is she pouring into his ear?

He didn't have to wonder for long. After ten minutes, the girl smiled, pecked the Dean on the cheek and started to make her way back to the van. Her head was up now and she was looking very pleased with herself.

Julian had his first twinge of doubt. Maybe she isn't such a fool, he thought. Perhaps she'd done something right for a change. Then he thought, impossible. She's too dumb for that.

Linda was back at the van now, and Julian leaned out.

'Do you mind telling me what the hell's going on?' he demanded. 'I didn't tell you you could go anywhere.'

The blonde smiled. 'Sorry if I was out of line,' she said, 'but I think I've made the Dean see sense. He's going to let us in.'

For a moment he thought he was hearing things.

'What on earth did you promise him?' Julian demanded.

'My body,' she told him. 'Why else do you think we're being allowed through?'

He didn't take her up on it. She was having him on, teasing him for treating her like dirt for the past couple of days. In his heart he couldn't blame her, for he'd fallen into the oldest trap of all and judged the girl on her appearance. He'd decided that because she wore a tight skirt and garish make-up, she had to be somehow less competent than anyone else.

Now Linda was teaching him a lesson. Whenever he tried to say something to her, or catch her attention, she studiously ignored him. She kept up the act all the way back to Manchester.

In the end he decided it had gone on long enough. As they were going into the editing room, he stopped her.

'We seem to have got off on the wrong foot,' he said, feeling a fool. 'Would you let me buy you lunch tomorrow, to straighten things out?'

Julian took Linda to the steak house in the centre of town. It was an expense account haunt for fat businessmen, all white tablecloths and polished crystal, and she was immediately ill at ease. It was as if the restaurant somehow belittled her.

Julian was intrigued by this trainee. She had the courage of ten men, yet she couldn't hold her head up in a steak house.

Over lunch, he asked Linda about herself. Where did her parents come from? What had she done before she joined the programme?

She hung her head and looked miserable.

'I was a secretary,' she admitted finally. 'Dad lives in Epping and drives a minicab when he's not on the dole.'

Suddenly he remembered who she was. David Berger, his news editor, who had interviewed her, had told him the whole story. She was a working-class girl with a brilliant instinct for a story. He was so excited by her ability that he broke all the rules and offered her a job.

And here she was in Manchester exhibiting that famous ability of hers, and Julian hadn't even seen her coming.

He turned to her. 'I don't give a stuff what your father does for a living,' he told her. 'What you do is what counts here. And your performance yesterday earned everybody's respect.'

The colour came back to Linda's face and she picked up her untouched glass of wine.

'Do you want to know how I pulled it off?'

'Of course I want to know. Why do you think I asked you here?'

Now she was smiling and he knew that lunch would be all right after all.

'I found something out about the University before we came,' she told him. 'I discovered they have a sports day next month that they are desperate to get on television, only nobody will touch it.' She looked nervous. 'So I'm afraid I stuck my neck out.'

Julian looked at her unbelievingly. 'You didn't offer the Dean a deal, did you?'

She nodded. 'What else could I do? Either I promised we covered their wretched sports day, or we didn't get in to see Eric Morecambe pick up his gong.'

Julian sighed. If he was doing his job properly he should have lectured her against taking events into her own hands. She had no authority to promise air time to anyone, but he had a hunch she'd make one hell of a reporter.

19

LONDON, 1988

Susan Stone sat in make-up at six o'clock in the morning and wondered just how much longer she could go on taking it. She had got out of bed two hours earlier, crept into the bathroom so as not to disturb her husband and gone about her morning routine.

Chris was awake when she finally emerged and she felt instantly guilty.

'Go back to sleep,' she whispered. 'I'm just off to the studios.'

But the man she had shared her bed with for the last twelve years wasn't listening. Instead he sat bolt upright and rubbed his eyes.

'We're having dinner with the bank tonight,' he reminded her. 'So don't get waylaid after the show. I don't want you sitting in meetings till all hours.'

Susan went over and put her arms round him, promising to be home by five at the latest. Then all at once she was overcome with the irresistible desire to climb right back into bed.

It would be so easy, she thought. I could just wriggle out of this dress. Get under the duvet and I'd be back to sleep in five minutes.

She wrenched herself away from her husband, summoning up all her discipline. I'm the star of *The Morning Show*, she told herself. There are dozens of people driving into work right now who depend on me to be there. There's no way I can let them down.

She was there on the dot of six o'clock, the way she had been every morning for the past seven years. And now she was sitting in make-up wondering what the hell she was doing there.

Half an hour later, when the paint and the powder had been applied, Susan felt slightly better. The reflection staring back from the mirror in front of her was of a dark, intelligent woman of around forty. She didn't look matronly yet, the way her two elder sisters did, though she knew it was only a matter of time. She shrugged. When that happens, she thought, the make-up girl will just have to work a little harder.

In the mirror Susan saw one of the researchers staggering through the door, weighed down by a tray full of coffee and croissants and hot buttered toast.

Now she felt much better. Make-up, then breakfast always restored her. By the time I get on the set, I'll be a new woman, she thought.

She watched as the girl set everything up on the table, meticulously, arranging the crockery like a waitress, and Susan felt a rush of warmth towards her.

Holly Fielding tried harder than most of the researchers who worked for her. She was a little disorganized and she lacked the charm she needed to get on in the business, but the girl was a trouper. Susan would rather have one of Holly than half a dozen of the usual deadbeats they inflicted on her.

'Is Steve here yet?' she asked.

Holly nodded and informed Susan that her co-presenter was outside in the gardens that surrounded the riverside studios.

'What the hell is he doing out there?' she asked. 'It's freezing cold and blowing a gale.'

The girl looked uncomfortable. 'Hasn't anyone told you?' she asked.

Susan started to get irritated. 'Hasn't anyone told me what?'

Holly got up from where she was sitting and started to

126

back away. 'You're filming outside today,' she said nervously. 'Our new hotshot director thought it would give the show a bit of atmosphere.'

The presenter sighed. This was all she needed – Bobby, the boy genius, giving the whole team a dose of pneumonia to satisfy some whim.

'I hope somebody's told him it won't work,' she said.

The researcher hesitated on her way out of the door. 'Everyone's told him,' said Holly desperately, 'but he won't listen.'

She fled before Susan could get any more information out of her.

Susan arrived on the set just before seven. Most of the cameras were set up around the long white sofa, now in the garden, on which she and Steve usually did the show. The wind, which was coming in gusts, was shaking the camera moorings and Susan worried that at any minute one of them could come crashing to the ground.

It's not my problem, she thought. I'm going to have enough trouble just coping with the show.

In her hand she had the call sheet that had been drawn up the night before. She and Steve were interviewing a socialite who had just written a novel. Then they were hosting a discussion group about a new ruling on primary school education.

After that there was a five-minute cookery spot, followed by their resident exercise lady. That will bring us up to the news headlines, Susan thought. If we survive that long in this wind, then we're home and dry.

She was going through the format with Steve when she saw the director approach. He was a tall, thin man who had come up in commercials and didn't want anyone to forget it. He still dressed as if he were in advertising, in a Ralph Lauren blazer and twill slacks, and he had the supercilious air of someone used to getting his own way.

Susan got straight to the point.

'Bobby,' she said, 'if you keep us out here much longer we're all going to die of exposure.'

The director wasn't amused. 'You're behaving like a prima

donna,' he told her. 'There's no room in television for that kind of temperament.'

The remark riled her the way it was meant to, but Susan knew better than to let it show. She gave him her most professional smile.

'I've been on this show for over seven years,' she said, 'and there's more than enough room for me.'

He looked at her for a long hard moment. 'That's what you think,' he said.

The gloom Susan had felt earlier returned in spades. Bobby wanted her off the show. She'd known it for months now. He wanted her out, so he could put in some little protégée of his own. She wouldn't let him get away with it. But the sheer effort of fighting her corner was making her tired. For the second time that day she asked herself what she was doing.

It was a tough morning's work. The wind made the technicians nervous and more than once the presenter was made to blink as a misdirected light was shone into her eyes. The weather conditions upset the guests as well, and when the first break came, Susan was more than ready to throw in the towel.

Yet she kept going. Her years of experience lent her stamina and by some miracle both she and Steve got through the show without any obvious hitches. When it was all over, they threw their arms round each other.

'We did it!' Susan said, congratulating them both. 'We survived it, wind and all.'

She didn't see the director approach until he was standing beside them.

'You didn't do it,' said Bobby. 'You both looked terrible on the monitor.'

Susan started to get angry. 'You didn't give us a chance,' she told him. 'What the hell did you expect?'

She knew she shouldn't have risen to the bait. Arguing with Bobby was the surest way to disaster, but it had been a terrible morning, the worst she could remember, and she was at her wits' end.

The director flicked an invisible piece of lint from his lapel. 'I'll tell you what I expected,' he said tightly. 'I expected the kind of polish that Susan Stone is well known for. That was a tacky performance and if you start to moan about the wind one more time, I'll recommend you take a refresher course in on-screen technique.'

It was at that moment Susan realized she had had enough. The early start, the wind and Bobby's rudeness had finally worn her down.

She struggled off the white sofa and stood to look Bobby straight in the eye.

'You can stuff your refresher course,' she said. 'And while you're about it, you can stuff your job as well.'

Then she turned on her heel and walked off the set.

Like everyone else on *The Morning Show*, Holly wondered who was going to take over from Susan. While they were waiting for her replacement, one of the presenters of the six o'clock news stood in for her.

No one took her seriously. No matter how efficiently she did the job, the presenter hadn't been chosen by Bobby, so she wasn't going to last.

In the weeks following Susan's departure, Holly kept her ear to the ground. She hung around the wine bars and the BBC Club in Broadcasting House listening to gossip. Susan Stone's departure had made the national press, and because *The Morning Show* was suddenly headline news, nobody could stop talking about it.

Holly heard several versions of the now famous falling out between Susan and director. In one the presenter was supposed to have struck Bobby round the face, calling him a bastard and other unmentionable names. It was a popular story amongst the broadcasters, who loved a bit of drama. The girl refused to believe it.

Even though Susan was history, Holly had a loyalty to her. She had been making the presenter's breakfast for nearly a year, ever since she had left school, and Holly couldn't pretend that Susan was dead meat just because she had left the corporation. The woman had talent. She'd seen that with her own eyes.

She'll surface again, somewhere else, the girl consoled herself. One day she'll pop up as the anchorwoman on one of the top ITV shows and everyone will eat their words.

After a while, Holly started to hear a different piece of gossip. The powers that be were instituting a search for a new girl. Several names were bandied about the BBC Club. Anne Diamond was being considered, as were Anna Ford and Patti Caldwell.

Holly realized the BBC was near a decision when the shortlist appeared in the *Daily Express*.

Everyone on the programme kept a close eye on Bobby, but the director wasn't giving anything away. They'd decided on someone, he was prepared to admit that much, only he wasn't saying who.

He managed to keep it quiet for twenty-four hours. Then some secretary in the Director General's office told her closest friend on the lunchtime news who the new presenter was going to be.

When Holly heard the name in a pub behind Portland Place, she was totally confused. The girl they were bringing into *The Morning Show* was an unknown from Manchester. She was called Linda Beattie and she had been on some current affairs programme for the past few years.

Nobody knew any more about her, except she'd once worked at the BBC in London, as a secretary on the six o'clock news.

That piece of information somehow made Linda Beattie more human. She wasn't some career bitch with a fancy degree and a string of credits to her name, she was an ordinary girl who'd started the hard way. Some of Holly's anguish over losing Susan Stone started to evaporate.

Linda might just be all right, she thought.

Holly hadn't wanted to go into television, not in the beginning. Her big ambition had been to study Classics at Oxford and run with the intellectual crowd.

Then she got her A level results and she realized her ambitions were in need of a rethink. She'd scraped a pass in

English and another in History and that was all. She could probably get into a minor college, but Oxford wouldn't touch her.

For a whole week Holly mourned her lost dreams. Then she went to see her headmistress and told her she wasn't interested in a university place after all.

After that she decided to consult Jason, but as always he was travelling round the country looking at new productions, and she had to wait a week until there was a free evening in his diary when he was in London. She grabbed the slot, instructing his secretary to pencil in her name. Then she relaxed and rehearsed what she was going to say to him.

She definitely wanted a career. She had a good brain and she wanted to be somebody in her own right, instead of just somebody's daughter. Most of all, she didn't want to settle for marriage and the suburbs.

She wondered how her father would take her last reason. He was forever dragging her off to parties and introducing her to the sons of his friends. Occasionally he would ask her if she was seeing anyone serious. And when she told him no, he would look crestfallen.

It was ludicrous, of course, but she didn't fight him. She simply bided her time until she'd made up her mind what she was going to do with her life. Then she pounced.

'Daddy,' she told him, when they finally got together, 'I want to talk about my future.'

Jason looked vague and took a sip of the whisky he was nursing.

'What do you mean?' he asked.

'Well, I can't sit around the house the rest of my life. I want to do something.'

'Like what?'

'Like a job,' she said, 'what else?'

He put down his whisky and looked thoughtful. 'I suppose you want me to pull a few strings?'

The way he said it made her feel like a spoiled brat, and for a moment she almost dropped the idea.

'Look,' she told him, 'you don't have to stick your neck

out. There's a careers mistress at school. She's bound to come up with something.'

Jason regarded his daughter. He could just see what the expensive school he'd sent her to would suggest. She'd be teaching at the Montessori, or cooking executive lunches. In a year or two she'd be speaking with a plummy accent and wearing an Alice band in her hair. The idea appalled him.

'I know I don't have to find you a job,' he told Holly, 'but I'd like to. Anyway, I think I know just the thing.'

The girl was all ears. 'Is it in show business?'

'Sort of. It's with the BBC. A chum of mine who's on the Board of Directors tells me they're short of researchers. You'd have to start off making the tea and running errands, but once you've got your feet under the table, I'm told it gets more interesting.'

Holly went for it. And three weeks and several interviews later, she found herself on *The Morning Show*.

Jason had been right about her having to run around. As well as making breakfast for Susan Stone, she found she was at everybody's beck and call. If a producer wanted coffee or the morning papers in a hurry, Holly was the one who went to get them.

When a celebrity came into the studio, Holly brought them to hospitality and poured the drinks. It was her job to relax the stars and tell them the sort of things the presenters would be asking.

It was fun at the start. Holly loved the buzz of the television studios, and she worshipped Susan Stone, for whom she worked her socks off.

Then Susan walked out and imperceptibly Holly started to get bored. There was no one to try for any more, her job began to seem pointless. What was she doing anyhow but working as a lackey?

She told her father as much one night, and he reminded her that she had to serve her apprenticeship before she got to do her own projects.

Although Holly knew he was talking sense, Jason's words

132

made no impression on her. In her entire life, she had never had to stick at anything, for she knew she could have whatever she wanted just by asking. So instead of doing the best she could, Holly started to walk through her job. She sometimes turned up late in the mornings, occasionally she mislaid things, and once or twice she completely forgot to do what she was asked.

They were all petty crimes and she got away with them because everyone was too busy to pull her up.

This is money for old rope, Holly thought. Yet she wondered how long things could go on this way.

20

Linda didn't sleep a wink the night before her first appearance on *The Morning Show*. She lay tossing and turning on the hard hotel bed the BBC had provided for her and wondered how she'd ever survive the experience.

I'm not equipped to handle this, she kept telling herself. I'm not even ready for it. Why on earth did they choose me?

She had been in this state ever since David Berger had told her the news of her appointment. It had been a week ago and she was still reeling from the shock.

When her name was put up by her programme chiefs, Linda had been amused. It's their way of patting me on the head and telling me I'm doing a good job, she thought.

She stayed amused until the news came that she had made the final shortlist. Then the smile left her face. What if I get it? she wondered. What if some bigwig in Broadcasting House has an error of judgement and I'm suddenly lumbered with *The Morning Show*?

The idea was too ludicrous to entertain. She was up against serious competition. Whoever was in charge was bound to go for a big name like Anne Diamond. Linda started to relax. There's no way it can be me, she thought.

But she was wrong. According to Julian, the director of current affairs had taken an interest in her career in the last couple of years. She had covered half a dozen stories that had made the network news. They had been important stories and back at head office her name had been noted and the powers that be had kept an eye on her.

When she heard this, Linda was pleased, but the final decision still didn't make sense.

'Why didn't they choose a big name?' she asked.

The director shrugged, and admitted he had no answer for her, so ever since she had been torturing herself with the question.

'Somebody somewhere has made a terrible mistake,' Linda thought, churning up the bedclothes in her antiseptic London hotel room. She felt her stomach give a disturbing lurch. 'In just a few hours they're going to find out just what it is they've done.'

She must have dozed off, for she was jangled into consciousness by the alarm clock. It was four thirty. Time to get up and face the music.

She called room service for a pot of coffee and forced it back while she was having her bath. Then she threw her clothes on, pulled a brush through her hair and made for the door. If she hurried, she'd be at the studio before six.

As she made her way into the grey London morning, Linda noticed the butterflies in her stomach had stopped dancing the tango. She felt the beginnings of relief. The fear that had been roaring through her was losing its grip. She was still nervous, but she wasn't hysterical any more.

Maybe there's hope for me, she thought. But she wasn't counting on it.

When she arrived, she went directly through to make-up as she had been instructed. She was early and nobody else was there yet so she made the girl rush her through. She needed to get straight out on the set and familiarize herself with its dimensions, and by six forty she was sitting discussing the schedule with the producer. She had been in the afternoon before, so there were no surprises. Her confidence started to return.

'Is there any chance of breakfast?' Linda asked.

The producer looked surprised. 'Didn't Holly bring it when you were being made up?'

Linda shook her head. 'Nobody came in when I was there, though they might have missed me; I was a bit early.'

135

Her companion grabbed hold of a messenger as he crossed the floor.

'Go and find Holly, will you?' he asked. 'And tell her our new presenter is starving hungry.'

Ten minutes later a bad-tempered-looking girl with a shock of dark hair appeared with a tray. She put it down on the coffee table in front of Linda and asked if there was anything extra she wanted.

'This is just fine,' Linda said. She extended her hand. 'I'm Linda Beattie, the new presenter.'

The girl took her hand. 'Holly Fielding, official breakfast maker and general dogsbody.'

'Good,' said Linda crisply. 'Then maybe when you draw up your next rota, you'll put my name on it. It's tough going to work on an empty stomach.'

Up in the gallery above the studio, a whole host of people were watching Linda. None of them looked at her directly. Instead, three men and one woman studied her image on the monitor screens, which took up the entire wall in front of them.

The lighting man was the first to zero in on Linda, twiddling the knobs on his console until he got the balance he was looking for. It wasn't a difficult task. The new girl had a face that was made for the small screen.

It's her features, he thought. The eyes are nice and wide apart and exactly the right shade of smoky grey. That tiny little nose doesn't do her any harm either. He took in the whole blonde picture of her and smiled to himself. I know why she got the job, he thought. They wanted a looker to wake up the audience in the morning.

The sound man hardly noticed Linda's face. If she had looked wrong, he would have registered it immediately, but this girl had the same wholesome blandness of every presenter he had ever seen.

He adjusted his instruments and listened to her voice. It had a good pitch. That was the first thing he noticed. There were no jarring notes he had to compensate for.

As she introduced her first guest, he concentrated on her accent. He knew Linda had been in Manchester for years, so he expected a northern accent, but the new girl sounded as if she had been born and bred in London — the East End, or was it Docklands? She wasn't a broad cockney by any means.

He listened harder in an attempt to identify where she came from. Slightly common, very confident, her voice was the kind he had heard in labour politicians and something in him responded to it.

She's good, he thought. The man in the street will identify with her.

He glanced across to the duty editor to see what effect Linda was having on her. Brenda Sykes was notoriously difficult to satisfy. As a rule she hated most of the women who worked with her because she believed they pandered to the male egos in the studio.

'What do you think of the new girl?' he muttered. 'Do you think she'll pass muster?'

Brenda frowned. 'She looks like a Hollywood floozie,' she said, 'but at least she's making some kind of sense. Some of the questions she's asking are quite intelligent.'

She didn't pass any more opinions because she didn't want to ruin Bobby's concentration. He was holding the programme together now, barking instructions to the camera team and occasionally talking to Linda and Steve through the microphones they wore in their ears.

They were onto their second spot now, cross-questioning a city tycoon about his dealings in a recent insurance scandal. The man was reluctant to talk. Whatever either presenter said to him, he parried, and the duty editor was reminded of an agile trout doing its best to wriggle off the hook.

For a second, Bobby took his eyes off the monitor screens and consulted his notes. Then he spoke into the microphone Linda wore in her ear.

'Your guest served a three-month jail term for tax evasion back in the sixties,' he told her. 'Raise it as soon as you can. It will knock him off balance.'

Linda did as she was told and the money man started

getting rough. Before he went on he had insisted they stay away from sensitive areas and he felt Linda had violated the agreement.

The team in the gallery held their breath. If Linda gave in and apologized, the spot would count for nothing. But what else could she do?

Bobby didn't wait to find out. There was a piece of film he was holding in reserve in case things went wrong and he started to give the signal to wind up the interview. Then just for a second he hesitated. The new girl was saying something that seemed to stop the money man in his tracks.

'It's all a matter of public record,' Bobby heard her tell him. 'You can't just pretend it didn't happen.'

If Susan Stone had hit him with that one, she would have made little impact, but Linda had a different kind of quality. There was something challenging and aggressive about her. She demanded an answer, almost as if it was her right. And she got one.

The man sitting beside her on the white sofa started to explain himself. He talked about his past, something his PR man insisted he never do. Then he touched on his present financial difficulties.

Bobby forgot the film he was about to put on. What was happening in the studio was bound to make the later editions of the *Evening Standard*. It could even run over to the morning papers.

The director looked at his new girl with a certain possessiveness. He'd pushed her into this and it hadn't fazed her. She'd delivered the goods. With the right handling, he thought, she could have a future.

21

As the weeks progressed, more and more time was devoted to Linda and her interviews. There seemed to be a special chemistry between Bobby and the new girl, a chemistry based on danger.

Bobby knew Linda liked to be challenged, to fight her way out of difficult situations, so at the last minute he would make a sudden change to the running order. Instead of the guest they were expecting to see, Linda and Steve would be faced with the last interview of the day. Occasionally Bobby would put someone on neither of them was expecting. When that happened, Linda's eyes would sparkle and a smile would come to her face.

Her co-presenter took it differently. Steve thought what Bobby was doing was putting a strain on both him and the show. It was unnecessary and self-indulgent. He complained to everyone who would listen, but it made no difference.

The Bobby/Linda combination was starting to have an effect on the ratings. There was a feeling something exciting was happening on *The Morning Show*, and the viewers started to switch over to it.

Linda's face was becoming known. All of a sudden she was being compared to Anne Diamond and Anna Ford.

Holly watched the new presenter's success and wondered what her secret was. Linda had been a dogsbody once herself, fetching and carrying for all and sundry, but she'd managed to dig herself out of that hole.

Holly wondered how she'd done it. Then she remembered

a bit of gossip she'd overheard in the BBC Club. Linda had had an affair with one of her bosses. She'd given him a leg over and he'd given her a leg up.

The joke had made Holly laugh at the time but it also made her feel better about herself. How could she be expected to make her way up the broadcasting ladder, she reasoned, if she wasn't sleeping with the right man? Not that she was about to make herself cheap in order to get a more interesting job. No, Holly thought, I'll just go on the way I'm going. Something is bound to break sooner or later.

Something did break, but it wasn't what she expected.

It happened on one of her disorganized days. She'd got in late that morning and she was in such a rush that when one of the guests asked for a copy of his questions, Holly clean forgot to get it. The result was the eminent surgeon who was Linda's second interview refused to go on the show. The whole slot had to be scrapped and a rather boring film about otters was put in its place.

Bobby was furious, of course, but he wasn't as cross as Linda, who wanted to know precisely the reason the surgeon had walked out.

The duty editor, Brenda Sykes, took her to one side and tried to calm her down.

'One of the researchers fouled up,' she told her. 'It's a glitch. Forget it.'

But Linda refused to forget it. She demanded to know which researcher nearly wrecked the show.

'Does it matter who it was?' Brenda asked. 'The damage is done now. We have to put it behind us.'

Linda looked stubborn. 'Whoever it was could make the same mistake again. Surely we can't risk that?'

'I know her,' Brenda said. 'That kind of behaviour is out of character.'

For a moment neither woman said anything. Finally Linda said, 'I've got a fair idea who it might be.'

The editor was intrigued. 'Tell me about it.'

'It's Holly Fielding,' said Linda without preamble. 'She's been a pain in the arse ever since I got here. She never makes me a cup of coffee unless I go to her on bended knee, and if I ask her to find out something for me, she drags her heels. I've tried complaining about her once or twice, but I always get the same answer: "Holly's a good girl," or "Holly's a hard worker. You must have rubbed her up the wrong way." So when you told me just now that the researcher who messed up my interview didn't normally do that sort of thing, I knew it had to be Holly. I'm right, aren't I?'

Brenda got worried all over again. 'You're not going to do anything about her, are you?'

'I might,' Linda said.

'Don't even think about it. Holly – or rather Holly's father – has friends at court. It's rumoured he's close to the Controller. So if you upset her, you might just be looking for another job.'

Linda didn't appear the least bit worried. 'If I lost sleep every time I thought I was going to lose my job, I'd have bags under my eyes. Holly has to be dealt with, and if nobody else on the programme's prepared to tackle her, then I have to do the job.'

The older woman frowned. 'Promise me you'll be careful,' she said.

Holly knew something was up when Linda asked her to have lunch after the programme. People like Linda didn't fraternize with the likes of her. They went off with an important contact, on whom they lavished their expense accounts. Or they dropped into the Groucho with one of the big shots on the programme.

But lunching with a researcher was totally out of character, so she knew Linda had a bone to pick. She wondered which of her many crimes the presenter would zero in on. Would she go on about the fact she forgot to make breakfast twice last week, or would she take her up on something else? Ever since she had messed up Linda's interview with the surgeon Holly had been waiting for retribution.

She thought the duty editor would tick her off, but when Brenda didn't, Holly became worried. Other researchers had been fired for less, but Brenda and the team seemed to pussy-foot around her as if they had some secret they didn't want to share.

I know what it is, Holly thought. They want to get rid of me, but because of the unions they need a stronger reason than one botched slot. So Linda's got into the act. She's probably working on some plan to frighten me out of my job, some scheme that she perfected in the North.

All the way to Fortnum's Soda Fountain, where she was meeting Linda, Holly tried to visualize what lay in store for her. In one scenario, the presenter was polite and cool all the way through lunch, dropping her bombshell over coffee. In another, Linda yelled at her for all the things she had done wrong. And in a third, she didn't show up at all. When Holly got to the restaurant there was a polite note waiting for her, telling her she was being sacked.

When Holly finally walked through the glass door into the store, she was in a state of panic. The Soda Fountain was full of shoppers that day — fat housewives up from the suburbs jostled with American tourists — and Holly had to wait at the back of a long queue before she was shown to the table Linda had reserved.

Why did she pick here? Holly wondered. It's hardly a glamorous media haunt. Before Holly could ask herself any more questions, she caught sight of Linda. She had got them a table right at the back of the room, and she was sitting over a pot of coffee looking perfectly content. She could have been a young mother taking her toddlers out for a banana split.

Despite herself, Holly started to calm down a little. If the presenter was out to get her, surely she wouldn't have chosen somewhere so cosy?

Holly fought her way through the crowd, grabbing hold of the chair Linda pushed out for her.

'Sorry I'm late,' she said, 'the traffic was horrible.'

'The traffic was pretty much the same when I arrived, but it didn't stop me getting here on time.'

Holly's heart sank. So I'm going to get a hard time after all, she thought.

She sat down and asked if she could have a glass of wine. Linda signalled one of the elderly waitresses that seemed to have been serving here for ever.

'I'm not drinking,' she said, 'but could you manage a half-carafe?'

Holly nodded, feeling wrong-footed. You didn't drink in the Soda Fountain, you had a milkshake or a hot drink, but it was too late to change her mind.

When the wine arrived, Holly gulped back half a glass, then turned to Linda.

'You asked me to meet you for a reason,' she said.

'I wanted to talk to you about the job you're doing. Or rather not doing.'

Holly put her wine down, managing to spill what was left of it all over the white cloth.

'If you're going to fire me, why don't you just get on and do it? I didn't come to be cross-examined. I'm not back in school.'

For a moment Linda didn't say anything. Then she leaned forward across the table. 'If I was going to fire you,' she said, 'I would have got Bobby to handle it in the office. The reason we're having lunch is to salvage things.'

'Do you think it's possible?'

'Once I know what's going on, anything's possible.'

Linda sat back in her chair and regarded the girl. Holly was looking particularly dishevelled today. Her thick black hair was standing on end and she was wearing a pair of blue jeans with holes ripped in the knees. Holly was the height of punk fashion and Linda wondered if she was trying to make some kind of statement. She took her time forming the next question.

Finally she said: 'Would you be very cross if I said I'd been doing some digging into your background?'

Holly looked surprised. 'Why would you want to do that?'

'Because of the way people in the studio talk about you. When I sounded off about the cock-up you made with the surgeon who walked out, everybody told me to leave it alone.

Apparently your father is a power in the land. He could make waves.'

The girl was astounded. 'Is that why I get away with murder?'

'You bet it is. None of the other researchers botches things up on a regular basis, or haven't you noticed?'

Holly felt very small. 'So what have you decided to do about it?'

For the first time since Holly came in, Linda smiled. 'I'm not going to bawl you out, if that's what you're worried about, but I am going to find out why you're behaving like such a brat. I can't believe you're hiding behind your father the whole time.'

'I'm not,' Holly whispered. 'If he knew what was going on, he'd probably make me hand in my notice.'

'So why are you making such a hash of things?'

'Because there's no point,' Holly said, sounding hopeless. 'I've spent over a year running other people's errands and I don't seem to be getting any further. When there's a really interesting story to work on, one of the other researchers gets it.'

'Have you ever wondered why?'

The girl made a face. 'Maybe I'm not sleeping with the right producer.'

She expected Linda to get defensive. Instead the blonde threw back her head and roared with laughter.

'If it was as easy as that, I wouldn't have a night to myself – none of us would – but it doesn't work that way. The reason any of us get ahead in this game is because we have something out of the ordinary to offer. The researchers who get the interesting jobs usually come up with the ideas for those jobs in the first place.'

'You're talking about seniors,' said Holly. 'It's easy for the guys with fancy degrees to get listened to, but who wants to know about me?'

'Why not try coming up with something? Then you might find out.'

'You mean put my head on the line in morning conference?'

'Sure. You're not frightened of getting it bitten off, are you?'

Holly considered the idea. When she had started out in the job, she read all the morning papers religiously. She was positively bursting with suggestions for stories, but the other more aggressive members of the team pushed in ahead of her. So when it came to her turn everything worth doing had already been discussed. In the end she stopped searching through the papers. She virtually stopped doing her job altogether.

'If I have another go,' she said slowly, 'will you stop the others from shouting me down?'

Linda poured some more wine into Holly's glass and took a sip of it herself.

'I can't do that,' she told her. 'I'm not your nanny. You've got to jump in and fight for yourself.'

Holly regarded Linda across the table. Her shiny blonde hair was groomed to within an inch of its life, her make-up was flawless and if she had to present a programme right this minute, she could do so without blinking an eyelash.

It's all very well for you to tell me to fight for myself, Holly thought. You've been doing it all your life. And winning. It's not so easy for me.

'Do you ever get scared?' she asked Linda. 'Do things ever get on top of you?'

'Of course I get scared,' Linda replied, surprised. 'But I don't let it stop me doing my job.'

Holly sighed. She liked Linda, and she was starting to look up to her, but as long as she lived, she would never ever understand her.

22

Jason had been waiting for Holly to come out of the studio for ever. And he started to get edgy. What on earth could be keeping her? he wondered. She knows we have to leave London by five thirty if we're to stand any chance of making the party on time. And we have to be on time. Clement Dane simply wouldn't understand if we turned up in Bath after the line-up was over. He'd think we'd done it on purpose, to spite him.

That was all Jason needed – his oldest friend and premier client turning on him because he didn't make his birthday party. Clement would probably bitch about it all evening to his theatrical cronies. So when he and Holly finally did put in an appearance, they would be as welcome as slugs in a cabbage patch.

I should have known better than to rely on Holly, he berated himself. There are plenty of other girls I could have asked, even though Clem is her honorary uncle. Jason thought about the fashion model he'd been seeing on and off for the past few months; the PR girl he'd had an affair with a year ago and still kept in touch with; the stunning actress he'd met at a dinner party only last week . . .

Any one of them would have been only too glad to accompany him to one of the biggest theatrical gatherings of the season. They would chat up all the famous faces, bask in his reflected glory, and generally make the most of the situation.

And he'd feel used and embarrassed and wish heartily he

hadn't gone at all. No, Jason thought, at least my brat of a daughter won't badger anyone I know for a job.

Nervously he glanced at his watch. It was at least half an hour since he had arrived in this airless reception hall. The foam-filled sofa was giving his back all kinds of hell, and if Holly didn't turn up soon, then he would just have to go looking for her.

Jason was just about to start badgering the receptionist when he saw the solution to his problems. Linda Beattie had just pushed her way through the glass doors. She was looking very fetching in a dark tailored suit and high suede boots, but all this was lost on Jason. The only thing he registered was that Linda was the presenter on Holly's programme. She must know where his daughter was.

He got to his feet and went up to her. 'I need to get hold of Holly Fielding,' he told her. 'Can you tell me where to find her?'

The blonde looked at him curiously. 'You wouldn't be her father, by any chance? Holly was expecting you to pick her up after work.'

Jason smiled and held out his hand. 'Jason Fielding,' he said. 'Forgive me for not introducing myself. You must be Linda Beattie.'

She did everything she could not to stand to attention. So this was the influential man in Holly's background, the personal friend of the Controller.

She looked at him more closely, seeing a tall greying man somewhere in his forties. He had once been very handsome and you could still see traces of it when he smiled. But it wasn't his looks that fascinated her, it was the man's presence.

Everything about him, from the cut of his suit to the way he held his shoulders, indicated that he had seen it all and done it all and nothing much impressed him any more. This man would be at ease in a North African souk or a gentleman's club. Linda liked that – enough to get involved in his search for the tiresome Holly.

'I've got a hunch your daughter's involved with some

147

problem back in the studio. If you'd like to come through, I'll see what I can do to find her.'

Jason had been on enough sets in his time not to want to bother. He always managed to trip over a cable, or wreck a carefully placed piece of scenery.

Then he thought, if I don't get Holly out of here in the next five minutes, I'm going to run straight into a Westbound traffic jam. So he smiled as pleasantly as he could and took Linda up on her offer.

He couldn't see his daughter anywhere on the floor, so Linda offered to go up to the gallery and look for her there. Five minutes later she came back empty-handed.

'I'll look in the editing suites,' she offered. 'She's bound to be hunched over a piece of film somewhere.'

Jason was near to losing his temper. 'Why would she be doing that? She promised me she'd be ready to leave the minute I got here.'

The blonde grinned. 'Working women,' she said, 'are a law unto themselves.'

The agent felt depressed. Holly certainly was a law unto herself. Ever since her mother left, the girl had become a wild child. She was probably doing this on purpose, he thought. She knew he was anxious about Clement's party so she'd bunked off somewhere just to tease him. Any minute now, she'd turn up looking as if butter wouldn't melt in her mouth, knowing full well he wouldn't have the heart to bawl her out.

But Holly didn't turn up. Instead, Linda Beattie came back looking worried.

'Your daughter seems to have disappeared into thin air,' she told Jason. 'I've looked everywhere and there's no sign of her.'

She saw the desperation in Jason's face and realized she'd landed herself in the middle of a family crisis. If she'd been smart, she'd have walked away as fast as she could, but there was something about this man that intrigued her, and she decided to stay.

'There's one last place where she could be,' she said. 'I

148

could kick myself for not thinking of it before. Holly's probably in the ladies' room, getting changed out of her work clothes.'

He looked relieved. 'That sounds like my daughter,' he said. 'Would you awfully mind going along and telling her to get a move on?'

Linda smiled. 'No problem,' she said.

Linda saw Holly as soon as she opened the door of the washroom. She was sitting in front of the chipped mirror that ran the length of the room, but she wasn't changing, nor was she checking her make-up.

She was doubled up on the wooden stool, her hands clutching her knees. Her face was a kind of grey colour and Linda knew without having to ask that she was in a lot of pain.

She went over and gently brushed the hair out of Holly's eyes.

'What is it?' she asked. 'What's wrong?'

Holly let out a little cry. 'It's my stomach,' she said, 'it's killing me.'

'Have you been sick?'

The girl managed a weak grin. 'Only all the time. But it doesn't seem to make it any better.'

'Can you move?'

Once more she gasped. 'No, it hurts too much.'

Linda thought hard. The girl had probably eaten something bad, and now she was paying for it. But what if it wasn't just food poisoning? What if there was something seriously wrong with her?

She took another look at Holly and decided to act on her instincts.

'Stay right where you are,' she instructed. 'I'm going to call an ambulance.'

She sprinted out of the washroom at top speed, hurrying down the corridor until she found a phone in one of the empty offices. Then she dialled 999 and explained what the problem was.

The ambulance crew arrived within fifteen minutes, whisking Holly away to a hospital in Putney. It was one of the big teaching hospitals with a rabbit warren of different departments on every floor. If Linda hadn't insisted on coming along with him, Jason would never have found his way to the ward where Holly had been taken.

As it was, the presenter gave the staff of the Putney General such a hassle that they almost led them by the hand to the right place.

Linda's instinct had been right. Holly had a burst appendix. If Linda hadn't got her to hospital as fast as she did, the girl might not have survived.

The duty surgeon made this plain to Jason when he finally got out of the operating theatre.

'Your daughter's going to be fine,' he said, 'but she's been through a bad time, so I wouldn't do any visiting until tomorrow at the earliest.'

Jason sat down heavily on the hard hospital bench and put his head in his hands.

'Holly could have died,' he said over and over again. 'What would I have done if she died?'

There was such an air of desolation about the man that Linda started to feel worried. He seemed to be taking this crisis entirely on himself, as if he was in some way responsible for it.

This is silly, Linda thought. Jason's not her only parent. She sat down beside him, putting a tentative hand on his shoulder.

'If you give me the number,' she said, 'I'll call your wife. She needs to know what's going on.'

His head came up then, and she knew just from looking at him she'd put her foot in it.

'I doubt if she'd care all that much,' he said harshly. 'She walked out on us several years ago.'

Now the whole thing started to make sense. And Linda wondered why she hadn't seen the truth before. No father she'd met was as anxious as Jason had been when his daughter went missing for ten minutes. And no father would be so utterly stricken over an illness from which his daughter would quickly recover. This man had brought Holly up on his own for the last few years. And the strain was clearly getting to him.

'Is there anything I can do?' she asked.

'You might stick around until I pull myself together,' Jason said. 'Unless there's somewhere else you have to be.'

Linda shook her head. 'You've got me at a good time. I was going home anyway.'

'Then you could probably use a drink.'

She smiled. 'We could both use a drink.'

He took her to the Chelsea Arts Club, a few hundred yards from the King's Road. It was a ramshackle place made out of several old houses knocked together. The entrance hall was like walking into somebody's front parlour, and the whole layout, with its crowded bar, its billiard room and its tatty, down-at-heel dining room, reminded Linda of the kind of place English gentlemen retreated to when they wanted to get away from their wives.

Jason bypassed the bar, which seemed to be full of drunken bohemians, and led her to one of the tables grouped in front of a fire.

Then he went and grabbed a bottle of wine and two glasses and for the first time that evening Linda started to let go.

For a while they talked about the worlds they each inhabited. Now he was away from his daughter, her companion seemed to expand, and Linda started to find out who he was.

She found him surprisingly sophisticated. All the men she had known in television were simpler than Jason. They were educated and hard-working, but none of them had ever come face to face with the real workings of the world. Now, as they talked about the theatre and the people who inhabited it, Linda felt him getting her attention.

She could have listened all evening to Jason's stories about the business. He was an amusing raconteur and she guessed he was in the habit of entertaining women.

But she wanted more than to be entertained. Ever since she saw him break down at the hospital, Linda had been curious about this man. She wanted to know what had happened to his marriage and why his wife had left him to bring Holly up on his own. Most of all, she wanted to know how he'd managed.

Linda started to probe Jason about his life. Her experience as a reporter taught her to be subtle, but as soon as she broached the subject of his marriage, he was on to her.

'I don't normally discuss my private life,' he said.

It was a rebuff and most girls would have backed off. Linda wasn't so easily deterred.

'Maybe you should open up a bit more,' she told him, calmly refilling both their glasses. 'You might find it helps you to cope.'

Jason looked irritated. 'What exactly do you think I have to cope with?'

Now she knew she was on dangerous ground, but Linda couldn't stop herself. She wanted to get through to this man. She needed him to know she wasn't just another pretty face to be flattered and patronized. She took a deep breath.

'I think you have to cope with a daughter who has more problems then you know about. I think half the time it gets you so confused, you don't know where to turn.' She paused. 'I also think you need help.'

Suddenly, unexpectedly, he started to laugh. 'Has anybody told you you're very pushy, or are all your friends too scared of you for that?'

She straightened up in her seat. 'I'm not pushy,' she protested. 'I'm concerned. There's a difference.'

Jason looked at the open-faced blonde sitting beside him. Linda wasn't his type at all. There was something bright and well informed about her that made him nervous. A girl like that wouldn't let you get away with anything.

He took a deep pull on his drink. I'm resisting her, he thought. I've been resisting her ever since she picked me up at the TV studios. The notion surprised him, women didn't usually get him this defensive.

'Why are you so interested in helping me?' he asked. 'Don't you have enough problems of your own?'

152

How it was her turn to laugh.

'I'm soft,' she said, 'or haven't you noticed?'

To his surprise he realized she meant it. She didn't seem at all interested in using him to further her career. She'd hardly mentioned her job. All Linda seemed to want to do was listen to him. And tonight, he decided, she was welcome.

He had kept it all in for too long now. His women friends didn't want to know about his domestic life and the couples he knew had troubles of their own. In a way Linda was ideal and the fact that she was a complete stranger only added to her charm. He could say what he wanted without the slightest risk of being judged. Then he would walk away and go on with his life without the embarrassment of having to run into her again.

He started to talk about his marriage to Eve. It had been perfect, he told her, until Holly started to grow up and make demands.

'Eve couldn't cope with that,' he told her. 'Her career in the theatre was taking off and she simply didn't have the time to take Holly to the doctor when she had whooping cough. So I was the one who had to step into the breach.'

'Did you mind that?'

Jason smiled, remembering. 'Not really. I love my daughter, though I didn't love some of her problems.'

'Which problems are we talking about?'

'You name it. She was lonely and needy, and because she couldn't run to Eve, she came to me for everything. Often I'd stay up half the night listening to her and calming her worries. It nearly drove me insane, but I couldn't ignore her.'

The presenter remembered how demanding Holly could be, expecting her to fight her battles with the other researchers.

'You shouldn't give in all the time,' she observed, 'or she'll end up a spoiled brat.'

Suddenly Jason caught sight of the clock above the bar. He'd been bending this woman's ear for the best part of two hours. She was probably starving hungry by now.

He asked her if she'd like to have dinner. And she smiled

and said she couldn't think of anything she'd enjoy better.

For a moment Jason felt a twinge of conscience. He was wining and dining Linda as if they were on a date, building up her hopes that there might be more to come. Yet at the end of the evening he had made up his mind he would wave her goodbye and never see her again.

He wondered if she'd understand.

23

Jason dropped Linda home around midnight, but he didn't make any move to come in. She liked him for that.

It was obvious he found her attractive, but he wasn't going to jump on her. She gave him her best smile and thanked him for a memorable evening.

Then, as she swung her way out of the front seat of his Daimler, she looked over her shoulder.

'Call me,' she said, all innocence and invitation. 'I'm in the book.'

The next day Linda didn't hear from him. She checked her messages several times, but her secretary always came back with the same answer: 'Sorry. There's been no Mr Fielding for you.'

Linda wondered if she'd been too flippant. Maybe she should have written the number down and pressed it in his hand. Then she thought, I don't have to crawl. If a man wants me, he comes after me.

Two more days passed with no word from Jason. It was excruciating. Linda would sit by the phone willing it to ring, and when it did, it was always someone she didn't want to speak to. An advertising man she thought she liked invited her to go to the races on Saturday; she was asked to Sunday brunch by Bobby, who cooked up a storm at weekends; a girlfriend wanted her to go shopping. She said no to all of them.

Somewhere in the back of her mind, she was still convinced she would hear from Jason, so she kept her weekend free.

By Friday she knew she had been waiting in vain. The man wasn't going to call – now or ever. He had other things to do.

She realized she had been behaving like a fool. He's an agent, she thought, a big noise in the theatre. I bet every ambitious actress in town is trying to get her hooks in him. He probably has a list of them in his little black book. One for every night. She picked up the phone and dialled the advertising man's number. Who knew, he might still want to take her racing.

On Monday Linda's secretary came in and told her Mr Fielding had called and left a message. Relief flooded over her.

'Did he leave a number?' she asked. 'I'll call him back.'

The girl looked confused. 'You don't have to,' she said. 'The message was about Holly. She's going to be in hospital for another two weeks so Mr Fielding said not to expect her in till the end of the month.'

'Did he say anything else?' Linda enquired. 'Or was that it?'

'That was it.'

Linda was tempted to put the whole business out of her mind. Then she thought about Holly. If she had to stay nearly three weeks in hospital, then she must have been pretty ill. She remembered the girl's ashen face when she found her in the ladies' room.

Poor little thing, Linda thought. I bet she's feeling really sorry for herself.

She decided to call the hospital to find out if she needed anything, but when she got through to the ward sister, she was sorry she'd bothered.

'I can't get Holly to a phone,' the nurse said. 'We're all too busy at the moment.'

Linda curbed her temper and asked how the girl was. This time the sister was even ruder.

'She's fine,' she said, 'and she'd be even better if people like you left her alone.'

'I'm sorry,' said Linda, 'but I don't know what you're on about. I work with Holly. This is the first time I've called.'

The voice on the end of the line sounded indignant. 'Half

the time I don't know what to believe. Ever since Holly's been in here the ward's been full of showbiz riffraff. How do I know you're not one of them?'

'You'll have to take my word for it,' said Linda sharply.

There was a short silence while the nurse considered.

'Well,' she said finally, 'just as long as you're not going to come barging in to see her, I suppose I can discuss her case.'

It was this last remark that got to Linda. She hadn't planned to go anywhere near Holly, but now the bossy nurse was denying her access, it was a different story. Nobody told Linda what she could or couldn't do.

'I've changed my mind,' she told the sister. 'I've decided to come barging in after all.'

Holly listened to her father talking about his latest discovery and felt slightly bored. He had been dredging up stories about his business for over a week now and she wished he wouldn't try so hard.

Then she saw the concern on his face and she knew she was being a bitch. It must be bloody dreary for him coming here night after night, she thought. And for what? To see me sitting up in bed moaning about my operation.

She did her best to pay attention to what Jason was saying. He'd been to some fringe production at the King's Head. The drama was all about a boy dying of AIDS and Jason hadn't expected much of it – until he saw the boy playing the AIDS victim. Instead of being turned off by the whole thing as he had expected, Jason found he was fascinated.

'The boy was a complete unknown, yet he had the same quality that Richard Burton had. I was absolutely mesmerized.'

Holly caught a whiff of her father's excitement and marvelled at it. All the years of her childhood he had told her tales like this. There was always some talented nonentity coming out of nowhere, just waiting for him to wave his magic wand.

'Did you sign him up?' she asked Jason, knowing the answer in advance.

157

He nodded. Then he embarked on a detailed agenda of what he had lined up for his protégé.

Jason was so wrapped up in what he was saying that he didn't see Linda pushing her way past the nurses' station. She was carrying a pile of glossy magazines, and Holly saw she'd also brought a huge box of chocolates.

Saved by the bell, Holly thought. If she'd had to endure another five minutes of her father's boy wonder, she might have thrown up.

'Linda,' she said brightly, 'what a lovely surprise.'

Then she turned her face up to be kissed and indicated a chair on the other side of her bed. 'I want to know everything that's been happening in the past week. You've no idea how boring it is in here.'

Jason watched his daughter as she prattled on. Her eyes were sparkling with interest and he noticed there was a little colour coming into her complexion.

She needs a woman to confide in, he thought. I do my best, but I don't really reach her.

He had no idea when he started to feel in the way. Was it when Linda swept past him, barely acknowledging he was there? Or when Holly showed how much she preferred talking to her workmate?

I've been dumped, he thought, feeling vaguely irritated. My dear little daughter has found someone more interesting to talk to and now I no longer exist.

He thought about leaving, knowing that neither of them would mind if he did. Then he took another look at Linda and decided to stay where he was.

She was more attractive than he remembered. Soft and almost touchable.

Before, when they had met, she was such a tight little career girl, all power-dressed and full of good works. Intent on saving him from his divorce and his wild child of a daughter.

Now he wasn't so sure. He glanced at his watch and saw it was getting on for seven thirty. If Linda had plans for dinner, Jason thought, she would have made a move half an hour ago. But the only plans she seemed to have were entertaining his daughter.

'I hate to break up the party,' he said, 'but experience tells me we're about to be thrown out. They always get rid of visitors about now.'

The blonde looked disappointed. 'What a shame,' she said. 'Holly and I were just getting down to cases. She knows things about the programme I never even suspected.'

'We can do it again,' Holly said. She hesitated. 'If you can find the time.'

Linda beamed. 'Of course I can. I'll come by after work tomorrow if you like.'

'Promise me?'

The presenter held out her hand. 'I promise.'

After they left the ward, when they were walking down the corridor to the lift, Jason turned to Linda.

'What made you come in here today?' he asked. 'I didn't know you and Holly were close.'

Linda shrugged. 'We're not particularly, but I got a feeling she might need me.'

Now he was curious. 'What made you think that?'

'Talking to the ward sister. She nearly chewed my ear off when I told her I was a friend of Holly's. According to her the girl's been inundated by half the actors in *Spotlight*, and she thought I was one of them.'

'So you decided to come and rescue her.'

'Somebody had to,' Linda said. 'Holly must be sick and tired of seeing you parade all your clients past her bed.'

Jason felt angry with her all over again. There was something about this woman that got under his skin. She seemed to know exactly what he was up to and, what was worse, she didn't always approve.

He felt a sudden need to explain himself. 'Look,' he said, 'I brought all those people in because I wanted Holly to have a fuss made of her.'

'And did it convince her? Did she really believe that all those actors really cared about her being ill?'

He thought for a moment. 'I don't suppose she did,' he said, 'but that's not the point.'

'It *is* the point. Look, Holly isn't my best friend, not by a long chalk, but at least I know her. I'm genuinely sorry for her. The mob you brought in were simply obeying orders. I bet she felt as patronized as hell.'

She was right, of course. Only Jason didn't want her to be right. What he wanted of a woman was a little reassurance.

He nearly reconsidered asking her out to dinner. Then he thought, no. I like being around Linda. I like listening to her, even though she says things I don't want to hear.

'What are your plans tonight?' he asked.

Linda looked weary. 'I've got a stack of work waiting for me at home,' she told him. 'I'll probably make myself a cheese sandwich and get down to it.'

'Why don't you give up and let me take you to Langan's instead?'

'I'd love to, but I can't. Thanks all the same.'

Before Jason could persuade her further, the lift arrived and they were absorbed into the crowd of departing visitors.

When they got outside the hospital gates he made one last attempt to get her attention.

'My car is down the road,' he said. 'Can I give you a lift home?'

She smiled her apologies. 'I drove here as well,' she informed him.

Linda started to visit the hospital regularly. It was clear Holly didn't have any close friends and apart from her father, nobody much seemed to care about her.

She was a difficult girl – Linda knew that just from working with her – but there was something else about her, a loneliness, a need for acceptance, that struck a chord in Linda.

She had been on her own once. When she started at the BBC. Just to get someone to have a drink in the local wine bar was a major effort then, so she understood what Holly was going through though she didn't have a clue why she was so friendless.

It's got to be something to do with her mother, Linda decided. A fractured relationship early on in life sets up destructive patterns. She probably finds it impossible to get through to people.

This particular line of thought wasn't exactly original. Linda had learned about people's innermost conflicts as a result of an affair she had had in Manchester with a professor of psychology, and in her idle moments she liked to apply what she had learned.

Jason, for example, had obviously been spoiled rotten as a child. The women in his family had doted on him, which was why he took them so much for granted in his adult life. The theory would have fitted him like a glove, if it hadn't been for Holly. His daughter was the one woman he didn't treat casually. Whenever Linda turned up at the hospital, Jason was always there, the model doting father, fussing around her and doing his damnedest to engage her attention.

It wasn't appreciated all that much. Holly was at the stage when she wanted to talk about clothes and boys and the latest pop video, so Jason didn't really stand a chance.

In a way Linda felt sorry for him. When she was around, the girl simply ignored her father and prattled on to her. She hoped Jason didn't hate her for it.

In a way it was Linda's guilty conscience that prompted her to accept a lift home when he asked her next. She had mentally written him off, but the man looked so beaten by the way his daughter was behaving, she didn't have the heart to turn him down.

It was early in the evening when she climbed into his wine-coloured Daimler. And as they drove over Putney Bridge, she saw the beginnings of a truly beautiful sunset. For a moment, she felt sad.

If only things had worked out between us, she thought, we could have driven down to the river and had a drink in one of those pretty little pubs.

He must have been reading her thoughts, for he asked if she had any plans for the evening.

Linda hesitated. This man had injured her pride. He had picked her up and dropped her as if she was some available bimbo, and now he was doing it all over again.

'I'm not sure,' she said cautiously.

He turned to her. 'Don't give me the line about having a lot of work piled up at home, because I won't believe you a second time. If you don't want to get involved with me, just say so. I'll understand.'

The harshness of the statement pulled her up short.

'I didn't know you were that bothered,' she said, doing her damnedest to keep the interest out of her voice.

For the first time that evening he smiled. 'To tell the truth, neither did I. You must have grown on me.'

She began to realize how silly she had been to expect a knight on a white charger. He'd clearly been through a horrible time with the actress he'd been married to. Maybe he didn't trust women any more. She decided to find out.

'You said something about getting involved,' she probed. 'What kind of involved?'

He looked at her for a full second and during that time she felt her heart stop.

'Use your imagination,' he said.

They had dinner in a Greek restaurant behind the Bayswater Road. It wasn't the sort of place Linda associated with somebody as smooth as Jason, but he was clearly a regular visitor, for the patron greeted him like a long-lost brother and showed them to the best table.

Linda couldn't remember much about the evening except there was a lot of food, which kept arriving on individual plates. There were dips, several varieties of seafood, great piles of salad. And when she thought there was no more room on the table, meatballs and lamb on skewers arrived.

'You don't expect me to eat it all?' she laughed.

'Of course I don't. I'm just doing this to impress you.'

She knew where the evening was heading – she would have been a fool not to – and she suddenly realized she didn't care any more. It's what I want, isn't it? she asked herself.

She remembered the way he'd looked at her in the car when she'd asked about getting involved.

'Why don't we give the coffee here a miss?' she said. 'I make it better than the Greeks do, and my flat's only round the corner.'

Jason was impressed with the way she lived. In the last few years he had been in enough bachelor girl flats to know what to expect, but Linda surprised him.

She inhabited a ground-floor apartment in one of the big blocks at the top of Queensway. It was a tacky neighbourhood, yet when you got through her front door, you stepped into another world.

The whole place was painted white and Linda, or somebody who knew what they were doing, had stripped the floorboards. It gave the place a rustic, almost cottagey look. She had stayed with the feeling and kept everything pared down to a minimum.

There was a big Conran sofa, a glass coffee table and two or three rattan chairs. Apart from the prints on the walls and the Turkish rugs, that was all.

'You really made something of this place,' he said approvingly. 'Who's the interior designer in your family?'

Linda made a face. 'If you'd met my family, you'd know that was a silly question.'

'Why do you say that?'

She looked at the tall, well-groomed gentleman sitting on her sofa and wondered whether to destroy the illusion she had created. If she told him she came from the buildings, would he still want to know her?

Jason saw her hesitate. 'You don't have to talk about it if you don't want to.'

She remembered the last time they had had dinner. She was the one who had done the probing then, digging into his marriage and his past until she got the story of his life.

I guess it's fair to return the compliment, she decided.

She went into the kitchen and returned with coffee and a half-bottle of brandy she had left over from a dinner party.

Then she sat down beside him on the sofa and told him her story.

She didn't try to edit it or pretty it up. There wasn't much you could do with a childhood on a council estate in Epping.

After a bit, Jason interrupted her.

'Was it really necessary to live there?' he asked. 'Your father worked, didn't he?'

'Dad drove a minicab when the spirit moved him, which wasn't often. He preferred to live off the state and let my mother go out cleaning for any extras. Then there was what I brought in. I got a job banging a typewriter the moment I left school.'

'You're not telling me your father took your salary off you?'

'You bet he did. How else do you think I kept a roof over my head?'

'You mean they would have turfed you out?'

She shrugged. 'If I hadn't got pregnant and managed to get a council flat of my own. That's the way girls like me usually survive.'

Jason picked up the brandy in the crystal glass in front of him.

'So what made you different?'

'I hated everything about the life I had. I hated the yobbos that lived beside us on the landing. I hated the lifts that stank of stale pee. I hated my father for being too lazy to get himself a full-time job, and my mother for putting up with the situation. All I ever wanted to do was earn enough money so I could leave the whole lot of them behind me. And I did.'

She saw him give her the same look he gave his daughter.

'Do you ever see any of them now?' he asked her.

'Occasionally, when somebody dies or somebody gets married. I haven't cut myself off completely, though I don't think any of them would cry if I did. You see, I'm not like them any more. And they rather resent me for it . . . I often think I'd have seen more affection from my mother if I'd had three children by three different fathers. At least she could have understood that. My job in television is totally beyond her.'

Jason put his glass down and started to stroke her hair.

'Poor Linda,' he said softly. 'I had no idea.'

She brushed his hand away. 'What did you expect?' she asked.

Jason thought about the bossy, dominating bitch he'd been running away from, the one who was going to take over his life and tell him what suit to wear with what tie. The girl he'd discovered this evening was nothing like that and for the first time ever he doubted his judgement. He took hold of the hand that had dismissed him so abruptly.

'If I told you what I expected,' he said gently, 'you'd probably never talk to me again.'

Then before Linda could ask him anything more, he gathered her in his arms and started to kiss her.

The violence of her response surprised her. She had been kissed before and she knew the rules, but this man woke something in her that she had never acknowledged. She had never felt so hungry, so greedy, and as she reached blindly for Jason, she felt vaguely ashamed.

They didn't make it to the bedroom. There was no time. All either of them wanted to do was to get close. So close they lost themselves in one another.

He made love to her on the floor, urgently and without finesse. And when the moment of union came, Linda gave herself so completely that for a moment she lost all idea of where she was.

Jason looked at the woman lying in his arms and marvelled at her. Each time they met, he thought he understood her. Then something would happen that changed his mind completely. One minute she was a bitch, the next a waif. Now she had become a goddess.

She's like quicksilver, he thought. Elusive and constantly changing.

He started to stroke the delicate skin at the base of Linda's throat, moving the tips of his fingers right down her length. She seemed to be covered all over in blonde down. It was so translucent you could only discover it by touching her. He let his hands linger in the curve of her waist and the swell of her buttocks, like a sculptor discovering clay for the first time, and he wondered why no other women had had this effect on him. Then he saw her smile and he threw all the other women out of his mind.

'I'm going to go on doing this all night,' he told her. 'So we might find somewhere more comfortable.'

Linda got up then and led the way into her bedroom. Like the rest of her apartment — like Linda herself — it was simple and superbly elegant.

I'm going to enjoy discovering this woman, Jason thought. There's more to her than anyone I've ever known. Even Eve doesn't begin to compare.

Linda woke before Jason, automatically bracing herself for the long drive to the studio. Then she saw she wasn't alone and the memory of the night came flooding back to her.

For a few moments she replayed it, bringing Jason back the way he had been just a few hours ago. She felt like waking him so they could go on loving, but reality changed her mind.

She had to be out of here in half an hour, showered, dressed and ready for the cameras. She crept out of the room and put herself together as silently as she knew how.

Much later, when the sun was up, Jason woke up in a strange bed and discovered he was alone. For a moment he panicked, wondering what the hell was going on. Then he remembered Linda worked for a living.

He looked at his watch and saw it was past nine. He wandered into her drawing room and turned on the television, and she was there, up on the screen, the way he knew she would be.

All at once he felt lonely. Linda had come into his life, altered all his plans, and now she had left him here alone. In a few minutes, when her first guest comes on to the set, she'll forget I even exist, he thought.

He clicked off the set and made his way into her kitchen. And that's when he saw the note she had left.

'Sorry I had to leave you so early,' she wrote, 'but duty called. If you're around this evening, I'll cook for you.'

A smile broke across his face and he made a mental note to cancel anything he had planned for that night and all the nights after.

24

Holly knew her father had a girlfriend when she found the Calèche. It was hidden away on the top shelf of his bathroom cabinet and without hesitating she took it down and sampled some.

Her nose twitched at the smell. There was something heavy and sour about it. The woman it belonged to knew her way around. Without thinking, Holly started to hate her.

It wasn't fair, of course. Daddy had every right to a sex life. But when the sex life started taking up residence, Holly's hackles rose.

There was only space for one brand of perfume in this bathroom: Joy – the scent Eve used. Her mother had trailed it through the house all the time she'd lived there, leaving traces of it on her pillow when she kissed her goodnight. Even when Eve was away, it lingered on the air.

There wasn't a vestige of it now, of course – there hadn't been for years – but that didn't stop Holly from dreaming, for she had never really understood what drove her parents apart.

They were like Liz Taylor and Richard Burton, she thought. Famous lovers, fated to stay together forever, but now they were living miserable separate lives – half-lives really, because neither existed properly without the other.

When she got depressed about it, Holly would fantasize about her parents getting together again. They would run into each other somewhere familiar – the Ivy, where they always held court, or the stage of the Adelphi – and their eyes would meet and they would remember how happy they had once been.

At this moment in her dream, Holly usually had music swelling in the background, something by Cole Porter or Irving Berlin, schmaltzy and full of show biz. In the final reel her parents would fall into each other's arms and swear never to spend another moment apart.

Standing in her father's bathroom, Holly tried to imagine how life would be with her parents back together again. The house would be full of hangers-on, of course, all stopping by for champagne on their way to the theatre. There would be extravagant parties every weekend. And she would feel special again.

Her friends at school always said she lived in an enchanted circle, and when her mother was there, it was true.

The bottle of Calèche in front of her brought Holly back to earth. Her mother had a rival and she was living here in London. Soon, Holly knew, she would be summoned to meet the bitch – she was sure the woman would be a bitch – and the two of them would go through the pantomime of pretending to like each other. The girl sighed. It wouldn't last long, thank God. Not going on her father's past form.

Then Holly was struck by an irrational worry. What if this new love of her father's didn't fade away? What if she hung on and finally supplanted her mother? The thought was too horrible to contemplate.

Before she could stop herself, Holly reached out and took hold of the bottle of Calèche. Then she removed its top and carried it over to the sink. Finally, with great deliberation, she poured the lot of it away. When the new girlfriend needed to dab something behind her ears, she would go into the bathroom and find the empty bottle. And unless she was a complete dummy, she would realize she wasn't welcome here.

Two days later, right on cue, Holly was asked to meet her father's new girlfriend. The three of them were to have dinner at San Lorenzo. Holly noted with satisfaction that her father never changed. He always paraded the new love in some smart restaurant where the noise level was deafening. That way they could all sum each other up without having to make too much effort at conversation. In San Lorenzo, on the right night, you can get through an entire evening without having to say anything at all.

Holly wondered what she was going to put on for the great event. Whenever she felt unsure of herself, she usually went for tight jeans and ultra-smart jacket. The jacket covered her fat bits, and the jeans emphasized the length of her legs. If she was going to make some predatory new girlfriend feel small, she had to show her she'd been around and she knew what worked. Saint Laurent and blue jeans did the job perfectly.

They got to San Lorenzo late, and when Holly walked in the door the first person she saw sitting at the bar was Linda.

'It's great to see you,' she enthused. 'You've no idea what a grim evening Daddy's about to put me through.'

Linda looked over the girl's shoulder, trying to locate Jason.

'Where is Daddy?' the presenter asked with just a trace of irony.

Holly looked distracted. 'Parking the car,' she replied. 'Do you think he'd mind if I ordered myself a drink?'

'I shouldn't think so.'

Holly leaned across the tiny bar and asked the waiter for a Campari. When it arrived she returned to what was troubling her.

'Jason's got a new girl,' she said confidentially, 'and tonight I'm being dragged along to meet her.'

Linda raised an eyebrow. 'Is that so terrible?'

'Of course it's terrible,' Holly almost shouted. 'Have you any idea what it's like to be looked over by some woman who just happens to be sleeping with your father.' She made a face. 'They're always super sweet and it pisses me off because I know they couldn't care less whether I live or die. Daddy's the one they've got their sights on and they think they can get to him through me.'

'I can see I'm going to have to watch my step with you,' Linda said.

Holly looked confused. 'What are you talking about?'

'I'm talking about us,' Linda said carefully. 'You, me and Jason.' She paused, letting the words sink in. 'I'm the girl your father's bringing to dinner.'

'You're Daddy's new romance?'

Linda looked nervous. 'You're not going to hate me for it, are you?'

'Of course I'm not. You can't start hating somebody you already like.'

Holly grinned, noticing for the first time how wound up Linda was.

'I'm sorry if I was horrible about Daddy's exes, but they really were a shower, you know. There was nobody half as nice as you.'

'You really mean that?'

'I wouldn't say it if I didn't mean it.'

All the same Holly was knocked for six. It seemed so improbable, Daddy and Linda. All her father's other women had been leggy showgirl types with cut-glass accents. They were forever talking about Mummy and Daddy in the country, occasionally dragging him off to the family home where they rode to hounds and shot pheasants.

Holly smiled. One thing was for sure in this new relationship: there was no chance her father would be dragged off to meet Linda's parents. From what she knew of them, they were best kept hidden.

Just as she was about to suggest they had another drink, Jason came bustling in. If anything, Holly thought, he was even more nervous than Linda. He made a big deal of greeting Mara, the owner's wife, kissing her hand like an Italian, then he joined Holly and Linda at the bar, ordering a bottle of champagne before they could tell him they were drinking Campari.

'I expect this has come as a surprise to you,' he said to Holly.

'Of course it's a surprise,' she said, feeling slightly sorry he had got himself into such a state. 'But I'm not against it. Linda knows that.'

Holly saw a look pass between the two of them and just for a second she felt terribly left out. They'd obviously spent hours working out just how she'd take this new arrangement, and now she didn't look like making trouble, they were quietly congratulating themselves.

Holly decided to go along with their mood. If Daddy had to have a girlfriend, it might as well be Linda, she decided, though she was curious to know how it all happened.

When they finally got to their table, Holly turned to her father and asked him. Then she wished she hadn't because he looked so embarrassed.

'Linda and I got to know each other when you were in hospital—' he started to say.

Then Linda cut in: 'Darling, it was before that. Remember how I tried to find Holly when she went missing in the studio?'

Holly tuned out. The pair of them were indulging in the game all new lovers play, dragging up magic moments when they first discovered each other. It was boring as hell, and if Holly hadn't been so fond of Linda the whole thing would have got under her skin.

As it was, she just felt sorry for her. Linda was obviously gooey-eyed about Jason. She might even have gone the whole hog and fallen in love. Only it wouldn't come to anything. Her father had given his heart years ago to her mother. They may be estranged now, but Eve would always be part of him, just as he would always be part of her.

Any woman who tried to get between them was riding for a fall.

25

Holly knew it was the beginning of the end when Linda found dust under the drawing room sofa.

She hadn't seen it coming, because Linda had been so well behaved until then. The presenter seemed to understand that the big house in St John's Wood was Holly's territory and she went to great pains not to crowd her.

Apart from the appearance of a new bottle of Calèche — Linda didn't say a word about the disappearance of the old one — she hardly made her presence felt at all. She was just a visiting girlfriend who moved in at weekends, then disappeared on Monday morning.

Holly might have known it was too good to last. The first signs that things were getting serious was when the weekends got longer. These days, Linda didn't move out until Tuesday or sometimes Wednesday, and because she was around such a lot, certain changes started to be made. One Saturday she and Jason came back from the shops clutching a huge canvas. Linda had bought it in Cork Street and they were both really excited about it. They started taking down some of the pictures to see where they could put it. And in the end the big oil painting of Mummy, which hung over the mantelpiece, was the one to go.

Jason moved it to a dark place over the stairs and put up Linda's picture in its place. Holly thought it looked completely horrible, but she didn't say anything until Linda found the dust.

The blonde had been messing around in the main drawing

room repositioning the sofas, and when she stood up to take a breather, she saw both her hands were covered in black grime.

She didn't complain about it. Linda wasn't the type to make a fuss about a bit of dust. What she did was to grab a pail of water and a scrubbing brush and deal with it.

Holly watched her scrabbling around, and felt mildly irritated.

'If I were you, I'd leave the cleaning to Lola,' she said. 'It is her job after all.'

Linda looked up, scarlet from her exertions. 'Well, she's doing a bloody terrible job. Someone ought to tell her.'

At first Holly didn't take the episode seriously. Lola had always ruled in the house. Ever since Holly was tiny and Mummy had to go away a lot, Lola did the scrubbing and that was the end of it. Holly explained all this to Linda one night when they were having supper, but Linda didn't grasp the importance of what she was saying.

'I think you've both let Lola get away with murder. She's sloppy as hell.'

Holly started to grin then, which really got up Linda's nose.

'It's not funny,' she said sharply. 'If things are left to get dirty, one of us could pick up a germ, and that's the last thing we need—'

Jason cut in on her. 'Surely you're exaggerating. Lola always seems to keep the house beautifully.'

'That's because you don't look too closely. You have a problem, believe me.'

Holly brought the cup of coffee she was pouring to the table and sat down.

'Are you going to talk to Lola about this problem?' she asked her father.

'Wouldn't it be better if a woman handled this?' Linda asked.

Jason considered for a moment. 'You're right,' he said. He turned to his daughter. 'Darling, you've known Lola since you were a baby. Do you think you could manage a quiet word in her ear?'

Holly said she would, and that's how they left it.

However, when Holly actually told Lola what Linda had said about her, the Spanish woman went spare.

She shouted, cursed and wept, and when she had finished expressing herself, she turned round and demanded an apology.

'I want Linda on her bended knees,' Lola told Holly. 'Otherwise I go on strike.'

Holly relayed the message to Linda, who seemed unmoved by it.

'I won't be dictated to by servants,' she said. 'You can tell Lola I meant everything I said. You can also tell her that the bathrooms are filthy and I want to know the reason why.'

Holly expected a major eruption when she tackled Lola again, so she talked to her father instead. Once he realized how close they were to a shutdown of all services, he would talk some sense into Linda. But Jason refused to do it.

'Can you see Linda apologizing to my housekeeper?' he demanded. 'I wouldn't subject her to that kind of humiliation.'

'If you don't,' Holly said, 'we're all going to suffer. I know Lola; she's perfectly capable of retiring to her room and leaving us to it.'

Jason looked dangerous. 'If she does that she'll be in trouble.'

Holly felt her heart lurch. 'You wouldn't throw her out?'

'Try me.'

Now Holly was really frightened. Earlier, it had all been a game, a silly domestic squabble. Now there was much more at stake, for Lola wasn't just the housekeeper. Lola had always been there for Holly. Holly thought back to the worst time in her life, when she was starving herself to death, and she remembered how Lola had cooked up a storm. She hadn't given Holly a bad time, or lectured her about what she was

175

doing to herself, she had simply done her damnedest to get her to eat.

Through the terrible years without Eve, Lola had been in the background. When Holly first went to bed with a boy, it was Lola she told. And when the boy ditched her for her best friend, it was Lola who wiped her tears away and told her he wasn't worth it.

Lola was there when Holly smoked her first joint and made herself ill — just as she was there when the girl landed her job in television. Lola was sad when Holly was sad, and happy when Holly was happy. And when Holly most needed her, she would open her arms and let the girl rest there for a while.

Eve had never cuddled her the way Lola did — not even Jason gave her this much comfort — and Holly knew she had to fight to keep her.

Holly concentrated all her attention on her father. They were in the drawing room having the first drink of the evening while Linda was fussing about in the kitchen.

'Daddy,' Holly said, keeping her voice down in case it carried down the hall, 'if Lola goes, my life will never be the same. How do you think I'm going to cope without her?'

Jason looked at his daughter and wondered what the hell he was going to do. The little speech she'd just delivered was pure emotional blackmail. Holly would cope very well without Lola once she got used to being without her. She coped without her real mother, hadn't she? And she'd made enough fuss about Eve leaving at the time.

All the same, he knew if he got rid of the Spanish woman, he would hurt his daughter, and he wondered if there was a way out of it.

I could force Linda to climb down, he thought. Once I've explained how close Holly and Lola really are, she'd understand.

Or would she? This new woman of his had a will of her own. If he sided against her with his daughter, she was perfectly capable of walking out.

176

The idea appalled him. Whether he wanted to or not, Jason was falling in love with Linda, and he wasn't going to do without her – not for Holly, not for Lola, not for anyone.

He turned to his daughter. 'This is a very silly situation,' he told her, 'and I'm sorry you had to get caught up in it. There's only one thing we can do now: I have to go and talk to Lola myself. She has to know that Linda is entitled to her opinion. And she has to respect that opinion.'

When Lola walked out, Holly mourned her. Even though she was no longer in the house, her presence still inhabited it. Holly would walk into the kitchen and stop in confusion when she didn't see the sturdy Spanish woman bent over the sink. Sometimes when she heard the Hoover in the hall she'd hurry towards the sound, then stop when she was greeted with the sight of an unfamiliar cleaning woman.

Linda was responsible for the new cleaner, and in the normal way of things, Holly would have been grateful to her for helping them out in their hour of need, but she wasn't grateful, for without Linda none of this would have happened.

When she thought about it, Holly realized Linda had been creeping up on them. She had been so charming when she first declared herself.

'I hope you won't hate me,' she'd said in San Lorenzo after it was plain she was Daddy's new girlfriend. The remark had disarmed Holly, who'd actually felt sorry for Linda, thinking she couldn't cope.

Now Holly laughed at her own naivety. Linda couldn't cope the way a praying mantis couldn't cope. The minute she'd set foot in the house, she'd staked it out. This was going to be her territory from now on and she'd set about making it so. Mummy's portrait was the first thing to go, and now Lola had been shown the door. The girl started to feel cornered. How long, she wondered, before Linda starts to exert her influence on me?

She'd tried to talk to Jason about the way their lives were changing, but he wouldn't listen to her.

'I've waited for someone like Linda for a very long time,' he told her. 'Anything she does around here is fine with me.'

The words were like a warning shot across her bows, Holly realized. Jason had as good as told her Linda was more than just a passing fancy. Not that he needed to. After Lola's departure Linda had virtually taken up residence. Now she didn't just stay for long weekends, she stayed all week, making the odd trip back to her flat for a clean change of underwear, or an evening dress for some do Daddy was taking her to.

For the first time since it started, Holly began to worry where the relationship was going. Linda had already far out-distanced any previous girlfriend of her father's. She was the woman of the house now, casting a spell over Jason and all the things he used to care about didn't seem to matter any more. He'd even stopped working every hour of the day, and Holly knew what the next move was going to be.

She's going to push to get married, Holly thought. It's obvious she wants to replace my mother and what better way than becoming the new Mrs Fielding?

She thought about how things used to be when Daddy and Mummy were the talk of the town. The family meant something then – they were legendary – and now Linda wanted to turn them into ordinary, everyday sort of people.

Well, Holly wasn't going to let her get away with it. Right at this minute she had no idea how she was going to stop Linda but she knew, if she put her mind to it, something would turn up.

Three weeks after Lola's departure, Holly had a letter from her mother. For the first time ever, Eve was taking time off from the theatre. She was going to be kicking her heels all summer long and she wanted Holly to come over and spend the time with her.

Holly folded the letter away and considered the idea. She hadn't been to New York in ages because it hadn't been working. She and Eve always ended up bickering and she wondered if it would be any different now.

There was only one way to find out. She hoped Linda wouldn't pull any tricks while she was away.

26

Eve was wearing wrap-around sunglasses, a tightly belted raincoat and a soft felt hat that partially concealed her face. Nobody walking past her would have the slightest clue as to who she was, and that suited her down to the ground.

Ever since the film opened across America, Eve had been mobbed wherever she went. She couldn't cross the street without some complete stranger thrusting an autograph book into her face, or even worse, asking questions about her private life. She was famous; she now counted as public property. Though there were days when she loved it, today wasn't one of them.

Eve was meeting her daughter today and she didn't want anything to go wrong. She sighed, pulling the raincoat tightly round her. How many times had she felt this way? How many times had she turned up at Kennedy determined that this visit would be the one when they finally understood each other? And how many times had she found she'd been chasing rainbows?

She made her way to the arrivals hall, and as she did so, she went over the wreckage of the last few years. She had started out with the best intentions – they both had – but the work had always come between them. There simply wasn't time to play the devoted mother and appear in a hit play.

And in the end, Holly had got bored with her. Her visits were fewer and fewer every year, and when she left school, they dwindled away altogether.

Eve knew then that if she didn't do something, she'd lose her daughter altogether, so she took the summer off. She booked herself out so she could give Holly her undivided attention. She just hoped she hadn't left it too late.

Above her the Tannoy crackled into life. The London plane had touched down. Any minute the passengers would be pouring into the terminal.

As quickly as she could, Eve made her way over to the barrier. She wanted to be there when her daughter came through the doorway. She wanted to pick her up and hold her in her arms and tell her how much she'd missed her. The first passengers were coming through and Eve craned her neck searching for the familiar face.

The first thing Eve noticed was Holly's style. She wasn't a power dresser, that was for sure, but there was a confidence about her that was new.

As the girl got nearer, Eve saw the reason why her daughter was walking tall. She had turned into a beauty. The dark, unruly hair that was always pulled back, was set free now. It bushed out around her shoulders, giving her a foreign, almost exotic, look. If she had put a flower behind her ear, you might have thought she had ancestors on some tropical island.

Holly played up her unusual looks. Instead of wearing some neat little suit she was in tight pants and a spectacular jacket that looked as if it came from Paris.

She's sexy and she knows it, Eve thought. For no reason at all she felt slightly shocked.

Jason didn't tell me she'd grown into a woman, she panicked. What am I going to do with her?

There was no time to deliberate on this, for Holly had seen her mother and was making her way over to the barrier.

'Mummy,' she said, 'you look like something out of *Sunset Boulevard*. What's all the heavy disguise about?'

Eve laughed. She might have changed her style, but Holly was still her daughter.

She turned her face up to be kissed. 'I'm famous now,' she said, 'or has the fact escaped you?'

The girl ducked under the rail separating them. She pecked her mother on the cheek, and before Eve could stop her, she reached up and whipped off the dark glasses.

'I don't detect anyone famous,' Holly said wickedly. 'Just a perfectly ordinary parent who hasn't bothered to put her make-up on today. You can't kid me with the dark shades routine.'

Eve was exasperated. 'Hasn't anyone told you about the film?' she asked, thinking immediately: I'm pushing my career down her throat again. There's time enough to go into what I'm doing.

She took her daughter's arm and signalled a porter.

'There's a car waiting for us outside,' she told her. 'Let's get you and the bags into it. Then we'll talk.'

Holly let her mother lead her outside. She hasn't changed, she thought. She's still completely obsessed with herself — more so now she's a movie star.

She wondered whether to tell Eve she had seen her film at a private screening Jason had organized, or whether to pretend she knew nothing about it. That would cut Eve down to size, of course, but was it worth it? If she wasn't careful Holly would be spending her first night in New York knee deep in her mother's press cuttings.

No, she decided. It's easier to tell the truth.

On the way into the city, she confessed about Jason screening the film. To her surprise, Eve seemed pleased.

'I'm glad he's keeping you in touch with what I'm doing. It's a good thing I didn't fire him after the divorce.'

'Were you going to?'

Eve raised her eyebrows and Holly noticed a sudden rash of lines on her forehead.

'I was once,' she replied. 'I thought it might be better for both of us if I found someone else to handle my business, but nobody else understood me the way your father does so in the end I left things the way they were.'

'Has it worked for you?'

Eve smiled. 'What do you think?'

Holly regarded her mother. She still had an enviable glamour, but she was older now. She wondered how Eve would feel about the advent of Linda.

'You do know that Daddy's seriously involved with someone?'

Eve seemed unperturbed. 'You're talking about Linda,' she said. 'Jason told me about her last time he was over here. He was wondering whether to move her in.'

The admission unnerved Holly. She suddenly had the feeling that all the grown-ups were together in some elaborate plot against her.

'I suppose you know about Lola then,' Holly said.

Eve shook her head. 'Tell me.'

Holly launched into the full story, missing out on none of the details. She gave particular emphasis to Linda's neurotic need for cleanliness. If Jason hadn't told Eve about Lola, then no doubt he hadn't given her the full picture of his new girlfriend.

Eve seemed fascinated, nodding sympathetically at every twist and turn of events. Holly noticed she didn't say a word against Linda, yet the girl knew her mother wasn't exactly pleased about the way things had turned out.

'Do you still keep in touch with Lola? ' Eve asked, looking concerned. 'She was very important to you when you were growing up.'

Holly nodded. 'I go and visit her in Blackheath where she lives now. She hasn't got another job yet, and when I told Daddy about it, he didn't seem all that interested.'

'Your father's got other things to worry about,' Eve said. 'Listen, if you give me Lola's new address, I'll see what can be done about the situation.'

'You're not going to send her money, are you?'

Eve grinned. 'Hardly, but I might try explaining things properly the next time Jason comes over.'

'So that he can send money?'

For a second, Eve looked distracted. 'Something like that.'

They had reached the city now, approaching it from the river, and Holly was reminded how tacky New York was.

All the buildings seemed to be run down and on the verge of collapse. There was dirt and debris blowing around the streets, and she wondered how her mother stood it.

She thought about the shabby old-fashioned apartment on the West Side. Had Eve managed to fix the air conditioning, she wondered. Last time she was there it was so noisy you got a headache if you left it on too long.

Holly sighed. Welcome to migraine summer, she thought. There's no way we're doing without a cooling system in this heat.

She noticed they were going a different way across the city. Normally they went down Seventh Avenue and through the garment centre. But this time they seemed to have passed it by. She glanced through the window and caught a glimpse of the Park.

'Where are you taking me?' she asked her mother. 'This isn't the way to the apartment.'

'It isn't,' Eve agreed, 'but I don't live there any more.'

The girl felt the beginnings of hope. 'You don't mean to tell me you've found somewhere civilized at last?'

'I think it is,' Eve said mysteriously, 'but you'll have to see it and make up your own mind.'

After that she clammed up. Despite all Holly's demands she refused to say where her new home was, or even what it was. She could have been living in a basement or a brownstone for all the clues she was giving. In the end Holly stared out of the window and tried to work things out for herself.

They were in the eighties now, just past the Met, and the limousine turned away from the Park and headed down one of the streets. It was an elegant neighbourhood full of grand apartment blocks with awnings and men on the door. They pulled up to one of the biggest right at the end of the street and despite herself Holly was impressed.

'How can you afford it?' she demanded.

'I didn't exactly get peanuts for starring in a Hollywood film,' Eve replied.

Holly could see that the minute they walked into the lobby. It had a marble floor and a huge reception desk with three

184

people behind it. All of them knew her mother. They kept calling her by her stage name, which irritated Holly.

Now I know why she moved here, she thought balefully. There's a ready-made audience right on the premises.

They hung about for what seemed like half an hour while Eve went into long explanations about Holly being her daughter who lived in England. Finally, when Holly felt as if she had shaken hands with every porter in the building, the keys to the apartment were produced. Then she and Eve bundled into a mahogany-lined elevator, along with the head doorman, who seemed to think they needed an escort.

Just for a moment, Holly felt a deep longing for the West Side apartment she had despised earlier. It was cold in winter and oppressive in summer, but at least it was private.

When they got through the front door, Holly brightened up a little. The first impression she got was one of space. The hall they stepped into could have been a room in itself, for it was high and wide and seemed to go on for ever.

Before she had time to take it all in, her mother had hurried her through to the main room, which Holly knew without being told was her pride and joy. It was the picture window that made it. It ran the whole length of one wall and very nearly its height. Looking through it, it was as if someone had commissioned a painting of the city, for here it was, spread out in front of them in all its glory.

Holly went to find her room after that and discovered it was one of three spare bedrooms, each with its own bathroom. Hers was the grandest, right down the hall from her mother's, and, like her mother's, it was decorated in pale lemon. Along one wall was a swish of silk curtains and facing it, covered in the same fabric, was the biggest bed Holly had ever set eyes on. She threw herself down on it, revelling in its soft, expensive luxury.

I'm going to like it here, Holly thought. I was right to come after all.

Her first week passed in a whirl of lunches and parties and shopping trips.

185

Eve's star status seemed to have attracted hangers-on in even greater numbers than before. Wherever they went, they were surrounded by a crowd of writers and designers, and actors between plays. It was like being at the centre of a kaleidoscope, for the crowd changed all the time – with two exceptions: Ida and Justin.

They were her mother's bosom buddies, the inner circle who stayed with her come what may. To Holly they were a mystery.

Ida, whom she had met when she first came to New York, had absolutely nothing in common with Eve. She was a loud, vapid blonde who lunched incessantly when she wasn't sitting on charity committees. After being exposed to her for half an hour, Holly realized that Ida couldn't give a stuff about the theatre, and only trailed around after Eve because she was a celebrity.

Justin's existence was just as difficult to understand. He was a pouting, posy queen with one of those affected camp voices that made Holly's hackles rise. His job on a New York paper gave him access to all the dirtiest gossip in town, which he repeated with relish. No one was immune from Justin; he slandered everyone he knew.

One day, when she had her mother to herself, Holly asked why she gave him house room. It nearly caused their first falling out.

'Justin is very dear to me,' Eve told her sternly, 'because he doesn't play games the way most men would. If I want him to escort me to a matinée or a benefit, he'll drop everything at five minutes' notice and be there.'

'Of course he does,' Holly said. 'Justin's a showbiz journalist. It's his job to be at the centre of things.'

But Eve wouldn't see the truth about him, and she forbade her daughter to discuss him again. Justin was a necessary part of Eve's life and that was the end of it.

Holly marvelled at the way her mother had changed. In the old days she wouldn't have been seen dead with either of these characters. But in the old days there were always boyfriends to fill the gap in her social life.

Holly wondered if Eve was losing her touch. Then she thought, no, the most likely thing was that Eve was having one of her secret affairs with somebody famous and rich and very married, and she was just using Ida and Justin to act as covers for her.

The idea that Eve was up to something intrigued Holly. She knew she had to find out what was going on, but how? Her mother was hardly likely to confess to a secret lover. They didn't have those kinds of conversations.

No, the only way Holly could catch her out was by snooping. She had to go through her private drawers, her letters, her underwear. Then she'd know her mother's secrets.

Her chance came when Eve announced she was going to spend the day in the beauty parlour. From breakfast time to after tea, she was going to put herself in the hands of the hairdresser, the masseur and the beautician.

'If you want,' she told Holly, 'you can come along and do the same. Or you can stay in the apartment.'

Holly opted to stay where she was. It was the perfect opportunity to find out the identity of the mystery man.

She felt no guilt about what she was about to do, for she had been snooping on her mother ever since her childhood. It started the day Eve missed her ninth birthday. Mummy said she was too busy with her play. And Holly had believed her until she turned on the television and saw her chatting to Prince Charles at a polo match.

After that she hadn't believed a word Eve had told her. She started checking up on her, going through Eve's diaries when she was out of the house, and though most of it was pretty boring stuff about the theatre, there were one or two things that caught Holly's attention.

Eve was always interested in her leading men — not as actors, but as men. The diaries never went as far as describing an affair, but Holly knew her mother was capable of it. When the drama over Brett had happened, Holly hadn't really been surprised. She'd just wondered why her mother had taken so long to get round to it.

After Brett, Holly hadn't been able to snoop any more, but

187

then she didn't really have to. Now Mummy was becoming a big star in New York, her love affairs were pretty well covered by the press. She had a fling with a pop singer years younger than she was, which rather shocked Holly. Then there was a boring rich banker, which surprised her because the man was quite old.

After that she became hardened to what her mother did. She didn't actually care what Eve's lovers were like, but she did want to know about them. In a way she felt it was her right to know, which was why, half an hour after her mother had left for the beauty parlour, Holly was going through the guest room.

At first she didn't find very much. She knew her mother had visitors, but the maid must have been very carefully briefed to clear up after them, for there was no trace of any of them.

Holly was about to give up when she noticed a cupboard tucked into the corner of the room. It was easy to miss, for it was made of the same dark wood as all the other cupboards, but this one was locked.

She knew without a doubt all the answers to her questions lay behind its doors, but where was the key?

Holly racked her brains, dredging up her mother's habits and little rituals. Then she remembered: all Mummy's really important belongings were kept in a little glass dish on her dressing table.

She hurried through to Eve's room, hoping her mother hadn't changed her routine. She hadn't. The same little glass dish she had had on her London dressing table was here in New York.

Holly recognized the diamond earrings her mother never seemed to get round to putting in the safe. There was her favourite lipstick and the ballpoint pen she always used, which had been stolen from some hotel. And there were a collection of keys. Holly took them through to the guest room and tried all of them before she found the one she was looking for.

When the right key fitted smoothly into the lock and

released the cupboard door Holly felt a sense of victory. No matter how hard she tried, her mother couldn't keep anything secret from her.

With growing excitement, Holly started to riffle through the suits she found hanging inside. There were three of them and on a separate hanger there was a whole selection of ties. She went for the ties first. You could tell a lot about a man from his ties.

The first thing Holly discovered was they were English ties. There was a Royal Solent Yacht Club tie, a Garrick tie and one that belonged to an old Etonian. She recognized them because her father had exactly the same ones.

Obviously her mother's new boyfriend couldn't be American. No American she'd ever heard of belonged to two English clubs and had been to Eton. No, the man was some kind of English toff.

She wondered if his suits lived up to the image. Very carefully she eased the jackets off their hangers and lay them on the bed. They had Savile Row written all over them and must have cost a fortune. She picked one up to see if the name of the tailor was stitched just above the inside breast pocket.

It was. What was even more of a coincidence was that the firm was the same one Daddy went to. Mummy's new boyfriend belonged to the same clubs as her father, he had gone to the same public school, and he even used the same tailor in Savile Row.

All of the sudden Holly felt an idiot. It can't be, she thought. Their relationship is strictly business.

Then she remembered how much Eve knew about Linda, and she started to get excited.

Daddy's confiding in her again, Holly thought, the way he used to.

She knew now she was on to something. Her hands were shaking when she took hold of the jacket nearest to her. There had to be something, some clue that would give proof to her suspicions. She went through the pockets and when she found nothing, she grabbed hold of another jacket.

She found what she was looking for in the third. Nestling

in the inside pocket of a Prince of Wales check suit was a lighter her father used. He had half a dozen of them, all with his initials engraved on the bottom.

So it's true, Holly thought. Mummy and Daddy are finally getting together again.

She wondered how long it had been going on. Had Jason been staying here for months or was it years? And why on earth did neither of them say anything about it? They had to know how delighted she'd be about the whole thing.

Then she remembered Linda, the praying mantis. It was obvious Daddy didn't want to hurt her feelings. Holly could understand that. Once upon a time, she had liked Linda — more than liked her, she'd admired her and looked up to her. If Linda hadn't made such a dead set at Jason, they might still be close, but that wasn't possible now.

All Holly could hope was that Daddy let her down as lightly as possible. That way the presenter wouldn't be on her conscience when her parents made it the second time round.

27

Holly decided to have the whole thing out with her mother. It was the only course she could take, the only way she could really find out what was going on. She was having a tough time working out how to go about it. If she told Eve she had found a closet full of her father's suits, how was she going to explain what she was doing going through the closet, particularly when her mother had so carefully locked it.

'I was just checking up on you, Mummy,' she could hear herself say, 'and guess what I found.'

No, that wouldn't do at all. She decided on a different approach. When she and Eve were alone together, Holly brought up Jason's name. They had been talking about something that happened in her childhood, and Eve had been perfectly happy to reminisce with her.

When Holly thought her mother was totally at ease talking about her father, she started to bring things up to date. As casually as she could, she enquired how often her father saw Eve when he was visiting the city.

'Why do you ask?' Eve said.

Holly started to feel foolish. 'I was just curious,' she said. 'You told me you and Daddy were friends again. I wanted to know how friendly.'

A shadow passed across her mother's eyes, making her look blank and slightly irritated.

'I don't think that's any of your business,' she said, bringing the discussion to a close.

After that Eve wouldn't be drawn into any more conversations about Jason. It was as if the entire subject was forbidden territory, and Holly felt utterly frustrated.

If she hadn't insisted on being taken to Zabar's deli, things might have turned out differently. She might have got round to quizzing her mother about the suits in the locked closet. She might have persuaded her to explain what was going on.

Only she did go to Zabar's, and what she found there distracted her so completely that all thoughts of her mother's secret life flew out of her mind.

They were standing in line at the main counter when Holly spotted him.

He was wearing faded jeans and a baggy sweatshirt, and his blond hair was dirty and slicked back. But she would have recognized him anywhere.

'Mummy,' she said, 'isn't that Brett Weston?'

Eve looked slightly shaken. Then she peered myopically across the store.

'It can't be,' she said. 'He's in California these days taping a series.'

Holly felt impatient with her mother. She knew Brett Weston was taping in California – the whole world knew. *The Silent Detective* was one of the top rated shows both sides of the Atlantic. But the fact remained that right at that moment, Brett wasn't in LA. He was standing by the smoked fish counter in Zabar's and if Eve didn't pick up on the fact, then Holly would have lost her chance to meet him.

'Mummy,' she said urgently, 'Brett Weston is my ultimate hero and he's standing ten yards away. I'm absolutely positive about it.'

Eve sighed. 'I suppose you want to go over and say hello.'

Her daughter looked at her, suddenly realizing what she was asking. 'Not if it's going to be difficult for you.'

She saw her mother pull herself together, assuming her public persona the way other people shrug on a shirt.

'Of course it's not going to be difficult,' Eve said crossly. 'Whatever happened with Brett was years ago. It's all gone and forgotten now.'

192

Before Holly could say anything else, Eve had her by the hand and was marching her across the store.

Holly started to panic. When Eve was in this kind of mood, anything could happen. All I need, she thought, is a drama in the middle of a delicatessen.

She needn't have worried. Brett and Eve were clearly used to playing this kind of scene, for the instant they saw each other, they fell into each other's arms with loud cries of surprise and delight.

'Eve, darling,' Brett said, 'what on earth are you doing here?'

Holly saw her mother screw her face into a kittenish pout.

'I'm showing my daughter the sights of New York.'

He made an exaggerated gesture, as if he was on stage and needed to tell the audience he had just remembered something.

'I showed you Zabar's once,' he said. 'And Joe Allen and the Russian Tea Room . . .'

'And the Bowery and every off-Broadway show playing in New York,' Eve chimed in.

Holly watched her mother going through her auld lang syne routine and decided she didn't like her very much. Eve and Brett were replaying their sordid little affair as if it were a musical comedy. It was disgusting. Holly decided to get the hell out before she threw up on the spot.

'Come on, Mummy,' she said. 'We've got shopping to do.'

Brett regarded her as if she had just swum into his vision.

'Don't disappear,' he said. 'I haven't even met you yet.'

If he had been anyone else, Holly would have come back with some smartarsed remark and walked away, but the actor had a curious effect on her.

It was as if her whole body had decomposed into a kind of jelly which she had no control over any more. She stifled the urge to throw herself at his feet. Instead she extended her hand.

'I'm Holly,' she said. 'I'm visiting for the summer.'

He caught her hand in both of his, turned it over and deposited a kiss on the palm.

She felt herself blushing. Then she saw her mother staring at her and she wished the ground would open and swallow her whole.

'Do you always behave this way with other people's children?' Eve asked caustically.

Brett smiled like a Cheshire cat. 'Not really,' he said in the husky, languid voice that was famous across two continents. 'I only flirt with the pretty ones.'

Eve decided it was time to change the subject.

'Darling,' she said, 'you still haven't told me what you're doing in town. I thought you were confined to the coast.'

'Only when I'm taping the series,' he told her. 'I get time off in between, when I try to tuck in a little theatre. I don't do anything as grand as Broadway,' he added quickly. 'What I like to do is fringe.'

Eve remembered something she had seen in the evening paper. 'You're opening on Monday in that Russian thing, aren't you?'

He nodded. 'Why don't you come along and see it, if you're not doing anything else?' He looked across at Holly. 'Why don't you both come?'

If Eve picked up on the electricity that was passing between them, she kept it to herself. Instead, she fished in her handbag for her diary.

'The date looks clear,' she said, flicking over the pages. 'I take it we can pick up the tickets at the box office? There is a box office, isn't there?'

He gave her an old-fashioned look. 'It might be fringe,' he said, 'but we're not complete amateurs. Of course there's a bloody box office.'

Eve snapped the diary closed and returned it to her bag.

'Then we'll be there,' she said. 'Both of us.'

Holly wanted to know all about Brett Weston — how her mother met him, what kind of man he was, why Eve had been attracted to him.

Eve co-operated, but only up to a point. She told her daughter everything she wanted to know, but she coloured her account so that Brett came out of it badly.

She had seen the way Holly was looking at him in Zabar's and it bothered her. There's no way I want her to get involved with the likes of Brett, she thought. I'm going to have to destroy him, before he destroys her.

She started her character assassination by taking Brett's acting apart. He was selfish on stage, she told her daughter. All the rest of the cast had to compensate for him and carry him.

Holly found this difficult to believe. 'If Brett was so awful,' she said, 'how come he's an international star?'

Eve looked scornful. 'What's he an international star in?' she demanded. 'Some television soap. You don't have to be all that good for the small screen. All you have to do is look good, and Brett can do that all right.'

'But I've watched him,' Holly protested. 'He's good. He really can act.'

Eve prayed for patience. 'He only looks as if he can,' she said. 'That flawless performance you see is the result of hundreds of takes. On film you can botch it up umpteen times and the director just makes you do the scene again until you get it right. Brett isn't a good actor, he's a lucky one, that's all.'

When she was satisfied her daughter believed her, Eve got more personal. Her memory of Brett was of a randy young actor who had used everything he had to rescue her performance, but she didn't present him like that. For Holly really to hate him, Brett had to be a lady-killer, so she painted a portrait of a sexual junkie — insatiable, ruthless and dangerous.

Eve watched her daughter's face as she trashed Brett's reputation, but what she saw there confused her. The girl didn't look shocked, or even mildly upset at some of the stories her mother was telling. Instead she was spellbound.

I'm exciting the hell out of her, Eve realized. She sees him as a huge, sexy challenge. I'd have been better off to tell her the truth, she thought mournfully. At least there might have been a chance she wouldn't be turned on by it.

For Brett's opening night, Eve decided there would be safety in numbers. Justin, Ida and Ida's husband were summoned. Eve organized a restaurant directly after the show, so there would be no excuse to linger in Brett's dressing room. Then, just as she was starting to relax about the evening, the unthinkable happened.

She woke up on the morning of the play with the mother and father of all headaches. The only way she could cope with it was to swallow the best part of a bottle of painkillers, and retire to bed with an icepack on her head.

Which was how Holly found her when she got back from a shopping trip that evening.

'Good God, Mummy,' she said, taking in the pale unmade-up face, 'what on earth's the matter?'

Eve took the icepack off her forehead and sat up in bed.

'It's a bloody migraine. I've been getting them ever since I came here.'

'So you won't be coming out tonight?'

There was disappointment in Holly's voice and Eve felt immediately guilty.

'Darling, I can't,' she said weakly. 'But you can still go. Maybe Justin will find a friend to take my seat.'

Holly contemplated the idea. If Justin's friends were anything like Justin, she would be spending the evening with the boys in the band. And Ida. There had to be a way out of it.

'I don't think any of your friends will be that keen to go without you,' Holly pointed out. 'It's only a fringe production, after all.'

Eve looked wary. 'So what are you suggesting?'

'I thought I might go on my own.' Holly put on her most innocent face as she said it, but it didn't fool her mother for one second.

She wants to go on making eyes at Brett, Eve thought. Over my dead body.

'I can't allow you out without an escort,' she told her. 'The city's too dangerous at night.' She saw her daughter's face and relented slightly. 'I'll tell you what,' she said. 'I'll put Ida off. Then all you have to deal with is Justin. That won't be too difficult for you, will it?'

It will be a nightmare, Holly thought, but she didn't say it. Her mother didn't look as though she could cope with a serious disagreement.

'Justin's no problem,' she lied. 'We'll have a great time.'

197

28

The theatre in Greenwich Village had once been a cinema and still looked like one. There was something brassy and down-at-heel about it and Holly half expected to see Brett sharing the bill with Tom and Jerry.

As she and Justin walked into the lobby, the girl made a quick inventory of the crowd. There was nothing brassy about them.

As well as the usual bearded intellectuals and their blue-jeaned girlfriends, there was a generous sprinkling of café society. She spotted a couple of Hollywood actresses, a well-known agent her mother had once introduced her to, and a group of Wall Street types.

She turned to her companion. 'I see the Park Avenue crowd are out in force tonight.'

The journalist shrugged. 'It's to be expected. There's always a shiver of excitement when a well-known television face has a go at something serious. And they don't come more serious than *Mother Russia*.'

Holly was curious now. 'Tell me about it.'

While they waited their turn at the box office, Justin did his best. *Mother Russia* was an attack on the communist regime. It was passionate, it was wordy and they were both going to have a tough time making sense of it.

'Why on earth is Brett doing it? There must be easier things,' said Holly.

Justin looked smug. 'Sure there are easier things, but they don't have a role that allows the leading actor to hog the stage

198

for nearly two hours. This is Brett's big chance to remind the world that he might earn his bucks from television, but underneath the plastic exterior, there's a serious actor bursting to get out.'

Holly remembered what her mother had told her about Brett's acting ability.

'I didn't know he was any good in the theatre.'

Now Justin looked really surprised. 'Brett Weston played Broadway for years before he sold out to the networks. He may not be Tony Hopkins, but he's competent. Whatever gave you the idea he couldn't hack it?'

Holly shrugged. 'It was just a bit of back-stage gossip I heard. There's probably nothing in it.'

When they got their tickets, Justin suggested they go straight in and claim their seats. Being fringe, it was first come, first served, and he didn't want to risk being shoved into the back row.

Holly didn't object. The fewer people who saw her with Justin, the better, she thought, for he was a sight for sore eyes. He had somehow got hold of the idea that going to the Village to see a play was slumming, and had dressed appropriately in threadbare jeans and a black leather rocker's jacket. A younger man might have looked stylish in the clothes. Justin merely succeeded in looking as if he were wearing fancy dress. He should have stuck with Brooks Brothers, Holly thought. I could have put up with him coming on like a preppy queen, but this is seriously weird.

She cursed her mother for landing her with this impediment. How could she go backstage with Justin? How could she go within ten miles of Brett? She stared hard at the make-shift stage and just for a moment she felt totally desolate. She was under the same roof as a man she privately worshipped – she would probably spend the best part of the next two hours just yards away from him – yet that was as close as she was going to get unless she could get rid of Justin.

She made her mind up. By the end of the evening, she promised herself, I'll be out from under.

The play was as terrible as she knew it would be. If anyone

but Brett had been in it, she would have fallen asleep by the middle of the first act.

As it was, she couldn't take her eyes off the stage, for the actor mesmerized her. Justin had been right about Brett's hogging most of the action. The play *was* him, and that's what saved it.

Brett Weston was quite simply magnificent. Every step he took, every speech he made, was nothing short of masterful and Holly realized her mother had been having her on about him. She wondered why Eve needed to say those things.

Holly glanced at her watch and saw the curtain would come down in the next ten minutes. Damn, she thought. What am I going to do about Justin? How am I going to dump him?

When it came to her, the solution was so simple, she wondered why she hadn't thought of it before. After the curtain came down and the audience were all queuing to get out, she would turn to her unwanted escort and say she had to go to the loo. Then she would disappear into the crowd, and while no one was looking, she would slip backstage. After that she had no idea of what would happen, but it didn't matter. At least she would be over the first hurdle.

Her plan worked perfectly. As soon as she made her excuse, Justin told her he would see her in the lobby – and Holly scampered through the exit sign vowing she would never set eyes on him again.

Backstage was tatty, dirtier and more run-down than any of the theatres her mother had ever played in. Holly wasn't bothered by it. She had been working behind the scenes for nearly two years now and she was used to seeing the downside.

If anything worried her, it was getting in to see Brett. This was his first night, after all. He would be surrounded by management and well-wishers. Who knows, in the excitement of it all, he might not even remember who she was.

For a moment, Holly hesitated. It was all very well chasing after one of Mummy's old boyfriends, but she didn't want to make a fool of herself. Then she remembered how she'd got rid of Justin and all the agonizing that had gone into it.

I've come this far, she decided. I might as well go the whole distance.

Holly looked around her and found she was standing at the beginning of a long corridor. Peering down it, she saw that it branched into two at its far end and she guessed the dressing rooms would lie somewhere beyond that.

She was correct. As she approached the place where the corridor divided, she heard the sound of voices. Somewhere down here, a whole group of people was having a party.

She turned the corner and found herself slap-bang in the middle of it.

The Park Avenue crowd Holly had seen earlier were all there guzzling champagne. And to the right of where she was standing she saw a huddle of people lined up outside a door. It was Brett's dressing room, she knew it instinctively, and she made for the door knowing the crowd would sweep her through it.

It took ten minutes to get right inside, but once she was there the crowd thinned. Somebody who could have been a dresser was making sure that every visitor got a drink and the statutory few seconds with the great man.

When it was Holly's turn, she was grabbed by the wrist and gently pushed in the direction of a big easy chair where Brett was holding court.

She was pleased to see he had taken off his make-up. Only egotists wore it to the first night party. He looked as if he had taken a shower as well, for he was in a towelling robe.

Holly offered her hand. 'Remember me?' she said. 'We met a couple of days ago in a delicatessen.'

For an instant Brett did nothing. Then he leaned forward and took her hand in both of his, turning the palm upwards. Then he kissed it the way he had done the first time they met. Holly's heart stood still.

'So you did remember,' she said weakly.

The actor threw his head back and roared with laughter.

'No,' he replied, 'I always get fresh with girls I don't know.' He pulled her towards him. 'I was wondering if you were going to turn up. I had a suspicion Eve might call things off at the last moment and I'd never see you again.'

Holly was light-headed with relief.

'Mummy did call things off,' she admitted, 'but she let me come on my own.'

'That was big of her.'

The girl wondered whether to level about Justin. If she wasn't careful they could just bump into him.

'Actually,' Holly said, 'I'm not exactly on my own. Mummy provided me with an escort.'

Brett was intrigued. 'Where is he?'

She told him how she had given Justin the slip. She very nearly confessed what a nerd he was, but she decided there was no need to put herself down completely.

'Well,' said Brett, 'now you're on the loose, how about coming on to supper. A group of us have got a table at Joe Allen. We won't have much of a chance to talk, but it could be fun.'

Holly looked at him, noticing for the first time he had freckles and gold flecks in his eyes. She liked that. She liked the way his hair grew long and straggly over his collar. She liked the faint musky, masculine smell he exuded.

The only thing she didn't like was the fact that he had once belonged to her mother. I guess I can work that one out, she thought lazily. I've got a whole evening to do it in.

When Holly was a little girl and her parents were still together, they used to take her to Joe Allen whenever they visited New York. It was the sort of casual hamburger place you took kids to, and if you were in the theatre there was a double plus because the restaurant was a hang-out for actors.

All the posters for the new shows were plastered across the red brick walls, and it always turned out that your particular waiter was a dancer or an actor who was temporarily at liberty.

The minute Holly pushed her way into the crowded room, she realized the place hadn't changed at all. Everything was exactly as she remembered it except for one thing: she was different.

Before, when she'd come here, she'd been an extension of her famous mother. Tonight nobody but Brett knew who she was, and he wasn't telling.

As far as the producer, the director and the cast of *Mother Russia* were concerned, Holly was a television researcher on vacation.

She'd told Brett about her job in the cab coming over to the restaurant and it had impressed him.

'So you are real after all,' he had observed.

She was annoyed. 'What did you think I was? I figment of your imagination?'

He put his arm around her. 'Don't be silly,' he said. Then he looked serious. 'If you want me to be honest, my first impression of you was that you were some rich brat living off your parents' success. Now I know that's not true, I'm rather relieved.'

It was a long, slightly drunken evening with everyone telling their own personal anecdotes about the theatre, and because she'd been through this sort of thing hundreds of times before, Holly knew exactly how to handle it. Everyone at the table was looking for applause – Brett most of all – so she supplied it. He had pleased her earlier on by acknowledging her as a woman in her own right. Now she hung on his every word, laughing at all the familiar punchlines as if she were hearing them for the first time, and he responded by moving closer to her, signalling to the rest of the table that she was his girl.

Just for a moment, Holly wondered if Brett had behaved this way with her mother. Had he sat with her in intimate little theatre restaurants acting as if he owned her, as if he had chosen her specially?

She needed to know. Very casually, she brought her mother's name into the conversation.

Brett didn't react. Instead he turned to the guy sitting on the other side of him and started to ask about the film he was shooting in the summer.

Holly bit her lip. Was Brett evading her? Or was he genuinely curious about the film? When she had his attention, she tried it again, only this time she was more direct.

'You used to come here with Mummy, didn't you?' she said.

For the first time that evening, Brett looked irritated. 'What is it with you and your mother?' he demanded. 'I thought you wanted to get away from her. The way you're carrying on, she might as well be sitting across the table from us.'

If she'd had any sense, Holly would have backed off there and then, but she couldn't. Eve's shadow still lay between them and it made her nervous.

'Look,' she said, 'I'll never talk about it again, but I have to get this out of my system. I need to know if it was serious with Mummy.'

He leaned towards her and for a moment she was frightened he would hit her. Then he relaxed.

'Why is it so important to know about what happened in the past? Eve and I have been history for years. I've been married and divorced since I last saw her.' He picked a stray hair out of Holly's eyes. 'There's nothing as dead as an old love affair,' he told her. 'If you hadn't been there in Zabar's the other day, Eve and I would have waved at each other and gone our separate ways. I probably wouldn't even have asked her to my first night.'

Holly started to feel better. She didn't have to feel guilty about being here any more. Mummy wasn't the threat she thought she was.

Holly asked him about his origins and how he got into the business, and she realized she was finally on the right track with him. Brett loved talking about his success. It was a trait she had seen in other actors, and she picked up a glass of wine and settled back in her seat. This could take some time, she thought, but I'm not going anywhere.

He started out by telling her how he grew up surrounded by a family who loved the movies, worked in them and wanted him to follow in their tradition. So he went to stage school the way they wanted him to, then started looking for a job.

'Reality hit me then,' he grinned. 'There were hundreds of kids just like me hanging around the studios and the agents' offices. I couldn't get arrested, much less get a job of work.'

Holly had heard the joke before, but she smiled to show she was paying attention.

Brett looked at the eager young woman sitting beside him and remembered telling the same story to her mother – except this wasn't going to be the same story. He'd lived down his nude modelling days. Over the years most people had forgotten that time had ever existed. What they knew about Brett was what they read in the fan magazines and that was the version of his life he decided to tell Holly tonight: he'd been a fringe theatre actor, touring America in obscure productions before finally making it to Broadway.

'Appearing with your mother put me on the map,' he told Holly. 'I didn't have to hang around with the second division any more. I was in a hit, so I could take my pick of the agents. I signed with one of the biggest almost immediately and never looked back.'

Holly looked dubious. 'It sounds to me as if you used Mummy.'

'How come?'

'Mummy was the star of that show. None of the critics really noticed anyone else. It wasn't until you and Mummy had that affair that the newspapers were full of you.'

Brett smiled, remembering how Eve couldn't function until he started sleeping with her.

'Let's say we both used each other,' he said.

She was about to press him for details when she remembered how irritated he'd been the last time she started probing, so she shut up and looked miserable.

Her attitude wasn't lost on Brett, who reached over and took her hand in his.

'I'm going to promise you something,' he told her. 'I'm going to swear right here and now that whatever happens between us, I'll never use you. You're not an actress and you're not your mother.'

Holly looked as if she might throw herself into his arms in front of the entire restaurant. And Brett congratulated himself for talking his way out of a tight spot.

If he went on the way he was going, he might even convince the girl he was some kind of hero.

29

Justin rang at ten thirty to say that Holly had gone missing. At first Eve didn't believe him.

'What do you mean she's gone missing?' she demanded. 'She can't have disappeared into thin air.'

Justin, who was standing in a bar where the television news was on full blast, began to feel desperate. He was never going to be able to explain himself on the phone. Yet the prospect of facing an irate Eve at this time of night was not one he relished.

'Holly went to the loo,' he said, doing his best to sound calm, 'and after that I didn't see her again.'

Eve went very quiet and for a moment Justin wondered if she was still there. Then she came back in force.

'Either I come down to the theatre,' she told him, 'which means getting out of bed, or you come up to me and we sort the whole thing out.'

The journalist realized he didn't really have much choice. He knew Eve well enough to know she would never get out of bed once she was settled, so he sighed and told her to expect him in twenty minutes.

When he finally got to the apartment, Eve was looking like the wrath of God. She answered the door in a terry towelling robe and Justin noticed she hadn't bothered to put on any make-up.

She might have done something with herself, he thought, looking at the grey, slightly mottled complexion. The poor cow looks nearly a hundred.

He did his best not to stare too hard as she led the way into the main drawing room. Then he relaxed. Eve had turned the lights down low so that the whole room was illuminated with the glow of the skyline coming through the picture window. She had effectively upstaged herself with the panorama of New York, and Justin smiled to himself. How clever of her, he thought. By the time I go home, I will have quite forgotten how ghastly she looks.

He turned his attention to the table in front of the long leather sofa. Eve had set it up with coffee and little snacks that looked as if they had been hastily sent round from the nearest deli. He sat down and helped himself to a Danish. Then because he couldn't avoid it any longer, he addressed himself to the problem of Holly.

After she had disappeared, he told Eve, he had searched the theatre. Not only that, he had questioned the box office staff and the programme sellers, but nobody could tell him anything. There had been no sight of a lone teenager wandering around the auditorium. And in the end he had gone in search of a phone and called Eve.

While Justin was telling his story, Eve's mind went down a different track. Girls don't get abducted from fringe theatres, she reasoned. I bet my daughter deliberately gave Justin the slip and sneaked backstage.

'Did you try going round the dressing rooms?' she asked.

'I didn't see any point. Holly doesn't know anyone in the cast.'

Eve started to hear alarm bells. 'She knows Brett,' she said.

'No, she doesn't. Brett's your friend. Holly went to some lengths to point that one out.'

I bet she did, Eve thought. She didn't want you spoiling her plans by letting on that Brett had more or less invited her to this first night.

Eve got up and poured herself some coffee. Then she settled back in her chair and started to think aloud.

'If Holly had gone backstage,' she said, 'she would have seen Brett. And if things went the way they seemed to be going when they met last week, he would probably have asked her to join him for dinner—'

Justin interrupted her. 'If you're right, she could be anywhere.'

'Not true,' Eve said. 'Brett would go to one of his favourite spots. My guess is that they're either in a little Italian joint on the West Side, or Charley O's, or Joe Allen. If one of us went round those places, we'd be bound to bump into her.'

Justin wasn't fooled by the royal 'we'. What she's angling for, he thought, is for me to trail round Manhattan in search of Holly.

He glanced at his watch. 'It's gone eleven,' he said. 'It's been a long day and I'm wiped out.'

'So you don't want to help me find her?'

Justin sighed. He'd wasted his evening in unfashionable theatre squiring Eve's brat. As far as he was concerned he'd done enough.

'If your daughter's having fun at a party,' he said, 'she's not going to appreciate me or anyone else dragging her off home. Why don't we give it a bit longer and let her turn up in her own time?'

There was sense in what he said – Eve could see that – but at the back of her mind there was a nagging fear. What if Brett asked Holly to come back with him to his apartment? Would she let him lead her there? Would she allow him to seduce her? Brett could be very persuasive when he wanted to. She frowned, remembering just how persuasive.

'I'll give it another hour,' she told Justin. 'Then I'm going looking for her.'

Holly came home at just after midnight. She had planned to go straight to her room, where she would sit in glorious isolation and go over the evening. She was half-way down the hall when she heard voices coming from the main room. Her mother was with someone – a man. Before Holly could work out who he was, Eve's voice came echoing after her.

'Holly,' she called, 'is that you?'

209

Who the hell else would it be, the girl wondered. Aloud she said, 'Yes, Mummy. I'm coming.'

There was nothing for it, she was going to have to brazen this one out. Going up in the elevator she had concocted a story about how she had been parted from Justin by the crowd surging out of the theatre. Just how she had run into Brett and ended up in Joe Allen, Holly couldn't quite work out, but she was sure something would come to her.

Then she walked into the sitting room and saw Justin. It's not going to work, she thought. He's got to Mummy with his story first.

For a moment she considered running out of the room and finding somewhere to hide. Then she thought, I can't do that. I'm not a little girl any more.

She squared her shoulders.

'Sorry I'm late,' she said. 'I was having dinner with Brett.'

She saw a look pass between Justin and Eve. I'm not telling them anything they don't know, she thought, and the realization gave her courage.

'I guess you must be ticked off with me,' she said, looking across at Justin. 'It wasn't very nice, standing you up like that.'

'Not very nice is playing it down a bit,' the journalist sulked. 'Have you any idea what it was like standing around in the lobby like a spare part?'

He was still in the ridiculous black leather biker's jacket, so Holly had every idea, but she decided to skip over it.

'I had to see Brett,' she told him. 'And I wanted to do it alone. You must understand—'

Her mother cut into the conversation then. 'I think we all understand what you were up to,' she said. 'You were doing a good job of making yourself cheap.'

In the silence that followed, Justin stood up. These two were going to be at each other's throats all night – he could see all the signs. The best thing he could so was to get out of the apartment before they came to blows. He made his farewells, blowing kisses across the room to Eve.

'I've got an early start in the morning,' he said. 'I can see myself out.'

The moment Justin was out of the door, Holly turned to her mother. Eve was good and mad, but Holly had expected that. There was no way she could waltz off with Eve's ex-lover and not get a hard time.

'I suppose you'd better tell me what's bugging you,' she said. 'Brett isn't exactly your property any more.'

Eve regarded her daughter in her tight Lycra leggings and high boots. 'Are you saying you've made a takeover bid?'

Holly steeled herself. 'Sort of.'

'So you don't care about Brett's reputation or the fact he could hurt you?'

Holly wondered whether her mother would ever stop trashing her ex-lover.

'He's not as bad as you say he is,' she insisted. 'We spent a long time getting to know each other tonight and he didn't hide anything from me. When I asked him about you, he admitted you used each other.'

'Was he equally straight about his murky past?'

'What murky past?'

Eve looked savage. 'You mean Brett didn't tell you about his days as a nude model? He was quite an attraction in the soft porn magazines.'

Holly's legs felt wobbly and she grabbed hold of the sofa for support.

'He told me he was a fringe actor,' she said weakly.

'He told the same story to all the fan magazines,' Eve said. 'His publicist dreamed it up to make him look like a nice guy.'

Holly saw the triumph in her mother's face and felt queasy. Eve had deliberately set out to destroy Brett, to rip him to pieces, and she would have got away with it if Holly hadn't known better. But she'd been on to Mummy right from the start, even before she'd seen Brett on stage.

Eve had been too nasty about him, too over the top — almost as if he was an enemy instead of a guy she'd once had a convenient affair with.

211

'I don't give a damn what you say about Brett,' she said. 'I'm going to go on seeing him.'

Eve stared at her daughter long and hard. 'Not as long as you live here, you're not.'

30

Brett rang three days later when Eve was out.

'What would you have done if Mummy had answered the phone?' Holly asked him.

The actor laughed. 'I would have been my usual charming self and given her hell for not turning up at my opening night. She would have been so distracted, it wouldn't have crossed her mind I was calling to speak to you.'

'But how would we have spoken?'

'Give it a rest, Holly. We *are* speaking. Stop inventing problems that don't exist.'

They made a date for the following night. Holly was to meet Brett at the theatre after the show, then they would go somewhere quiet for dinner. All she had to do was find a way of concealing it from her mother.

As soon as Eve got back, Holly told her there had been a call from an Arnold Rubinstein.

'He's a friend of Daddy's I promised I'd look up when I was over here. He wants me to have dinner tomorrow night.'

Eve looked curious. 'Jason never mentioned anyone of that name to me.'

'I think he's more of a business contact than anything else,' Holly said quickly.

'Then I don't understand why you have to see him.'

Holly shrugged. 'Nor do I, but I said I would and now I can't get out of it.'

There was a pause.

'What does this Arnold Rubinstein do exactly?'

Now Holly was really in a corner. She wasn't practised in deception, so she hadn't thought the thing through.

'Arnold's a lawyer,' she said, grabbing at the first thing that crossed her mind. 'He and Daddy are working on some show together.'

'That's interesting. Does he live in the city?'

It was becoming more and more like an inquisition. She'll be asking for his address and telephone number next, Holly thought. She realized she'd have to make Arnold difficult to find.

'Actually I don't think he lives anywhere near here. He mentioned he had a place in Westchester, but I didn't get any details.'

Eve nodded. 'I don't expect you would,' she said. 'I suppose you'll be picking him up at his office.'

'I said I'd be at the Chrysler Building at the end of the day.'

This seemed to satisfy her mother, for she didn't ask any more questions.

When Holly got herself ready for dinner that night, she almost believed she was going to meet the fictitious lawyer she had created.

Brett had arranged to meet her in an Irish bar two blocks from the theatre. The curtain came down on the dot of nine and he fully expected to be there in twenty minutes.

He was true to his word. Holly had barely arrived when she saw Brett come striding through the door. She noticed his hair was still damp from the shower and there were traces of make-up which he had overlooked around his chin. He came up to the counter where she was standing and put his arm round her shoulders.

'What will you drink,' he asked, 'or have you already ordered something?'

She told him a glass of white wine was on its way and he smiled and organized himself a beer.

Then he talked about the play. It was an ordinary matey sort of conversation, the sort he might have with another member of the cast, and Holly felt relieved. She had geared

214

herself up for this date. She'd set so much store by this working out that the whole thing had got blown up in her mind. All the way over to the theatre she had been rehearsing what she was going to say to him, how she would impress him, and now they were actually together, there was no need for any of it. All she had to do was just be her natural self and go with the flow.

They stayed drinking and talking until past ten. Then Brett glanced at his watch and pulled a face.

'I'd no idea it was so late,' he said. 'You must be starving.'

Normally Holly would have agreed with him, but tonight, she didn't seem to care about eating. Left to her own devices she would have been quite happy to have spent all evening in the bar.

Then she thought: this is only my second date with Brett. If I look too relaxed, he'll think I'm moving in on him.

'I wouldn't say no to dinner,' she said, 'though we'll have to find a late-night place.'

Brett knew of any number of late-night places all within a dozen blocks. But he feigned ignorance.

'We could have a long search finding somewhere decent.' He looked at her face, trying to measure the extent of her trust. 'There is another option, of course.'

'What's that?'

'I could cook you a meal. It wouldn't be anything fancy, but if you're prepared to take pot luck I can guarantee you'll get fed.'

Holly suddenly felt happy. This evening was turning out better than she'd imagined.

'I'll go along with that,' she said.

Brett lived in a faceless black glass apartment block somewhere near the United Nations Plaza. It reminded Holly of the sort of hotel high-flying businessmen use and she asked Brett what made him choose to live there.

'I didn't chose it,' he told her. 'The girl who works for me at the studios made all the arrangements.'

They were standing waiting at the desk for the keys to the

apartment and Brett made a great show of looking around the bland pastel carpeted lobby as if he were seeing it for the first time.

'I guess it isn't very homely,' he said, 'but it's central and secure, and that counts for a lot in this city.' He grinned. 'If you want to see how I really live, you'll have to come out to the coast.'

All the way up in the elevator, Brett described the splendours of his house in Beverly Hills. There were three acres of garden containing a swimming pool, a tennis court and a hot tub. Inside he had his own private screening room and the top of the house had been turned into a games room with a full-sized pool table.

Holly started to feel uneasy. She could cope with the man she met in New York, the dedicated actor who liked Irish bars and Joe Allen, but the Hollywood Brett was another matter. She wondered if he changed in some subtle way when he arrived in Los Angeles. Did he metamorphose into some glossy playboy when the plane touched down at LAX?

It's none of my business, she thought. The guy had offered to cook her dinner, not ask for her hand in marriage.

As soon as they got into the apartment, Brett headed for the kitchen where he went in search of something to drink. Finally, after much rootling around, he produced a bottle of Californian Chardonnay, which he thrust into her hands along with a bottle opener.

'Get started on this,' he instructed, 'I'll organize the food.'

From what Holly could make out, Brett was cooking Italian style that night. There were great pans of pasta on the boil and Brett was chopping and frying and doing things with herbs that put her in mind of one of those cooks you see on television. It was as if he was acting the cook, rather than actually cooking, and Holly began to worry about the food. The pasta was going to be overdone by the time the sauce was ready. And the sauce itself looked suspect. Brett had added the contents of half a dozen jars to the pan and the result was an evil-smelling brew.

Holly started to feel slightly sick. If he expects me to eat this, she thought, he's going to be in for a disappointment.

To play for time, she poured them each another glass of wine.

'Why don't we go into the other room while this is cooking?' she suggested. 'It will take a while to finish.'

He took the hint, leading her out of the kitchen and down the hall. She had expected to be shown into a drawing room something like her mother's, all glass coffee tables and splashy abstract paintings. Only the room Brett was showing her into was nothing like that. It had a double bed, a television set and a walk-in wardrobe.

'I think we're in the wrong place,' she said, confused.

Brett laughed. 'That depends what you want to do with the rest of the evening.'

If Holly had been in her right mind, she would have told him to behave, but he looked into her eyes before she could say it and she was lost.

She was dressed in her usual jeans and jacket, and Brett reached out casually and eased the jacket off her shoulders.

Then slowly, as if it were the most natural thing to be happening, he started to undo the buttons of her blouse. They came apart surprisingly quickly, and she tensed, remembering she wasn't wearing a bra. It was then she expected him to make his move. The other men she had known went crazy when they saw her breasts, tearing her clothes off with a kind of desperation.

Only Brett kept his cool, studying her minutely as if he were about to paint her portrait. Then he went on undressing her and, when she was totally naked, he took hold of her and led her over to the bed.

'Lie down,' he said.

She did as he told her, feeling both aroused and faintly ridiculous. Then he leaned over and started to touch her.

He began at the base of her neck, moving his hands downwards until they were resting on her breasts. Then with great delicacy he took each nipple between his thumb and forefinger and brought it to life.

217

Holly felt the first strong stirrings of excitement, yet as she did, she realized something was wrong.

She and Brett were engaged in the most intimate of encounters, but he hadn't kissed her and he was still fully dressed.

He must have seen the question in her eyes, for he came closer. She closed her eyes, expecting to feel his mouth on hers. Instead he kissed her temples and her neck, her breasts, letting his mouth take over from his fingers, suckling each nipple until she thought the pleasure would drive her mad.

She arched her back, willing him to go further and, as if in reply, she felt his hands on her body again. This time they were bolder, passing quickly over the curve of her stomach until they reached her mound.

Her legs came apart then and she felt his fingers at her entrance, probing and exploring. At that moment, she knew she was ready for him. She looked into his eyes.

'Now,' she begged. 'Please, now.'

He still had his jeans on and her hands went to the fastening, opening and undoing until he was finally released.

Then she let her hunger do the rest, guiding him to the entrance between her legs and drawing him into her.

Her first orgasm happened very quickly. As did her second and her third. But Brett stayed the course, pushing into her slowly and purposefully as if he knew her final excitement was a long way away.

There were times that night when Holly thought she would die of love or exhaustion or both, for Brett was like a stallion. He knew every position, every intricacy in which two bodies could be engaged, and he took her through each one of them like an instructor.

Holly followed where he led, dimly wondering where all this was heading. Then from somewhere deep inside her she felt a new sensation.

It was like a fire slowly building its heat, making every part of her seem somehow more alive. She cried out to Brett, with passion and ecstasy and yearning, and he held her tight, responding with his own need.

They clung to each other for what seemed like an eternity.

Then she felt the beginnings of release. It came flooding through her and as she spent herself, she felt Brett's own release merging with hers. For an instant in time they were like one being. Then the moment passed and Holly returned to herself. Except she didn't entirely.

In the heat of their final coupling, she left something behind. A minute portion of her soul belonged to Brett now, and because of it, he could do with her exactly what he wanted.

She hoped he would show her some mercy.

31

Eve turned restlessly in bed, reaching out for the sleep that seemed to elude her. She had taken her pills expecting oblivion, but tonight they didn't seem to be working.

Damn Holly, she thought, finally sitting up and turning on the bedside lamp. Damn the mixed-up little monster. Until she deigns to put in an appearance, there's no way I'm going to get any rest at all.

She pushed aside the covers and struggled to her feet. Then she picked up the terry towelling robe from the chair, put it round her, and decided to make herself a pot of tea.

If a hot drink didn't calm her down, then at least it would give her something to do while she waited up for Holly. I'm turning into my mother, she thought. She used to sit up just like this when I went out on dates.

But she isn't on a date, Eve reminded herself. Holly is visiting some business acquaintance of Jason's. So why do I get the feeling she's on a date? And why isn't she home when it's way past midnight?

Eve went through to the kitchen, turned on the lights and picked up the kettle. Then when it was filled and heating, she watched it, waiting for it to boil.

I'm turning into a neurotic, she thought. Holly's probably sitting in some nightclub being bored to tears by an elderly lawyer.

Eve started to wonder about Arnold Rubinstein. If he lived in Westchester, what was he doing in the city at this hour? His last train would have gone ages ago.

Maybe, she rationalized, he has an apartment in Manhattan. A lot of hard-working businessmen do.

On impulse she went to find the New York telephone directory. Then she riffled through the pages until she got to the Rubinsteins.

There were hundreds of them. They went on for page after page. The As alone took up two columns. Eve had visions of herself calling all the A. Rubinsteins in the book, searching for an Arnold who worked as a theatrical attorney.

Then she had an idea. There was no need to waste precious hours ringing the whole of Manhattan. She could get hold of Arnold's wife in Westchester and get the number from her.

She glanced at her watch. It was twelve forty-five. What possible reason did she have to wake up some suburban housewife she didn't even know?

Then Eve thought about her daughter. What if she wasn't still having dinner with Arnold Rubinstein? What if the man had caught his last train home and Holly had been mugged or raped trying to reach the apartment? The thought of Holly lying bleeding and abandoned on some sidewalk propelled her into action. Mrs Rubinstein, whoever she was, was going to have to understand.

Eve ploughed through the Long Island directory, finding Westchester, then R. There wasn't a Rubinstein to be found.

It was at that moment that she realized she had been a fool. Of course there were no Rubinsteins in Westchester. Rubinstein was a Jewish name and Westchester was as Waspy as hell.

Eve wondered if Holly had made a mistake. Maybe Jason's friend didn't live in Westchester after all. Maybe she'd mixed it up with some other district.

A nagging, disloyal thought crept into her mind. Maybe Arnold Rubinstein didn't exist.

There I go again, Eve thought, the neurotic mother. But her mind wouldn't let go of her suspicions.

She'd consumed an entire pot of tea, and it seemed to have jolted her into some sort of hyperstate. She couldn't just sit and worry about her daughter any more, she had to do something about her worries.

She tried to remember where Arnold Rubinstein was supposed to work. Didn't Holly mention she was going to the Chrysler Building to meet him? She wondered how she could trace all the law firms that operated out of there. Then she thought, no, that's as silly as ringing all the Rubinsteins in the New York phone book.

There's only one sure way to solve this mystery, Eve decided. I'm going to have to talk to Jason.

She made a swift calculation and realized it would be early in the morning in London, just before breakfast. Well, at least she would be guaranteed to reach him.

Jason answered on the second ring, sounding sleepy and bad-tempered. Then he heard Eve's voice and seemed to pull himself together.

'Eve,' he said, 'what is it? What's the matter?'

She smiled inwardly. They had been divorced for years now, she was calling from another continent, yet he still managed to be able to read her mind.

She didn't waste time on small talk.

'It's Holly,' she said. 'I could have a problem with her.'

'What sort of problem?' he asked.

Eve started to feel silly. Her daughter had gone out to dinner and she wasn't back yet, that was all. When she told Jason that Holly was dining with Arnold Rubinstein he would probably roar with laughter and tell her not to be a goose. She decided to give him the opportunity.

'Holly's out with one of your old business friends,' she said. 'I'd like to know what kind of man he is.'

'Tell me his name.'

Eve hesitated for a moment. 'Arnold Rubinstein.'

When Jason spoke again there was a note of confusion in his voice. 'I don't know any Arnold Rubinstein.'

'You must do. He's a big New York attorney. Holly tells me you've been dealing with him for some time.'

There was another silence while Jason figured out what to say next.

'I think our daughter's having you on,' he said finally. 'The lawyers I use in the States are based in California, and none of them is called Rubinstein.'

Eve got off the phone as quickly as she could. This was her problem and she wasn't ready to share it with Jason yet.

So Holly lied, she thought. She wasn't seeing Arnold Rubinstein at all. She invented Arnold Rubinstein because she didn't want to admit what she was really doing tonight. So what's she up to? And who is buying her dinner?

The image of Brett flew straight into Eve's mind – randy, predatory Brett in his too-tight jeans. It can't be, she thought. If he'd called, Holly would have told me.

She knew she was fooling herself. After the ultimatum she'd given her daughter, Holly wasn't going to tell her anything any more.

32

Holly arrived back at her mother's apartment as dawn was breaking over New York City. If the situation had been different, or the man had been different, she would have felt frightened as she put her key in the door.

As it was, the prospect of facing her mother gave her no terrors at all. She had grown up last night, suddenly and joyfully, and today she was surer of herself than she had been in her whole life.

Eve could say nothing to dent this new-found confidence because none of her judgements meant anything any more. All her mother was was another woman with her own set of opinions and prejudices. Holly would give them a hearing — that was only fair — but she didn't have to take them to heart.

It was in this mood that Holly let herself in, marched down the hall and made her way into the kitchen. She hadn't expected to see Eve there — it was miles too early for her — yet there she was, sitting in her terry towelling robe looking like the grand inquisitor.

In the old days Holly would probably have stood there hanging her head while Eve made some sarcastic remark about her morals, but the old days were over and done with.

'I suppose,' said Holly, 'you want to know where I was last night.'

Eve pursed her lips and Holly noted it made her look about a hundred.

'As you are my daughter and you happen to be in my care right now, I don't think it's too much to ask.'

224

The girl sat down and helped herself to a piece of toast from the pile in front of her mother. She took her time covering it with low-calorie spread, while she worked out exactly what she was going to say. Finally she had it off pat.

'I wasn't with Arnold Rubinstein last night—' she told Eve.

Her mother cut in on her. 'I know that,' she said. 'I spoke to Jason last night.'

The toast was half-way to Holly's mouth. Now, instead of eating it, she put it right back on the plate.

'You mean you were checking up on me? Of all the low-down, suspicious—'

'Before you go off the deep end,' Eve said patiently, 'try to see it from my point of view. You'd gone out for the evening with somebody I'd never heard of. Then you didn't bother to come back all night. Of course I checked up on you. Any mother would.'

Some of Holly's confidence started to ebb away. She had come prepared for a fight, a gloves-off, screaming, shouting match, but it didn't seem to be going that way at all. Eve was doing a good imitation of Mother Theresa, so Holly decided to push things.

'Do you want to know where I really was last night?'

Eve felt her heart lurch. 'Of course I do,' she said.

She saw her daughter sit straighter in her chair as if she was preparing some kind of announcement. It took all Eve's strength not to put her hands over her ears.

'I was with Brett,' Holly said. 'We went to bed together and it was like nothing I have ever known.'

Eve pulled a face. 'Spare me the details. I do know what it's like.'

Holly leaned forward. 'No, you don't know what it's like,' she said. 'You've no idea what it's like. If you did you'd be pleased about Brett. You'd wish me well.'

Eve got up and went over to the window where she'd left a pack of cigarettes. It took the utmost concentration to get one out and light it without her hand shaking, but she managed it. Then she turned to her daughter.

'The way I see it,' she said slowly, 'you've spent all night fucking your brains out with some little playboy who should know better.' She took a deep drag on her cigarette. 'I can't stop you doing that,' she went on. 'You're a big girl now. But don't expect me to applaud every time you take it into your head to behave like a whore.'

Holly tensed. 'If I behaved like a whore last night, what does that make you? You slept with Brett as well.'

Eve held on to her temper. If she showed any emotion now, she would have lost this argument, and maybe her daughter as well. She smiled. 'Sure I slept with Brett. Everybody including your father and the divorce lawyer knows that. What they don't know is how long it took to seduce me. When I met this man you're so crazy about, I didn't lay down and beg for his favours. I played him along, gave him a run for his money, so when he finally nailed me, he was damn grateful for the opportunity.'

She paused, grinding her cigarette out in a saucer on the counter in front of her.

'If I have any quarrel with what you're doing, it's this: you've made it too easy for Brett. If the sex is as good as you say it is, he probably won't drop you immediately – you can count on a few more hot nights – but the next time you're in his bed, remember this. No man takes a pushover all that seriously.'

The girl suddenly felt very small and very alone. Only an hour ago she felt she could take on the whole world, starting with her mother. Now she knew it was an illusion. Eve was a bitch to end all bitches and Holly hadn't lived long enough or travelled far enough to master all her tricks.

Holly got up from where she was sitting, scraping the chair across the polished wooden floor.

'I hate you,' she said, turning on her heel. 'I hate you and I despise you and I wish you were dead.'

Then she got out of the room as fast as she could. There was no way she wanted her mother to see she was crying her eyes out.

*   *   *

Holly hardly slept for what remained of that night, and when she did manage to doze off, she would wake a few minutes later rigid with worry.

What if Mummy went round to see Brett and told him not to see her again? What if she rang Daddy and got her hauled back to England on the next plane? The tiny, nagging fears chased each other round her brain until she thought they would drive her mad.

Finally it was time to get up, and once she was on her feet with a strong cup of coffee inside her, Holly began to make sense of the situation. She'd already decided to apologize to her mother.

She wouldn't mean a word of it, of course, but it would clear the air and stop the war, and give her a little breathing space until she heard from Brett again.

Eve must have known what was on her mind, for she wasn't convinced at all that Holly was sorry.

'How do I know you won't do exactly the same thing the next time my back is turned?' she asked.

They were sitting in the kitchen eating breakfast. Holly felt a wave of misery wash over her. There was nothing she could say to her mother without getting into even deeper water, so in the end she fudged it.

'Give me a break,' she wailed. 'I didn't sleep at all after all those terrible things you said. My head feels like someone is drilling a hole in it.' She noticed a slight thaw in the atmosphere, so she went on playing the little girl. 'Would you be very cross if I didn't come shopping today? I don't think I could face it.'

As soon as the words were out of her mouth, Holly realized she was home and dry, for Eve suddenly looked very worried and started rushing around searching for painkillers.

Only when Holly had swallowed two paracetamol and wrapped herself in a blanket did she finally get left alone.

'I'll be out till four,' Eve told her. 'Are you sure you'll be able to manage?'

Holly said she'd try, and after a bit more fussing and strict instructions to get lunch sent in, Eve was finally on her way.

When her mother had left, Holly wandered aimlessly around the apartment. She turned on the television and flicked from channel to channel before she realized that nothing interested her in the slightest. She attempted to tidy her room, only to find the maid had got there before her. She even thought about washing her hair, and it was at that moment she realized she was trying to kill time.

What am I waiting for? she asked herself, but she knew the answer. She was waiting for Brett to come and rescue her.

Holly glanced at her watch and saw it was half past eleven. Brett might not call until the afternoon. He might not call until the evening. He might not call until the next day.

She started to feel frightened. What if he didn't call at all? Mummy would have been proven right then, and Holly would be faced with two more weeks in New York listening to her mother say 'I told you so'.

She couldn't bear it. If push came to shove, she'd rather go home early. She thought about calling her father in London – she even picked up the phone and started dialling the number. Then she stopped.

What am I doing, she thought, admitting defeat before I've given Brett a chance? I've been away from him a matter of hours, and already I'm behaving as if last night never even happened.

She suddenly realized she was being very silly. She didn't have to sit by the phone wondering if it was going to ring. She could take the initiative and call the man herself. He was her lover, after all, not some stranger she'd met at a party.

She did it before she could lose her nerve. To her relief, Brett answered on the second ring.

His voice was abrupt, as if he were in a hurry, so Holly said who she was as fast as she could and hoped he wouldn't put the phone down.

He didn't. Instead he sounded pleased it was her and said he was going to call.

'I had a couple of work things to sort out first,' he told her, 'but I was going to touch base around seven.'

'By then it could have been too late.'

'What do you mean it could have been too late?' There was an anxious note in his voice and it reassured her.

'I could have been on my way back to London.' She told him. 'I had a fight with my mother this morning and it's not too comfortable here any more.'

There was a brief silence, then Brett said, 'Where are you now?'

'I'm still in the apartment.'

'And your mother?'

'She's out for the day.'

'Then this is what you do. Throw some things into a bag and be ready to leave in half an hour.'

'What happens in half an hour?'

'I'll be on the doorstep.'

Holly hardly dared to breath. She'd fantasized about this, and now it was actually happening.

'Are you going to take me back with you then?'

He answered her with a roar of laughter. 'Well, I'm not going to take you to the airport, that's for sure.'

33

When she had first gone to Brett's apartment, Holly hadn't taken in much of it. She was, she reflected, there to be seduced so there was little point to a guided tour.

Now it was different. From the minute he turned up at her mother's place, Brett made it clear he was carrying her off into his life. So when she got to the United Nations Plaza, Holly made a careful note of her surroundings.

The block was as faceless as she remembered it – all neutral colours and doormen standing to attention, but she ignored all that. She wasn't going spend her time in the lobby. If things went as she hoped, she would be welcoming all Brett's friends to the penthouse on the fourteenth floor.

As she walked through the front door, she almost held her breath. This is my first real home, she thought, the first place where I'm totally in charge, with no Linda or mother or even Lola to tell me what to do.

Brett saw her slightly glazed expression and asked her if she felt quite well.

Holly turned round in the narrow hall and threw her arms about him.

'I feel brilliant,' she said. 'It's not every day Sir Galahad bears me off to his castle.'

The actor laughed. 'Allow me to show you around the estate,' he said, leading her into the main room.

Holly had expected something modern and sleek, something that befitted the star of a top-rated show, but what she saw surprised her.

It was a smallish space, dark and rather pokey, with a sofa and a couple of shabby armchairs grouped around a television set. She couldn't entertain here, she thought, unless the people Brett knew went in for TV dinners. She did her best to hide her disappointment.

'Let me look at the kitchen,' she demanded. 'I expect that's where I'll be spending my time.'

For a moment Brett seemed confused. 'I don't think so,' he told her. 'I always eat out when I'm in New York.'

'What about last night, when you brought me here?'

He smiled, remembering his attempts at Italian cooking.

'I was bent on impressing you,' he admitted. 'I wanted you to think I could toss off a little cordon bleu confection any time I wanted.' He made a face. 'It's a good thing we never got round to eating dinner. You'd have found me out in seconds.'

Holly resisted telling him she suspected he was a rotten cook all along. Instead she said: 'I think it's time you let me impress you. I'm not bad when you let me loose with a saucepan.'

Brett regarded Holly for a moment. She was a pretty thing if you liked them rounded and young. It would be the easiest thing in the world to give her carte blanche, to let her cook for him and look after him and generally spoil him rotten.

But he couldn't do it. He was going back to the coast in a couple of weeks and he needed to travel light.

'This apartment isn't a home,' he said, more sharply than he intended. 'And I don't want you turning it into one.'

Holly looked stunned. 'So what am I doing here? Why did you take me away from my mother's? I mean, what's the point?'

Brett counted to ten in his head. The problem with young girls, he thought, is they're all overdosed on romantic fiction. If I'm not careful she'll expect me to go down on one knee.

He took Holly firmly by the arm and led her through to the open-plan kitchen where she would never make a meal. Then before she could say anything, he started to explain himself.

'The moment I first saw you,' he told her, 'you knocked me out. You were so young and so fresh and so damn sexy that it was all I could do not to rush you straight back to my apartment and ravish you. And when I finally got round to ravishing you, it was so sensational, I never wanted to stop.'

Brett leaned towards her and stroked her cheek, smoothing out the fine down that seemed to cling to her skin like gossamer.

'None of this means I've fallen in love with you,' he said gently. 'I don't want to walk you down the aisle and give you babies. What I do want to do is spend time with you, know you better. Damn it, woman, I want to enjoy you.'

She regarded him, big-eyed and doubtful. 'You want something casual, no strings attached – a sort of series of one-night stands.'

If he had been honest, he would have gone along with her. A series of one-night stands was exactly what Brett had in mind, but he knew that if he admitted it, Holly would be out of the door in seconds. So he lied a little.

'I told you when we first met I wouldn't use you and I meant it. You've got to trust me.'

'I don't know,' she said, fighting back tears. 'I don't know anything any more.'

He went over to where she stood and gathered her in his arms. Then very lightly, very expertly he started to kiss her.

At first she didn't respond, as if making like a marble statue would convince him she didn't give a damn. But Brett knew her better than that. Without drawing away he started to unbutton the top of her shirt, dipping his hand into her bra, until he was cupping her breast. He put his tongue in her mouth then, and felt a long shiver of desire ripple through her.

She was his. So long as he took her to bed right now.

With any luck, he decided, Holly would be so carried away with the excitement of it all, she would forget to ask what happened next.

*　　*　　*

Holly's days fell into a kind of pattern. At seven thirty a man came in to shave Brett and barber his hair. Sometime in the middle of that the maid would arrive laden down with carrier bags containing breakfast. Then Brett would give her detailed instructions as to what he wanted and how she should prepare it. It turned out he was a health freak and would only touch certain foods. So if the maid couldn't find fresh fruit that morning, there would be one hell of a row and Brett would sulk and have herbal tea on its own.

After breakfast Ziv, the personal trainer, arrived. He was a beefy Israeli who travelled with his own set of weights, which he humped around in a huge canvas holdall. He was also, Holly suspected, something of a sadist, for he positively enjoyed the sight of Brett heaving and straining his way through the gruelling routine which looked as if it had been designed for an Olympic athlete.

The second day he came, he invited Holly to join in, but she ducked out, hastily inventing a bad back.

If Brett asks me to come to Hollywood, she decided, I'll do my damnedest to fit in. I'll enrol in a gym and eat wheatgerm till it comes out of my ears, but right now I'm still in New York, so I might as well make the most of it.

After Ziv had done his stuff, Brett liked to go through his post, usually with a girl from one of the secretarial agencies. Then it was time for lunch. Whatever else was going on, they always had it alone in one of the little neighbourhood restaurants. For both of them it was an oasis in the middle of the busy day and they used the time to catch up with each other.

Brett seemed endlessly fascinated by tales of Holly's childhood. She could tell him anything, even the silliest details, and he was never bored. He wanted to know how it was growing up in the shadow of a famous mother. When she told him about the tours when she never saw Eve, the West End openings when she couldn't get past her mother's entourage, Brett was surprisingly understanding.

'It was rough for your mother as well,' he told her. 'All

233

the years when she was building her name she was being pulled in two directions. There was her career and then there was her family. It always amazes me she survived as well as she did.'

'But she didn't survive,' said Holly. 'Eve's all alone now. She hasn't got a man in her life – at least not a permanent one – and this trip is the first time I've seen her in ages.'

Brett did his best to be patient. 'Has it occurred to you Eve wanted it this way? Acting was always the biggest force in her life, and now she's finally admitted it. Your mother doesn't need the clutter of a family or even a steady boyfriend. It gets in her way, it distracts her.'

Holly suddenly felt vulnerable. She'd known the truth all along, of course, but having it spelled out to her by Brett was something she didn't need.

'Are all actors like this?' she asked. 'I mean, can you do without people the way Mummy does?'

Brett laughed and took her hand in his. 'I'm not as dedicated as your mother,' he told her. 'I earn my living doing soaps and commercial crap. It's not as satisfying, but I get to live a little.'

Hours later, when Brett had left for the theatre, the conversation played on Holly's mind. It was the first time she'd talked about her mother for a week – the first time she'd even thought about her – and now Brett had forced the issue she couldn't stop.

In her mind's eye she saw Eve come home from her shopping trip and discover she wasn't there. She would have been puzzled by it, because Holly had said she was ill.

After a bit, when Holly didn't come back, Eve would have gone into her room. Then she would have known Holly had moved out, for she had left nothing behind her.

Holly wondered what her mother had done then. Had she called the cops, or Justin, or her father in London? Or had she simply gone on with her life as if nothing very much had happened?

All of a sudden it became terribly important to find out.

Without hesitating, Holly went over to the phone and started punching out Eve's number.

Her mother didn't seem all that surprised to hear Holly's voice. She didn't gasp or start ranting and raving. Instead she calmly enquired how things were going with Brett.

'How did you know I was with Brett?' Holly demanded.

'Where else would you be? You didn't go home to your father – I checked with him – and you don't have any friends in New York, so moving in with Brett seemed the most logical thing to do.'

'Weren't you worried?'

There was a sickening silence and when her mother came back on the line, she sounded fainter.

'Of course I was worried. I was worried sick, if you really want to know, but there was nothing I could do. If I rang you, you'd only think I was hounding you. So I just sat tight and hoped you would call.'

Holly felt very small, yet at the same time she felt a curious sense of relief. No matter what Brett said about the theatre being all important to Mummy, she really did care, otherwise she wouldn't have got herself into such a tizz.

'Mummy, I don't want you to worry about me any more,' Holly said. 'I'm truly happy with Brett. In spite of all the things you said, I think I've finally found the right man.'

'Then I'm happy for you too, though I don't suppose I'm going to get the chance to see you after today.'

'What do you mean?'

'I mean you're probably all packed up and ready to go to Los Angeles. Brett starts filming his detective series again next week.'

Holly felt as if she had been punched in the stomach. Brett was about to leave for LA and he hadn't even told her! She must have been standing there speechless for a long time, for she heard her mother's voice in the receiver.

'Darling, are you all right? I haven't said anything out of turn, have I? You do know about Los Angeles?'

Holly felt a burning need to get off the phone as fast as she could.

'Of course I know about Los Angeles,' she told her mother crossly. 'Why shouldn't I know?'

34

There came a moment when New York started to get to Brett. It was always the same: he'd look up at the sky one day and suddenly get depressed that he couldn't see the sun. A vagrant would come up to him in the street and demand a hand-out and he'd panic he was going to get mugged. Then he'd start to yearn for Beverly Hills.

Beverly Hills, where it was clean and rich and he could swim all the year round in the pool in his own back yard. Where he could walk into any top restaurant and get a table without having to wait. Where he had friends. Where he could play tennis. Where he had a girl waiting.

The thought of her put Brett in mind of another girl. Holly was in the apartment right now, expecting him to come back from the theatre and tell her what was on the agenda for the evening. He felt sour.

Goodbye is on the agenda, he thought, goodbye and good luck and I'll see you next time round.

He knew it wouldn't wash, though. If Holly had been some bimbo, it would have been so simple. He could have slid out of town behind the promise of an introduction to a powerful agent or a pair of diamond earrings, and there would have been no trouble at all. A bimbo would disappear back into the woodwork until he decided to call her again.

Holly won't do that, he told himself. She'll shout and scream and cry her eyes out. She might even threaten suicide. She was young enough for that.

The sour feeling intensified. Brett was going to have to

think up a way of letting Holly down lightly. I've got to dump her, he thought, but at the same time, she has to believe it isn't really the end. I have to leave her with some hope.

For a brief moment he resurrected the idea of diamond earrings. No, he thought, that's a kiss-off present. Even a kid like Holly would know that.

He thought of inviting her to the coast in six months' time, when he was out of her system, but his life was too complicated for that.

Then the solution came to him: he would leave Holly the apartment in New York. It was still his for another week, so she could take a little holiday at his expense.

Now the idea was firmly in his head, Brett wondered how he could deliver this little present and still make her believe the affair wasn't quite over.

I know, he thought, I'll tell her I have some problems to sort out in LA – personal problems. Then when everything's hunky-dory, I'll get on the phone and send for her.

Brett wondered what Holly would do when she found out the truth of the situation. He decided not to worry about it. The minute he was on the plane to the coast, it ceased to be his problem.

The week passed in a kind of dream. Now Brett was gone, Holly's whole reason for living seemed to have gone as well. There was no maid, no personal trainer, no barber arriving every morning. Instead, the day stretched ahead of her, murky and featureless.

She stayed in bed, caught up in a kind of inertia, almost as if she had been injected with a sleeping drug, and she took refuge in it.

In a way sleep was a solution to all Holly's problems, for when she was asleep she couldn't think about Brett, or worry about why he had left her. It also stopped her worrying about why the phone didn't ring, for since Brett had gone to the coast, she hadn't heard a word from him.

In the first couple of days, it didn't panic her. Brett had a lot on his plate when he started filming. After he'd cleared the decks a bit, she knew he'd be in touch.

But he wasn't. Holly wondered what could have happened to him. Had something gone wrong with *The Silent Detective*? Were there problems with the series Brett hadn't told her about?

Then she wondered if he was ill. There were a number of flu bugs going around New York and Brett could easily have picked up one of them before he left.

After six days another possibility occurred to her. Brett mentioned he had a couple of personal problems to sort out. Was 'problems' another word for girlfriends? Was he surrounded by clinging starlets? She rejected this last idea as ridiculous. Brett had more on his mind than sex. Anyway, he was committed to her. Hadn't he promised to send for her?

Holly decided she was being neurotic. Brett was simply immersed in the demands of his life. In a day or so the phone would ring and she would be making arrangements to move to California.

The next day the phone did ring, though the call wasn't from Brett. It was from some real estate agency who wanted to repossess the apartment.

She told them they were mistaken, of course. This place was on permanent loan to Brett Weston. Why didn't they check with Mr Weston's agent at International Management and he would explain the situation?

The woman on the end of the line refused to be fobbed off so easily.

'We've just been talking to Jack Chaplin,' she informed Holly. 'He was the one who hired the apartment in the first place.'

Holly fought down her growing irritation. 'Then Jack Chaplin must have told you there was someone living here.'

She thought that would get rid of the real estate agent, but it didn't. The woman seemed to know all about Holly. She also knew about Holly's plans.

'Mr Chaplin told us you would be moving out tomorrow. He wasn't expecting you to be staying beyond then.'

When Holly put down the phone she was totally confused. Why did Brett tell his agent she was going when he hadn't told her? There had to be a rational explanation for it all. A few days ago they had been making plans to spend their lives together, and yet to all intents and purposes he was now throwing her out on the street.

This can't be happening, Holly thought. Somebody somewhere has got their wires crossed. Brett would never do a thing like this to me. The agent obviously has it all wrong.

Holly decided to call Jack Chaplin herself. To her surprise she could not get hold of him. The operator gave every impression he was there, yet when Holly gave her name, the woman seemed unwilling to put her through. Mr Chaplin was either on another call or in a meeting, and Holly was fobbed off with one of his assistants.

Every time she called she was handed on to a different assistant, all of them equally unhelpful. Finally she lost her temper.

'I need to get hold of Brett Weston,' she screamed into the receiver. 'Do something, will you?'

The man on the end of the line failed to react. 'If you write a letter and send it to this office,' he told her, 'I'll see it gets to Mr Weston.'

Holly really blew her top after that. Without being asked she told the bland young assistant exactly who she was and why she needed to talk to Brett.

'I'm being turned out of my apartment,' she said, 'the apartment Brett rented for us both. Now will you do something?'

For a moment nothing was said, then she heard whoever it was whispering to a colleague. Finally, after what seemed like hours, the man came back on the line.

'There seems to be some sort of misunderstanding,' he said. He cleared his throat. 'I would like to tell you what's going on, but I'm not authorized.'

Holly started to feel like the victim of a practical joke.

'Then tell me who is authorized,' she demanded. There was another round of throat clearing.

'Jack Chaplin is the only one who can discuss Mr Weston,' came the reply. 'I'll have him call you when he gets back to his office.'

Holly rang off, defeated. She had to leave the place by tomorrow morning, unless Brett intervened, and how could he do that when he obviously didn't know what was going on? When his minions and underlings were doing their level best to screen her out of his life?

Holly knew she had to get round them. Writing notes and leaving telephone messages was no good any more. Hollywood stars like Brett had an invisible fortress around them, and if she was to scale that fortress she had to do so in person, physically to turn up on his doorstep and throw herself on his mercy. After that she would be home and dry, for she knew, without a doubt, he couldn't resist her. Whatever else was happening in Brett's life, it would all grind to a halt once she had arrived.

But how do I get there? she wondered. I don't even know his address. She decided against getting back to Jack Chaplin's office. It was unlikely they would divulge Brett's whereabouts.

There had to be somebody else who knew where to find him. And then she had it: Justin. He was a newspaper columnist. He and his colleagues would know the exact location of every major celebrity in the States. It was their job, after all.

Holly looked up the number of the *New York Daily News* in the phone book, then put in a call to Justin. This time she didn't get the brush-off. If anything he seemed pleased to hear from her.

'How's the big romance?' he asked cheerfully. 'Eve tells me you've moved in together.'

Holly felt her courage begin to desert her, then she took a hold of herself.

'There's been a bit of a mix-up,' she said cautiously. 'Brett

241

flew down to the coast a few days ago, leaving me in the flat, and I haven't heard from him.'

Justin chuckled. 'Movie stars behave like that,' he told her. 'Why don't you call him?'

There was a short silence while Holly wondered how much to admit to.

Finally, she said, 'I can't call Brett. That's the problem. You see, I was so sure he would be in touch it didn't occur to me to get his number, or even the address of the house.'

Justin reached over his cluttered desk and grabbed a pack of cigarettes.

'Tell me,' he said slowly, 'do you think the guy's trying to get rid of you?'

'Don't be ridiculous,' Holly burst out. 'Brett cares for me. He told me so. No, he just got busy and he needs reminding.'

Justin thought for a moment. It was obvious what was happening: Brett Weston had made his conquest and now he was moving on, but Holly wasn't going to let him get away with it.

Justin's mind went into overdrive. Holly was Eve Adams' daughter. If she started making trouble for Brett, the situation had the makings of a first-class scandal.

There was caution in Justin's voice when he spoke next. 'You told me Brett needs reminding about you. How do you plan to jog his memory?'

Holly giggled. 'Once I find out where he is, I'll go and see him, of course. Can you think of a better way?'

No, darling, he thought. The way you're laying it all out for me is absolutely perfect.

Aloud he said: 'You can stop worrying about Brett's whereabouts. I can get that for you. When are you thinking of making this trip?'

'The sooner the better. If I can get on a flight later on today, I'll go for it.'

It was in the bag now. All Justin had to do was go on playing the helpful uncle and the story was all his.

'If it helps, I can book your airline ticket,' he said. 'The *News* is good at that sort of thing.'

There was a yelp of delight on the other end of the phone.

'Justin,' Holly said, 'you wouldn't really do that for me, would you?'

'Of course I would,' he replied. 'Eve's family to me and so are you.'

35

Holly arrived in Los Angeles in the early evening. It must have been peak time for travellers that day for the whole airport was teeming with men in suits on their way to meetings, groups of tourists and the odd impoverished-looking chicano who was probably employed at one of the million-dollar mansions up in the hills.

Most of them trod on her feet in the baggage hall where one of the conveyor belts wasn't functioning, and Holly had to stand around for nearly an hour until she managed to retrieve her case. She was hot and tired and sweating slightly when she finally got out onto the concourse. And that's when she saw him – a tall greying man with a Zapata moustache, carrying a placard with her name on it.

She wondered who on earth he could be and as she hurried over to him, the man's face broke into a broad smile.

'You must be Holly Fielding,' he said. 'I'm Steve and I was told to expect you.'

'Who gave you that order?' she asked.

The smile under the drooping moustache didn't slip. 'Justin Grey at the *Daily News*. I always meet his visitors when they come through. It cuts out a lot of struggling.'

Holly looked beyond them to a whole bunch of people trailing baggage behind them. Some of them were shouting and waving their arms at a procession of battered-looking cars. She turned to her companion.

'The taxi queue?' she said.

He nodded. 'Let me take you away from all this.'

Holly stopped arguing and let Steve lead her to a limousine with tinted windows. Then she slid into its cool leather-lined interior and realized the car Justin had laid on came equipped with air conditioning.

There was an array of buttons on a console in front of her, and she pressed one or two and found they worked the windows and a stereo system. Finally she found the button that operated the partition that separated her from Steve.

'I want to go to North Foothill Drive,' she told him. 'And make it fast.'

Holly looked out of the window and realized she was asking for the moon. It was peak traffic time and the cars were bumper to bumper on the freeway. She would be sitting here for hours, she realized, staring out at the pale blue sky into which thousands of tons of petrol fumes were pouring. She'd flown out to the coast expecting azure swimming pools and acres of manicured lawns and all she'd found so far was a gridlock.

She turned away from it in disgust and saw the driver catching her eye.

'Stop hating it,' he said, 'you've only just got here.'

The remark woke her up. She hadn't talked to anyone since she left New York and now this friendly inquisitive man was putting her on the spot.

Normally she would have told him to shut up, but she was alone in a strange town and she felt the need for company, so she started to ask him about LA.

Steve was a mine of information. He'd lived here for some years, so he knew where the movie colony hung out and where the ghettos were. The whole area was a mishmash of contrasting cultures. There was Venice, with its surfers and dropouts, Bel Air where the rich hung out in police-patrolled estates, and the city itself where the Koreans and the chicanos and the blacks crowded together at the bottom of the pile.

Holly was curious to know how he knew so much, so Steve started telling her about his life.

He was currently married to his second wife, Doe, who had been an actress.

245

'She only ever got bit parts, but she was invited to all the parties so she saw a fair bit of life. Some of the things she told me made my hair stand on end. When we were married, I made it a condition that she would give the whole thing up.'

'Did she mind?'

'I don't think so. By the time she'd met me, she'd had the film business up to here.'

There was something about Steve that was curiously relaxing. He wasn't trying to sell himself all the time and because he was so laid back, Holly felt easy about telling him her own story. She was quite open about the way she felt about her mother, and how she'd walked off with her old boyfriend.

As Holly talked about Brett, she felt all the tensions of the past week begin to disappear. The man sitting in the front seat seemed to understand what she had been going through.

'You sound like you fell hard for the guy,' Steve said. 'I hope it works out for you.'

'So do I,' she said.

Then Holly told him all about the last week of her life. The air conditioned limousine was anonymous in the same way as a psychiatrist's couch, so she didn't spare him any of the details.

Her voice choked a little when she got to the part about how Brett's agent had tried to turn her into the street, and Steve slowed the car and turned round for a moment.

'You poor kid,' he said. 'You've really been through the mill. Hollywood agents can be grade A bastards when they put their minds to it.'

'But why would they turn against me like that?'

'They're protecting their own interests. Anyone who gets between them and their client is a threat. It's a risky business being a movie star's girlfriend.'

Holly started to feel reassured. Steve obviously knew what he was talking about.

'I was lucky to get you to drive me,' she told him. 'You've no idea how nervous I've been about this trip.'

'Well, you can calm down now,' Steve told her. 'We're coming into Beverly Hills. Pretty soon we'll be right outside Brett's house.'

He paused for a moment. 'I take it the guy's expecting you?'

The question stopped Holly in her tracks. She'd kind of assumed Brett would be sitting in his Hollywood house waiting for her to turn up. Now she realized how stupid she'd been.

He could be anywhere, she thought. He could be at the studio or having drinks with friends. He might even have gone away for a few days.

'Actually,' she admitted, 'Brett doesn't know I'm coming. What am I going to do if he's not there?'

'It's not a problem,' Steve told her. 'You're my last passenger today so I can wait with you in the car until lover boy turns up.'

They were turning into a wide leafy suburban boulevard with houses set back from the road. The sign on the corner told them they were in North Foothill Road and Holly's heart quickened.

She had rehearsed what she was going to say a thousand times, yet now they were actually pulling up outside Brett's house, all the speeches and the explanations flew out of her mind.

She pressed the button that lowered the window to give a clear view of where she was heading.

It was a sprawling white building half hidden by palms and hedges. All around it were high wire security fences. Holly started to panic.

'It looks as easy to get into as Fort Knox,' she told Steve. 'How do I know the doorman will let me through?'

'Just tell them your name,' said the driver. 'Whoever operates the gates will have to check with Brett and you'll be home and dry.'

Before she could change her mind, Steve was opening the car door for her.

'Good luck,' he said, 'not that you're going to need it.'

247

It was as easy as Steve said it would be, and within minutes the gates clicked open and Holly found herself standing in Brett's front porch. She wasn't sure what she expected when the door opened, but the sight of a butler in full livery took her breath away.

'I'm here to see Mr Weston,' Holly said, expecting to be turned away any minute.

The servant smiled and ushered her inside to a large white marble hall filled with flowers. At one end she could see a sweeping wooden staircase leading to upstairs rooms. The butler took her to a downstairs conservatory leading out on to a swimming pool. He indicated a sofa covered in tiger skin.

'If you wait here,' he said, 'Mr Weston will be with you. He's just come in from playing tennis, so he could be a few minutes. Can I get you a drink?'

Holly felt overwhelmed by the unexpected opulence of Brett's life. He'd told her in New York he lived in style, but this kind of style was totally outside her experience.

She looked up and noticed the butler was waiting for her instruction.

'I'll have a glass of white wine,' she stammered.

She felt relieved as he retreated from the room. Butlers, she thought, marble halls . . . whatever next?

What happened next was the appearance of a statuesque Chinese girl. She had clearly been on the tennis court with Brett, for she was still in her shorts and sweat shirt. Without introducing herself she collapsed into a wicker chair and started fanning her face.

'I'd kill for a Perrier,' she told Holly. 'You don't know where Henry is, do you?'

Holly assumed she meant the butler.

'He's gone to get me a glass of wine,' she said. 'I expect he'll be back any minute. By the way, my name's Holly.'

'I know,' the girl said. 'Brett told me.'

Holly started to feel nervous. 'Did he tell you anything else?'

The girl sat forward in the chair, running her hands through damp black hair.

'He said you were a groupie,' she said flatly, 'and you were making a nuisance of yourself.'

Holly felt shame burn itself all the way up her neck and into her face. Brett, her Brett, had told this stranger those stupid lies about her. She had to be hearing it wrong.

'I'm no groupie,' she said with as much dignity as she could muster. 'When Brett gets here he'll tell you so himself.'

He arrived as if on cue, dressed in a towelling robe with his hair all spikey from the shower.

'So you two girls have met,' he said a little too heartily. 'Is all going well?' He turned to the Chinese girl. 'I take it you've organized drinks for everybody?'

Holly looked at the pair of them. There was a sort of relaxed intimacy in the room. It was almost domestic and she realized this girl, whoever she was, had been organizing drinks for Brett for quite some time.

Now Holly felt really uncomfortable. 'Do you think,' she said, sitting up very straight on the tigerskin sofa, 'do you think somebody might tell me what's going on here?'

Brett smiled. 'I might ask you the same question. I left you in New York a week ago, imagining you were on your way back home to England. Suddenly you arrive on my doorstep.'

Holly felt her eyes prickling and to her horror, she realized she was crying.

'How can you say that?' she demanded. 'We were lovers when you left me in New York. You were going to send for me and bring me out to this house.'

Holly saw a look of surprise on the Chinese girl's face and realized Brett hadn't levelled with her at all. He'd said she was a groupie and a nuisance. What he'd left out was that she had actually moved in with him.

She knew her hunch was spot on when the girl got out of her chair and marched over to Brett.

'So that's why you never let me come up to New York,' she

said, looking dangerous. 'You were shacked up with Holly.'

Brett started to back away from her. 'It didn't mean anything,' he said weakly. 'All it was was a fling.'

Brett's girlfriend made as if to scratch his eyes out, but instead of grabbing hold of her and putting a stop to her nonsense, the actor inched further away from her.

At that moment, Holly realized Brett was terrified of the slim, black-haired girl. And all her illusions about him finally went out of the window. Brett wasn't a hero at all. He was just a cheat who had been caught in the act, a cheat who was going to have to pay for what he had done.

Holly got to her feet.

'I think I'll leave you two beautiful people to sort out your relationship,' she said. 'There's no point in me staying here any more.'

But the Chinese girl had turned away from Brett and was advancing on Holly.

'Oh no you don't,' she said. 'I want to know what's been going on while my back was turned.'

For the first time that day Holly felt in control of the situation. She was going to use this girl to even the score.

'Where would you like me to start?' she began, but Brett had had enough. He wasn't going to stand there and watch two prize bitches carve him up.

He took hold of Holly by the arm and started to push her towards the door.

'I want you out of here,' he said, 'before you can make any more trouble.'

Her anger rose up inside her. She had been used by this man, used and betrayed, and now he was throwing her out of his house like a pile of dirty washing.

She pulled away from him. Then before he could make another move, she turned and belted him right in the kisser. When her hand came away, she was pleased to see an ugly red welt burning across his cheek.

That will keep the make-up boys busy for days, she thought.

He tried to make a grab for her, but she was too fast for

him. All she wanted to do now was to get the hell out of his sight and never come back.

Her heels clicked across the shiny marble floor as she saw herself out.

I'm free, she thought. I don't love Brett any more – I don't even like him very much – and I owe him nothing at all.

Steve watched helplessly while Holly sobbed her heart out in the back of his limousine. Only when she showed signs of slowing down, did he get out of his seat and climb in beside her.

She looked up at him and attempted a smile.

'Sorry about the dramatics,' she said, 'but I've had a horrible time.'

The driver reached out and put an arm round her.

'Would it help if you talked about it?'

So Holly talked, leaving out nothing. Steve knew how to listen without judging. If she'd told him she'd just committed murder, the driver would probably have seen it from her point of view.

As it was, all she had to confess to was belting Brett across the face.

'He had it coming,' she told Steve, 'and it bloody well served him right. Next time he thinks about messing around with two girls at once, he'll remember what happened the last time he did it.'

She looked up to see Steve lost in thought. He was listening to what she was saying, but he was staring out of the window at the same time, almost as if he was in another world.

'Is something the matter?' she asked.

The driver clicked to attention. 'I was just thinking about Brett,' he smiled. 'I don't think he's going to forget this little drama for a very long time.'

Steve drove Holly to a Mexican restaurant in one of the back streets behind Beverly Hills' main shopping centre. It was the kind of touristy place where the food was better taken away, but she couldn't say that to Steve, not when the head waiter

251

greeted him like a regular and showed them to a quiet booth at the back.

Looking at the menu, Holly felt as much enthusiasm for it as she had for the plastic airline meal she'd left on the plane. She glanced across to Steve and saw he was concerned.

'I get the feeling this isn't your kind of thing,' he said wryly.

All of the sudden she felt guilty. Steve didn't have to take her to a restaurant tonight. Any other chauffeur would have dumped her at the nearest cheap hotel and left her to get on with it.

'I adore Mexican food,' she said firmly, 'and I'll feel even better about it when you tell your wife where you are. She must be expecting you.'

He stood up and slid out of the booth. 'Why don't you order for both of us while I look for a phone? I'll only be a few minutes.'

Steve was gone for longer than Holly expected, so she passed the time looking at the other diners. There were three or four half-shaven men in blue jeans and expensive leather jackets standing round the bar, a crowd of business types in sober suits on the big table in the middle of the room, and in the booths were a number of couples who could have lived locally.

Her eye was taken by a grey-haired man and his wife sitting across from her. There was something about the woman that made Holly look longer than she normally would. She was beautiful in a dark-haired, pale-complexioned sort of way, but it was her expression and the way she moved her hands that interested Holly. Her mother acted that way in restaurants.

Just for a moment, Holly wondered what Eve was doing and whether she'd tried to contact her at Brett's.

She'll have a surprise if she does, Holly thought. Brett will probably damn me to hell the minute she comes on the line.

It was then that Holly decided she had to come clean with her mother. It wouldn't be easy, of course. She would have to admit that Eve had been right all along and that Brett really was a prize shit. She would make herself look small in the process, but it had to be done. She'd put her mother through hell. The least she could do now was atone for her sins.

I'll go straight round her to her apartment the minute I get back to New York, Holly decided. Then we'll get the whole thing out in the open.

The prospect of making peace with Eve made her feel better. Ten minutes previously the waiter had deposited a plate of pancakes in front of her, and though they were congealing on the plate, she piled into them.

By the time Steve came back from calling his wife, she had devoured the entire plate of pancakes and was busy ordering another.

'So you really do like Mexican food,' he grinned.

They stayed in the booth eating and talking for another two hours. Steve seemed anxious for her to go over the encounter in Brett's mansion, almost as if he were committing it to memory.

He's probably going to tell the whole thing to other drivers in the depot, Holly thought. It will make him look as if he hobnobs with the stars. Though she hated being gossiped about, she obliged the chauffeur, filling in the gaps in the story, embroidering the conversation with the Chinese girl, so the whole thing sounded more interesting.

She might have gone on for longer if she hadn't been so anxious to get back to New York.

She glanced at her watch and saw it was past six. Steve seemed to read her mind.

'There's a plane leaving around nine. If we get going now, I should have you at LAX in plenty of time to catch it.'

She gave him her best smile. 'You've done so much for me,' she said. 'How can I ever thank you?'

36

Holly arrived back at Kennedy around midnight, found a payphone and called her mother. To her relief, Eve answered almost immediately.

'Mummy,' she said, 'it's Holly. I'm back in New York.'

'Darling, that's wonderful. When do I get to see you?'

There was a brief silence.

'How about now?'

For a moment Eve hesitated. 'Have you and Brett had a row or something?'

'It's worse than that.'

'How much worse?'

'We broke up. I left Brett in Los Angeles.'

Holly expected her mother to crow, or at least to say, 'I told you so.' Instead she sounded concerned.

'So you're all alone at the airport. Do you want me to come and get you?'

'I think I can find a taxi.'

'Then hurry. I want to know what's been happening to you.'

All the way to the apartment, Holly wondered how she was going to explain herself. Did she tell the truth and confess she'd been taken for a sucker, or did she invent a lover's tiff? That would be easy enough to get away with, and it would save her face.

She'd almost decided to do it – she would have done it – if Eve hadn't been so damned understanding.

The moment she walked through the door, Holly was

pushed into the drawing room where there was hot coffee and Danish waiting for her.

'Sit down and kick your shoes off,' her mother instructed. 'You look like you need to catch your breath.'

Before she could say a word, Eve thrust a steaming mug into her hands and started to ask about her journey.

It was small talk, of course. Eve wasn't interested in the flight from LAX, but she went on with it because she didn't want to put Holly on the spot about Brett.

In that moment all the lies Holly had invented flew out of the window.

'Mummy,' she said, 'I think I should tell you what happened in Los Angeles – or rather what didn't happen.'

Eve looked confused. 'I thought you set up home there?'

Holly shook her head. 'I dreamed of setting up home there but it didn't come to anything. I've been in New York all week waiting for Brett to give me the word.'

Holly was sprawled out on a rug by the fire and now Eve kneeled down beside her and took her hand.

'He didn't call you, did he?' she said softly.

'How do you know?'

'Because I know Brett. He's always had a girl in every town, and I bet there was one waiting for him in LA.'

Holly started to cry. Silent tears rolled down her cheeks and she made no attempt to wipe them away. Eve grabbed hold of her then, pulling her into her arms so she was surrounded by her warmth.

'Save your tears,' she said, stroking her hair. 'He's not worth it.'

Later, when she was herself again, Holly poured them both some more coffee. Then she told her mother everything that had happened in the last twenty-four hours.

None of it surprised Eve. She'd heard it all before. What did intrigue her was how Holly found Brett in Los Angeles.

'Justin didn't tell me he gave you Brett's address, and he should have done, particularly after all the trouble he went to laying on a driver.'

Holly looked curious. 'When did you last talk to him?'

'Around tea time. You were probably with Steve when we spoke.'

'Why would he keep quiet about it? He's your best friend, isn't he? Wouldn't he want you to know what was going on with me?'

Eve reflected for a moment. Then she looked sad. 'What we mustn't forget is that Justin works for a newspaper. However much he loves me, he loves a good story more.'

'You're not telling me I'm a good story?'

'You're not just a good story, you're a wonderful story. Brett's a household name. Even if you were nobody and got tangled up with him, it would make headlines.'

'But I'm not nobody, am I? I'm your daughter and your good friend Justin will throw that into whatever story he's doing.'

Eve got to her feet. 'It's very late,' she said, 'and we're all imagining things that might never happen.' She put an arm round Holly. 'Come on, let's go to bed. We've both had enough for one day.'

The papers arrived at seven in the morning, and Holly, who normally didn't open her eyes until eight thirty, was right there waiting for them. She carried the whole pile through to the kitchen where she put on some toast before settling down to read them.

At first she couldn't find the *Daily News*, and she panicked, thinking the delivery boy had forgotten to put it in. Then she came to it, sandwiched between *Vanity Fair* and one of her mother's trade papers.

She rescued it, scanning the front page to see if she could find anything about Brett. What she was looking for was in the bottom right-hand corner. It was a small flash, flagging a story on an inside page: 'Brett Weston in love triangle . . . See page 7.'

Holly flipped through the paper until she got to the story. Then it hit her right between the eyes.

There was a big picture of Brett arm in arm with the Chinese girl. Underneath it was one of Holly.

But it was the headline that really finished her. 'Star's daughter says: "Cheating Brett got everything he deserved."'

Underneath, almost word for word, was the story Holly had told Steve in the Mexican restaurant. He must have been taking notes, Holly thought.

Then the whole thing came to her. Steve wasn't a chauffeur at all. He was a gossip-hound posing as a chauffeur. Justin must have called him at the *News*'s LA office the minute Holly got on the plane.

She felt bitter. All the guy had to do was turn up and play fairy godfather and I was putty in his hands, she thought. I was so completely out of it, I would have told him anything he asked me without suspecting a thing.

Her eyes returned to the saga in front of her. Justin, whose name featured prominently at the top of the page, had stopped at nothing to sensationalize it. The whole sordid business with her mother and Brett had been dragged up again. Justin had even hinted that Brett had been the cause of Eve and Jason's divorce. Holly felt sick.

It was tough luck that she'd been made to look cheap. In a way she'd deserved it, but her mother didn't. And not by a friend she'd trusted.

Holly folded the paper back together again, and pushed it to the bottom of the pile. Maybe Eve wouldn't get to it today.

The minute her mother appeared in the kitchen, however, she asked if there was anything in the *News*.

Holly looked shifty. 'Just a small item. Nothing very important.'

Eve grabbed hold of the morning papers. 'I'll be the judge of that . . .'

While she was reading the story, Holly prepared breakfast. She put muesli into two bowls, cut up fruit to go on top, warmed croissants and buttered toast.

In the end it was Eve that stopped all the frantic activity. 'Come here and sit down,' she said softly. 'We have to talk.'

Holly dragged herself to the kitchen table and grabbed the

chair opposite, but try as she might she couldn't meet Eve's eyes.

'I expect you're furious with me,' she said finally.

Eve reached out and touched her daughter's face.

'I'm not furious with you, darling. You're the innocent in all this. The person I want to murder is Justin. He might have warned me this was about to happen.'

'If he'd done that, you'd only have tried to stop him.'

Eve shook her head. 'Not true. You can't prevent this kind of dirt getting out. All you can do is make sure you're out of town when the story hits. That way you duck all the other newshounds on the lookout for a follow-up. Justin knows the game. He could have protected me from that.'

Holly looked stricken. 'He wasn't much of a friend, was he? And I wasn't much of a daughter playing into his hands like that.'

Holly had prepared an absolute feast and brought it to the table, but Eve noticed she hadn't got around to swallowing a mouthful. I can't have her blowing this out of proportion, she thought. If this little episode stops her eating, we'll be right back to her old starvation days.

'You've got to stop punishing yourself for Brett,' Eve said gently. 'It happened, you made a mistake, but it's not the end of the world. We'll all survive it.'

'But what about the story? Won't it hurt your reputation?'

For a moment Eve looked genuinely amused. 'If my reputation got hurt every time a bit of scandal appeared, then I would have stopped working years ago. What do you think happened the first time the Brett affair appeared in print? When your father and I were getting divorced?'

'Tell me.'

'I got asked to do a musical comedy and a television soap. The scandal made me bankable. Don't ask me why, but it did. That's the way this business works.'

'And you can live with that?'

Eve wondered whether her daughter would ever see the world as it really was.

'I have to live with it. It goes with the territory. Look, not every bit of publicity I get is damaging. Some of it makes me look better than I am — most of it, actually — so when something like today's story happens, I put a brave face on it and wait till it blows over. It always does, you know.'

Holly looked doubtful. 'You're sure of that?'

'I'm certain of it.'

37

The nausea hit Linda the way it always did the minute she woke. As calmly as she could she went through her deep breathing exercises. It was no use. She was going to be sick and there was nothing for it but to make a dash for the bathroom while she still could.

Linda edged her way out of bed, taking care not to wake Jason. Then she ran the four-minute mile to the lavatory where she retched her heart out. She was so concerned with her discomfort that she didn't hear the door open behind her, so when she finally got her head up she was surprised to see Jason rubbing the sleep out of his eyes.

'How long has this been going on?' he asked her.

She tried to make light of it. 'I must have eaten something that disagreed with me. I'll be better now it's all gone.'

Jason took her by the shoulders and led her back to the bedroom. Then he sat her on the bed and looked at her sternly.

'There's no point in lying to me,' he told her. 'I heard you being sick yesterday morning and the morning before. It takes more than a bad oyster to do that.'

Linda put her head in her hands.

'I guess I was going to have to tell you sooner or later. It's just I wanted to be sure.'

'Sure of me? Or sure of the baby?'

She looked up, startled. 'How did you know about that?'

He sat on the bed beside her, drawing her close.

'We've been virtually living together since the beginning

of the year,' he said gently. 'I know if you're getting a headache or you've had a bad day. I even know when you're
expecting your period, so how could I not know if you were
pregnant?'

She didn't say anything for a few minutes, and it was Jason
who finally broke the silence.

'You are pleased about it,' he said anxiously, 'aren't you?'

Linda smiled. 'Of course I'm pleased. I'm over the moon
about it. I just didn't know how you'd feel about starting
another family.'

'Do you want my honest opinion?'

She nodded.

'I'm not happy about the idea.'

She started to interrupt but he stopped her.

'What I mean is, I'm not happy about you having babies
unless you're married to me. I know it's old-fashioned, but
there it is.'

Linda drew away from him. 'Is that a proposal?'

'Of course it's a proposal. I'm in love with you, Linda, or
hadn't you noticed?'

She came right back into his arms, holding him so tightly
that all the breath went out of him.

'I accept,' she said joyfully, 'and I'm very glad you decided
to be old-fashioned.'

He started to make love to her then, caressing her ripening
body with such tenderness that she felt herself melt into him.

It was going to make her late for work, she knew it and
she should have been worried, but ever since this child had
been growing inside her, she had let go a little. It doesn't
matter any more, she thought. Nothing matters any more
except for Jason and the baby.

Later, when Linda was standing under the shower, the
reality of what she had agreed came home to her. She would
be married to Jason now, not just living with him. She would
be Holly's stepmother, and she wondered how they were
going to break the news to the girl.

Holly was due home any day now, and if her mother was
anything to go by, she wouldn't be at her most receptive.

Some man had walked away from her, some Hollywood stud she'd been silly enough to fall in love with. And now her father was about to do the same thing.

If Linda and Jason weren't careful, Holly could cut up rough and that was the last thing they needed.

Linda turned the shower off and wrapped herself in a huge terry bathtowel. Then she padded back to the bedroom.

Jason was putting on his shoes when she came in, though when he saw the expression on Linda's face, he stopped.

'What on earth's the matter?' he asked.

Linda sat down beside him. 'I've been thinking about Holly,' she said. 'After the time she's been through in America, she's not going to be in any shape to take our news.'

'Why not?' Jason demanded.

Linda did her best to be patient. 'Because her security's taken a bad knock. The Brett Weston business has completely thrown her. If you suddenly up and announce you're marrying me, she'll feel abandoned by every man she's ever loved.'

'So what do you suggest we do?'

'I think we should give it time. Let her settle in here and get comfortable again. Then when she's got her bearings, we can break the news.'

'But I don't want to keep our marriage a secret, or our baby. It's the best thing to happen in a very long time.'

Linda was tempted to go along with him. Anyway, Holly was old enough to look after herself.

She pulled herself up short. I was Holly's age once, she thought, confused and muddled-up. If I tread on her feelings now I could ruin her. She set her face.

'I hate to do it,' she told Jason, 'but we don't have any choice.'

Holly had never been so pleased to be anywhere. She was in her own room with her own things around her. If she wanted a glass of water in the night, she could walk through to her bathroom in her sleep, she knew the way so well. If she needed to wash her hair, she knew exactly how the shower unit worked, how hot she could get it, where it leaked, how much pressure she could expect. These were such stupid things, such trifling details, she never really missed them until she was away from home. Now she was back, she vowed she'd never take them for granted again.

This house was her womb. She realized that now, and she wanted nothing to alter it. So instead of bickering with Linda over the way the house was run, she held her fire. She didn't mention Lola once, and she kept a curfew the way Linda wanted it, getting home before midnight most evenings.

Holly's behaviour met with approval, not just from Linda, but from Jason as well. Since she'd been away the two of them seemed to have grown closer, and she wondered what it was all leading to.

Daddy couldn't be thinking of anything permanent, she knew that, for if he was, why would he still be seeing Mummy? Why would he be shacking up with her every time he went to New York?

The question preyed on Holly's mind. She hadn't thought about it much in the first week after she got home, but now things were back to normal, she was worried.

I could go on fretting about this for the rest of time, she told herself, or I could get it out in the open. I could ask Daddy what he was up to and refuse to be fobbed off the way I was in New York.

Now her mind was made up, Holly started to make a plan. She needed to get Jason on his own, somewhere where they could have a private conversation. Linda would go nuts if she had any idea what Jason was up to, and Holly didn't want to risk that. There was no point in her inflaming Daddy's girlfriend until she knew exactly what was going on.

Holly decided to get Jason to take her out to lunch. They hadn't had much chance to catch up since she'd been back, so she picked a Saturday when she knew Linda would be at the hairdresser's.

'Why don't we go to Drones today?' she suggested early

on. 'You always used to take me there when we needed to talk things out.'

Jason regarded his daughter with surprise. 'Is there anything special on your mind?' he asked.

'Not really, except I never told you exactly what went on in New York and I thought you might be interested to know.'

Jason looked weary. 'I did hear it chapter and verse from your mother. She even sent me a copy of the newspaper story, so I think I'm in the picture.'

'Are you cross about it?'

'Of course I'm not. I just think we've all given Brett Weston enough time and emotion.'

He saw how disappointed she looked and realized he was being harsh.

'That doesn't mean I won't take you to lunch,' he told her. 'There are plenty of other things we can talk about.'

Holly brightened up. You bet there are, she thought. We can start with the subject of your suits and what they're doing in Mummy's closet. And when we've finished with that, we can move on to what you're doing with Mummy.

In its heyday, Drones in Pont Street was crowded out with the beautiful people. Now only hairdressers and football players seemed to patronize the pastel coloured restaurant.

That suited Jason fine. It meant he could ask for a quiet table in a corner and not be told Sharon Stone had booked it three weeks ago.

When they arrived he got his wish. A table under the stained-glass window had just come free. All they needed to do was wait in the bar until it was made ready for them.

Jason and Holly sat down on the velvet banquette that ran all the way round the tiny area and Jason ordered the drinks. They had been coming here so long now that he automatically knew what his daughter wanted. And when two bull-shots arrived in tall, frosted glasses he was relieved to see she hadn't changed her tastes.

Jason picked up the drink and saluted her.

'Here's to you being home,' he said. 'I missed you.'

'I missed you too,' Holly said, looking sad. 'More than you'll know.'

Jason looked into his glass. Fate had handed him the perfect opportunity to tell Holly about his impending marriage. He'd actually planned to break the news once they got to the table, but in this present mood she'd be in tears before they got there.

'I couldn't have made things better even if I'd been in New York with you,' he said softly. 'There are some experiences you have to go through on your own.'

She made a face. 'I suppose you're going to tell me it's all part of growing up.'

'Actually I wasn't. You're bright enough to know that for yourself.'

Jason stood up and indicated it was time to go into the restaurant, and they both made their way to the table.

It was full that day with weekend shoppers, and everyone was chattering at full volume. Holly seemed to be impervious to the crowd, concentrating instead on the contents of the bread basket.

She grabbed a roll from the top of the pile and started to tear it apart. There was something greedy about the way she was devouring it, and Jason began to get irritated.

'If you go on doing that,' he said, 'you'll ruin your appetite.'

She glowered at him, but didn't stop eating. So he said: 'You'll ruin your figure too, if you're not careful.'

At least this time he got a response.

'I suppose you think I'd look better if I was skin and bone like Linda.'

'Linda isn't skin and bone, far from it. She's getting rounder every day.'

'Why would she be doing that? Linda's a diet junkie.'

Jason looked at his daughter. She'd put down the half-eaten roll, so at least she was listening to him. He decided to make the most of the moment.

'Linda's putting on weight for a very natural reason. She's pregnant.'

Holly was dumbfounded. She'd come to lunch expecting to hear Linda was leaving to make way for her mother. And now Daddy goes and announces she's having a baby.

'How long has this been going on?' she demanded. 'And why didn't you tell me about it before? I've been home nearly two weeks now.'

Jason looked embarrassed. 'Linda didn't want to spring it on you,' he said finally. 'She knows you've been going through a bad time, so she thought she'd leave you to settle down first.'

'That's very big of her,' Holly said. 'Is there anything else I should know, now you've decided to level with me?'

She noticed her father really was having a problem now. He'd gone bright red in the face and was busy pouring more wine into his glass.

He's going to tell me he and Linda are getting married, she thought, only the poor thing's got himself in such a twist, he can't get the words out. She decided to put him out of his misery.

'You're going to make an honest woman of Linda, aren't you?' she said softly.

'Would you mind if I did?'

Of course I mind, she thought. Things were going so well until now. Mummy and Daddy were back in bed together. I could almost see us being a family again.

But I bargained without Linda. She must have known the quickest way to get a man was to get pregnant, and now she is, there's nothing that can be done about it.

She looked at her father. 'How is this going to affect things with Mummy?'

Jason seemed surprised. 'It shouldn't make any difference. Mummy and I have a business relationship now, that's all.'

'That's not how it looks to me.'

Holly saw the surprise on her father's face change to horror.

'Would you mind explaining exactly what you mean?'

So she did. She described the day she spent alone in her mother's apartment, and how out of curiosity she wandered into the spare room and started to go through the closets.

'I found your suits then,' she confessed. 'Your suits and your ties and a pair of your shoes—'

Jason interrupted her. 'So you instantly assumed my things were there because I was sleeping with Eve.'

'What did you expect me to think? I hardly imagined you were trying to save money on hotel bills.'

Jason suddenly felt helpless. If he told his daughter the truth he would be going back on his promises. And if he didn't . . . He shrugged. If he didn't, they all looked silly. There had to be a way of defusing the situation.

'I don't blame you for thinking what you did, but you're way off the mark.'

He reached out and took his daughter's hands in his. 'Darling, I can't tell you the real situation, at least not now. But what I can promise is that now Linda and I are getting married, I won't be seeing much of your mother any more.'

Holly looked at him in disbelief. 'Is that it? Mummy gets the boot because you've found a newer model? Or is it because the newer model's suddenly pregnant?'

Jason fought off exasperation. 'I told you before, things aren't the way they seem. How I feel about Eve and how I feel about Linda are nothing to do with each other.'

Holly sighed. She could go on fighting for her mother, but she knew she was on a loser. Daddy had made his choice. He was going to stand by Linda and the new baby. They would all make a future together and she knew she'd have no place in it.

She wondered how soon it would be before she was asked to leave home, and began to feel panicky. She wasn't ready to be pushed out just yet. She needed time, and the best way to buy it was to have her father on her side. She turned to him.

'Would it make you feel any better if I forgot what I saw in New York?'

Jason was visibly relieved. 'It would solve a lot of problems.'

'Then you've got it. I wouldn't want to mess things up with Linda.'

38

Linda and Jason got married in the registry office on Marylebone Road. Neither of them wanted to make a fuss about it: Linda because her pregnancy was just beginning to show; Jason because this was his second time round and he felt foolish about going through an elaborate pantomime for the sake of all the relations.

Holly thanked her lucky stars they both felt that way. She had nightmares about being dressed up in some frilly horror of a dress and made to perform the role of chief bridesmaid. Now they were playing the whole thing down, she could turn up looking tailored and sink into the background.

This was more difficult than she expected. Apart from Linda's parents, who insisted on witnessing their daughter's wedding, and Jason's best man, Clement Dane, the distinguished Shakespearean actor, Holly was the only person there.

She stood behind her father while he and Linda took their vows, and wondered what the hell she was doing. She hadn't wanted to come along today and she had already come up with an excuse, saying she felt she'd be in the way, but Linda wouldn't hear of it.

'You're going to be my new family,' the presenter had told her. 'You must be there.'

So Holly had shown up in her best Armani jacket and now she wished she'd found something else to do.

The whole ceremony seemed so phoney in her eyes. These were two grown-up people who had lived together for the best part of year, and here they were solemnly swearing vows to each other. The stupid thing about it was that they looked so sincere. Linda, despite her widening waistline, looked positively dewy-eyed. And Daddy was behaving as if he were in church, saying the words of the ceremony with a reverence Holly had never heard before.

She might not have been able to take it if it hadn't been for Linda's parents being there, but they looked as disbelieving as she did, which cheered her up.

Right from the moment when they turned up at the municipal building, Ron and Sally Beattie had been a source of fascination to Holly. They were so unlike Linda.

Holly regarded the presenter's mother, with her peroxided hair and garish make-up. She was straight out of *EastEnders*, right down to the too-tight skirt and stiletto heels.

Ron was, if possible, even more embarrassing. He was balding on top, but he had combed his hair very carefully over the naked bit, which made him appear a complete wally. The two of them together looked like a couple of passers-by pulled at random off the street to act as witnesses.

Holly wondered how Linda felt about them being there, because they weren't doing her any favours at all.

She thought about the party her father had organized at the Connaught afterwards. There was to be champagne and canapés in one of the private rooms. With all Daddy's show-biz friends and all Linda's television friends, Ron and Sally would stick out like a sore thumb.

Holly was beginning to enjoy the prospect of Ron and Sally's debut at the Connaught when she caught sight of Linda. The nuptials were over, the couple had signed the register and now Linda's mother was expressing her congratulations.

It was a grisly sight. The elderly woman had enveloped her daughter in a bear hug and was planting her heavily rouged mouth all over her face. Linda didn't exactly flinch, Holly saw, but what she did was worse in a way: she pretended she was enjoying it.

Holly caught sight of the wedding photographer and

realized Linda's ordeal was only just starting. She would have to go through the whole pantomime again on the registry office steps.

Holly shrugged and followed the party outside. Linda will cope, she thought. She copes in front of cameras every morning.

The party at the Connaught was in full swing when they arrived. The room at the back of the restaurant was jam-packed and Holly was tempted to hang around and see how Linda handled being the new Mrs Fielding; then she decided there would be plenty of time for that later. She had just spotted a group she used to work with, and the need to be with people of her own age overwhelmed her.

Before long Holly was surrounded by her old colleagues, knee-deep in gossip. A tall good-looking boy who looked as though he had gone to public school came over to join them. For a moment there was an embarrassed silence. Then the producer's secretary leaped into the fray.

'Meet Harry. He took over your job when you went off to America.'

Holly knew she was meant to feel put out about Harry, but seeing somebody else in her job didn't bother her at all. She'd never really enjoyed it that much. What interested her was whether Harry enjoyed it.

She quizzed him about what he was doing, noting how cool he was. Most researchers she worked with were permanently on the defensive. It was part and parcel of the life they led. Harry didn't look as if he had a care in the world.

He had just come down from Edinburgh with a First in Communications, so a job in television was everything he had been looking for. Holly listened while he went on to describe what he was doing on *The Morning Show*, and she realized with a pang that none of his duties included making the coffee.

She was tempted to tell him that if he'd been a girl, making coffee would have accounted for most of his activities. Then her father came over and the moment was lost.

'I see you've been introduced to each other,' he said, putting his arm round Harry, 'though by rights that shouldn't be necessary.'

'I don't know what you're talking about,' Holly said.

Jason grinned. 'You mean to say you don't recognize each other? I find it hard to believe. You both went to the same parties for the first ten years of your lives. Harry's father is my best buddy.'

It all came into focus now. Clement Dane, Uncle Clement, Daddy's best friend and best client, had a whole brood of nasty little boys who had terrorized her during most of her childhood.

Holly looked at Harry and tried to remember which one he was. Was he the rude, spiteful one who put his pet earwig into one of her shoes? Or was he the piggy one who always seemed to eat all the smoked salmon before she could get a look in? There were twins as well, she remembered, wiry little things who liked getting into fights.

She shook her head. None of these monsters looked anything like the self-assured blond standing in front of her.

'Are you sure you're one of the Danes,' she asked, 'or did they adopt you later on?'

Now it was Harry's turn to grin.

'You don't remember me because I was a different shape in those days. I used to eat rather a lot.'

'Piggy,' said Holly, delighted now. 'Who would have thought it?'

She was about to start on a whole raft of reminiscence when the master of ceremonies called for silence.

The time for speeches had come. Holly knew her father was going to say something, and that Clement Dane would do his bit, but she had no idea who else would get a word in.

Then she spotted Linda's father, studying a great sheaf of paper, and she had her answer. Ron was going to speak up for the Beatties — if he could get the words out, for even from where she was standing, it was clear the man was drunk.

He had gone bright red, and even though he had loosened

his collar it didn't help. His half-undone shirt and flapping tie made him look even more pissed than he really was.

What the hell are we going to do about him? Holly thought. He can't go on like that. He'll make fools of all of us.

She decided it was Linda's problem, and sped over to where the bride was standing.

'You've got to have a word with your father,' Holly said urgently. 'You can't let him do his speech in the state he's in.'

The blonde looked helpless. 'What can I say to him?' she demanded.

'Tell him the truth. It's always the best way.'

'I can't do that. He'll throw a fit.'

At that moment Holly realized Linda was in no state to cope with anything. The baby and the excitement of the wedding had completely knocked her for six. Left to her own devices, the blonde would simply stand by and let her father do his worst.

Well, Holly couldn't allow that. Somebody had to save the day, and she realized she was that somebody.

She looked up and saw Clement was beginning his speech. He was standing slightly in front of the wedding cake, telling an endless stream of theatrical anecdotes. Holly knew it was going to take hours. When he got started, it was hard to switch him off, but for once she was glad of it. It would give her the time she needed.

As stealthily as she could, Holly pushed her way through the crowd until she got to where Linda's father was standing. He hadn't spotted her and was engrossed in the typewritten sheets she'd seen him with earlier.

What am I going to say to him? she wondered. Do I tell an absolute whopper and pretend Linda has to hurry away early? She glanced at Ron and thought better of it.

This man had been around. He might be out of his depth at the Connaught, but there was a shrewdness about him that would see right through any lie she could concoct.

He looked up and saw her standing beside him.

'I've got to talk to you,' Holly whispered urgently.

Ron looked impatient. 'Can't it wait?' he asked.

She shook her head, and before he could put up any more objections she had hold of his arm and was propelling him into the corridor.

She had the initiative now, and while Ron was gathering his wits, Holly ploughed on with what she wanted to say.

'You can't make that speech,' she told him.

'Why not?' he demanded.

'Because it would destroy your daughter.'

'Don't be silly,' he said. 'There's nothing I can say about Linda that would do her any harm.'

'If you were stone-cold sober, I'd agree with you, but you're not. You could come out with all sorts of silliness right now. You might even wax strong about the baby.'

Ron, who still had hold of his glass, took another big swig of champagne.

'What's wrong with talking about the baby? All Linda's sisters were pregnant before they settled down.'

Holly started to get desperate. There was no reasoning with this man. To him, it was perfectly normal to get up at a wedding half-cut, just as it was usual to have babies without fathers.

'So you're determined to go through with it?'

'Whose to stop me?'

'Nobody. Only I doubt if Linda will ever forgive you.'

The old man swayed slightly, letting his eyes go out of focus. Then suddenly, with a superhuman effort, he pulled himself together.

'The problem with you,' Ron said finally, 'is that you're a rotten little snob. And Linda's just as bad. She's ashamed of where she comes from, and she's ashamed of her mum and dad. I saw it the moment we walked into the registry office.'

He drew himself up to his full height. 'I'm not going to make this speech,' he said, 'not because of what you want, or what Linda wants either. I'm standing down because I'm buggered if I'm going to waste any more of my time here.'

With that he strode past Holly back into the party. She

274

followed in time to see him grab hold of Linda's mother and hustle her out of the door.

Holly started to feel guilty about what she'd done. She hadn't meant to offend the old man. All she'd wanted to do was shut him up.

She hurried over to her new stepmother to explain herself. 'You mean Dad won't be making his speech after all?'

Holly nodded miserably. 'He's gone home in a huff.'

Linda looked at her new stepdaughter and felt torn. Part of her was glad her father had stormed out. She'd never have lived it down if he'd passed out half-way through the wedding speech. But there was another part of her – the part that had once lived in Essex, the part that loved her parents. The part that felt ashamed.

I bet Dad was mortified when Holly told him he was too pissed to make sense, she thought. Nobody ever accused him of that before. Even when he's shifted a whole lot more booze than he did tonight.

'Dad will get over it,' she said to Holly. 'But if you ever run into him again, make sure you apologize for what you did.'

39

Pregnancy slowed Linda down. Where she once bounced out of bed at six in the morning, now she crawled. The sickness had gone, but it had been replaced by a lethargy which was quite unfamiliar to her.

The old Linda would have shaken it off with an aerobics class or a course of medication. But she wasn't the old Linda any more. She was a heavy, slow-moving creature who had to sit down whenever she felt she was doing too much.

They were very nice about it in the studio – or they put on the appearance of being nice, fluttering around her as if she was going to give birth any second. But underneath all the concern, Linda sensed the powers that be were becoming impatient with her. Bobby, the director, whom she trusted implicitly, was starting to complain about the shadows under her eyes and Linda noticed that she was starting to appear less and less in close-up.

She had promised herself early on that she would work right up to the last moment, but now she realized she was being unrealistic. She was too far gone to anchor a programme that demanded she had all her wits about her. If she went on trying, she realized, she would do herself considerable harm, so she bowed out with all the grace she could muster.

Towards the end of the week Linda took Bobby out for a drink and told him she was going home to wait for her baby.

The director was less surprised than she imagined.

'I thought this might happen,' he told her, 'so we've organized for someone to come and fill in while you're away.'

She might have slowed down, but Linda was still capable of looking over her shoulder, and she didn't like the sound of this new arrangement of Bobby's. She did her damnedest not to look anxious.

'Can you tell me who that someone is?' she asked as innocently as she could.

Bobby looked furtive. 'It's one of the girls who works for BBC North-West, Gail Roberts. She wants to get some experience on a network show, and we thought this would be a good chance for her.'

Linda nibbled the end off a perfectly manicured nail. Gail Roberts wasn't exactly a cub reporter. She was a couple of years younger than Linda and she was good – too good to stay in the North for the rest of her life. Linda's guess was that once Gail had got her feet under the table, she'd be making a bid to stay on *The Morning Show*.

'I will be coming back after the baby,' Linda told Bobby. 'Or weren't you aware of that?'

The director pursed his lips, which was a bad sign. When Bobby made that face, you knew you were in trouble.

'You say you're coming back,' he replied, knowing that he was treading on dangerous ground. 'Can I believe you? You've only just got married; you might find you like staying at home looking after hubby and the little one.'

Linda shifted uncomfortably in her seat. 'You're saying motherhood will change me.'

'It changes a lot of women.'

With a certain amount of effort, she summoned up the last of her energy.

'And a lot of women stay exactly the way they were. I'm not the type to start knitting, and I don't think I ever will be.'

Bobby patted her hand. 'Stop getting so worked up. I personally don't think you're going to turn into an earth mother either, but you can't blame me for hedging my bets. Gail's a good substitute. She hasn't got your polish or your sex appeal, but if push comes to shove, I can make do with her.'

Linda sighed. In the old days she would have gone to the Director of Programmes and made a fuss about Gail, but she was so big and so ungainly right now that she risked making a fool of herself.

Nobody's going to take me seriously when I'm like this, she thought. My only option is to go home, have this baby and get back to work as soon as I can.

Linda gave Bobby her nicest, most sincere smile. 'Give Gail my love,' she said. 'We knew each other when I was working in the North.' She paused. 'And tell her not to make herself too comfortable while I'm away. It won't be worth her while.'

Linda started to depend on Holly. She had no intention of imposing herself, but she was in need of a second pair of hands, and the girl was there.

Holly should have been looking for a job, of course. Ever since she came back from New York she'd been talking about it, but apart from reading the sits vac column in the media magazines, she didn't actually do anything about getting employed.

Linda thought about the way it had been for her. Her father wouldn't have allowed her to lounge about the house the way Holly was doing. She had had to earn her keep. She wondered if all this mollycoddling was good for the girl.

If Holly's allowed to get away with doing nothing, Linda thought, she's going to turn into a couch potato.

So she put her to work.

'As long as you're at home,' she told Holly, 'I want you to pull your weight.'

In Holly's case this meant going to the supermarket three times a week, cooking dinner most evenings and generally making sure the housekeeper Linda had hired was doing her job properly.

Linda half expected the girl to protest – she'd never had to lift a finger in the house before now – but to Linda's surprise, Holly settled down to the routine.

She even seemed to enjoy it, organizing Linda and Jason with almost military precision. Meals appeared like clockwork. Jason was banned from going to Linda's breathing classes, and Holly went in his place, so he could be in the office.

Linda gave in to all of it. In the last lazy months of her pregnancy, she handed over to Holly and was grateful the girl was so willing to help.

It was in this mood that, Linda finally confessed the truth about Harry Dane.

She brought the subject up when the two of them were sitting in the drawing room indulging in a cream tea, complete with chocolate eclairs. Holly liked to spoil her stepmother with treats like this, which made Linda feel even worse about what she'd done.

'Did you ever wonder how Harry Dane ended up with the job you used to have?' she asked.

Holly selected a mille feuille from the pile of cakes and put it on her plate.

'I don't give too much thought to my old job,' she said absently. 'All that happened a long time ago.'

'But it must have seemed odd about Harry,' Linda pressed. 'I mean, why him of all people?'

Holly dug into the cream sandwich with her fork, squashing it into two halves. Finally, when she'd taken a mouthful, she turned to Linda.

'I suppose I thought it was a coincidence when I ran into him at your wedding. But it didn't bother me.'

'Well, it should. You see, I fixed Harry up with the job.'

Holly regarded her stepmother with a certain curiosity. 'I don't think it's such a big deal. Obviously Harry was looking for a job and he must have asked all his father's friends for leads. You came up with something he wanted.'

'You don't think it was disloyal, touting your old job?'

Holly shrugged. 'If Harry hadn't landed it, some other clever clogs would have. Anyway, I didn't want to go back to the programme. I've had enough of television to last me a lifetime.'

Linda looked horrified. 'How can you talk like that? Television is the only work experience you've got.'

'So I'll get other experience.'

'At what? Waiting on tables? Serving in a shop? That's all you're qualified for.'

Holly pushed away the remains of her pastry and tried to look patient.

'I don't have to work,' she pointed out, 'so I don't have to grab the first menial job that's on offer. I can take my time looking around. Something will come up. You'll see.'

40

Jason did his best to control his temper, which was difficult when his wife was being irrational.

'You can't just invite Harry Dane to dinner out of the blue,' he told her. 'He'll think you're up to something.'

Linda would not be put off.

'I am up to something,' she protested. 'I want Holly to come to her senses. If she actually spends some time with this man who's taken her job, she might realize what it is she's lost.'

Jason remembered countless conversations with his daughter on the subject of her career.

'I don't think you understand Holly,' he said. 'She's bored with television. She thinks it discriminates against women.'

'Of course it discriminates against women,' Linda snapped. 'So do a lot of professions. But she can't just throw in the towel because of that.'

Jason reached out and took hold of the hand nearest to him, stroking and smoothing it, until he could feel Linda start to relax.

'Darling,' he said, 'stop getting into such a flap about my daughter. She'll sort herself out.'

'That's what she says. But I don't believe it. Things aren't as easy as when I left school. People are looking for degrees and qualifications, and what does Holly have apart from a couple of A levels?'

They were sitting in the back garden of the house in St Johns Wood. Spring was on its way and all around them she could see sticky horse chestnuts and great sweeping clumps of snowdrops. The gardener would have his work cut out in the weeks to come, Linda thought, and so will I. The baby's due at the end of the month. And I'll have to start getting back on my feet.

For a moment the idea of Holly's willing hands was almost irresistible. She was probably wonderful with babies.

Then Linda pulled herself up short. She was being selfish and she knew it, taking advantage of her stepdaughter's talent for domesticity.

I have to shake Holly out of this phase, Linda decided. I have to get her interested in working again.

'Holly can't spend the rest of her life mooching round the house,' she said to Jason patiently. 'She has to find some goal, some reason for getting out of bed in the morning.'

'And you think Harry spouting on about how much he loves television will do the trick?'

Linda frowned. Why did Jason have to be so difficult about a perfectly simple plan?

'I think Holly needs reminding how much fun her life used to be. I thought I'd ask Brenda Sykes from the programme as well. She lives with one of the anchor men on *Panorama*. When the whole group of them get together they'll talk television non-stop, and Holly will feel like an outsider. She'll hate that. She might also start feeling some healthy resentment for Harry while she's about it.'

Jason regarded Linda with a mixture of love and exasperation. She'd got the whole thing wrong, of course, because she'd made the mistake of thinking Holly was like her.

His daughter didn't give a damn about fighting her way up the television ladder, and Harry's challenging her about it wasn't going to make the slightest bit of difference.

Jason thought about the boy being dragged along to dinner under false pretences. Poor sod, he thought. He'll wonder what the hell's going on.

Ever since he left Eton, Harry Dane had been on the top of every ambitious mother's list.

He was invited to Ascot and Glyndebourne in the Season.

If a family had a country house, then Harry was asked for weekends. And every debutante who had a coming out ball wanted to dance the last waltz with him.

If Harry had been a conceited man, he might have put his sudden popularity down to his strong rugger-playing physique, or even his exam results, for most of his tutors predicted a brilliant future for him. But he knew none of it was true. Harry was the darling of the social set because he had a famous father.

Clement Dane, or Sir Clement Dane, as he had become, was one of the most distinguished actors on the British stage. When he played the lead in a Shakespeare tragedy, he spoke his lines with such passion, such clarity that even the longest speeches became instantly accessible.

All the years of his childhood, Harry grew up in the golden glow of his father's fame. He knew the family wanted him to follow him into the theatre, but right from the start he had rejected it. He adored his father, but he didn't want to be a second-rate clone of him. He went to Edinburgh University instead of RADA, and when he came down with a first-class honours degree, Clement was somewhat mollified. His first-born had it in him to succeed. Now what he needed was a job.

His old friend Jason solved that problem, obligingly fixing Harry up with something in television. Then, a few months later, Jason asked the young man to come over for dinner.

Harry rang to tell Clement about the invitation. Then, to his surprise, his son calmly added that he had no intention of accepting.

'Jason's trying to palm his daughter off on me,' Harry said. 'It's always happening and I'm sick of it. If I'm interested in a girl, I'll make contact. I don't want her parents pushing her at me.'

Clement understood what Harry was saying – but right now those girl problems were of little account. What mattered, what was totally unforgivable, was that his son was turning down a mentor. You didn't do that in business if you wanted to get on.

'I don't care how you feel about the girl,' Clement told Harry. 'I want you to say yes to that dinner.'

'Because Jason got me a job?'

'Precisely. It was a major breakthrough and, who knows, there could be more where that comes from.'

He sensed his son retreating from him as he spoke and he wondered why.

'Dad,' said Harry in a voice Clement recognized as dangerous, 'I'm not looking for favours. I would have preferred to find my own job in the first place, only you'd called all those people so I went along to the interviews to stop you looking like a fool.'

Clement could feel his temper rising. If he didn't have to be in full costume in an hour's time, he would have gone round to Harry's flat and given him an earful. As it was, he had to make do with the telephone.

'I suppose,' he said icily, 'you accepted the job on *The Morning Show* to stop me looking like a fool as well.' He paused for a moment. 'Come off it, lad. You've done more than well out of Jason, and now the time has come to pay off the debt. All I want you to do is to go along to dinner and be your most charming self.'

'But if I come running when her family click their fingers,' said Harry, 'Holly'll think I'm some kind of puppy dog.'

So that's the problem, the old actor thought. He's taken a shine to the girl, but he doesn't want to look too eager. Well, to hell with his pride. If Jason wants him to go to dinner, then to dinner he'll go.

'If you don't accept this invitation,' Clement said, 'you'll look a damn sight worse than a puppy dog. You'll look like an ungrateful hound. And no son of mine goes around behaving like that.'

When Harry's taxi pulled up in front of the grand house where he was having dinner, all his worst suspicions were confirmed. This was a rich family with a spoilt darling they wanted to get off their hands. He'd been through this routine so many times, he could almost predict what would happen.

Jason would give him a too-large drink, and before he was half-way through it, he would be thoroughly quizzed about his job and where he thought it would lead him.

If the old man was really desperate, he would probably offer to help him, suggesting business contacts of his that he could introduce Harry to. Then just when Jason thought he had him on the hook, the girl would appear, done up like a dog's dinner, ready to be wooed.

Harry shivered slightly as he got out of the cab and handed over his fare. This was going to be a short evening, he decided, short and sweet. At his age, he had no intention of being done up to the nines.

Linda answered the door, looking anxious and far too pregnant to be giving a dinner party. For a moment Harry felt concerned for her. Then he thought, to hell with it. She was the one who issued this invitation; she knows exactly what's going on.

He allowed her to take his coat and lead him through to the drawing room where he saw Brenda, his duty editor, a man he vaguely remembered seeing on some current affairs programme, and Holly. They were all standing in front of the fire giggling at something Brenda had said, and Harry guessed they were probably talking shop.

He made his way towards them, but was intercepted by Jason, who wanted to know what he wanted to drink.

Here it comes, the young man groaned inwardly, the cross-examination. But Jason wasn't in the least bit interested in what Harry was doing. All he wanted to talk about was Clement. The two of them had been King's Road cowboys in the sixties and for the next half-hour Harry was subjected to a blow-by-blow account of the girls they chased, the girls they conquered, the girls they shared.

He'd heard Clement tell these self-same stories time and time again, so he pasted a polite smile on his face and mentally tuned out.

On the other side of the room, Holly and the other two were joined by Linda who had stories of her own to tell. Harry watched helplessly while the four of them dished the dirt on the programme, the hierarchy at the BBC, and a colleague whose name he caught just before Jason's voice eclipsed the rest of the conversation.

It was so frustrating. Here he was, trapped in a boring discussion about his family, when he could be in the swing of things.

Without meaning to, Harry glanced across at Holly, who was at the centre of the group. She was looking surprisingly demure for a girl who was out to trap a man. She wasn't wearing any make-up and her long dark hair had been scooped back into a ponytail. Then he noticed she was wearing trainers — trainers and leggings and a long, baggy sweater that came halfway to her knees. For a split second, Harry wondered if Holly was staying to dinner. Then he thought, of course she is. Why else would they have gone to all this trouble?

After they'd all trouped into the dining room, Linda directed Harry to a place at one end of the table, where he found he was sandwiched between Holly on one side and Brenda on the other. Directly opposite them was the television man who had been introduced as Richard Davis from *Panorama*.

It was Richard who got much of Holly's attention. She seemed to know most of the BBC current affairs crowd and the two of them launched into an excited babble. If Harry had been working longer in broadcasting he might have been able to cut in, but being relatively new, he kept his mouth shut and felt a complete fool.

In the end it was Jason who came to his rescue. He started talking about the theatre. Harry had grown up surrounded by it all his life, so he could relax and talk about it with his old confidence. One of them told a silly story about Clement going to Hollywood for the first time, and after that there was no stopping them. The anecdotes, the scandals, the sheer bitchery of the theatre came pouring out, holding the rest of the table completely spellbound.

The caterers served the soufflés. Then completely unnoticed they took the empty plates away and replaced them with foie gras and salad. They could have put down pease pudding and chips for all the difference it made, for once the ice was broken everyone weighed in with their own memories of the theatre: Brenda had once dated a stand-up comic; Richard had started his life in drama school; Holly had Eve for a mother.

Childhood memories were irresistible, and Holly found herself pouring out those memories to Harry, who understood completely.

Holly realized she was looking into a mirror. Everything that Eve had done to her, Clement had done to Harry. He had experienced the same loneliness, the same hurts, the same feeling of being abandoned, and just for a moment she felt curious.

'Did your brothers go through all that too?' she wanted to know.

'No, they got off scot-free. I was the eldest, so I think I was the only one Father really focused on. He saw me as a younger edition of himself and for years he dragged me round the dressing rooms and the back stage parties, so I would know the world I was going into.'

He paused and took a sip of his wine. 'I hated it, of course. He pushed it at me too hard and I rebelled. When I was very little I vowed wild horses wouldn't persuade me to be an actor.'

'So you went into television instead.'

He grinned and some of his brashness dissolved. 'It was the first job that came up,' he admitted, 'but I wouldn't have said no to a job in journalism, or film if the offer was there.'

He went on about his ambitions, talking about what he wanted for the future and with a pang he realized he was doing all the things he vowed he wouldn't. He was telling the story of his life to some girl who could just have designs on him.

The thought distracted him and he stopped listening to what Holly was saying. In that instant he lost her. When he looked up he saw she had started another conversation across the table, and when he tried to cut in, it was no good at all. Holly was completely tied up with somebody else.

Just for a moment Harry wondered whether she really was after him. Most of the other girls who chased him certainly made more of an effort with themselves. None of them would consider coming to a smart party in trainers.

He looked at Holly babbling on to Brenda Sykes. No girl who was seriously out to nobble him would ignore him like this either. He didn't know whether to be relieved or furious. Then he listened to himself and realized he was furious.

He was just about to say something really rude to her, something that would stop her in her tracks, when he heard Linda bring up the programme he was working on. She was talking about the job he was doing, and suddenly he was all ears.

'Researchers on current affairs programmes can go a long way,' Linda was saying. 'It's a direct route to better things. I wouldn't be surprised if Harry doesn't make producer or even assistant director.'

While Linda was talking, Harry noticed she was looking directly at Holly. There was something aggressive about the way she was doing it, almost as if she were rubbing it in that Holly had once had the chance he had. And she had blown it.

He saw Holly flinch and look miserable, and all at once the fury he had felt at her earlier completely disappeared. Now he simply felt sorry for her.

Poor kid, he thought. She's been ignored all her life by her real mother, and the replacement, instead of supporting her, is out to get her.

He decided Holly needed someone on her side, someone who would come to her rescue, who would put her adversaries in their place.

'Harry,' Linda was saying, 'how do you feel about the chance you've been given?'

He took a sidelong look at Holly and decided this was the moment he had been waiting for.

'I'm grateful for the job,' he said, 'but I'm not going down on my knees.'

Linda looked at him sharply. 'Why is that?' she demanded.

'I would have thought a student with no experience would genuflect just a little bit.'

'That's where you're wrong. Students with no experience have all the options in the world. They can go abroad and rough it for a bit, they can follow in their father's footsteps, or they can grab the first job that takes their fancy and try to make a go of it. I went for the job, but that doesn't mean I did the right thing.'

Linda's voice was tinged with ice. 'Maybe you'd like to tell me what the job lacks.'

'The job doesn't lack anything. The lack, if there is one, will be with me. It could turn out I'm not suited to television. Or maybe this wonderful opportunity is beyond my abilities. There are no guarantees. You can't just sit there complacently and expect everything to work out as you'd planned.'

Jason cut in on him. 'Harry's right. I started out as an actor, but it didn't suit me at all.' He turned to his wife. 'You were one of the lucky ones. Not everyone is as sure as you were about what they wanted to do.'

Harry looked at Linda and realized he'd done what he'd set out to do. The woman was completely deflated. It would be a long time before she considered having another go at Holly, at least when he was there.

He checked to see how his little speech had gone down with Holly, but to his surprise he saw she wasn't impressed at all.

'I suppose you thought that was very clever,' she told him.

'I thought it was very necessary. Your stepmother was in danger of making mincemeat out of you.'

'So you zapped her for her own good.'

He looked deep into her eyes. 'I did it for you, actually.'

He thought she was going to hit him. 'You mean you humiliated Linda to score Brownie points with me. Give me a break, will you? There are easier ways to impress a girl.'

She was incandescent with rage and he felt like a hero in an old Hollywood movie. I should tell her she's beautiful when she's angry, he thought. Then I should kiss her.

He suddenly realized nobody else at the table was saying

anything and he looked up to see every eye was on them. Holly grinned and Harry realized she was laughing at him too.

He cursed himself for his stupidity. He'd fallen for this girl right under the eyes of her family, and it turned out that the girl herself couldn't give a damn whether he lived or died.

When the dinner party conversation went back to normal, Harry made a decision. He wasn't going to let Holly go — that would be cutting off his nose to spite his face — but from now on he was going to keep her at arm's length. Until she showed him she felt something for him, he would simply have to treat her like a little sister.

41

In the weeks before Linda's baby was born, Holly allowed Harry Dane to take her out to dinner a couple of times. He was surprisingly good company, and he seemed interested in what she had to teach him about television.

If she allowed herself, Holly could have become quite distracted by him, but there were other claims on her attention.

Linda was about to produce Holly's new brother – they'd known it was a boy for months now. And even though she knew he would push her out of the way, she couldn't help but be fascinated.

Hours after he was born, she rushed round to the hospital, curious to see her new rival. The moment she looked at him, all her resentment evaporated, for he was quite beautiful.

It was his eyes that set him apart. Other children had glassy, out-of-focus eyes. Linda's child had nothing of the sort.

For a start they looked different. They seemed a brilliant shade of violet, a bit like Liz Taylor's in her heyday. And there was an intelligence behind them. When Holly walked into the hospital room the baby looked at her. It was an intense, curious gaze, and when she moved around the bed to talk to Linda, the violet eyes followed her.

'Does he look at everyone like this?' she asked Linda, and her stepmother laughed.

'Tommy only does that with the people he loves,' she said.

It was the first time Holly heard his name, and she marvelled at Linda's fast decision making. Two days ago Jason and Linda had been at loggerheads over names. Now, without appearing to consult anyone, Linda had gone for Tommy, which nobody had even considered.

'What made you choose Tommy?' Holly asked.

'I opened the book with all the names in it, closed my eyes and stabbed a pin on the page. That was the name that came out.'

Holly was appalled. 'How could you do a thing like that? You might have lumbered the poor little mite with a name like Moses or Alphonse.'

Linda was unperturbed. 'If I had, it wouldn't have mattered. People become their names, not the other way round. If Tommy had turned out to be Moses, he would have been Moses his way. The name would have taken on a totally individual dimension.'

There was a long silence while Holly regarded her stepmother. Childbirth had clearly unhinged her. She was about to ask how much longer they would be keeping her in hospital when Tommy started to cry.

Linda seemed flustered by it. As if crying was something she hadn't read up on yet and didn't know how to deal with.

'Holly, darling,' she said, 'could you ring for the nurse? Tommy needs something.'

Holly hurried over to the cot. Then instinctively she lifted the baby up in her arms and held him over her shoulder. The child made little snivelling, choking sounds, so she rubbed his back until the wind came up. The crying stopped after that and Linda looked at Holly in total astonishment.

'Who taught you how to do that?' she demanded.

Holly cradled Tommy in her arms and said nothing, for she realized she must have been born knowing what to do when a baby cried. Some women are, and others, like Linda, would never really be at ease with their offspring no matter how many books they read.

Holly gently put the baby back in his crib. As she lowered him on to the blanket his eyes came open and the violet stare hit her with full force. She stared back mesmerized. Then Linda's voice broke the enchantment.

'You seem to have made quite a hit with my son.'

She spoke with a sharpness Holly hadn't heard before, almost as if she was jealous of the bond the girl had formed with the baby.

Holly straightened up then, tearing herself away from the violet eyes.

'He might be your son,' she said softly, 'but he's my brother. Let me love him just a bit.'

'I'm being silly,' Linda said, brushing away tears. 'The doctors warned me I'd be all over the place.'

Just for a moment, Holly felt sorry for her stepmother. She was so in control in the studio, so tight and buttoned up. Yet here, in an ordinary, everyday situation, she was marshmallow. Holly hurried over to Linda's side of the bed.

'Cheer up,' she said. 'Everything will settle down once you get home.'

'Of course it will,' said Jason.

He had come in silently, without either of them noticing, and now he was standing over the crib.

'How do you like your brother?' he asked Holly.

'I think he's lovely,' she replied. 'I like his name too.'

Jason looked momentarily confused. 'What name? He hasn't got a name.'

'Oh yes he has,' said Holly. 'Linda picked it out with a pin this morning. He's called Moses. Moses Alphonse . . .'

As soon as she got home, Linda did three things. She started a strict diet, went on a course of muscle-tightening exercises, and put an ad in *The Lady* for a nanny.

The ad produced results. During the next week or so a shower of applications arrived at the box number.

Holly helped Linda go through the letters and together they arrived at a shortlist of around a dozen possibles. Then the interviewing started.

Linda let Holly sit in while she was seeing the nannies, and she was pleased she did. Holly's experience as a researcher led her to ask the kind of questions nobody else would have dared.

The girl found out in record time whether or not the

293

candidate had a boyfriend, a drug habit, or an attitude problem. When Holly had finished there were only three left worth considering: a Norland nanny who went in for titled families; a motherly type who had dedicated her life to the very young; and a former nurse.

The Norland nanny ruled herself out when it came to discussing perks. It seemed the girl needed three nights off a week and her own bed-sitting room where she could entertain her friends.

The motherly type had a different problem. She wanted to be part of the family. The idea of staying in her room was anathema to her. If Linda was giving a dinner party or just watching television, Mrs Briggs wanted to be included.

'It's better for Tommy if we're all close,' she explained. 'He'll grow up knowing there's love in the house.'

After that Holly put on her most enquiring manner and asked a few more questions. It turned out that Mrs Briggs was a member of an outlandish religious sect which preached all men were brothers under the skin and should share and share alike.

After Linda showed her the door, they were down to the final name – Angela Collis, the former nurse.

Angela Collis couldn't have been more suitable if Linda had sat down and written out her CV herself.

She had trained as a nurse straight out of school and because she loved children she was put to work in the maternity ward of the local hospital in her native Glasgow. Five years later the department was closed down. Angela had applied to several other hospitals with maternity wards, only to find they were all fully staffed.

In the end it was one of her former colleagues who suggested nannying, after which she never looked back. To date Angela had worked for a vet with three daughters under five. From there she moved on to a belted earl whose second wife had recently given birth.

When the child was a toddler, Angela got taken on by a widower whose wife had left him to bring up twin girls who were still at the nappy stage.

She had been with that family for the longest – nearly seven years. Then her employer was given a posting to Canada and once more Angela was on the job market.

As Angela told them about her work experience, Holly could see her stepmother getting more and more excited. Holly could sense Linda was on the brink of offering Angela the job and she hoped against hope the former nurse wouldn't flunk out at the last moment.

'Do you have a boyfriend?' she asked Angela. 'I know a lot of nannies like their men to stay over.'

The girl blushed to her Presbyterian roots.

'I'm not keeping company with anyone at present.'

One down, one to go, Holly thought. She glanced at Linda, but the blonde had decided to take a backseat on the final negotiation. So Holly ploughed on.

'What about free time? I expect you'll want a few evenings to yourself.'

Angela didn't hesitate. 'I fit my time around the baby,' she said. 'If little Tommy needs me seven nights a week then I'll be there for him.'

'What about when he doesn't need you?'

'Then I'll have the usual two evenings whenever it suits your plans.'

Holly was dumbfounded. The woman was perfect. No matter what she asked her, there was no way she could trip her up.

She turned to Linda. 'I think you've found what you're looking for,' she said softly.

Linda nodded. 'I think I have.'

42

Linda stared at the phone in her hand before replacing it carefully on its cradle. What she had just heard was about to change the entire pattern of her life. Her new nanny had just told her she wasn't going to start work on Monday after all. A better job had come up unexpectedly, a job working for an industrialist who had a house in Belgravia and an estate in Wiltshire. He had made her an offer to take on the family's two small sons, and she had to look after her best interests.

At first Linda hadn't believed her.

'Do you want more money?' she asked desperately. 'I'm prepared to match whatever the new man is offering you.'

This made next to no impression on Angela. 'It's not just the money,' she said, 'it's the conditions. Mr Irving is giving me my own suite in the Belgravia house, with the same arrangement when we all go down to the country at weekends.'

'I suppose he's invited you on shooting parties as well,' said Linda sarcastically and immediately regretted it.

She had to humour this nanny if she wanted to hang on to her job. But she had gone too far. Angela informed her in no uncertain terms that she resented her attitude, and nothing in the world would make her change her mind.

In the end, Linda accepted defeat, after which she limped into the drawing room and poured herself a stiff whisky. Jason was out playing golf, so she had nobody to turn to in her moment of need.

All she could do now was to get slightly high on booze before she worked up the courage to call Bobby and tell him she wouldn't be coming into work tomorrow.

She could almost envisage his reaction. 'You're anchoring a networked show,' she could hear him say. 'You're not allowed to have nanny problems. Gail Roberts wouldn't behave like that.'

Bobby wouldn't fire her out of hand, of course. It wasn't the way he operated. He'd be patient with her while she got another nanny.

Then he'd bide his time until the next crisis. And there was bound to be one. Nannies who were any good at the job were notoriously fickle. Linda could get hold of an angel one day, only to find the angel had decided to emigrate to Australia two months later.

She took a large gulp on her whisky, and thought about the years to come when she would be dancing to the demands of whichever nanny deigned to come and work for her.

I'll never be free, she thought. These girls will hold me to ransom until Tommy is old enough to go to prep school.

The whisky was going to her head. She could feel her knees buckle slightly as she went over to the drinks cupboard to pour herself another. She was so intent on not spilling any of it that she didn't hear Holly come into the room.

'Drinking in secret?' the girl teased. 'The new nanny will never approve.'

Linda looked up. 'The new nanny isn't coming,' she said hollowly. 'Somebody else made her a better offer.'

Holly did a double take. 'You don't mean she took it? What kind of a person would do that at the last minute?'

Linda poured herself another generous measure of whisky.

'A nanny would do that,' she said wearily. 'That's the way they behave, or didn't you know?'

'You're taking this too much to heart. There are plenty of girls around who behave better than that.'

'Find one,' Linda said bitterly, 'as you're such an expert.'

Holly couldn't believe what she was seeing. The poised,

perfectly-in-control Linda was losing it, and all because she was scared shitless that Bobby would fire her once she told him her problem.

Holly went to where Linda was standing.

'Have you tried calling the agencies?'

'No, and I'm not going to. I don't want to put Tommy in the care of someone I've never met.'

'Right now you don't have any alternative.'

The blonde looked defiant. 'Yes I do,' she said. 'I can get you to look after him.'

Holly was rooted to the spot.

'How do you know I'll agree to do that?'

'You love your brother, don't you?'

'Of course I love him, but that's not the point. I'm not a nursemaid.'

There was a silence.

'Nor am I.'

It was blackmail, of course. Linda knew that if Holly turned her down, she'd have to look after Tommy herself. And that would mean kissing her career goodbye.

So kiss it goodbye, Holly thought savagely. There are more important things than television.

She looked at her stepmother then. Linda was flushed from the whisky and there was a desperate look in her eyes. If Linda loses her precious career because of me, Holly thought, I'll never be allowed to forget it. She'll cry on Daddy's shoulder about the sacrifice she's been forced to make, and before I know it, I'll be the villain of the piece.

The vision that had worried her before, of being turfed out of her home, returned to haunt her, for she had no doubts that Linda would want her revenge. Holly turned to Linda then.

'You can stop panicking,' she said. 'I've decided to help you out. But only till I find a job.'

She saw the relief on Linda's face. Then she saw something else, a kind of smugness as if she knew some secret nobody else was in on.

I can guess what it is, Holly thought. Linda thinks she's

home and dry. She's convinced I'll never find another job and I'll be her nanny for life.

She thought of telling her stepmother otherwise, but decided against it. There's no point in antagonizing her, Holly decided.

43

Mostly it was easy to cope. Tommy was a good-tempered little boy and, when Holly was around, not given to complaining.

When Linda came home it was a different story. If he was sleeping, he would wake the instant she got through the door and raise hell until she came to make a fuss of him.

Holly didn't believe it was possible, but she actually looked forward to Linda's arrival. There was something monotonous about the baby routine, with its endless round of feeding, burping, changing. At least when Tommy was being obnoxious, he was doing something.

She didn't admit to being bored because she loved Tommy. But she was bored — bored and torn in two. She needed to find a job, but the thought of handing her baby brother over to a total stranger worried her. What if they didn't understand that Tommy liked his milk cooler than all the books prescribed? What if they didn't hold him just right? What if his private, gurgling baby language meant nothing to them?

In the end she was so convinced that nobody but she could cope that she put her job-hunting on hold.

Then one day her little brother started to run a fever and Holly realized she'd been wrong all along.

It started early in the morning, soon after Linda left for the studio. Holly usually gave Tommy his first feed then, but he wasn't interested in his bottle.

She decided to leave him for half an hour while she got

herself some coffee, but that was almost impossible for the baby was making a noise fit to wake the dead.

Holly picked him up, put him over her shoulder and wondered what on earth was the matter. He was normally so placid. Nothing ever upset him, yet here he was grisling and choking and acting like the world was coming to an end. She tried him with the bottle again, but he smacked it out of the way, sending the whole thing down the front of her shirt, so she laid him down in his cot and felt his forehead. It was burning hot.

Holly ran into the bathroom and grabbed the thermometer. Then as gently as she could, she took Tommy's temperature. When the mercury shot up to 104° Fahrenheit she started to panic. He was sick, there was no doubt of that, but how sick? She'd read about babies running sudden fevers, then going back to normal after a few hours. She'd read about meningitis too. Ringing the doctor was the only thing she could do.

The paediatrician Linda used was out on house calls, but her receptionist was very sympathetic. She offered to bleep the doctor and said in the meantime Holly was to do nothing to excite the baby.

Holly looked at Tommy's face, which was as red as a tomato. What does she think I'm going to do? she wondered. Bounce him on his head to stop him screaming?

For the next half-hour she sat over the phone, but there was no call from Dr Summerfield. In the normal way of things she would have got hold of her father and demanded help, but Jason was thousands of miles away on a business trip and not due back until the end of the week.

Holly looked at her watch and wondered if she should contact Linda, who would be arriving at the studio now and on her way into make-up. The researcher on duty, probably Harry, would be filling her in on the programme order, and she would be concentrating on what questions to ask her first guest. The last thing she needed right now was a panic over Tommy, particularly if it was a false alarm. No, Holly thought, she'd give the doctor a bit longer.

Ten minutes later Dr Summerfield finally made contact. She was nearby in Lancaster Gate and when she heard what the problem was, she promised to be with Tommy as fast as she could.

By the time the doctor arrived, Holly was a nervous wreck. She'd tried picking Tommy up, she'd tried changing his nappy, she'd taken his temperature half a dozen more times, and he was still roaring.

Dr Summerfield, a tall thin woman in her forties, was appalled at his state.

'Haven't you tried to cool him down?' she demanded. 'A flannel soaked in lukewarm water would have helped.'

'Your receptionist didn't tell me that,' Holly said.

The doctor looked at her as if she was a complete fool.

'Nobody needed to tell you that,' she said scornfully. 'It's common sense.'

Then before Holly could say anything else, the doctor was ringing an ambulance.

'It looks like he's caught some bug,' she said, putting down the phone, 'but we can't be sure what it is until we get him into hospital.'

'I'll call his mother,' Holly said, terrified now.

For the first time since she arrived, the doctor nodded her approval.

'I'd get hold of the father as well,' she said. 'These infections can be dangerous.'

It was only then that Holly realized the baby could die. She was meant to be looking after him, and through her total ignorance of the simplest first aid, they were probably going to lose him.

The thought of it terrified her. She loved this little scrap more than anything she had ever loved in her life. And he loved her back, she knew that. He depended on her and trusted her, and in return all she had done was let him down.

I should have taken a course on child minding, she berated herself. If I'd done that, none of this might have happened. But I thought I knew it all.

The ambulance arrived before Holly totally lost control,

302

and Tommy was taken away. Dr Summerfield left Holly the name of the hospital and the number of her mobile phone. Then she hurried after her patient, leaving Holly to get hold of Linda and Jason.

Getting Linda was easier than Holly anticipated. The show had just come off the air and her stepmother was in her dressing room cleaning off her make-up.

When Holly told Linda what was up she didn't scream or carry on the way the girl thought she might. Instead she went terribly quiet and started asking for all the details. When she'd dredged everything she could out of Holly, she told her she was on her way to see Tommy.

'Find Jason,' Linda instructed her. 'His secretary will know exactly where he is.'

The girl in Jason's office, however, was maddeningly vague. She was prepared to divulge that Jason was in New York, but where exactly she couldn't say.

'But he must have given you the name of the hotel where he's staying?' Holly demanded.

The girl didn't say anything for a moment. Then she admitted: 'Mr Fielding isn't in a hotel. He's staying with friends.'

'Then give me the number of his friends. I'll get hold of him there.'

'I'm afraid I can't do that,' the secretary said. 'Mr Fielding left strict instructions to keep the number private.'

Holly lost her temper. 'Look,' she said, 'you're not talking to some out-of-work actress. It's his daughter here, and I'm calling because there's an emergency.'

The girl seemed unconvinced, so Holly told her about Tommy, adding that if Mr Fielding's only son expired, she would hold her personally responsible.

That did the trick. Without any further argument, Jason's secretary gave Holly the New York number where he could be reached.

'His last appointment's at three, so he should be there if you call in twenty minutes.'

Holly put the phone down and stared at the number she

had been given. There was something familiar about it and she went to her Filofax and checked it against a number she already had.

They were both the same. Jason was contactable at her mother's apartment.

Daddy lied to me, Holly thought. When I tackled him about Mummy he said it was all over and he was marrying Linda.

Only it wasn't over. Daddy was in New York and he was with Mummy. There was something fated about her parents, Holly realized. They could divorce each other, live in different countries, Daddy could even find himself another wife, but none of it made any difference.

They belonged together, and if both of them were too blind to see it, then she'd have to step in to do something about the situation.

She hesitated. Before she could start rearranging her father's life, there was another, far more pressing problem on her hands. Daddy had to be put in the picture about Tommy.

Holly dialled her mother's number and, to her relief, Jason picked the phone up.

When he heard Holly's voice, he immediately went on the defensive and demanded to know how she'd got hold of the number.

If she hadn't been so worried about Tommy, Holly might have got nasty and asked why he was keeping it a secret. As it was, she simply told him what had happened.

Jason asked her the number of the hospital, then told her he would be on the first flight to London, and she was to wait for him at the house.

'But I want to go and see Tommy,' she protested.

'You won't be allowed to,' her father informed her. 'They like to isolate very young babies so you'll be wasting your time kicking your heels at the hospital.'

Holly was about to reply that she wanted to be there all the same, but by the time she opened her mouth he had slammed the phone down.

Parents, she thought sulkily. Why can't they ever live up to your expectations?

In the end it was Linda who said Holly could come to the hospital, aware that it would kill Holly to sit at home not knowing how Tommy was doing. Neither Linda nor Holly got any sleep that night.

The doctor had been right about the infection. Tommy had contracted some kind of mystery bug that was running wild through his system. All anyone could do for him was to keep him stable and watch over him.

Every hour or so, one of the duty nurses would come out of intensive care and report on his progress, whereupon Linda would grab hold of the unfortunate woman and subject her to the third degree. Tommy continued to burn up, but he also continued to survive and Linda held on to that.

'He's my son,' she told Holly, 'and he's a fighter. He'll get through this somehow.'

'If he doesn't,' said Holly mournfully, 'it will be my fault. I should have spotted he wasn't well much earlier and done something about it.'

'What on earth could you have done?'

The girl told her about Dr Summerfield's idea for cooling him down with a flannel.

'Everyone does it,' she said. 'Everyone with the slightest idea about babies.'

To her surprise, Linda dismissed this out of hand.

'I've never heard such nonsense,' she told Holly. 'That's First World War stuff. The next thing you'll be saying is she recommended blanket baths.'

Linda took a deep breath to steady herself. 'Look,' she said, 'it's easy to be wise after the event, but the plain truth is that Tommy's got a virus that only Tommy can deal with. There's nothing you or anyone else could have done to change that. So you can stop blaming yourself right now.'

Holly regarded Linda with real affection. There's somebody good under that hard surface, she thought. What a pity she has to go out of our lives.

Jason got to the hospital at eight o'clock the following

morning to find Holly and Linda huddled together on a bench outside intensive care. They were both fast asleep and they looked so completely spent he didn't have the heart to disturb them. Instead he went to find the doctor on duty to ask how his son was doing.

The young man, who looked as if he barely qualified, was surprised at Jason's anxiety.

'Hasn't anyone told you about Tommy?' he asked.

'Hasn't anyone told me what about Tommy?'

The doctor passed a hand over his eyes. It had been a busy night. Still, he thought one of the nurses would have broken the news to the parents. He grasped Jason's shoulder.

'He's going to be all right,' he told him. 'The fever broke an hour ago, now all he has to do is repair himself.' He smiled. 'Babies are very good at that.'

The giddyness of Jason's relief swept away all the anxieties that had been crowding in on him. A few moments ago, he had promised himself he would tell Linda all about the problem with Eve. It was looming too large now. He couldn't be expected to cope with it all on his own. Now he knew that Tommy was going to live, it didn't worry him so much.

I'll tell her another time, he decided. Right now I have different priorities.

44

When Holly had a problem, the first person she went to was Harry. Over the weeks he had become one of her closest confidants because he treated her like an equal.

Other men she saw treated her like a fragile little girl, buying her presents and taking her out to the opera. Holly dismissed them all as phoney because she knew none of them really thought she was in the least bit helpless. All they wanted was to get into her knickers, which was a shame because none of them interested her.

The only one she might have said yes to was Harry, but she knew she had no chance there at all. He was too open with her, too brotherly to have any dark designs on her body, so she reluctantly put the idea to one side and concentrated on their growing friendship.

It had come to the point where Holly could tell Harry almost anything and not be laughed out of court, so she decided to come clean about what her father was up to in New York.

To her surprise he didn't react with the horror she expected.

'Are you sure about all this?' he said after he'd heard her out. 'I mean, have you got any proof your father and mother are back together again? Or is it just gossip?'

They were striding through Hyde Park on a windy spring afternoon. The Canada Geese huddled together on the edge of the Serpentine, fluffing up their feathers against the cold. Holly knew just how they felt. Here she was, confessing her darkest secret, and the reception she was getting was as bleak as the wind.

'You're fobbing me off,' she said angrily. 'You don't want to believe me because you're on Linda's side.'

They were approaching the boathouse and as they did so, the cold hit them. Instinctively Harry put out an arm and pulled Holly towards him.

'I'm not on anyone's side,' he told her. 'I just don't want to see your entire family pulled apart by something that might not be true.'

'It is true,' she said grimly. 'I saw the proof with my own eyes.'

She went on to describe how she had found her father's clothes in Eve's spare bedroom.

'I've always suspected my parents had something going and now I know I wasn't wrong.'

'Have you talked to your father about it?'

Holly made a face. 'Of course I talked to Jason. The minute I got back from the States I talked to him, but he clammed up on me. He gave me some nonsense about not seeing Mummy any more because of Linda, and I believed him.'

'And you don't now?'

Holly struggled free from the protection of Harry's arm. Walking on her own helped her to concentrate better.

'I don't now because I had to get hold of Daddy in New York when Tommy was in hospital, and guess what. His phone number was the same as my mother's.'

'You poor lamb,' Harry said. 'What a situation to be in.'

'I'd save your sympathy for Linda. She's the one who's going to need it when I tell her what's going on.'

All of a sudden Harry was standing stock still and looking at Holly in disbelief.

'You're not going to interfere in all this, are you? It's none of your business.'

Holly looked fierce. 'You don't know what you're talking about. Of course it's my business. It's been my business ever since my parents split up. Have you any idea how miserable it's been for them without each other? They've been like lost souls all these years.'

Harry gave her an old-fashioned look. 'Jason's misery didn't exactly stop him from getting involved with Linda.'

'She threw herself at him, and Daddy was so lonely he couldn't resist her.'

'Pull the other one. He married the girl, didn't he?'

'He had to. Linda was pregnant with Tommy.'

Harry started stamping his feet to keep warm. 'Come on,' he said, 'let's finish our walk at the Royal Lancaster. There's a decent bar there so at least we can go on with this over a drink.'

The bar was built like a conservatory and looked out over the park. At five thirty it was completely deserted. Holly could talk about her family to her heart's content and there was no risk of being overheard.

As soon as Harry had ordered them a bottle of white wine, she returned to the subject of Linda.

'You think I'm being cruel telling her, don't you?'

'I don't think you're being cruel. I think you're going over the top. Look, Jason and Linda and Eve sound like they've got themselves into a hopeless muddle, but it's their muddle for them to sort out.'

'But what if they don't? What if Daddy goes on acting like a coward and nothing happens?'

Harry picked up the chilled wine and poured them each a glass.

'It wouldn't be the end of the world,' he said. 'I imagine your mother is quite happy with the present arrangement.'

Holly stared moodily out of the window. Eve might be content to let things drift, but she wasn't. All these years she'd endured seeing her family split half-way across the world. Because of what? Pride? The inability to admit a mistake?

Well, she wasn't going to let them get away with it any longer. Mummy and Daddy needed each other. They'd proved it by shacking up together. Now the whole thing had to come out into the open.

Holly saw Harry was looking at her. 'You're not listening to me, are you?'

'No, I'm not. I've made my mind up.'

Harry picked up his glass and decided to have one last appeal to Holly's sense of decency.

'What about Tommy?' he asked. 'Linda's not going to put up with your father two-timing her. She'll walk out and take the baby with her.'

The girl looked stricken. 'I stayed awake nights thinking about it,' she told him. 'I can't bear the idea of losing him, and I hate the thought of him growing up without a father—'

'But you're going to leave him to his fate,' Harry interrupted.

'He's very young. He won't even know what's going on.'

She took hold of her glass of wine and downed half of it.

'Believe me, it's better that this happens now,' she said. 'If Daddy drags his feet, Tommy could be as hurt as I was when Mummy left home.'

Holly decided to tackle Linda when Jason was away. She needed her stepmother to herself when she dropped her little bombshell, for she needed to explain exactly what was going on and if Daddy was there, she might not get the chance.

So she bided her time. Ten days later Jason announced he was going to Edinburgh. He would be gone two nights at the very least. It would give Holly the opportunity she was waiting for.

The minute her father was gone, Holly told Linda they needed to talk. She must have looked nervous when she said it, for the presenter hesitated and put her bag down.

She was on her way out to the studio and normally nothing slowed her down.

'Is it important,' she asked Holly, 'or can it wait till I get home tonight?'

Holly thought about it. She wanted to get the whole business out of the way as quickly as possible, but rushing things wasn't going to help.

'Why don't we save it till dinner tonight?'

Linda looked relieved. 'I'll pick up a bottle of claret on my way home,' she promised. 'I've got a feeling we might have something to celebrate.'

Holly watched Linda leave the house and fought down mounting dismay. The woman was clearly expecting her to announce she was finally getting a job. Or worse, maybe she thought she was getting engaged.

All she was going to do was tell her her marriage was over.

Linda came back earlier than usual, carrying a packet of smoked salmon along with the wine.

'I know how you like it,' she said, 'so I thought I'd treat us.'

Her kindness was too much for Holly.

'Linda,' she said, 'I do wish you wouldn't do this. I don't have anything good to tell you.'

The blonde smiled. 'Then I'd better open the wine right now.'

Holly watched her as she went to the cupboard and selected two crystal glasses. Then she popped the cork and poured a generous measure into both.

'Here's to us,' she said, taking a sip, 'and to your news, whatever it is.'

Holly decided things had gone far enough. 'My news is about Daddy,' she told her.

Linda smiled brightly. 'What about him?'

'He's cheating on you.'

Linda didn't say anything. Instead she put her wine down and went over to where Holly was sitting on the sofa.

'That's a hell of an accusation,' she said gently. 'Where did you hear it?'

'I didn't hear it anywhere. I saw it. At lease I saw evidence of it . . .' Her voice trailed off and Linda put her arm round her.

'Suppose you tell me about it right from the beginning. Then at least I can get it straight in my own mind.'

She was so calm, Holly noticed, as if she were discussing the latest programme bulletin instead of losing her husband.

Maybe she'd change her attitude when she knew what was really going on.

Holly told Linda about what she found on her trip to see Eve. Then when the blonde didn't say anything, she went on with the rest of it. She told the whole thing very simply, missing out nothing. When she'd finished, she saw Linda had gone very white.

'I can't believe it,' Linda said over and over again, as if her not accepting it would somehow make it untrue.

'I spoke to Daddy only a few weeks ago in New York,' Holly insisted, 'and the phone he answered belonged to my mother.'

'But he wouldn't do that to me,' Linda said. 'He wouldn't go behind my back.'

Holly looked at her stepmother in despair. 'You've known Daddy under two years. How can you be so sure of him?'

'Because he loves me.'

Holly sighed. 'He also loves my mother.'

Linda put her head in her hands. The last remark of Holly's seemed to have hit home, for Linda didn't say anything for a good five minutes.

Finally, when the girl wondered if her stepmother was crying, Linda looked up.

'It seems I've been living in a dreamworld,' she said bitterly. 'How long have you known about all this?'

'Since last summer, though I was only really convinced a few weeks ago.'

'I have to make some calls,' Linda said shortly. Then before Holly could call her back, she hurried out of the room.

A few minutes later Holly heard Linda go upstairs and she knew she wouldn't see her again that evening.

Holly poured some more wine into her glass and wondered what Linda was going to do. Would she call Jason in Edinburgh? Or would she call her lawyer? And at the end of it, would any of tonight's events rebound on Holly herself?

She pushed the last worry to the back of her mind. She'd

done what she had to do. Now all that was left was to sit tight and see what happened.

Holly slept badly that night. Every time she lost consciousness she dreamed about Linda, and the dreams were so vivid and so shocking that they woke her up.

Once, when she opened her eyes, she realized she was crying. Yet for the life of her, she couldn't recall what had upset her.

In the end she got up to take a sleeping pill. As she crossed the landing to the bathroom where she kept them, she thought she heard Linda moving about above her. She checked the time. It was half past three. No, her stepmother would be dead to the world by now, just as Holly would be when she'd swallowed the Nembutal.

Holly was woken by the alarm in the morning. Automatically she struggled into her dressing gown and went down to the kitchen to make Tommy's first feed. While she was heating the milk, she noticed a difference about the house. It was quieter than usual.

Linda should be leaving for work by now, yet there was no coffee cup in the sink to show she had even got out of bed.

She probably overslept, Holly thought. Any moment she'll come banging down the stairs yelling for some file she mislaid last night.

There was no sign of Linda when she'd finished preparing the bottle, so she decided to look into her bedroom on her way up to Tommy.

She knocked twice, the way she usually did, and when there was no answer, she tried the door and found it was open. The sight that greeted her left her speechless.

Linda wasn't there, but the fact she had once been was only too evident. Every drawer and every cupboard was hanging open. When Holly went into the room and looked closer, she saw none of her clothes was there. Linda's dressing table was completely bare as well, and all her things had disappeared from the bathroom.

Holly ran out of the room and up the stairs, and even

before she reached the nursery, she knew Tommy was gone. By now he would be screaming his head off with hunger. There was only an empty silence.

She's taken him, Holly thought. She got all her things out in the middle of the night. Then she went back for Tommy.

The moment she got into the nursery she saw she was right. The place had the same deserted air as the bedroom. There was no Tommy, no cot, and all the frilly, flouncy things that went round it had gone too.

Linda's left nothing of herself, thought Holly. She crept away in the middle of the night without even saying goodbye.

For a moment she felt guilty. Then she stifled the emotion. She'd done what she had to do. It was painful and difficult, but in the end, when the dust had settled, Daddy would be grateful. They would be a family again. After years apart, Eve, Jason and she would be together the way they were always meant to be.

Holly visualized the way the press would take the news. Every showbiz editor in London would be begging for an exclusive on the reconciliation. The news magazines would want picture spreads of them taken at the house. They would be famous again and she would be back in the enchanted circle.

She looked around the deserted nursery for the last time. Then she walked out and closed the door behind her. You don't make an omelette, she thought, without breaking a few eggs.

45

Linda looked at her watch and breathed a sigh of relief. She'd managed to get clear of the house just in time. Holly would be up by now, looking for Tommy, and when she didn't find him, she'd raise the alarm.

She turned the car away from Swiss Cottage and headed towards the City. By the time Jason comes looking for me, she thought, I'll be long gone.

The thought of her husband brought a rush of tears to Linda's eyes. How could he be so utterly selfish, she wondered, running after me, making me pregnant, even marrying me, when all the time he was in love with Eve?

Ever since Holly told her, she'd tortured herself for not seeing things as they really were. I must have spent the last eighteen months in a trance, she thought. I must have been blind and addled. But she knew she was neither of these things. She had simply been in love and it had grounded her.

Linda sniffed and wiped her eyes. Well, she wasn't grounded any more. She was in full command of her senses and she was on her way home.

There was something almost Victorian about the situation, Linda realized. Some rotter of a man had let her down and she was running back to Mother, Mother and Father and the council estate in Essex.

She stifled her distaste at the prospect. They care for me, she told herself. They may not be rich or influential, but they still have the old-fashioned values. They'd both of them go to their graves defending me.

She remembered the way her father had sounded when she'd called in the early hours of the morning. He'd wanted to find Jason there and then. He was bursting to give him a piece of his mind and it was only when she promised to come home that he'd finally calmed down.

'We'll decide what to do about that husband of yours when you get here,' Ron had told her.

Linda looked at the signposts ahead of her and saw she was coming up to Aldgate. Soon she would be through the East End and Epping would be in her sights.

In the old days, when she was starting her job with *The Morning Show*, she dreaded these drives down to her parents'. They reminded her of all the things she wanted to leave behind her. Now she realized, too late, how stupid she'd been.

Epping was where she had been born. It was her roots, and she needed her roots now. She needed the comfort of knowing where she belonged.

She got to her parents' just before ten. Tommy was screaming his head off as she drove through the rabbit warren that led into the centre of the buildings. She looked at her son, purple in the face with grief and indignation and she knew just what he was going through.

'It's tough for me too,' she crooned softly. 'We'll just have to be brave together.'

She parked the car, worrying that it looked too new and classy, so she locked the steering wheel and all the doors. Then she put the alarm on. If anybody tries to steal it, she thought, at least I'll get an advance warning.

Her mother was overjoyed to see her and the baby.

She'd spent the morning so far making tea and fancy little sandwiches to revive them from the journey. Linda humoured her and tucked in.

She wasn't the only guest at the feast. Two of her sisters, trailing toddlers, crowded into the front room. Then ten minutes later her father arrived.

It was the signal everyone needed. All at once they started to ask Linda about her marriage. Did she know Jason was sleeping with his ex? Had she been in touch with Eve? Was she as glamorous as she looked in the movies?

Linda regarded her nearest and dearest with the beginnings of irritation.

'Stop putting me on the spot,' she protested. 'You're all treating me like a gossip item.'

Her eldest sister grinned at her. 'You are a gossip item. Not everybody gets two-timed with Eve Adams.'

Linda realized the story of her marriage must have gone all the way round the estate. Before she knew it, somebody would make a call to the *Sun*, and there wasn't a damn thing she could do about it.

She turned to her father for support and he rose to the occasion.

'Linda's tired,' he said, looking at her sisters, 'and that baby of hers sounds as if he needs his nappy changing. So go home the pair of you, and don't come back until I say so.'

There was a certain amount of protesting – nothing this exciting had happened in years – but they knew better than to fall out with Ron, so reluctantly they pushed off.

Afterwards, when Tommy was asleep in the spare room, Linda sat down with her parents. She'd promised her father a council of war and now was the time for it.

As accurately as she could she told the story Holly had presented her with last night.

When she'd finished, her mother looked at her.

'It's your own fault for marrying him in the first place,' she told Linda. 'Jason's way out of your class. I could see that at the wedding.'

Linda felt bitter. 'You think that's why he went back to his first wife? Because I'm not good enough for him?'

'Mother didn't say that,' Ron interrupted.

'Then what did she say? That I should have married the boy next door?'

Her father sighed and she could see for the first time how troubled he was. Linda reached out and took his hand.

'I'm sorry. I shouldn't bite your head off. None of this is your fault.'

317

'It is my fault,' he said. 'If I'd put my foot down and stopped you going to London, none of this would have happened.'

'But I wouldn't have had a career then. I wouldn't have gone on television and had my own morning show.'

Ron let go of her hand. 'Fat lot of good it did you. I told you a long time ago that if you went into television, you'd meet a whole lot of people who were way above your head, and I was right. That Jason of yours has made a proper fool of you and you couldn't even see it coming.'

Linda couldn't fault the logic of what he was saying and she wasn't going to try, but in her heart she knew her father had missed the point. She may have been out of her depth when she'd first joined the BBC, but it hadn't stayed that way because she'd learned. By the time she met Jason, she was more than equal to him.

He didn't betray me because I was the wrong class, she thought wearily. He let me down because I was the wrong woman.

Linda regarded her parents huddled together on the G-Plan sofa. Years of living on social security, of pinching and scraping, had left their mark. Both of them had aged beyond their years, and they had a frayed, slightly shop-soiled look.

She looked down at the toes of her polished Gucci boots. Without anything else she was wearing, the boots probably cost more than the total of her mother's wardrobe.

We could come from different planets, she thought. We hardly even speak the same language any more.

It was then that Linda realized she couldn't stay. Her parents would make her very welcome, she knew that, her father had promised her as much on the phone last night, but it wasn't going to work. She had been away from Epping too long now, and the world had made its mark on her. She turned to her father.

'I won't be here for long,' she told him.

He smiled and looked sad. 'I know that, lass,' he said. 'It's written all over you.'

Her mother chipped in then. 'Where will you go next?'

Linda considered for a moment. 'I was thinking of travelling up north. I spent a few years there learning to be a reporter and I liked it.'

The old woman nodded her approval. 'It's not such a bad idea. Did you know you've got an aunt in Newcastle?'

In a way it was Linda's mother that finally decided her. Going north had been a vague idea, a notion she'd tossed out on the spur of the moment, but now she knew she had family in Newcastle, it gave her a reason to go there.

'You'd better give me my aunt's address,' Linda said. 'I could just need it.'

Holly was there when Jason came through the front door, hovering about in the hall as if she had been waiting all day for his return.

Jason immediately smelled a rat. My daughter was never this anxious to see me, he thought. There has to be something wrong.

He put his arm round her. 'What's bugging you?' He felt her shoulders go rigid.

'Things happened while you were away,' Holly said.

Oh my God, it's the baby, he thought. He started to make for the stairs but Holly held him back.

'It's not Tommy.'

He let his breath out. 'So what is it?' he demanded. 'The house hasn't burned down, Tommy's okay. Any minute now you'll be telling me something's gone wrong with Linda.'

He was making his way down the hall as he spoke, going towards the kitchen where he expected to find her. She liked to sit surrounded by domesticity when she came home from work. It reminded her, she often told him, of the real world, the world beyond the cameras.

Today she wasn't sitting in her usual place, and Jason turned to Holly.

'*Is* there something wrong with Linda?' he asked. Then he saw the triumph on Holly's face.

'Linda's gone.'

'Gone where, exactly?'

Holly shrugged. 'I've no idea. All I know is she's gone for good.'

Jason sat down hard.

'Would you mind running that past me again? I don't think I heard you right.'

The girl came over and put her arms round him. 'Daddy,' she said, 'I've done something I should have done a long time ago. I told Linda the truth about you and Mummy.'

Jason pushed her away from him then.

'What the hell are you talking about?'

'You and Mummy getting back together again. It is true, isn't it?'

'No it bloody well isn't.'

Holly did a double take. 'Why do you have to go on lying to me?' she protested. 'I know damn well you've been shacked up in New York for God knows how long.'

Suddenly Jason was very still. 'Is that what you told Linda?'

'Somebody had to. You couldn't go on living a double life.'

He sighed. Holly was right, he had been leading a double life, but it was nothing like the one she imagined. He was about to tell her about it, but there was a more urgent priority.

'What happened when you told Linda?' he asked.

'She was shattered, of course. She had no idea you were still in love with Mummy.'

'So she stormed out?'

'Not immediately. She went to her room first and made a few calls. Then during the night, when I was asleep, she packed up everything. She even packed up Tommy. And she disappeared.'

Now Jason was really worried. If Linda took the baby with her, this was more than a fit of pique.

'Have you any idea where she might be?'

'Do you have to go on about Linda the whole time? What about Mummy? What about us being a family again?'

There was a short silence.

'We were never a family.'

'You can't mean that. It was all over the papers. You and Mummy were a legend.'

Jason got up and went over to a cupboard where he found a bottle of whisky. Only when there was a drink in front of him did he go on.

'You've got it all wrong about Eve,' he said finally. 'We looked like the perfect couple – it was good for business – but in private we were poles apart.'

'But you were in love, weren't you?'

He stared into his glass. 'In the beginning we were in love. But by the time you came along, things were cooling down.' He downed some of his whisky. 'Remember how lonely and left out of things you used to feel when Mummy was on tour? Well, it wasn't any different for me. If anything it was ten times worse. We did our best to paper over the cracks when Eve came home, for your sake more than anything else, but our hearts weren't in it.'

Holly suddenly felt very alone. All her life she had been sustained by the simple belief that her parents were meant for each other, that one day they would find each other again, and now the whole dream had been blown to pieces.

'Was there really nothing left when you divorced?' she asked weakly.

She saw her father attempt a smile, then think better of it.

'We were friends when we divorced. We still are friends. But that's where it ends. The woman I love, the one I really want, is Linda. Only you seem to have lost her for me.'

Holly felt tearful. She'd tried so hard to please her father, to make them all happy, but she'd gone and messed everything up, as usual.

'Daddy, I didn't mean it . . . I didn't know. God, I'm so sorry.'

'I'm sure you're sorry,' he said bitterly, 'but it's not going to bring Linda back.'

Holly was on her feet now, pacing around the kitchen. Thinking aloud.

'She could have put up in an hotel. I'll check everything in the centre, and I'll try the suburbs –'

Jason cut in on her. 'What about the airports? She might have gone abroad.'

Holly shook her head. 'She'll have run to her friends first. Brenda Sykes could be putting her up, or even Bobby.'

She thought through a list of Linda's nearest and dearest. Then she had an idea.

'What if she's gone home?'

Suddenly Jason was all business. 'You know Linda's father, don't you? I saw you chatting to him at the wedding.'

Holly tried to interrupt, but her father was up and running.

'If you drive down to Epping and pay the family a visit, I'll look after everything else. By the time you get back, one of us will know where she is.'

'You don't expect me to go now?'

Jason looked at his watch and saw it was getting on for seven.

'Not unless you've got anything better to do,' he said.

46

Ron Beattie didn't try to disguise his feelings. He was not pleased to see Holly and he made no bones about it.

'What do you think you're doing here?' he said, opening the door to her.

She started to feel sheepish, remembering the last time they had met. He'd been pissed then and she'd virtually ordered him out of the Connaught.

Now he was cold sober, but it didn't make him any more reasonable.

'I've come in search of Linda,' the girl said.

'Well, you won't find her here.'

Any minute he was going to throw her off the doorstep and this whole trek down to Epping would have been for nothing.

Holly put on her most ingratiating smile. 'Can we talk for a moment? There's so much I need to ask you.'

She saw Ron frown and the door start to close. Then she remembered what Linda had advised her to do the next time she ran into him.

'I want to apologize for the wedding,' she said desperately. 'To ask for your forgiveness.'

He hesitated for a fraction of a second, so Holly went on talking.

'I behaved like a cow,' she said humbly. 'It was no business of mine what condition you were in. I should never have stopped you making that speech.'

For about a minute nothing happened. Then, very slowly the door swung open again.

'Do you mean that, or are you just saying it?'

Holly looked into the leathery face of Linda's father. He looked wary, but there was something else, a kind of secretiveness, as if he were hiding something.

'I meant it,' she said as confidently as she could. 'Now, are you going to let me in?'

He stood aside, allowing her through to a room the size of a cupboard. A whole family live in this space, Holly thought. Linda can't be here.

Ron indicated a leatherette chair in front of the gas fire. When she was settled, he took the sofa.

'What do you want to know about Linda?' he asked.

'What do you think?'

The old man was silent. 'I can't tell you where she is,' he said finally. 'She made me promise not to tell anyone.'

'So you've seen Linda?'

'She was here yesterday.'

'So you know what happened with my father? You know why she left?'

Ron looked sly. 'I know some of it,' he said cautiously.

'Then let me explain about the rest.'

'You don't need to. For my money, Linda married the wrong man in the first place. Now she's well out of it.'

'I don't think you understand,' Holly protested. 'Daddy loves Linda. He had no intention of leaving her for my mother.'

Ron shifted about in front of the fire, warming his hands over the plastic coals.

'I don't think it matters now,' he said. 'It's over.'

Holly spent the next hour or so trying to talk Ron round, but there was no budging the old man. He seemed to have made his mind up that Linda was better off wherever she was. And in the end Holly realized she was fighting a losing battle.

As Ron showed her to the door, she made one last plea.

'Is there any chance we'll ever see Linda again?' she said. 'I need to tell Daddy something.'

There was the faintest flicker of a smile. 'Tell him to stop looking for her. He's wasting his time.'

During the next week, Ron Beattie's words came back to haunt Holly. No matter where they looked, no matter how many people they asked, Linda seemed to have disappeared into thin air.

Jason even went up north hoping that some of her old colleagues from *Manchester Today* would provide a few clues, but he came back with nothing. Everyone they talked to was terribly sympathetic and bent over backwards to help, but they simply didn't have any idea where Linda might be.

In a last desperate attempt, Holly went back to Epping. Only this time, Ron didn't even bother to ask her in.

'Linda doesn't want to see you again,' he told her crossly. 'Either of you. I would have thought you'd have got the message by now.'

This time when she went home, she was seriously worried. If she told Jason what she'd just heard, he might give up hope altogether – or worse, he might go to Epping himself to do battle with Linda's father.

As she let herself into the house, Holly sent up a silent prayer for Jason to be out, but as she walked into the large, formal drawing room, he was waiting.

Instead of his usual early evening whisky, he was drinking tea, and when she went to make a joke of it, he failed to see the humour.

He's going to bend my ear about Linda, she thought wearily. Then I'll have to come clean about where I've just been.

But Jason had chosen this moment to talk about her mother.

'You need to know what's been going on between us,' he told Holly.

She looked scornful. 'I don't think so. I know you don't love her any more. So if the two of you have some sordid, 'old-fashioned arrangement, I'd rather you kept it to yourself.' She saw her father look uncomfortable.

'Your mother and I don't share a bed, if that's what you're thinking.'

'Then why the hell have you been secretly shacked up with her?'

Jason didn't reply at once. Instead he poured out some more tea and passed her a cup.

Finally he said: 'I've been staying in Eve's apartment because she needed me. She didn't want you to know this, but she's been terribly ill.'

Holly cast her mind back to last summer in New York. She'd never questioned it at the time, but whenever they planned an evening out together, Eve always cried off with a sick headache.

'Was this illness something to do with her migraine?'

'Your mother wasn't suffering from migraine.'

There was a tight feeling in Holly's chest. 'What was she suffering from?'

'Cancer.'

The word filled Holly with fear, and suddenly she knew why her father had started this conversation.

'She's going to die, isn't she?'

'I had a call from New York this afternoon,' Jason told her. 'Her doctor seems to think it won't be very long now.'

The sheer brutality of the statement took Holly's breath away.

'How long have you known about this?' she asked.

'About a year. Your mother told me she was in trouble around the time Linda moved into the house.'

He stopped talking as the memory of Eve's frantic phone call took over. She had come through on his private line just before lunch.

'I need to see you,' she said.

He thought about his crowded schedule and his new girlfriend and started to tell her it wasn't possible, but Eve didn't seem to hear him.

'I wouldn't ask you if it wasn't important. When can you come over?'

Something in her voice warned him not to argue with her. When she sounded like this, Eve meant business.

He sighed and opened his diary.

'I can come to New York at the beginning of next week. Is that soon enough?'

She said it was and told Jason she'd meet him in the Plaza around lunchtime. This is a new departure, he thought. Eve only drinks in little theatrical bars. But he didn't question her. If his ex-wife wanted to act out of character, it was her prerogative.

She was already there when Jason arrived, sitting at a little table in the Oak Room bar, nursing a glass of wine. He noticed she looked even more beautiful than he remembered. And it was nothing to do with the thousand-dollar jacket she wore.

There was a haunting, forlorn quality about her that was quite new. He wondered what the hell had gone wrong with her life.

He didn't have to wonder too long, for Eve came straight out with what was bothering her.

'I've got cancer,' she said quietly, 'and I don't know what to do.'

They'd talked about it for hours after that. Jason wanted to know how bad it was and if she had a chance of beating it. And she told him if she was prepared to go through with the treatment, then the odds were in her favour.

After that he went with her to see her doctor. The treatment was worse than he imagined and he wanted to know if she had been told about it. The consultant said Eve knew what she would be going through, but he feared she would have a tough time on her own.

It was then he knew he couldn't abandon her. The passion between them was over now and there was someone else in his life, but that didn't mean he absolved all responsibility for Eve. They had shared their youth. They'd had Holly together. He couldn't just forget all that and walk away.

Jason made a plan with Eve. He would be there once every three weeks. It was easy enough to invent a show on Broadway that needed help with the cast. Just as it was easy to lie to his secretary and his staff.

The system worked like a dream. Jason was there for Eve when she needed him, and Linda didn't ask questions about his being away so much because she was busy with her own career. If Holly hadn't decided to poke her nose into his business, Linda would still be none the wiser.

Now Jason looked at his daughter. 'I suppose you want to know why I didn't tell you about any of this?'

'Of course I want to know. Eve is my mother.'

'I know, darling, but my hands were tied. Eve insisted that you weren't to be told. She wanted to protect you from the awful news. You'd suffered enough and she didn't want to burden you with the worry of it. Anyway, last summer, she was convinced her treatment was working and the problem would go away.'

'Only it didn't.'

He nodded. 'In the end the disease was stronger than your mother.'

Holly felt the tears trickle down her cheeks. A few days ago she'd lost Linda. Now her mother was bowing out as well.

'How long does she have?' Holly asked in a whisper.

'A week, maybe two.'

The finality of it made her crumple. All her life she'd known how tough her mother was, how nothing could defeat her or even make her pause in her stride. But in the end, Eve was as mortal as everyone else.

Holly suddenly realized she'd never really known her mother. They were starting to get close at the end of her last visit, but that was over Brett, and there was so much more they had to talk about.

She looked back over her lonely childhood and saw that half of it had been her own fault. If she'd been interested in her mother's career, instead of resenting it, they might have started talking years ago. Now there was no more time left.

Holly pulled herself up short. Of course there was time. Her mother wasn't dead yet.

'How soon can I get to New York?' she asked her father.

47

The door to the apartment was answered by a nurse in a starched white uniform.

'You must be Holly,' she said. 'Your mother's expecting you.'

Holly followed the nurse down the hall, not knowing what to expect. Everything was exactly as she remembered it. Fresh flowers still arrived daily. There was a bottle of champagne in an ice cooler on the drawing room table. Holly half expected her mother to come out of the bedroom, dressed to the nines and ready to go to a premiere.

But that wasn't going to happen. It's all an illusion, Holly thought savagely. She's dying and she can't bear to admit it.

When she came through the door, Holly realized she had been right, for the woman propped up against the pillows was just the same as she was when her daughter had last seen her.

Her dark, lustrous hair fell loose around her shoulders, her face was thinner, but still radiant, and she was even wearing a designer nightie.

Holly ran to the bed and put her arms round her.

'Mummy,' she said, 'I'm so sorry.'

Her mother's body felt fragile and birdlike, as if the girl was holding a doll, and Holly shifted out of the embrace so she could take a closer look.

She wished she hadn't. The luminous woman she had seen when she walked in was a total illusion. Skilful make-up had given her an animation she no longer possessed. Now Holly was near to her, she caught a whiff of fixative. She reached out to touch the thick hair and her hand encountered a wig.

Holly saw her mother watching her, and realized too late she hadn't tried to cover her feelings.

'You're shocked,' Eve said, 'aren't you? You don't think I should take all this trouble to look human.'

Holly bit her lip. 'It's not that,' she told her mother. 'I just don't understand why you still care.'

Eve placed her hand lightly on her daughter's shoulder and pushed her away from the bed.

'Go and sit on the visitor's chair,' she said, indicating a wicker construction half-way across the room, 'and I'll tell you.'

Holly did as instructed.

Then her mother said, 'I don't suppose you have any idea what I'm like under all this?'

'Daddy told me some of it.'

Eve laughed derisively. 'What would he know? This is the only way I've allowed him to see me.'

Holly felt totally confused. 'But why? You were married to Daddy for years. He won't think less of you if he sees how ill you are. He loves you. I love you too. You don't have to do all this.'

She saw the glint of tears in her mother's eyes.

'You're wrong,' Eve said sadly. 'I learned a long time ago in the theatre that people believe in what they see. They look at your face and your hair and the way you wear your clothes, and they assume that's who you are. More often than not they're right.'

'How can they be? There's more to you than just a surface.'

'I wouldn't bet on it. I've been an actor all my life. The only time I'm real is when I'm being someone else.'

Holly looked at her mother. She took in the ridiculous wig and the theatrical make-up and she decided she was over-playing it. She also decided if she let her get away with it, she'd go on talking nonsense. Holly got out of the uncomfortable wicker chair and went over to the bed.

'I don't believe a word you're saying. You weren't born

an actress. You had a life before you went on the stage. Or so Daddy always told me.'

Eve pushed herself up against the pillows and started to look interested.

'What did Jason tell you about my childhood?'

Holly racked her brains. The truth was, her father had always been evasive about Eve's early days. And the only other link with the past, Eve's mother, had died when Holly was very small.

'I never got much out of Daddy,' she admitted. 'I just kind of assumed you had a normal, suburban kind of upbringing like everyone else.'

'Well, you assumed wrong. I didn't grow up like everyone else. I only wish I had.'

As she started to talk about her life in Purley, Eve could almost see the rows of little semidetached houses. They were so neat, so predictable with their net curtains and crazy paving. Who would have thought that behind the respectable, middle-class façade there was a whole family who broke the rules.

No, she thought. I'm being unfair. It wasn't the family who were at fault. She and her mother knew exactly how to behave. Her father was the one who was out of line.

He had worked as a junior partner in a firm of accountants. It was a detailed, rather boring job, made worse by the fact that he didn't get on with any of his colleagues. He would harbour fantasies that there was a plot to oust him from his partnership. Night after night he would come home ranting about the injustices visited upon him during the course of the day.

But some nights Daddy didn't come straight home. Some nights he'd go to the pub with his cronies. Those were the nights Eve dreaded.

Being in the pub seemed to make her father angrier than usual. He'd come crashing into the house late, usually after Eve had gone to bed, and the minute he got through the door, he'd pick a fight with her mother.

Eve would hear them shouting at each other for hours on

end. Then the beatings would start. She always knew when her mother was getting a pasting because her voice would change. Instead of sounding angry, she would start to whimper and beg. Then there would be a loud crack and the whimpering would change to crying.

Eve had known about the beatings for years. It was hard not to know when she had to face her mother in the morning and listen to her trying to explain the bandage on her wrist, or the shining black eye that had mysteriously arrived during the night.

When she was twelve, her mother finally told her what she already knew.

'I want you to listen to me very carefully,' she said. 'You're growing up now, and your father could easily come after you.'

Eve didn't want to show her terror, but she couldn't help it. The thought of enduring what her mother had endured over the years was too much for her.

'We have to run away from here,' she decided. 'If we stay, Daddy might just kill one of us.'

It was over-dramatic, but Pearl Adams took her daughter's point. The next day she went to the post office and drew out her savings book. Then she hired herself a local solicitor who instructed her to make a formal complaint to the police.

Eve's father moved out that evening. Months later she and her mother went to court where the whole shameful story was paraded in front of a judge and a group of locals, some of whom Eve recognized from church.

The worst part was having to stand in the witness box and tell everyone about her father. Out of the corner of her eye she saw him looking at her from one of the benches in front of the court and she was truly convinced he would come over and set about her.

Then she saw her mother and she knew that even if Daddy throttled her, she had to go on with her story.

It was her testimony that got her mother divorced. Daddy was ordered never to set foot in the house again. He was also told to pay for their support.

He kept to the letter of the law on the first instruction, for neither of them ever saw him again. They never saw his money either. From the day the divorce was made final, not one penny went into Mummy's bank account.

The court tried to trace him, but they didn't have much luck. He simply seemed to have disappeared off the face of the earth. And there was nothing anyone could do about it.

Mummy made the best of things. She sold the house, and when she'd paid off the mortgage there was enough to support them in a little flat in Croydon. Then she set about finding a job.

While she was growing up, Eve saw her mother do a variety of things. In the beginning, she cleaned other people's houses, then worked as a receptionist in a succession of grey office blocks on the fringes of the town. It gave them enough money to eat and enough money for Eve to go to drama school. Then Jason came along, and her mother was history.

'But didn't you feel bad about pushing your mother out of your life?' Holly asked after Eve had told her story.

Eve shrugged. 'Not at the time. I wanted to get on and Mummy was in the way. It was only years afterwards, when she still wasn't speaking to me, that I started to worry about it. In the end, of course, you solved the problem. Mummy was thrilled about having a grandchild, so we settled on an armed truce.'

Just for a moment she looked sad. 'We were very civil to each other after that, almost too civil. But I knew that behind her smile, Mummy never really forgave me.'

48

Now Eve had started to open up, the memories came pouring in on one another. There was Jason and the little flat they shared together right at the beginning. All she'd wanted to do then was look after him.

She'd lost the stage for a while when she'd lost her nerve, so everything she had was concentrated on making a life with the man she loved.

Holly sat spellbound while Eve talked about those days. The girl wanted to know every little detail now. It was as if she were a detective looking for the vital clue that would solve a mystery, and the mystery was the theatre itself. What was the secret of its hold on Eve? Why did she walk away from everything that mattered, from everyone that mattered, when it called out to her?

Holly interrupted Eve in the middle of a story about her father and a picnic in Hyde Park. She liked these harmless, happy tales, but she needed to know more now. She needed to know why the honeymoon had to end.

'What made you go back to the stage?' she asked. 'You had everything you wanted.'

Eve looked vague. 'You know, I've really got no idea. One day I just knew it was time. It was like a holiday coming to an end and there was no choice but to go back to work.'

'How did Daddy feel about it?'

'He wasn't all that bothered. I didn't work that much in the beginning. There were bits and pieces of TV, I did a provincial tour, but I was lucky if I scraped a living.'

'Something must have happened to change that.'

Holly saw a glow come into her mother's face then, and she realized that the memory of Eve's first success still had the power to light her up from inside.

She started talking about the Noël Coward revival. A West End management were putting it on a couple of years after she'd last been in the business, though at the time she didn't give it much thought. The backers would be looking for stars. She knew it and Jason knew it, so she was surprised when he came home one night and told her he'd put her up for one of the cameos.

'They're looking for an unknown,' he told her, 'an unknown with hidden star quality that this part will bring out.'

At first she'd laughed at the idea. 'All the wannabees in London will be going after it. I won't stand a chance.'

Jason agreed with her. 'You probably won't. But it will be good experience for you.'

To the astonishment of both, she made the shortlist. Eve and three other actresses were being called to the final audition to see how they played against the leading man. It was then Jason decided he had to be there. Eve was nervous at the best of times. Now she needed all the support she could get.

He arrived at the theatre late to find they'd already started. For a moment, he panicked. If he'd missed her, she'd never forgive him, and if she didn't get the part, she'd blame him for not being there.

He hurried over to where the director was sitting and asked what was going on. The man, who had known Jason for years, grinned like a schoolboy.

'Stop faffing and sit down,' he said. 'Eve's not on till last.'

Jason wedged himself next to the director and focused his attention on the stage. The girl, whoever she was, was putting on a good show. She'd obviously been in rep for years and it showed.

Could Eve pull off anything this professional? Jason wondered. But even as the thought crossed his mind, he knew

336

she couldn't. Her technique had stood her in good stead so far, but how would she fare when she was up against an experienced actress?

The next two girls were pretty much in the same mould. They all knew the tricks and the inspired little bits of business, and they played them for all they were worth. Eve's instincts had better be spot on this afternoon, Jason thought, otherwise she's dead and me sitting here won't make a blind bit of difference.

For the fourth time that day, the leading actor went into the introduction to the scene. Eve was to make her entrance in tennis whites, simpering and silly, yet at the same time utterly adorable. Jason was so worried about whether or not she could do it, that he almost missed her entrance, which would have been a pity, for it set the comic pace for the whole of the next twenty minutes.

He promised himself that he would concentrate on everything she did. He would evaluate her voice, the way she projected, the way she moved on stage. He would even test her memory to make sure she stuck one hundred per cent to the script.

But Jason did none of these things. He simply watched Eve play a flapper. Somewhere during the course of the scene he stopped doing even that, for Eve ceased to exist. All there was out in front of him was a dizzy debutante with a knack for putting her foot in it.

Once or twice he laughed out loud when she said something particularly witty, or did a bit of business that surprised him. Then the scene ended and she stopped. She turned off the magic, and all there was was a bare rehearsal stage and Eve, his protégée, standing in the middle of it.

He wanted to run up and take her in his arms. He wanted to tell her she was the best, the most exciting talent he'd ever had the privilege to watch, but he had no wish to make a complete fool of himself so he sat where he was and listened to everyone else's reaction.

Eve had no idea whether Jason was horrified or thrilled with what she had done. He simply looked stunned. In the end, she stepped down into the stalls and asked him what he thought.

Before Jason could answer the director and the leading man came crowding in on them.

'Darling, you were wonderful, the best, a complete natural . . .'

The compliments piled up on each other, making her dizzy. Eve had got the part. They were making that clear.

She reached out for Jason's hand, searching for his approval, looking to share her success. And he was there for her, her lifeline, the rock in the centre of everything . . .

Now Eve stopped talking for a moment and regarded her daughter. Should I admit the truth? she wondered. Should I tell her I was a fool not to have left Jason then? She looked back over the wreckage of her marriage – of her life – and felt depressed.

The hell with it, she thought. There's no reason to bring Holly down too. I'd rather she held on to her dreams.

She glanced at her watch and saw it was lunchtime.

'We should eat something,' she said, 'and I should get out of bed.'

'Are you sure you feel up to it?'

Eve grinned. 'There's nothing more uncivilized than picnicking in the bedroom. Unless you're with a lover.'

Holly got the nurse and together they moved Eve into a chair, which they wheeled into the drawing room. It was a slow, painful operation, and twice Holly wanted to call a halt and send Eve back to bed, but she knew she shouldn't do that. Reliving the past seemed to have given her mother a new vitality. It wasn't going to last forever, but while it was there it was silly not to make the most of it.

After they'd eaten, Holly pressed her mother for the rest of the story. She wanted to know what happened after she landed the part in the Noël Coward play.

Eve told her everything – how she made her name on the West End stage. How quite suddenly Jason was besieged with parts for her.

How, for the first time, she started to come alive.

338

'It was as if I had been sleepwalking for years. I'd been going through the motions of living, without actually noticing anything. Even when I got together with Jason, the world was still in black and white. And now suddenly it had changed to glorious technicolor.'

Eve paused. 'I know this is going to sound corny, but when I made it as an actress, I realized it was what I had been born to do. Beside it, everything else seemed trivial and unimportant.'

She saw her daughter looking at her, and realized she'd gone too far.

'Now I know why you ignored me all those years when I was growing up. I didn't really exist for you, did I?' said Holly.

Eve held out her hand and motioned her to come and sit beside her.

'Of course you existed for me. You were a part of me, but the theatre was a bigger part.'

She reached up to her daughter's hair and brushed it out of her eyes. 'Do you want me to lie to you?'

It was in that moment that Holly saw her mother clearly. She wasn't like other, ordinary people. She was possessed. Her talent turned her into something else. Holly thought about Van Gogh, and Mozart and all the other gifted misfits who were driven by the fires inside them. Mozart didn't put his family first when he was writing an opera. He couldn't afford to — any more than Eve could afford to when she was playing the lead on Broadway.

Why didn't I realize that before? Holly wondered. Why does it have to be now, when we have so little time left?

Later on that night, when she was in bed, Holly was wakened by the nurse.

'Your mother wants to see you,' the woman told her.

Holly didn't ask why. In the back of her mind she had been waiting for this moment. Waiting for it and dreading it.

As quickly as she could, she pulled on a dressing gown and hurried to her mother's room.

All the lights were on and Eve was sitting bolt upright. Holly did a double take. It was three o'clock in the morning, yet Eve hadn't attempted to remove her make-up or the wig she insisted on wearing.

It was as if she knew she was going to die and she wanted to look her best for the occasion. Holly felt sad. Eve had to play a part, right to the end. Even for her own daughter.

Holly took her mother's hand.

'You asked to see me.'

Eve nodded. 'I wanted to talk about your father. I wanted to know if he was happy with Linda.'

For a moment Holly was nonplussed. It was the early hours of the morning. Her mother was getting weaker. And now she wanted to discuss Linda. Holly decided not to tell her about the drama of the last few days.

'I think Daddy's happy with her,' she stammered. 'Why do you want to know?'

'Because I'd like to think Jason has a second chance. I made him miserable for years and he deserves better.'

Holly was sad that her mother was being so hard on herself. Daddy was a big boy when he took her on. He knew what he was doing.

'You didn't make him miserable,' she said. 'He was lonely sometimes – we both were – but we put up with it because we loved you.'

Eve's voice was a whisper now and Holly had to lean closer to catch what she was saying.

'But he didn't go on putting up with it, did he?'

Holly knew she had to console her mother now. She couldn't let her die thinking she didn't matter to anyone.

'You pushed him out of your life,' she said softly. 'Just as you pushed Pearl out, just as you tried to get rid of me, but you didn't succeed with any of us in the end. We went on loving you just the same.'

It was exactly what Eve wanted to hear. Out of nowhere she mustered a watery smile. It was her best smile, her stage smile, and for a brief second the girl stopped seeing the skeletal face under the stage make-up. There was no wig

340

any more, and no pain. All she saw propped up on the pillows was a lovely woman in the prime of her talent.

Much later, when it was all over, Holly remembered that last moment. By some trick of theatre, Eve had imprinted on her daughter's mind the image she wanted to leave behind. For the rest of her life, Holly would carry it around with her.

49

LONDON, 1991

It was a long shot, but these days Jason was following up everything. A contact on Channel Four had unearthed an old friend of Linda's. Apparently he had once been a boyfriend and from time to time he still talked about her.

Jason had no wish to meet him, but you never knew. If Linda wanted to pick up her life again, Edmund Stern could be someone she wanted to know.

Jason discovered Edmund worked for an independent production company which made gardening programmes for the networks. What on earth was Linda doing with a nonentity like this? he wondered. Then he pulled himself together. A lead was a lead. He owed it to himself to see it through to the end.

He and Edmund met in Jules Bar on Jermyn Street. Jason got there first and spent the next half-hour perched on an uncomfortable bar stool wondering what the hell he was doing. He was due at a casting at three. If he had to hang around for much longer, he would end up missing lunch again.

Still, lunch wasn't such a big deal. He couldn't remember when he'd last had time to eat it.

He was thinking of ordering another drink when a tall balding man came striding into the bar. He was obviously looking for someone and Jason got to his feet.

'Edmund Stern?' he asked.

The man nodded and Jason pulled up another bar stool and introduced himself.

Then he went through the preliminaries. He had been

sounding people out for weeks now, and there were certain questions that had to be asked: When did you know Linda? How well did you know her? Had she been in touch recently? Do you know how to get hold of her?

It took one drink to discover Edmund was a dead end. He'd known Linda years ago, when she was still a secretary and he hadn't had sight of her since.

Jason checked the time. He had to be on his way in fifteen minutes. He tried one last question.

'Were there any mutual friends Linda might still be in touch with?'

Edmund smirked. 'Unlikely,' he replied. 'Linda and I didn't really mix in the same circles.'

Jason should have left it there, but this guy's attitude rubbed him up the wrong way.

'What do you mean, you didn't socialize together? I thought she was your girlfriend?'

Edmund hesitated. 'You're married to her, aren't you?'

'What's that got to do with it?'

'A great deal. Look, I don't want to offend you, but the girl I dated and the girl you married were poles apart. I knew Linda when she'd just got out of Essex. She was rough and tarty as hell in those days. If you'd known her then, you wouldn't have wanted to be seen in public with her.'

Jason fought down the impulse to grab hold of his guest by the scruff of his neatly barbered neck and throw him into the street. 'You're talking nonsense,' he said. 'Linda was never tarty. She doesn't have that kind of mentality.'

'Well, she certainly convinced a lot of people I knew.'

Jason got to his feet and made to leave. He had heard all he needed to hear from Edmund Stern. He slapped some change down on the counter and turned to his guest.

'Do stay and finish your drink,' he said. 'I've just remembered an urgent appointment.'

The rest of the day was ruined. Edmund was one more disappointment in a succession of dead ends. Jason had pulled every string he knew, tapped every contact in his address book, yet the trail stayed frustratingly cold.

Sometimes he imagined Linda had taken off for some remote desert island. He had visions of her hiding in a shack on a windswept beach away from every kind of communication. It was just the sort of thing she would do if she didn't want anyone to find her. And if her father was to be believed, that was the case.

Jason wondered if it was worth his while to pay a visit to Ron Beattie. Then he thought: what's the point? Holly had been there twice now and had no joy. He's not going to go out of his way to make me welcome.

He might have gone on brooding for hours, if his assistant hadn't come into his office.

'How was the casting?' she enquired.

Jason looked blank. 'I didn't take in much of it, but if I'd seen anybody good, I would have noticed.'

In a pig's ear you would have noticed, the girl thought. You've been oblivious to anything other than Linda ever since she disappeared.

She turned to Jason. 'I assume Edmund Stern was a blind alley.'

'The blindest alley yet. I sometimes think I'm wasting my time.'

She was tempted to agree with him. Then she saw how miserable he looked.

'Something will turn up,' she told him. 'It's too early to throw in the towel.' She paused for a fraction of a second. 'Meanwhile you've got a business to run.'

Jason ran his hands across his eyes. 'Give me the urgent priorities. The ones I can't hand over to somebody else.'

The girl read off from a list she held in front of her.

Andrew Lloyd Webber wanted to sound him out about a new musical; a couple of actors he'd spotted in a fringe production wanted to make appointments; Sue Davis, one of his biggest clients, had fallen out with her director, and he had been asked to find the lead for a new production of *Time and the Conways*.

Everything his assistant told him had to be done yesterday, but the pressure didn't bother him. When he was working

344

flat out, there wasn't time to think. He didn't have to feel guilty about Eve dying without him. He couldn't go on brooding about Linda. With luck there wouldn't even be the chance to worry what effect this was all having on his daughter.

'Get Andrew on the phone right now,' Jason said. 'After that, call Sue and tell her to come and see me first thing. Fit the fringe guys in when you can. And I'll read the Priestley play tonight when I get home. There's a copy in my study.'

Jason was home by ten and made straight for his den at the top of the house. *Time and the Conways* was a wordy play, and he knew it would take him till well past midnight before he'd read it all.

He'd plough through the first act, he decided. Then he'd go down to the kitchen and get a sandwich and a cup of coffee. If he didn't eat soon, exhaustion would get the better of him.

Jason took his jacket off and threw it over a chair. Then he went in search of the play.

The heavy oak bookshelves that lined Jason's study contained most of the classic plays. At one time or another he had been called upon to cast most of them and he kept them in alphabetical order. It wouldn't take long to locate the Priestley play. But it was not in its usual place. He found two of Priestley's other plays – he found a Harold Pinter lying next to them – but *Time and the Conways* was missing.

Jason walked along the length of his bookshelves wondering if he could have put it back in the wrong place. And it was then he noticed that the play he was looking for wasn't the only one missing. There were half a dozen gaps he hadn't seen before, and that bothered him. His collection was sacrosanct. Nobody, not even a cleaning woman, was allowed in to dust it. So who had sneaked in and helped themselves?

He thought about the coffee he had promised himself and decided he needed something stronger. A whisky would clear his mind, maybe even help him remember where those damn plays had got to.

When he got to the drawing room, Jason found Holly curled up in one of the sofas. She was reading something that clearly possessed her, for she didn't even look up.

After he got his drink, he went and sat down beside her, and that's when he saw what was taking his daughter's attention.

She was reading one of his missing plays, a piece by Noël Coward. If he hadn't been so irritated, he might have wondered why she was interested in it, but he was tired, he was hungry, and after the disappointment with Linda his nerves were on edge.

'What are you doing with that?' he said, snatching it out of her hand. 'I didn't say you could walk off with my property.'

Holly looked startled. 'It's not exactly the crown jewels,' she protested.

The edge on her voice pulled Jason up short. Holly's nerves weren't in great shape either since her mother died. He felt like a heel for shouting at her.

'I'm sorry, darling. I shouldn't have done that.'

She gave him a weak smile. 'And I shouldn't have gone through your bookshelves without telling you.'

He put his arm round her. 'No, you shouldn't. I've been looking for *Time and the Conways* and going mad because I couldn't find it.'

Holly reached forward to the pile of books on the table in front of her. She picked off the top one and handed it to him.

'Your problems are at an end.'

If he hadn't known his daughter better, he would have taken the Priestley play and gone back to his study, but he knew Holly well enough to realize she was up to something.

'Why this sudden interest in my old classics?' he asked gently.

She looked at him levelly.

'Mummy started it,' she said. 'When I was out there that last time we talked a lot about the theatre, and it fascinated me.'

Jason smiled, remembering. 'It was your mother's life, you know.'

'She told me. I think she felt sorry it overtook everything else, but she couldn't help it. It cast a sort of spell over her.'

'She told you that?'

'That and lots more. I heard all about how she grew up and what a bossy boots Granny was.'

'I suppose you heard how I took over her life as well?'

Holly thought for a moment. 'I did actually. It was a bit different from all the stuff that's been printed in the papers.'

'Of course it was different. Nobody, not even me, can create a star overnight. Your mother had to wait for her break, like everybody else.'

There was a short silence.

'You did love her, though?'

He looked worried. 'Why do you ask me that now?'

'Because you weren't there. Mummy was dying and you were so wound up with finding Linda that you didn't go to her.'

Jason took hold of his whisky. He had made it stronger than usual and now he was glad of it. As the alcohol burned its way down his throat, he wondered what he was going to tell his daughter. In the end he decided on the truth.

'I wanted to go to her,' he said finally, 'but I held back because of you. The two of you had a lot of sorting out to do. If I'd been there she wouldn't have opened up the way she did. I would have got in between you, as I always did when you were younger, and you would never have known who she really was.'

Holly moved up close to him then. Cuddling up like she'd done when she was a little girl.

'You did that for me?' she said with wonder. 'I had no idea.'

'There are a lot of things you don't know about.'

'Starting with the theatre,' she told him, 'but I'm going to put that right.'

Alarm bells started to go off in Jason's head. 'How exactly are you going to do that?'

Holly sat up straight now, her eyes sparkling, and he knew then his earlier suspicions were right. Holly *was* up to something.

'I plan to find myself a job backstage,' she told him.

'Why on earth do you want to do that?' he protested. 'You saw how the theatre ruined your mother's life.'

'It didn't ruin her life. It made it. The only time she was really alive was when she was on stage.'

Jason looked at his daughter with a mixture of love and despair. Eve had filled her head with dangerous dreams. It was his duty to explode them before it was too late.

'You're not your mother,' he said gently. 'You're not even an actress.'

She faced him out. 'I know that. But I want to understand what Mummy went through.'

'And you think shifting scenery will give you that insight?'

'Dammit, I don't know. But I've got to give it a shot.'

He wanted to shake her. He wanted to tell her she was a fool. He wanted to forbid her to go anywhere near a theatre for as long as she lived. But he couldn't. Instead, he played his last card.

'You won't get any work backstage without being a member of Equity.'

Holly grinned. 'I know that, but some of Mummy's friends have said they'll help me.'

Jason suddenly realized that events had overtaken him. Behind his back, Holly was creeping into the theatre. If he didn't move quickly, she'd have a job and be totally out of his control.

'Forget Mummy's friends,' he said shortly. 'I'll organize you a card when I've found you something to do on a production.'

'You mean you'll help me after all?'

He sighed heavily. 'What do you think?'

Three days later, Clement Dane called Jason at the office. He was taking his company on a national tour of the provinces, starting in Manchester.

'I aim to put on three classics, which I'll alternate,' he explained, 'and what I really need is a couple of strong male leads.'

'What happened to the last ones I found you?'

Clement sighed. 'Television,' he said.

Jason smiled. Clement's sudden need for a couple of leading men put the agent in a bargaining position. Normally he wouldn't ask his friend for an out-and-out favour. But an exchange of favours — that was different.

'How are you off for ASMs?' he enquired.

Clement sounded vague. 'I leave that all to Joe Briggs. He's been running that side of things for years.'

'But do you have your quota of backstage help?' Jason pressed.

Now Clement didn't sound vague at all. He sounded petulant.

'You're after something,' he said. 'I can see it a mile off. You want to fix some chum up with a little light scene shifting.'

'Actually it's not a chum. It's my daughter.'

There was a stunned silence.

'But Holly's an airhead,' Clement protested. 'She's not interested in working.'

Jason took a deep breath. 'Are you saying she's not capable of being an assistant stage manager?'

'Of course I'm not. Anyone can do it if they put their minds to it, but Holly won't concentrate. I know her.'

'So she'll make a mess of it.'

'You said it, I didn't.'

Jason let it go for a moment. Then he said: 'I was rather hoping she would make a mess of it.'

There was a groan on the end of the line. 'What kind of friend are you? You want me to hire Holly so she can sabotage my entire production? You must be out of your mind.'

'Actually I'm not.' Jason wondered how he was going to explain the situation. Then it came to him.

'Clem,' he said, 'have any of your children wanted to do things you were dead against?'

349

'All the time.'

'How do you handle it?'

'I let them go ahead and hope their lack of experience will screw them up.'

'That's exactly what I'm attempting to do with Holly. She's set her heart on the theatre because of some nonsense her mother fed her and I can't talk her out of it. All I can do is find her a job and hope like hell she's miserable doing it.'

Clement laughed. 'I can promise you if she screws up on my tour, she'll be more than miserable. Her life won't be worth living.'

'You'll personally guarantee that?'

'I haven't told you I'll take her on yet. This is my livelihood, you know. I can't afford to carry any dead wood on an expensive tour.'

This was the moment Jason had been waiting for, the clincher.

'You mentioned you were looking for leading men?'

Clement sighed. 'You're not going to tell me you can provide them in exchange for hiring Holly?'

'That's exactly what I was going to tell you . . .'

50

Holly clambered out of the taxi on to the station concourse, dragging her suitcases behind her. Practically everything she owned was inside them. All her clothes, her hairdryer, her diary, the new Jilly Cooper she was half-way through. She had even packed a month's supply of her favourite biscuits, just in case she couldn't get them in the provinces.

When she paid off the driver, she grabbed hold of her luggage and marched up to the station noticeboard. The Manchester train was leaving from platform 13. She hoped it wasn't a bad omen. She really needed this job to work out for her.

Daddy had put himself on the line this time, asking Uncle Clement to take her on. Harry told her how bad-tempered his father had been about it, moaning about her lack of experience.

'I wouldn't let it worry you, though,' he'd told her. 'Father always moans about everything at the beginning of a tour. Once you get to grips with the job, it'll be a doddle.'

Now, as she walked up to the station barrier, she wondered whether assistant stage managers had such an easy time. It was the least glamorous aspect of the business and she would be at everyone's beck and call.

Memories of her stint in television came back to haunt her. I'll be back in the old routine, she thought, making tea and running errands. The idea depressed her so much that she nearly turned tail and ran back home. But she'd left it too late. The guard at the barrier was already demanding to

351

punch her ticket and she had no choice but to hand it over. She was directed to go to one of three reserved carriages, so she hauled her cases down the platform and climbed into the first one, which was completely empty.

It didn't stay empty for long. Five minutes later two girls in jeans and cowboy boots joined her, followed five minutes after that by a tall bearded man, a flashy, actressy-looking woman and a boy in a duffle coat who looked like a student.

Everyone there seemed to know each other and for the next half-hour, as the train pulled out of London, the carriage was filled with greetings.

From what she could catch of the conversation, Holly made out that all the people there had either worked with each other or been at drama school together. Yet they were so curious about each other. The actressy woman, whose name was Rose and who turned out to be the leading lady, was subjected to a cross-examination of the last two years of her life. When they had finished with her, the bearded man came in for a grilling, which is how Holly found out he was the stage manager. And when the boy's turn came, she knew without having to listen that he was the other ASM.

Holly stared out of the window. She didn't belong here. This was her mother's world, not hers. It had been silly of her to think she could just barge into it and make herself at home.

Self-pity was about to engulf her when she realized that someone was trying to attract her attention. One of the girls was shaking her shoulder and asking if she wanted a sandwich.

She came back to reality to see everyone had lunch packets on their knees and were passing round the contents. Rose had a whole cooked chicken which she was busy dividing into portions. The stage manager was handing out tomatoes and wedges of cucumber, and the scruffy girl sitting beside Holly was waving sandwiches under her nose.

Holly suddenly felt a complete idiot. She'd packed every-thing but the kitchen sink, yet she had forgotten all about lunch today. She looked at her companion with genuine regret.

'I'd love one,' she said, 'but I can't offer you anything in return.'

The girl was unfazed. 'Don't worry,' she said, 'we've all got a mountain of food between us. If you don't help us out, we'll have to throw most of it away.'

Holly took her at her word. She'd forgotten to eat breakfast and now she was absolutely starving, so she piled into the sandwiches, helped herself to a chicken leg and polished off everything else on offer.

The food had a relaxing effect. She found herself talking quite naturally to the girl sitting beside her and when the stage manager joined the conversation, she introduced herself with no trouble at all.

'I think I'm going to be working for you,' she told him. 'My name's Holly Fielding.'

The bearded man extended a hand. 'Joe Briggs,' he said, 'and you're the new assistant stage manager. You've no idea the fights I had with Clem over hiring you.'

The sense of doom she felt earlier came back in spades.

'I suppose you were wingeing on about my lack of experience,' she said.

'How did you guess?'

'It wasn't difficult. Uncle Clem has been complaining about it ever since he hired me.'

The word 'Uncle' had a magical effect on the rest of the compartment. All at once Holly found the occupants were hanging on every word she said.

'Clement didn't mention he was your uncle,' Joe Briggs said, looking annoyed.

'He was probably trying to protect me,' said Holly sweetly.

The stage manager pulled out a cigarette and lit it. 'I don't believe a word of it,' he said. 'The next thing you'll be saying is Edith Evans was your grandmother.'

'She wasn't actually,' Holly said quietly, 'but Eve Adams was my mother.'

There was a silence while everyone looked at everyone else. Finally it was Rose who spoke.

'I know who you are,' she said. 'I read all about you in New York. Didn't you have a fling with that awful shit Brett Weston?'

Normally Holly would have clammed up. She never talked about Brett, but if she went silent now, this group would lose all interest in her. It was very important to keep their attention, so she admitted to the affair.

I've done it now, she thought, looking around the carriage. Everyone's going to think I'm a first-class slut or a complete fool.

But they didn't. It turned out that Rose had also had a fling with Brett and had been bruised by it.

As soon as Rose finished her confession, the other girls, who were both actresses, started on about their experiences. The theatre, it seemed, was full of absolute bastards. Sexy bastards, but bastards all the same, and the girls described blow by blow exactly what had been done to them in the name of love. It was like being back at school. No detail, however grotty, was disguised or held back.

Holly started to feel better about Brett. What had happened to her wasn't so unusual after all. Other people got hurt, but if those other people were in the theatre, they made the experience work for them.

As the journey went on, Holly listened to the girls describing the way they used their bruised emotions in the roles they played.

Eve had done the same, of course. Holly would be watching her play some dramatic scene and she'd realize she'd seen it all before. A quarrel on stage would have the echo of a fight she'd overheard at home. The words would be different, but the feelings would be identical.

Mummy stole from life, Holly thought. They all do. The notion that was once shocking now seemed perfectly natural. After all, what was the point of life if it couldn't be plundered for the sake of art?

I'm learning, Holly thought. I don't know much yet, but

I've got my toe on the ladder. I could belong to this world if I wanted to.

Sunday was the worst day of the week, for it was the day they moved. All the scenery, the huge flats that dominated the stage, the props, the costumes, had to be loaded into a removal van and taken to the nearest railway station.

Once there, everything was put into a special compartment where it was transported to the next town.

The whole operation was Holly's responsibility. If a prop went missing or the train was late, Holly had to explain the situation to Clem, who would be tough with her because of who she was.

She got a dressing down every Sunday because there was always something that went slightly wrong. And when it happened, when Clem humiliated her in front of the entire company, she would bite her lip and say nothing.

In another job, Holly would have never taken it, but this wasn't really a job — it was a way of life. Now she was in the middle of it, she couldn't imagine how she could have existed any other way.

She was actually being paid to do what she would have done for nothing. For all her chores, even the Sunday move, had a magic about them. She supposed it was something to do with the fact that she was important. She was part of a team where every member depended on her. If she was in the prompt box and accidentally gave the wrong cue, the play could be thrown out of balance. If the coloured water in the stage wine glasses was stale, performances would suffer.

Everything she did, from pulling down the curtain to calling the actors on stage before a performance, was vital, and because she knew it, she put every ounce of her energy into getting things right.

Clement Dane watched Holly's progress with a certain amount of curiosity. He had been convinced that she wouldn't last five minutes. He had done his damnedest to frighten her out of the job by criticizing her every move, but he had failed to make any impression on her whatever.

The girl fitted in like a dream. If Joe Briggs had hand-picked her, he couldn't have been more satisfied. Clem wondered what the hell he was going to say to Jason.

When Jason called him at the end of the week, Clement was cautious.

'Holly seems to be working out okay,' he said. 'But it's early days.'

At the end of the second week, he was a little tougher on Jason.

'I think you might have been wrong about your daughter,' he told him. 'She shows a real aptitude for the theatre.'

Jason didn't say anything to that. Holly had shown a real aptitude for television until the going got tough. He decided to bide his time. He didn't get in touch with Clement for another ten days, though when he did, there was still no change.

'Are you on my side or aren't you?' he demanded. 'I thought you were going to make it difficult for her.'

'I did make it difficult for her, and she handled it like a trouper. Even Joe Briggs was impressed.'

Now Jason was really stymied. This was the last thing he imagined would happen.

'What are we going to do about her now?' he demanded.

'We're going to do nothing,' Clement told him. 'Holly's a good kid and she's finding her feet. I think it's time you allowed her to be herself.'

'I don't like the sound of that at all,' Jason said.

51

Five weeks into the tour, Clement had a visit from his stage director, who was looking harassed. All the actors were tightly stretched with three plays to perform, and one of the less experienced actresses objected to being landed with understudying.

'Normally I'd tell her to get on with it,' he said, 'but if I did I'd be taking a risk. The girl is very highly strung. Pushing her too hard could affect what she does on stage.'

Clement considered the problem. He could take on an understudy, but it went against the grain. The tour was only just breaking even. Another salary would put him in the red.

He looked at the other option. The ASM traditionally took on this kind of work, but most ASMs had been to drama school and could handle themselves on stage. Holly couldn't act her way out of a paper bag.

He pulled himself up short. How did he know that? He'd never heard her read. The girl could be perfectly adequate; she'd been around the profession long enough.

He decided to float the idea past his director, and to his surprise the man looked relieved.

'I'd hoped you might think of Holly,' he said. 'She's standing in for Annette in rehearsals, and she's not bad.'

The actor hesitated. It would be easy to go along with the situation. Too easy. He had to be sure they were doing the right thing.

'I'll tell you what,' he said, 'make Holly learn all the part. Then when she's word-perfect, take her through one of the

357

key scenes and I'll be watching from the back of the stalls.'

The director looked impatient. 'We're not auditioning a leading lady,' he said irritably. 'Why don't you take my word she's okay?'

Clement got to his feet and ushered the director out of his office.

'If Holly was anyone else I would,' he said, 'but she's Eve Adams' daughter. I don't want to find myself insulting the lady's memory.'

The play was a slight thing by Noël Coward. Clement had only put it in the repertoire because he knew it was a crowd puller, but he wasn't entirely happy with the decision. His company were fine in Shakespeare and Ibsen, but they lacked the subtlety for light comedy.

Now his director was thinking of letting Holly understudy one of the leads. If the girl ever had to go on, the whole play would come apart at the seams.

Clement wondered why he'd agreed to the scheme in the first place. Then he looked at his watch. Holly was due on stage about how. He supposed he'd better go and have a look at her.

She didn't come on immediately, so Clement imagined how she should play the scene. She was meant to be a flapper, simpering and silly, yet at the same time utterly adorable. Gertrude Lawrence had done it a million years ago and got the role off to a T. He sent up a prayer that somebody somewhere had told her about Lawrence's techniques.

Then he stopped worrying and settled back in his seat. If the worst came to the worst, he would just have to dig into his pocket and hire another professional.

Clement forgot all about a professional when Holly came on stage. He simply watched her play a flapper. Somewhere during the course of the scene he stopped even doing that, for Holly had ceased to exist. All there was out in front of him was a dizzy debutante with a knack for putting her foot in it.

She even made him laugh out loud when she said something particularly witty or did a bit of business that surprised him. Then the scene ended and she stopped, she turned off the magic. And all there was a bare rehearsal stage and Holly, his ASM, standing in the middle of it.

Clement got out of his seat and ran up the aisle. 'How did you do that?' he demanded. 'Who's been giving you lessons?'

'Uncle Clem,' Holly said, surprised, 'I didn't know you were watching me.'

He went up to her then. He wanted to examine this marvel closely. He needed to know how she functioned, and most of all, he needed to know what tricks she'd been up to when his back was turned.

'You haven't answered my question,' he said. 'How did you learn how to do that?'

Holly grinned. 'It was one of Mummy's favourite parts,' she admitted. 'She sat me down once, and told me how she made it work. I guess I just paid attention.'

Clement looked at her. She'd done more than just pay attention and he realized he'd been an idiot not to see it. The girl was her mother. It was simple as that. She had her magic, her timing, and that ridiculous, dog-like, slavish love of the theatre. That had belonged to Eve as well.

He took both Holly's hands in his. Then very slowly, very theatrically, he brought them to his lips.

'Welcome home, Holly,' he said.

52

Clement let Holly do the Coward play. It was hard on the actress who had been hired to do it, but she had two other pieces to appear in — and even if she hadn't, he would still have done it. It was his company. He was the one who was paying the salaries. And that entitled him to a bit of favouritism.

Not that Clement showed Holly any special preference. If she knew, if she even suspected how good she was, she would be impossible. He knew that much from Jason. So he went on being tough with her.

She still had to move the scenery every Sunday and account for every prop — and on top of all her other chores, she now had a part to learn.

The Coward play went on twice a week, and Holly was expected to be word-perfect two days after Clement had decided to give her a chance.

She didn't let him down. Like Eve she was a quick study, and by the end of the week she was champing at the bit. She wanted to go on stage. Now she knew she could do it, she wanted to prove to the world and to herself she was an actress.

Clement didn't give in to her. He needed her to work on the part and he personally supervised every one of her rehearsals. When he had first seen her, she had been brilliant, but she had been giving the performance her mother gave. What he wanted from her was her own performance, so slowly and systematically he destroyed what she was doing.

Only when there was nothing left and Holly was thoroughly confused, did he attempt to put the whole thing back together. And as he did, Holly began to show what she was capable of.

She has the makings, Clement thought, but there's a long way to go. She'll be fine playing in Noël Coward. I could put her on tomorrow and she'd bring the house down, but that's not what I want of her.

He thought about the great dramatic parts that he could coach her in – the Shakespeare heroines, the Ibsen bitches, the tragic pathetic waifs that came out of Tennessee Williams' pen. All these belonged to her by right. He had a responsibility to deliver them into her hands.

Clement thought about Jason. He would want some say in his daughter's career. Then he realized that Jason didn't know anything about Holly's career. As far as he was concerned, she was doing a runaround job which was shortly to come to an end. Any day he was expecting a call from Clement to tell him she was more trouble than she was worth.

He'll hear from me, the old actor decided, but I won't be sending his daughter home. I'll be insisting she joins my company on a long contract.

He wondered how Jason would take it. His old friend didn't want Holly anywhere near the theatre. He'd told him so in words of one syllable. And now she was acting, doing the one thing guaranteed to give Jason nightmares, they were well on course for an almighty row.

Then Clement had an idea. Jason had never seen Holly in action, so how was he to know the girl was born to act? Once he senses her power, Clement thought, he won't be able to deny her. Nobody could.

He decided to let Jason see Holly in the Coward piece, but not straight away. She had to get her stage legs first. He thought about the next few weeks. They would be hitting Edinburgh next. Then, town by town, they would be working their way down the country, ending up in Brighton. That's where I'll do it, Clement decided, the Theatre Royal, Brighton. Holly will be at her best then. She'll have had just enough experience to look confident. She'll have the measure of the other players and she'll be able to handle an audience.

When Jason sees her in Brighton, he'll see a great actress in the making and if I know him as well as I think I do, he'll probably insist on handling her.

He sighed. This whole exercise was going to cost him a fortune.

Holly was made up and ready to go on half an hour before the performance. Everyone else was still in their dressing rooms, but she was too excited to hide away until the last moment. She wanted to be where the action was, on the stage, peeking through the heavy velvet curtain so she could get a good fix on the audience.

She had appeared in the play three times so far, and already she knew the key to her success was the people out in front. If they were in a good mood and out to enjoy themselves, she would have it easy. But if they were tired, or if it was raining and their journey to the theatre had been difficult then she would have to work a little harder for her living.

Holly looked around her and saw she was all alone on the stage. So she held her breath and counted to ten. All she needed was Clement appearing out of nowhere and giving her a lecture on the wickedness of what she was about to do. But the coast was clear, so she stood on tiptoe and gently pulled the heavy drape until it opened a chink. A chink was all she needed. Spread out in front of her was the best Newcastle could offer on a Saturday night.

There were factory workers and their wives all done up in their best dresses, local traders in their dark, badly cut suits. And in and among them, looking slightly patronizing, was the cream of the county set.

It was a full house that night, Holly noted with satisfaction. The front circle was chock-a-block and there was standing room only in the stalls. She was about to pull the curtain to, when she did a final quick check of the first three rows.

That's when she saw Linda.

She had put on a bit of weight since Holly had last seen her, and she had lost her glossy cover-girl look, but there was no mistaking her.

Holly held her breath and gave the curtain another tug. She needed to be absolutely certain about what she saw. So intent was she on making sure it was Linda that she didn't hear the footsteps behind her until it was too late.

Clement's hand descended on her shoulder and pulled her away from the front of the stage.

'What on earth do you think you're doing?' he whispered. 'Do you want to bring bad luck down on us?'

Holly whirled round then, and he could see from her expression she didn't give a hoot about theatre tradition.

'I've just seen Linda,' she said. 'She's in the second row of the stalls.'

Clement started to pay attention. 'Are you sure?'

The girl gave him a little push in the direction of the audience.

'Take a look for yourself.'

Against every instinct, Clement Dane peered through the curtains. One look was enough. Visibly shaken, he took hold of Holly and propelled her towards the prompt side.

'We've got to do something about this,' he said. 'Jason would never forgive me if I let her get away.'

Holly struggled to keep a straight face. 'What have you got in mind?' she asked. 'Do you plan an abduction in the middle of the first act. Or will you just send her a note summoning her backstage?'

The actor looked at his watch. 'We've got twenty minutes to curtain up. Why don't you slip down there and try to attract her attention?'

Now Holly thought she'd heard everything.

'I'm in full costume,' she protested. 'If I did that, Linda wouldn't be the only one who noticed me.'

She wondered what to do next, then realized they were both being silly. If Linda had bought a ticket for the play, then she had to know Holly was in it.

'My guess,' she said to Clement, 'is that Linda doesn't

want to run away from us. If anything, this is her way of making contact. Listen, why don't I send her a note saying I know she's here and I'd like to see her?'

'What if she turns tail and makes a run for it?'

Holly shrugged. 'Then you'll just have to go after her. You said you weren't going to let her get away.'

Clement knew when he was beaten. He delved into one of his pockets and extracted a crumpled envelope.

'Scribble something on the back of this,' he instructed, 'and I'll get someone to take it out front.'

They both held their breath while the ASM made his way down to the auditorium. Holly could just see the boy struggling along the second row. Then Linda had her note. She didn't seem in the least surprised to get it, and Holly knew her hunch had been right: Linda wanted to be found.

She peered through the folds of curtain, mesmerized as to what her stepmother would do next. Then she saw her turn over Clem's envelope, write something on the other side and hand it back to the ASM waiting nervously in the aisle.

He seemed to take forever before he got back to them. When he finally approached, Clem grabbed the note out of his hand.

'What does it say?' Holly demanded.

The actor looked as if a weight had been removed from his shoulders.

'She wants to meet you after the play. She says she'll come to your dressing room after the final curtain.'

'But I don't have my own dressing room. You put me in with three other people.'

She could tell she was getting on his nerves for he wore that irritable look he used when she'd mislaid one of his precious props.

'This is no time to start bleating about the facilities,' he told her. 'If you're really worried about your precious privacy you can use my dressing room. I'll go and sit in the bar until you and Linda have finished whatever you've got to say to each other.'

Holly thought about Clem in full make-up lording it up

at the bar and she wasn't fooled by the sacrifice. He'll love every minute of it, she thought. I'd better make sure I have a good long session with Linda.

The first thing Linda did when she came through the door was to rush up to Holly and engulf her in a bear hug.

'I've been so worried about you,' she said. 'I read about Eve in the papers and realized you must have been knocked for six.'

Holly disentangled herself and regarded her stepmother with a certain curiosity.

'Is that why you turned up?' she asked. 'To find out if I was okay?'

'Of course it's why I turned up. Is there anything wrong with that?'

Holly found a couple of bucket chairs and pulled them in front of the gas fire. Then she waited while Linda settled herself, noticing the blonde was still wearing the wedding ring her father had given her. Linda had been cruelly betrayed, yet she still wore the damned ring.

Remorse overwhelmed Holly. I've behaved like a bitch, she thought. If I don't make amends this minute, I'll never forgive myself.

'There's something I have to tell you,' she said.

Linda looked at her. 'Is it about your mother?'

Holly nodded. 'I got it all wrong about her, you know. Daddy wasn't in love with her at all. He was years ago, but by the time he married you it was all finished.'

She waited for Linda to ask her for more details, but the blonde said nothing so she gritted her teeth and ploughed on.

'The reason Daddy kept going over to New York was because Mummy was ill. She'd had cancer for ages and there was nobody she could turn to. So Daddy had to look after her. That's why he was staying at the apartment.'

Linda leaned back in her bucket chair and looked at Holly. 'I should murder you for all the trouble you've caused me.'

For the first time that evening, Holly felt nervous.

'I'm sorry,' she said, 'but I didn't know what I was doing.'

'Are you quite sure of that?'

Holly wondered whether to tell Linda everything. Then she thought, the hell with it, why not? I owe her that much.

'Actually I wasn't the total innocent,' she confessed. 'I wanted Daddy and Mummy to get back together again, so when I discovered Daddy was actually staying with her, I put two and two together and invented a happy ending.'

She folded her arms round herself, expecting Linda's anger. It never came. Instead the blonde looked stunned.

'You silly girl,' she said. 'You silly, silly girl. What am I going to do with you?'

'You could forgive me.'

Linda reached across to where Holly was sitting. Then she took her hand and held on to it while she thought.

Finally she said: 'I'm willing to forget the past, if you are.'

'You mean we could start afresh?'

Linda nodded.

A feeling of glorious relief swept over Holly. Everything was going to be all right after all.

'So you'll come home?'

Linda hesitated. 'I don't know about that. A lot of water has gone under the bridge since I left.'

Some of Holly's relief started to evaporate.

'You haven't found somebody else?'

'Of course I haven't, but I'm concerned about your father. My guess is he's pretty shell-shocked right now. He might not appreciate me turning up out of the blue.'

Holly couldn't believe what she was hearing. 'Daddy would be over the moon if you came back,' she said quietly. 'He's been out of his mind with worry about you and Tommy.'

Linda looked doubtful. 'Isn't he just a tiny bit fed up that I ran out on him in the first place?'

Holly let go of Linda's hand and got out of the chair.

'The one he's fed up with isn't you,' she said. 'When he came home and I told him what I'd done, I thought he'd never speak to me again.'

366

She paced up and down, remembering the endless fruitless searches for Linda.

'He calmed down a bit when I did everything I could to find you, but he won't be the same until you come home.'

She turned to Linda. 'Look, I'm not trying to push you, but if you want to move back in without any fuss, there'll be a chance in three weeks' time. Daddy will be away in Brighton seeing me then.'

Linda smiled and stood up. 'I'll think about it.'

Now Holly was really worried.

'At least tell me where I can find you. You do live somewhere around here?'

Linda was edging towards the door now, slipping out of Holly's life the way she had done before.

'I'd rather stay anonymous for the time being,' Linda told her, 'but I'll be in touch, I promise.'

Before Holly could stop her, she was gone. And by the time the girl made it to the door, the corridor was empty.

She considered calling her father and telling him what had happened but she dropped the idea. Linda knew the score now. If she wanted him, she'd go and find him. If she didn't, it was better he knew nothing about her sudden reappearance.

Holly hurried out to the bar to tell Clement what she had decided.

53

It took half an hour to find a space in the multi-storey car park and Jason wondered what he was doing there. He didn't need to be in this gloomy building in the middle of Brighton. He didn't need to be in Brighton at all. He was up to his ears casting a film and his presence was required in Los Angeles. When he told Holly that, she had carried on as if he was threatening to cut her out of his will.

'It's my first acting part in my first play,' she had wailed. 'If you don't come down, I'll never talk to you again.'

He'd caved in, of course. LA could wait a few more days. His only daughter was doing a walk-on in a provincial tour and she needed encouragement.

He got out of his car and walked towards the central lifts that led to the street. The whole place smelled of rotting garbage and he had to hold his handkerchief over his nose to prevent himself from being sick.

I must have been mad to let her talk me into this, he thought. Stark raving bonkers.

Then he thought about his old friend Clement and realized he wasn't the only one who belonged in an institution. Soon after Jason had put the phone down on Holly, the actor had called.

Clement wanted to be sure he was coming to Brighton.

'What's all this about?' Jason had demanded. 'First I get Holly threatening to cut me out of her life if I don't see the play, and now you pop up. You're not up to something, are you?'

Clement had hummed and hawed about Holly really minding about his opinion. Then he started waffling about parents and their responsibilities. In the end Jason told him to shut up.

'I'll be there,' he promised. 'Just don't nag.' And he had been as good as his word.

The whole front of the theatre was festooned with posters advertising the play, and out of habit Jason checked out the billing. Clement was right on top, of course. Then under the title were the other names. There was Rose, the resident leading lady, followed by the two character juveniles, and right at the bottom was a fifth name: Holly Fielding.

What the hell's my daughter doing on the bill? Jason thought. Only lead players get that kind of projection.

Then the penny dropped. Holly wasn't playing the maid after all. For some reason he couldn't quite work out, Holly, the junior ASM, had landed herself a plum role.

He ran into the lobby and bought himself a programme. If his daughter was a leading player, then she must be in there.

She was. The cast list told him she was playing the soubrette part, the one Eve had made famous when she was just starting out. Jason groaned under his breath. This was all he needed – Clement taking advantage of Eve's reputation.

It was an old trick, the oldest in the book. You get hold of a distant relative of a famous star who happens to be in the theatre. Then you put them in the star's part and pull in the box office returns. You could always count on people's curiosity. They'd come to see a public hanging if you could guarantee them a ringside seat.

He thought about his daughter and felt slightly sick. In a way, putting her on tonight was a bit like a hanging. The audience would gawp and whisper when she came on, and when she showed her inexperience, as she was bound to, they'd enjoy it even more.

What was Clement playing at, he wondered, selling the

369

family name down the river? Frowning, Jason made his way to his seat. It was obvious the tour was in serious financial trouble. That was the only reason his old friend would stoop to this.

Ten yards from the fourth row where Jason was sitting, Holly was peeking through a gap in the curtain. So he had come after all, she thought. Now all I have to be is absolutely brilliant.

Her heart gave a dangerous lurch. What if I'm not brilliant? she panicked. What if I make a total fool of myself?

She started to tremble. I can't do it, she thought, not tonight. Not with Daddy sitting in the fourth row.

She felt herself being pulled back from behind the curtain.

'How many times,' Clement said, 'do I have to tell you about doing that? One night when you least expect it, you're going to scare yourself silly.'

She turned round and held on to him for dear life.

'I've gone and done it,' she blurted out. 'I've just seen Daddy out there.'

The old actor looked at her coldly. 'Well, that's your tough luck,' he said, 'because you're on any minute now.'

Before she could tell him she'd changed her mind, he shoved her roughly to the side of the stage. Then he assembled the cast and signalled for the curtain to go up.

Holly thought she was going to be sick. Rose was half-way through her opening speech and Holly's cue was about to come up. I'll dry, she thought. I'll go out there and I won't be able to remember any of the words.

She stood there frozen to the spot, listening for her entrance. Then it came, and something else took over.

She was a twenties flapper now, simpering and brainless and she sashayed onto the stage and fluttered her eyelashes at the audience. A ripple of laughter greeted her first bit of business. It was cautious, restrained laughter, but it was laughter all the same. And she was off.

She played the part as if she owned the stage, as if all the other actors were there for her benefit. Yet she wasn't selfish. Somebody else with her skill could have easily taken over, but instinct told her not to. The play had a rhythm and she knew if she imposed herself on that rhythm, she would destroy it. So she went with it and as she did she began to feel the effect she was having. She had started with a weak laugh and she had built on it. Now, as she delivered Coward's lines she realized she had the theatre in the palm of her hand. She could do what she liked with this audience, and for the first time ever she knew what it was like to be in control.

At the end of it, when she was taking her curtain calls, she remembered her father was in the audience. Did he like what I did tonight? she wondered. Or did he just compare me to Mummy? Suddenly, none of it mattered.

Whatever his opinion, she had found what *she* wanted to do. It had taken her a long time and caused her a lot of pain, but she had arrived now and there was no budging her.

She came off the stage and hurried down the corridor to her dressing room. Daddy can rant and rave all he likes, she thought, but he can't take me away from the theatre. It's inside me. It's welded to me. If he wants to stop me acting, he'll have to stop me breathing.

Jason came into Holly's dressing room when she was half-way through taking off her make-up, and she wished he had given her more time. How could she think when her face was covered with cold cream? How could she defend herself?

She looked at her father over the pile of damp cotton wool and realized he knew this was a bad moment, but he was going to say his piece anyhow.

There was no way she could avoid this confrontation.

With her free hand, she indicated a chair propped in the corner.

'Why don't you grab hold of that,' she suggested, 'before someone else bags it? Then I'll organize a drink for us.'

Jason ignored the chair and perched himself on the counter in front of his daughter.

'Do you know what you're letting yourself in for?' he demanded. 'Have you any idea what kind of life you're going to have?'

Holly had been prepared for this, and she came right back at him.

'I'll have a job,' she said. 'That can't be so bad.'

'That's what you think,' he said grimly. 'The theatre isn't like any other employer you've ever had. It won't settle for your talent, or the hours you put in. It won't be happy until it consumes your entire life.'

She sprinkled skin tonic on a fresh tissue and looked up at him.

'That's being a little melodramatic, isn't it?'

He passed a hand over his eyes. 'No, it isn't being melodramatic. It's being honest. Since you were a little girl, I've always avoided being too candid with you. I was frightened of destroying your confidence. Well, now I'm finished telling you lies. If you go on doing what you did tonight, the whole of your future will be lived in squalid little dressing rooms like this one. Your home will be a series of hotel rooms and the men you love will change with every tour.'

'That's nonsense,' she said. 'Lots of actresses marry and settle down.'

He attempted a laugh, but it didn't quite come off.

'Name me one actress, one working actress, who made a success of settling down. The poor things don't have a chance. There's always a tour or a film that demands they be away from home. Look at your mother. She was hardly there when you were growing up. The theatre had first call on her time, and in the end, when we made too many demands, it took her away completely.'

Holly moved closer to her father.

'Does it always have to be the way it was for Mummy?' she whispered. 'Is there no chance of living normally like everyone else?'

He shook his head.

'Not a chance,' he told her. 'Anyway after a bit, you won't want to live normally. You'll be so tied up with what you're doing that the real world will seem out of step with you.'

He paused, wondering whether to go the whole way, then he thought, what the hell? Holly's started on this course. She might as well know what's in store for her.

'When you begin to get well-known,' he went on, 'there'll come a time when you make your own rules. You'll take a new lover every time you start a play and you'll drop him at the end of the run. All your friends will be involved in the business because that's all you will want to talk about. And you'll stop celebrating Christmas because you'll either be working, or you'll be getting ready to work.'

The girl was silent for a moment while it all sank in. Then she turned to her father.

'There's one thing you haven't told me,' she said. 'You didn't say whether or not I was any good.'

Jason smiled. He had been right about her all along. She really was a player, and because of it he knew what to say to her for the first time in his life.

'You were sublime, darling,' he smiled. 'Your mother would have been proud of you.'

She frowned slightly. 'And you,' she demanded, 'were you proud when you saw me today?'

He gave his best agent's look, admiring and ever so slightly deferential.

'How could I not be?' he told her. 'You acted everyone else off the stage. Even Clem had his work cut out keeping up with you.'

It was what Holly wanted to hear, for she let go of the tension that had wired her up since she came off stage. She signalled to her dresser to come over, and told him to go out to the bar and fetch some drinks.

'My father will have a whisky,' she instructed, 'and I'll have—'

Jason cut in on her. 'We'll do nothing of the sort. Tonight

calls for a bottle of champagne. Several bottles. Fetch whatever there is on ice and tell Clem to come and join us.'

54

Holly, Jason and Clement had a late supper at the Metropole where Jason was staying. The maître had given them the best table in the restaurant, bang in the middle of everything, and because the hotel management knew Clem and Holly were on at the theatre that week, they put themselves out.

There was yet more champagne — compliments of the Metropole. And on top of it, a group of admiring waiters were asking for autographs. Jason began to think somebody had turned the clock back twenty years.

I used to go through this with Eve, he remembered, and out of the blue he started to feel depressed. This is meant to be a party, he thought, a celebration of Holly's first big success, so why the hell do I feel like committing suicide?

He signalled to the waiter to pour the wine. Then he ordered lobsters and smoked salmon for them all. It was an extravagant gesture, designed to lift their spirits, and it worked for everyone but him.

He watched under a black cloud while Holly prattled on about her new career. It had been agreed that she joined Clem's touring company, and now it was cast in stone, she was full of plans for the future.

She was going to take voice lessons and movement lessons. She wanted to learn how to sing and she needed a whole new wardrobe if she was going to live out of a suitcase.

She sounds as if she's well and truly on her way, he thought morosely.

All at once Jason realized why he was so down. He was

losing his daughter, the last of the women he loved. He thought about Eve and Linda, his two wives. They'd walked away from him the minute they stopped needing him. Now Holly was doing the same.

In a moment of self-pity he wondered what there was about him that repelled women. He wasn't weak, he wasn't stupid and he'd been earning a more than decent living for over three decades. Yet every time he gave his heart, it got trampled on.

He looked across the table in time to see Holly sign her name for a couple who had been at the theatre earlier. She was grinning from ear to ear like a pools winner and he realized he couldn't stay angry with her for ever.

He smiled and forced himself to join in the banter, but his heart wasn't in it. All he really wanted to do was go to his room and consume enough whisky to send him into a dreamless sleep.

As soon as he decently could, he pleaded an early morning meeting in London. Then he signed the bill and left Holly and Clem to finish what remained of the champagne. He noticed neither of them looked up as he left the room.

Jason's mood persisted all the way back to London. It was irrational, he knew it, but he felt as if he had been dumped, and this latest defection ignited all the other hurts he had suffered over the years.

The memory of Eve and the way she cheated on him came back in full force.

She took me for a fool, he thought, and she really believed she could get away with it, except that from that break up there were only casualties.

Jason thought about Tommy then, the latest victim of his failure with marriage. The baby was so young, so trusting, so open to damage. How would he fare without a father? In years to come, when Tommy had grown into a man, what would Linda say about his father? Would she paint him as the villain? Or would she merely present him as a weak womanizer who couldn't resist the charms of his ex-wife?

The whole scenario depressed him utterly. It was bad

enough losing Holly, but at least she was a grown woman. Tommy was still a toddler and the knowledge that he would never see the child again left a gaping hole in Jason's heart.

He got into London just after eight and he reckoned that if he made a detour and went home, he could change into a clean shirt and still make the office by the time it opened.

He turned and headed north for Swiss Cottage and as he did he started to sift through the detail of his coming day. He had a staff meeting which was going to take up most of the morning, then lunch with the head of drama at Thames. And in the afternoon he was seeing actors. He made a mental note to check his LA trip was all booked. The thought of getting away cheered him up. He might be all alone in the world, but at least when he was abroad he wasn't constantly reminded of the fact.

Jason got home at eight thirty and decided to grab a cup of coffee before he changed. When he got to the kitchen, he realized he wasn't the only one who had coffee in mind. The percolator was full and bubbling on the stove. A jug full of milk stood on the table, along with an empty cup and a plate with a half-eaten piece of toast and honey.

Linda always used to have that for breakfast, he remembered, and as he stood there wondering what was going on, he caught a whiff of a familiar scent. It was Spanish castille soap he hadn't smelled for ages because you couldn't buy it here. Linda always used to order it from a store in Madrid, because she refused to use anything else.

Linda, he thought. She must be here in the house. Either that or I've got a pretty exotic burglar.

He called her name, running up the stairs two at a time, and she came out on to the landing.

Jason had often wondered how he'd feel when he saw her again. There had been so many false starts, so many Linda lookalikes, that he had no idea how he'd react to the real thing.

But this Linda wasn't anything like the real thing. She was wearing jeans instead of her usual designer suit, and she had a healthy, rather hefty look about her that he didn't recognize at all.

Jason made his way cautiously up the last few stairs.

'What are you doing here?' he asked.

'What does it look like I'm doing?'

He sat down on the top step and put his head in his hands.

'You left something behind and you've come back for it.'

Linda sat down beside him. 'Try again,' she said.

He turned to her then and the bath soap he'd smelled in the kitchen was stronger now. He suddenly felt weak and totally unable to cope.

'Don't you think I've suffered enough,' he said bitterly, 'without having to play guessing games?'

She put her arms round him then, pulling him close, and he suddenly realized that Linda hadn't changed at all. She might look different, but that was the outside. The real Linda, the essence of Linda, was the same as it always had been.

He held her tight for what seemed like hours, and when he finally released her he saw there were tears in her eyes.

He put his hand up to her face and wiped it dry. Then he looked at her anxiously.

'Are you here to stay?' he enquired. 'Or are you going to do another disappearing act?'

'I'm home,' she told him, 'if you want me to be.'

Jason felt an overwhelming urge to take hold of this big healthy housewife, remove her battered jeans and make violent love to her. But he held back.

Linda had hurt him very badly, worse than any of the other women he had loved, for there had been no reason for her to vanish without waiting for an explanation. He had to know what had gone on inside that addled, beautiful head of hers. And he knew that if it took all week and he had to cancel everything on both sides of the Atlantic, he would get the truth out of her.

He stood up and walked her down the stairs. Then he led her back into the kitchen, because he knew she felt at home there, and poured them both coffee.

'I need to know what happened,' Jason said, bringing their cups to the table.

Linda didn't say anything for a moment. Instead she picked up her hot coffee and warmed her hands.

'If I tell you, you're going to end up blaming Holly, and I don't want that.'

'Holly has her own life to live now. Whether or not I blame her won't make a blind bit of difference.'

Linda looked pugnacious. 'It will make a difference to me. Holly talked me into coming here today.'

Jason absorbed this piece of the puzzle and refused to let it confuse him.

'Go back to the beginning,' he insisted, 'otherwise I'm never going to understand this situation.'

So Linda went back. She recreated the moment when Jason was away in Edinburgh and Holly had broken the news that he was seeing Eve again.

'I had no idea,' she told him, 'that you even spoke to Eve, let alone saw her. But Holly said you'd been an item for ages.'

'Didn't it occur to you to question what she said?'

Linda looked down at her hands. 'I know you think I behaved like a complete twit,' she told him, 'but I think you forget how much I loved you. It drove me insane to think you might be going to bed with Eve. I wanted to kill you. Then I wanted to kill her. And when I'd got over that, I wanted to punish you. So I took your baby son and disappeared.'

'Where on earth did you hide?'

Linda smiled. 'I didn't really go that far, though at first I did consider Australia. Then when I thought about it, I realized you can hide anywhere so long as you go to a town, so I chose Newcastle because I have an aunt who lives there.'

Jason couldn't believe what he was hearing. 'You mean while I've been combing the globe, you've been two hours away by British Rail?'

'Four hours,' she corrected. 'Though if I'd stayed in London I doubt whether you'd have been able to trace me.

Millions of people live here. If I just kept my head down and didn't contact any of my friends I could have dropped out of sight.'

'What made you decide to come back?'

'A combination of things. I read about Eve's death in the papers and that started me thinking. I was worried that you and Holly might be suffering, so when I heard Holly was in a play that was coming my way, it seemed a good opportunity to make contact again.' She paused for a moment. 'Holly must have been feeling pretty guilty. The moment I set eyes on her again she was falling over herself to tell me what really happened.'

'You mean that little troublemaker actually did something right for a change?'

'Stop blaming her,' Linda said. 'She didn't mean any real harm. She just got her emotions muddled up.'

Jason smiled. For a hard-bitten career woman Linda was really rather innocent. Holly had been wantonly destructive and all she could do was make excuses for her. He suddenly felt ridiculously fond of his wife. He knew no matter what Holly did, Linda would probably go on defending her for the rest of her life.

He reached out and took her hand.

'Do you think you might tell me how Holly made you come back home?'

'It was simple really. She knew I didn't want any fuss or drama, so she tipped me off that you were going to spend the night away in Brighton seeing her play. It was the perfect opportunity to slip back, and it suited Tommy too. You've no idea how much of an upheaval this sort of thing is for a baby.'

The mention of his son's name brought Jason to his feet.

'You mean Tommy's here and you haven't told me?'

Without waiting for her reply, he ran out of the kitchen, up the stairs and along the hall until he got to the room his son used to use as a nursery.

He'd changed it into a study since Tommy's departure. Only Linda had rearranged things when she got in last night.

Now there was a single bed right in the centre of the room where his son slept.

Jason hardly recognized the little boy he found. For a good ten minutes he just stood and looked at him, taking in the changes of the last year. Tommy had a thick mop of blond hair now, the same colour as Linda's. He had Jason's nose, or would have when he got bigger, and from the set of his jaw he was unmistakably a Fielding.

Jason reached down and stroked the hair out of Tommy's eyes and the movement woke him. Just for a moment the child regarded Jason with surprise, then quite unexpectedly he broke into a brilliant smile and stretched his arms out towards him.

Jason scooped the boy up and swung him in the air. Then as if he had been doing it all his life, he sat Tommy on his shoulders and carried him down to the kitchen.

55

'The TV people offered Linda her old job back,' said Holly.
'They were all so excited she was back, she even got a raise
in salary.'

Harry was hanging on every word. 'So when does she
start?' he asked.

'She doesn't. Ever since the big walk-out she's discovered
she doesn't like working all that much. These days she's hung
up on being private.'

Harry looked disbelieving. 'Give your stepmother a break,'
he said. 'She's only been home a couple of months. Once she
settles down, she'll go back to her old habits.'

Holly got up from her chair and made her way across
Harry's tiny living room to the sideboard where she replen-
ished her glass of wine. Then she went over to where he was
sitting and curled up at his feet.

'Linda won't go back to her old habits, any more than I'll
go back to mine.'

Harry looked at her fondly. 'I should hope not. You hardly
behave like my little sister any more.'

He settled back on the sofa and remembered the night
that everything changed. He had gone to see Holly when the
company came into Richmond, and the moment she came
out on stage he could see she was different. Before, she had
been a girl — a very sexy girl, but a girl nonetheless. Now
she was a woman and it disturbed him.

It also filled him with curiosity. He had to see for himself

382

whether the change was real or whether it was just part of her performance.

So he took her out for dinner locally as a kind of test. It wasn't the best idea he had ever had, for neither of them managed to eat very much.

In the end, Harry decided honesty was the best policy.

'I think I'm in love with you,' he told her.

'What do you mean you *think* you're in love? Either you are or you're not.'

He felt embarrassed. 'You can't tell unless you've been to bed.'

Holly smiled. 'Then why don't we give it a try?'

They went back to his flat in Bayswater and somewhere in the middle of the night, when they were both naked and he was making love to Holly for the third time, Harry looked at her and grinned.

'What's so funny?' she demanded.

'Just the fact that we never did this before. If I'd known what I was missing, I'd never have stayed away from you.'

A look of sheer impatience passed across Holly's face.

'Well, get on with it,' she said. 'There's a lot of time to make up.'

They'd spent every night together since then. She'd even moved in half her clothes, which were currently draped all over his bachelor bedroom.

With a jolt Harry came back to the present. Holly's possessions wouldn't be with him for much longer. Neither would she. Any minute now his father was taking her off on tour again and Harry's life would go back to the way it was before.

The thought of it filled him with dismay. He had got used to having her around. He'd be lost without her. He must have shown his feelings, for he saw Holly looking at him with concern.

'What's the matter?' she asked. 'You look a bit down.'

He decided to level with her.

'It's the thought of your going away again. I'll miss you.'

'I'll miss you too, but there's no point in getting depressed about it. Playing the provinces is part of my life now.'

There was a silence while he got his courage together to say what he had to.

'You don't have to drag round all those tatty theatres,' he told her. 'You could always stay here and marry me.'

He expected her to hurl herself into his arms, the way most girls would when a man they love offers to make an honest woman of them, so he was a little put out when Holly stayed right where she was, sitting on the floor.

He frowned slightly. 'Come on, darling,' he said. 'You know it's the only solution.'

She took hold of her glass of wine and stared into its depths.

'It might be the only solution for you,' she said quietly, 'but it won't work for me.'

Harry felt irritated. 'What's the matter? Don't you love me?'

'Of course I love you,' she told him, 'but that's nothing to do with it.'

She remembered the conversation she had had with her father when he realized where her commitment lay. Now she knew she would have to let Harry down lightly.

'Listen to me,' she said. 'I'm just starting to do the one thing I'm good at. It's not that easy to walk away from it.'

'But you can walk away from me.'

Holly sighed. This was getting difficult.

'I'm not walking away from you,' she said patiently. 'We can still see each other. I'm not going a million miles away.'

'Then why don't you marry me?'

He looked stubborn now, and for a moment she was tempted to give in to him. She did love him and, who knew, they might just make a go of it.

Then Holly remembered her mother. She'd loved Jason, she'd died with his name on her lips, but she'd made a hell of a mess of being married to him.

She got up from where she was sitting and snuggled up to him on the sofa.

'Darling,' she said, 'I'm not going to marry you, but I'm

384

not going to marry anyone else either. Actors aren't very good at that sort of thing.'

Harry glowered. 'I suppose you'll be telling me next you're thinking of spreading your favours around the company?'

'Don't be an idiot,' she told him. 'My favours belong exclusively to you, for however long you want them.'

Harry was tempted to tell her to pack her bags and get out. Then he thought: what's the point? Knowing Holly, she'd do just that and I'll never see her again.

'So you're volunteering to be my bit on the side?'

Holly grinned. 'If that's the way you see it.'

He looked at her despairingly. 'Aren't you ever going to get sick of living out of a suitcase?'

Even as he asked the question he knew he was on a hiding to nothing. Holly was just like his father. She'd be dragging around theatrical digs for the rest of her life. And she'd adore it, every minute of it.

56

LONDON, 1994

The red Aston Martin roared into the Strand, slowing down as the traffic became one solid mass. Ahead of him, Harry could just make out the lights of the theatre where Holly was playing.

He'd been past it dozens of times since she opened, yet seeing her name up there still gave him a thrill.

I suppose I shouldn't be so damned pleased about it, he thought. After all, if she wasn't playing at the Adelphi every night, I might see a bit more of her.

He smiled, honking his horn at a passing cyclist who looked like running into him. It wasn't going to make any difference whether he was pleased or miserable about Holly's success. She'd still go on acting whatever he thought. She'd made that crystal clear to him three years ago when he'd first asked her to marry him. And she hadn't deviated one iota.

But she hadn't deviated from him either. When she'd promised to love him, she'd meant it. There had been no run-of-play affairs, no quick flings when she thought he wasn't looking. She was his girl, fair and square, and now he was going to make it permanent.

The traffic was starting to thin out and Harry put his foot down and headed towards the Savoy. He'd picked the Grill Room for dinner because he knew it had memories for her. Her parents, when they were together, had dined there regularly. They even had their own table which he had made a point of reserving. Everything was to be perfect. When he asked Holly to marry him tonight he intended to have everything working for him.

Another man, a less certain man, might have had doubts about putting himself up for rejection a second time, but Harry had no reservations.

He had seen Holly grow up almost in front of his eyes and he understood her. He knew how like her mother she was, but he also knew she had learned from her mother. She had lived through Eve's mistakes, had suffered because of them, and she had developed a quality Eve had never had: independence. The stage would never dominate Holly's life the way it had dominated her mother's because she didn't need it so badly.

Holly was perfectly capable of being happy even when she wasn't acting. Knowing this gave Harry the confidence he needed.

Tonight he would describe to her the life that lay waiting for them. He would tell her about the house he was buying, the company he was forming, the babies he would give her. When he'd finished, he had no doubts whatever she would belong to him.

He pulled up outside the Savoy, jumped out of the car and handed the keys to the doorman. He was just about to let the man go ahead and park the car when he remembered something.

Quickly he took the keys back and opened the front door. Then he reached under the dashboard and pulled out a square box covered in red velvet. In it was the diamond solitaire that Holly would be wearing at the end of the evening.

He tucked it into an inside pocket. Then he straightened up and strode purposefully into the hotel.

Holly was waiting for him when he got to the table and there was a glow about her he hadn't seen before. Maybe she's guessed, he thought. It can't be that difficult.

He kissed her very lightly on the lips, the way he always did. Then he sat down wondering how to start the conversation.

387

Holly saved him the trouble. Before he could open his mouth, she was up and running.

'I've just had some wonderful news,' she told him, 'something that's going to change my life.'

'Tell me about it,' Harry said.

Holly's lips curved into a smile. 'I only heard about it today, but I wanted you to be the first to know. The play is going to Broadway and I'm going with it . . .'

Harry looked at her. 'That's great,' he said. 'Only there's a condition.'

There was a pause. 'What condition?'

He reached into his pocket and pulled out the red velvet box.

'Marry me first.'

Holly opened the box and slipped the diamond on to her finger.

'I thought you'd never ask,' she smiled.

POCKET

B O O K S

THE HEADHUNTER

JULIETTE MEAD

CANDIDA:
Icily elegant, a clever, hungry, manipulative man-eater whose
cool strategies can make or break careers . . .

TEDDY:
Pretty and voluptuous, drawn into the headhunting game by
the fascination of stalking her prey . . .

The City is a jungle: a raw, hungry hothouse heated by the
octane of money and sex, and none is more adept at prowling
its byways than the headhunter.

Candida Redmayne's headhunting agency is the best - foolproof
and awe-inspiringly intellectual - and if Candida is playing a
game which has little to do with her professional targets and
everything to do with her personal, then no one guesses. No
one until Teddy Winnington: but she has her own problems to
resolve, her own scores to settle.

PRICE £4.99
ISBN 0 671 85231 0

POCKET
BOOKS

INTIMATE STRANGERS

JULIETTE MEAD

Would you open your house - and your heart - to a complete stranger?

For two couples, the challenge proves irresistible. Maggie and Oliver Callahan agree to swap their idyllic Wiltshire home with an American couple from North Carolina. The exchange covers everything . . . home, pets, neighbours, lifestyles. For the rest of the summer, two families who have never met will be INTIMATE STRANGERS.

Learning each other's secrets.
Exposing each other's weaknesses.
Opening each other's hearts . . .

PRICE £5.99
ISBN 0 671 85232 9

POCKET
B O O K S

NOT QUITE AN ANGEL

LUCINDA EDMUNDS

*With her angelic beauty and her talent for acting, Cheska
Hammond is an international movie star at the age of four.
Spurred on by the huge success and wealth, her mother, Greta,
dismisses Cheska's strange behavior - after all, she has never
lived a normal life.*

Cocooned in her childlike, fantasy world, as a teenager Cheska
has little idea of how to deal with the emotions she feels when
she falls in love for the first time; emotions that explode into a
nightmare both for Cheska and for her family, which leave her
desperate, disillusioned and full of obsessive hatred.

Years later, when things come to a head and history is
threatening to repeat itself, it is up to Cheska's own daughter,
Alex, to discover that her mother is both a dangerous liability
and the tragic victim of circumstances beyond her control - and,
most definitely, not quite the angel she appeared to be.

PRICE £5.99
ISBN 0 671 85256 6

POCKET
B O O K S

ENCHANTED

LUCINDA EDMONDS

*At just seventeen, Madelaine Vincent is tipped as the
most promising ballerina of her generation. In the heady
world of 1980s London, where anything seems possible,
Maddie and her childhood friend Sebastian, a composer,
plan a glittering future. But others will fight to see
Maddie's happiness destroyed . . .*

Forced to compete for her father's affection against a
vengeful stepsister, and her dancing career in ruins,
Maddie then discovers a secret that means she must
lose the second chance for happiness - but only time
will tell whether Maddie has the courage to take it.

`A glamorous yarn of bravery, betrayal, debt and
disillusion...Enchanted...has taken
(Lucinda Edmonds) right to bestsellerdom' She

PRICE £4.99
ISBN 0 671 85200 0